# Who's To Say Where The Stars Will Shine

PART THREE OF THE WHO'S TO SAY TRILOGY

# Carol Carpentier

BRIGHTON PUBLISHING LLC
435 N. HARRIS DRIVE
MESA, AZ 85203

# Who's To Say Where The Stars Will Shine

## Part Three of the Who's To Say Trilogy

### Carol Carpentier

Brighton Publishing LLC
435 N. Harris Drive
Mesa, AZ 85203

www.BrightonPublishing.com

Copyright © 2018

ISBN: 978-1-62183-512-7

ISBN 10: 1-62183-512-X

Printed in the United States of America

## First Edition

Cover Design: Tom Rodriguez

# Dedication

## BOB CARPENTIER

*To my loving husband, whose encouragement and belief in my story was validated by his devotion to the process of helping me put my thoughts into words. Without his creativity and hours of hard work, my trilogy would not have been completed.*

*Bob, I will never be able to thank you enough.*

## KATHLEEN MOHN

### MARCH 1947 - FEBRUARY 2018

*To my beloved niece Kathy, who always loved my storytelling when we were growing up together. I remember her words of encouragement:*

*"Everybody needs to hear your stories! You need to write a book."*

# Acknowledgements

I thank the following people for their invaluable input while on this journey through the lives of Laura and Liam:

My grandson Brent for the inspiration for my story.

My daughter Tammy and son Philip for all their help in promotion and sales of my books.

Lif Strand, my longtime friend and fellow Arabian horse breeder, who traveled many miles to bring skills so vital in transforming my vision into a novel.

Pat and Bob Radmacher, our dear friends and partners in the world of Arabian horses, whose companionship during the research in Ireland brought us a wealth of memories.

Susan, Una, Josie and Toppy of the Corcoran family in County Tipperary. By the warmth of their hearth, these Thoroughbred breeders and trainers entertained us with colorful tales of life on the Emerald Isle. Toppy Corcoran, the leading jockey during the period of my story, was an invaluable source of information about the world of Irish horseracing.

# ᴄ✤Chapter One✤ᴐ

The churning Irish Sea had thrust the ferryboat into yet another steep angle, revealing a blustery sky through a tiny porthole. Groping for anything to steady herself, Laura Meegan wondered how much more her stomach could take. This voyage was a far cry from the family pleasure cruise aboard the QE II. That younger Laura had found passage into a blossoming yet forbidden love between herself and Liam, followed by an unexpectedly safe kinship with new American friends Jon and Jen Bianchi.

Would it all come crashing in on them now, forever obliterating the lives of the young teens who had worked so hard to earn their heritage at Montrose Manor?

Laura groaned as Gretna Green now seemed impossibly out of reach, and with it the promise of being with Liam to start a new life together. If she could only turn back time… if she could only make her father see Liam for what he truly was: her savior, her protector, her soulmate. But Lord Aidan Meegan could only see Liam Delaney as the boy he had rescued from tragic loss, the boy he had brought into the fold of his own titled family, the boy who was now stepbrother to his only daughter.

✤

The feeling of someone touching Laura's arm interrupted her train of thought. Her eyes fluttered open and she realized they were damp with tears. The porthole came into view—but it was the window of a Boeing 707. The shaking sensation was turbulence on the flight from Florence to Dublin.

"Sweetheart, you must have had some kind of bad dream," Liam said as he gently swept her long blonde hair from her face. "I hope you're not still troubled by what happened in St. Moritz."

Laura threw her arms around him. "No, not that–the trip to Gretna Green."

Liam's eyes opened wide, and then he smiled to mask his concern. "That was ages ago, sweetheart. But thanks to our allies, your father included, we got through it, and we've been together ever since."

Her face brightened. "We do have quite a support team, don't we?" She glanced over at Jon, who was absorbed in the latest issue of *Rolling Stone* magazine, and his sister Jen, who was sleeping dreamily with her head on the shoulder of Danny Bailey, her fiancé. Like Laura and Liam, Danny called the southwest of Ireland his native land, and the 850-acre Montrose estate made it home sweet home.

Laura felt renewed contentment at that moment, with the image of fans cheering them on in a European nightclub still fresh in her mind. "When I think of all the things we've experienced since those days when we were nearly torn apart... and now we're all together."

Liam mused, "In a way, we may be closer because of the times we *weren't* together. Absence does make the heart grow fonder."

Laura frowned. "You're just saying that because you and Jon and Danny are going back to Trinity again, while Jen and I have to go back to St. Andrews."

Liam gazed down into her soft brown eyes. "Remember, your goal is joining us next year at Trinity. It means studying hard at St. Andrews–and it means you need to be patient. I will be there waiting with arms open wide." He leaned over and gently kissed her, and Laura's heart skipped a beat, as always.

Back at Trinity College in Dublin, Jon couldn't wait to tell bandmates Garrett and Brian about the gig at Le Voyage. He ran into Garrett after a morning class, and they had time for a cup of coffee. Jon excitedly told him about their performances, but left out any mention of the wild party episode in another band's hotel suite that resulted in intervention by both medical and law enforcement responders.

The slender young Irishman listened, but seemed preoccupied. When he finally spoke, Garrett's voice was somber. "We may have some problems with Second Wind doing the opening gig for Foolish Pleasure."

Jon's blue eyes flashed with alarm. "What's going on?"

"It's Brian. He got into some trouble when he was home in Belfast over Easter. I don't know all the details, but he was in some kind of fight, broke his arm and ended up in jail. I'm not even sure if he'll be back to Trinity for a while."

Jon threw his hands up. "I can't believe this! What was he thinking?"

Garrett sighed. "Brian's a good friend and a good student, but I'm afraid there's a dark side to him. His father sent him to university in hopes it would straighten him out, but Brian's political beliefs got the best of him. He's been involved with IRA sympathizers and their protests. I don't know what Second Wind will do without him on drums."

Jon ran his fingers through his long blond hair as he strategized to save the unique college rock band that was essentially his own creation. "Maybe Jen can fill in for him until he can use his arm again."

Garrett's wild hair tossed as he shook his head. "How's she going to learn our material? There's not much time–and her school is miles away." St. Andrews Catholic School for Girls was the residential preparatory establishment in County Tipperary, where Jen and Laura spent weekdays away from Jon, Danny and Liam. The two girls, in their mid-teens, were a couple of years younger than the boys.

Jon made his case to Garrett. "Jen already knows most of it, and she's a fast learner. Maybe she can come to Dublin on the weekends to rehearse with us instead of going to Montrose Manor. We can practice during the week without drums–Danny can carry the rhythm." Danny was the bass player in Second Wind, as well as the band The Siblings, which they had formed years before at Montrose Manor.

Garrett was skeptical, but didn't argue. "I guess we don't have much choice. We really don't have time to audition new drummers."

⚬⟋⟍⟋⚬

After classes Jon met up with Danny and filled him in on the situation. In a manner characteristic to him, Danny eyes were partially obscured by his strawberry blond hair as he offered his opinion.

"Of course I'd love to have Jen come here on the weekends, but you know we need to talk to Liam and Aidan first."

Danny's careful consideration was no surprise to the bolder American, whose reply came quickly. "I'll tell Liam, but I don't want to mention it to Aidan just yet. Let's keep the part about Brian being arrested out of the story–even when we talk to Liam."

4

Danny shook his head. "I hate to keep anything from Liam."

"Danny, he's such a worrier. Let's wait to tell him until we have all the facts."

They saw Liam later that day and brought him up to date, using the agreed-upon caution. But Liam had other considerations his friends hadn't thought of.

"What about Laura?" he asked. "She'll want to be part of it if Jen is."

Jon shook his head. "I'm just using Jen as a fill-in drummer."

"That's not even fair to Jen," Liam pointed out. "She'd be putting all this effort into it, but then Brian's arm mends and he just kicks her off the drum set?"

"I agree," Danny said. "The girls just gave an outstanding performance with us in St. Moritz. We can't just brush them aside arbitrarily."

"Thank you, Danny—well put."

"Jeez!" Jon cried. "I can't say no when you guys double-team me. All right, we'll ask both of them to come and rehearse with us. We'll take it from there."

"Of course we ask Aidan before we make any changes," Liam said firmly.

"I guess we'll have to," Jon sighed, rolling his eyes. "We would be asking the girls to come here on the weekends instead of going home to the manor."

<hr>

When Brian called Garrett from Belfast, the news wasn't good—his arm would need surgery. It was doubtful he would heal in time to open for Foolish Pleasure. Garrett told him about the plan to have Jen fill in for him.

"You've got to be kidding me! She can't kick those rhythms."

"Yeah, but neither can you, and we don't have any choice."

Brian cursed. "I've been playing in bands for years, and I finally get the opportunity of a lifetime... and what do I do? I blow it."

Garrett got firm. "I think you need to decide if you want to finish your education–and play with Second Wind–or be a protestor. We can't have you getting arrested and beat up all the time."

Brian hesitated. "I know. I have been doing a lot of thinking... but I just can't give up my beliefs. I'll try to stay out of trouble. I do want to graduate–I only have one year left. Did you tell Jon I was in jail?"

"Yes, but he only knows about *this* time. Man, aren't you going to be kicked out of Trinity for getting arrested again?"

"They just think I'm off for a broken arm. So keep it quiet, please." Garrett agreed and Brian told him he'd keep in touch.

To Jon's surprise, Aidan agreed to the girls' rehearsing with the band on weekends. The well-to-do Irish businessman had made his position known some time ago that conventional academic study was of the highest priority. But after carefully guiding his daughter and her extended family of teens, Lord Meegan had seen that they were all on the right paths. He had kept an open mind about their musical pursuits, and his voice now sparkled with a cheery timbre as he spoke to Jon on the phone.

"The girls were planning on going to Dublin next weekend anyway for Liam's birthday," Aidan said. "But you might want to consider not rehearsing on Saturday night. I bought a little present for Liam. You're all getting tickets to see the band U2. I bought six tickets–I took a guess that you might want to bring a date."

"U2? Wow! Thanks! This is so cool! Oh–and no on my bringing a date–but I know Garrett would like to go. Thanks!"

# Chapter Two

**D**anny and Liam met the girls Friday at Pearse Station in Dublin. It was only a few city blocks away from the Meegan's three-story brownstone that Lord Meegan referred to as Dublin House. Aidan had his staff set it up in autumn of the previous year so the three boys could be walking distance from their classes at Trinity.

Danny's brown eyes lit up as Jen stepped off the train, her short strawberry bangs bouncing with each step. He easily scooped her up with his rugby-player's arms.

The tallest of them was Liam, but he never had any complaints about how far he had to stoop over to give Laura a kiss. His only concern at that moment came when he reached down for her bag. "What have you got in this suitcase? It's so heavy."

"Shoes–and plenty of clothes," she said with a shrug. In fact, Laura's luggage contained presents for Liam, along with decorations and other items for his surprise party.

After dinner they went right to the task of rehearsing in the basement studio with Garrett. Jen did a remarkable job picking up the material that was new to her. Laura sang backup vocals and danced while shaking her tambourine.

"Not bad," Jon remarked. "Let's pick it up tomorrow–maybe a morning practice."

"I want to spend the day with Laura," Liam said. "Can't we do it at night?"

Jon shook his head. "I've got plans with Garrett."

"And I'm taking Jen out tomorrow night," Danny added.

Liam didn't say any more, but he was disappointed that no one had included him.

Laura noticed his frown. "I'm sure we can think of something to do together."

After the morning rehearsal, Laura took Jen aside and spoke softly. "Liam and I are going to the museum and the park. We'll be back at five o'clock. You're in charge of the banner and balloons–and make sure the cook has everything ready. Molly's making a chocolate cake. Father should be here by half-four."

Jen agreed and soon Laura and Liam left Dublin House. They spent an enjoyable afternoon together, and Liam didn't give his birthday a thought.

While they sat on a park bench two pretty girls approached. "Hello, Liam." The petite brunette batted her eyes and flashed him a smile.

He looked surprised. "Uh... hello."

"We just bought tickets to the Foolish Pleasure concert," she announced. "And the extra bonus is that your band is the opening act." Liam blushed while the girl moved in close to show him her ticket. "See? It's printed right here."

"Wow, I didn't know they would have it... publicized."

"I can't believe I go to school with a rock star," she giggled. Neither girl had acknowledged Laura's presence.

"I'm not a rock star," Liam stated. "This is my girlfriend Laura–she plays in the band, too."

"Oh. How nice. Well, bye!" The girls smiled sweetly at Liam and walked off.

Laura looked at him incredulously. "I can't take you anywhere."

"You have nothing to worry about."

Laura sighed. "I'm afraid this is only the beginning. You'll be a superstar soon, and I'll have to make an appointment to see you."

"Nonsense–I'll always have time for you, the one I love."

Suddenly Laura looked at her watch. "We'd better get back! It's nearly five."

"What's the big hurry? Everyone else seems to have plans."

"Um... I thought we could go back, change our clothes and... go see a movie. Besides, I need to put on something warmer."

"I'll keep you warm," he said, pulling her in.

Laura smiled, but stood up. "You can keep me warm while we walk back."

Aidan's car was parked in front of Dublin House, and Liam was surprised.

"I didn't know he was coming. I wonder why he's here."

"I think he has a meeting tonight or something…. Oh, Liam, I forgot my key. Do you have yours?"

Liam smiled and reached in his pocket. "What would you do without me?"

He was still looking at her when he swung the door open.

"Happy birthday!" half dozen voices screamed. Liam stood for a moment in shock, then smiled at Laura. "I should've known you wouldn't let my birthday slip by."

"We really got you, man!" Jon laughed. "C'mon, let's eat. I'm starving!"

Aidan's smile brought a glow to his soft brown eyes. He could always count on this youthful group to be entertaining yet respectful and appreciative of what he'd done for them through the years. With help from them all–but especially from Liam–his daughter had been able to heal after the grief of losing her mother when Laura was just eight.

A three-course dinner was presented by the capable staff of Dublin House, followed by one of Liam's favorite desserts: chocolate cake. Liam then opened gifts.

"Wow! It's that leather jacket I saw in Italy. Laura, you shouldn't have."

Jon grabbed for it. "I'll take it if you don't want it."

"I don't think so."

"And now for my present," Aidan said, pulling an envelope from his pocket. Liam was awestruck when he looked inside. "U2! For tonight? This is fantastic. It's sold out–how did you get these? How did you even know about it?"

Aidan smiled. "I've learned a thing or two hanging around you teens. Now, I think you should get ready to go–you don't want to be late."

The concert was soon underway, and after a three-hour performance, exceeded all expectations. The energy of U2 was electrifying, with each of the four musicians delivering strength and emotion in every song.

On the way home the teens couldn't stop talking about the show.

"I can't believe what a wonderful voice Bono has!" Liam exclaimed. "He sang every word in perfect pitch, and with such incredible power."

"And that guitarist–The Edge," Jon added. "He lives up to his name in how passionate and fiery he plays."

Danny put his hand on his chest. "Adam's bass feels like the pulse of a heartbeat."

Jen sighed. "Larry's drumming is unreal. I would love to play with him...."

Danny gave her a suspicious look. "I bet you would."

"I mean drum with him," she laughed. "Although he is pretty cute."

"You're stuck with me, darlin." Danny planted a firm kiss on her lips.

Liam noticed Laura's smile. "So, you think the drummer is a fine thing?"

"Yes, he's easy on the eyes. But Bono is more my type. You know–strong, sexy, handsome, an incredible voice." Liam pretended to be wounded.

Laura's brown eyes sparkled as she laughed. "I was talking about you! But, seriously, their whole sound was incredible. It was like they were taking us on a long voyage."

"Their lyrics are cool, too," Garrett said thoughtfully. "They're very socially conscious, and they have a real connection with their audience. I feel like I personally got the show of a lifetime. I think we should try to be more like them."

"I don't think we'll have to try," Jon remarked. "I have a feeling they're going to be a big influence on us."

# Chapter Three

It would only be five weeks until Second Wind opened for Foolish Pleasure, the American band whose popularity had led them to tour dates in the UK and Ireland. The connection between them and the younger members of Second Wind was multi-faceted, as they had met on the same QE II cruise where Laura and Liam had met Jon and Jen. Liam's talent as a young songwriter had so impressed Greg Watts of Foolish Pleasure that he had bought several of Liam's songs over the course of two years. Quick thinking and the art of persuasion had allowed Jon to secure the position of opening act for Second Wind.

With the tight rehearsal schedule in place, the girls continued to come to Dublin House on the weekends. Of course, the young musicians still had to finish term papers and study for final exams. It was more pressure than any of them could have imagined.

Finally the last week of school arrived. The members of Second Wind looked pale and undernourished. Every waking moment had been spent studying or rehearsing, and the short periods of sleep they did get were sometimes restless.

Even the celebration that normally comes after a final exam was not allowed by Jon, who the others saw as the official drill sergeant of the band. Their last finals would be on Thursday, and the first concert was Saturday night.

Laura called Liam from St. Andrews Thursday afternoon with upsetting news about her old pony.

"Lilly passed away. I need to go to Montrose."

"I'm sorry about Lilly," Liam said. "I know how much you loved her. I'll go home with you–we can come back to Dublin Saturday midday."

"You don't have to do that, Liam. I know Jon wants you there to practice."

"I want to be with you. They can rehearse without me, and I could use a break."

"I love you so much," Laura said. "You're so thoughtful."

"There's no place I'd rather be than by your side. See you tomorrow, sweetheart."

Jon had overheard the end of the conversation. "Where are you going tomorrow?" Liam explained the situation and Jon flipped out. "I can't believe you would desert us now!" Danny overheard Jon and came in from the next room.

"Hey, Jon, calm down. We can practice without them."

"Is this how our future with the band is going to be?" Jon shouted angrily. "The most important gig of our lives, and Laura needs to grieve over an old pony?"

There was a stunned silence. Liam's face turned red. Jon's callous remark had pushed him over the edge.

"Jon, you don't think I know that our music is important? Of course I do! But I will always put Laura's needs first. I don't see that I am letting anyone down. Besides, I need a break–you've been driving us too hard."

Danny stepped between them. "Enough! Liam, you go to Montrose, and Jon, you calm down. We are all as ready as we can be–you're only adding more stress. Look at you two, going at each other. You would never know you were best friends."

"You're right, Danny," Liam conceded. "I'm sorry for snapping, Jon, but I really do need a break. I promise we'll be back Saturday for an early practice."

Jon gave Liam a hug. "I'm sorry, too, Big Guy. I've been so uptight about this gig I can hardly think about anything else. I'm amazed I was ready for my finals. We'll be okay rehearsing without you, but there's going to be a big hole in our sound."

Liam smiled at the compliment. "I think we're ready–don't worry."

Liam boarded the train by himself at Pearse Station, feeling contented that soon he would see Laura but sad about the loss of her pony. Lilly had been in the family since Laura's mother Fey was still alive.

A rush of his own family memories came to Liam as he gazed out at the lush green of the Irish countryside. The heartache of having lost both his parents had diminished somewhat through the years, replaced by the ongoing process of counting his blessings. The bond he had begun making with Laura when they were just kids was the singular blessing that had seen him through his pain and given him hope for a future.

The sound of airbrakes from the slowing train brought him back to reality, along with the sight of the village station, the trusted rendezvous point for him and Laura when they were returning to the Montrose estate from different directions.

Liam waited on one of the benches until Laura's train rolled to a stop. He could see she had been crying as she stepped onto the platform, and he reached out to give her a gentle hug.

"Sweetheart, are you going to be all right?"

"I feel guilty I didn't pay more attention to Lilly. I should have been with her."

"There's no way you could have been with her–you were at St. Andrews." He could see she was still troubled, and he put an arm around her as they walked. "I want you to remember Lilly the last time we were with her. We had a picnic under the oak tree in her pasture. She followed us out there and you fed her part of our lunch. She got all the oatmeal biscuits, even mine. Remember you braided her long mane and put wildflowers in it? You have the pictures you took of her standing on our blanket, eating out of the picnic basket."

Laura managed a faint smile. "You're right. It's a lovely day to remember. You know, your voice on the phone isn't the same as seeing your loving eyes smiling at me." She gave him a tender kiss.

❦

Aidan met them at the door, giving his daughter a hug. "Laura, I know how much you loved Lilly. Remember, she had a good life and lived a very long time."

Laura's stepmother Hannah appeared and presented Laura with a bouquet of lilies. "Mr. Callahan cut some fresh flowers for you, dear."

"Thank you, Hannah. I will bring them to Lilly's resting place." She wiped her tears. "I hope Emily and the baby are doing well."

"They are doing fine. Thank you for asking, dear."

Hannah was aware that Laura, although polite enough to ask about her stepsister and the new baby, would not want to engage in a conversation about them just now. As expected, Laura and Liam went upstairs to their rooms for only a few minutes. Their next destination was Montrose's stately stone barn, where caring for the horses was the pride and purpose of each day.

Barn manager/trainer Patrick O'Brogan greeted Laura with gentle compassion. "I'm so sorry, but please know she didn't suffer any. She's next to Ol' Tommy and Kite." Laura could only nod.

Patrick escorted them to the big tree that stood guard over the final resting place of their old friends. Laura placed the flowers on Lilly's grave.

Liam looked at the handcrafted crosses made for his beloved dog Kite and the faithful draft horse Ol' Tommy. *Why do we have to lose the ones we love?* Tears welled up in his eyes as he again thought about his parents.

Laura finally spoke. "I think we can go now. I know Lilly is in peace."

They strolled leisurely back to the manor. "I really needed this time at home," Laura confessed. "Our lives have become so busy. It's nice to come back to Montrose and just enjoy what we have here."

Liam smiled knowingly. "I was so happy to be back in my old room, if only for a minute. I instantly felt... centered, you know. I like what we're doing with the band and our education, but I miss our simpler life and our time alone."

Laura kissed him on the cheek. "I don't want us to ever forget our times here."

"We won't forget, sweetheart. No matter where we are, I know we'll always have Montrose right here." Liam placed Laura's hand on his heart.

# Chapter Four

Saturday night had come quickly, and the members of Second Wind were prepared–but nervous. Jon was wound up like a spring, bouncing around, making sure everything was ready. The equipment was all in place on the Dublin stage, they had completed the lighting and sound check, and it was finally time to dress for the show. Most of all, Jon was intensely aware of the growing crowd, queued up and beginning to take their seats in the large stadium.

Aidan, whose guidance of the teens included management of their musical commitments, began his pre-show pep talk. "Remember, you have performed for some very sophisticated audiences in St. Moritz, and you even had to carry the whole show the last few nights. You were a big hit. Tonight's venue is larger, but most of the people in the audience are already fans. They're excited to see you perform and they'll love you. Now go out there and do what you do best!"

"Thanks, Aidan," Jon said. He turned to the band. "I've only got these words to say: Take no prisoners!"

The stage was dark when the young musicians took their places. Garrett opened with a progression of broken chords on the synthesizer. It was an exciting sound–an electronic blend of horns and strings. With a soft green spotlight on the keyboardist, the crowd was pulled into anticipation. A yellow beam began to illuminate Jen on the drum set and Danny, next to her, on bass. They built a steady pulse moment by moment.

A ray of pink captured Laura, frozen with her tambourine held high. Jon hit his first power chord, and the entire stage lit up. He struck each successive chord with a leap into the air. Laura came alive in a feverish dance, delighting the young men in the crowd.

Jon sustained the final chord in the progression. Jen hit two crash cymbals simultaneously and paused as they rang through. A beacon of blue revealed Liam as he stood alone on a raised platform. He hooked the crowd with his commanding voice, seeming to hold a single note forever. The stadium was electrified as Second Wind powered into a song that would set the pace for the entire night.

In the audience was a young reporter for the *Irish Times*, Eoin McKee. "These kids are amazing!" Eoin yelled to his date. "And they're the opening act!" She smiled and nodded dreamily as she watched Liam in his tight leather pants.

As Second Wind reached the end of their song list, Aidan felt a sense of pride and awe as he witnessed the audience respond with such enthusiasm.

The crowd demanded two encores, giving the band a standing ovation. As they finally left the stage, Greg from Foolish Pleasure was there to congratulate them.

"Wow! You guys are going to be a hard act to follow!"

Jon had a grin plastered on his face–he was so excited he could hardly speak. "We did it! They liked us! We did it!"

"I have to hand it to you guys," Garrett said. "I think this is the best night of my life! I've been struggling in bands for years, but you guys have made my dreams come true." Garrett looked right at Jen. "You were great! And much finer to look at than Brian."

Jen was thrilled with Garrett's approval, and Danny gave her a big hug. "He's right, darlin', you were hot tonight!"

"And Laura, you pulled it all together," Garrett added. "I had some doubts about the need for the dancing, but now I can't see us doing a show without you."

"Thank you, Garrett!"

"I couldn't be more proud of you all," Aidan said cheerfully.

Foolish Pleasure began literally with a bang, fireworks shooting off from behind the stage. They played many of the songs Liam had written, as well as Danny's song *Ocean's Apart*, which was his testimony to the heartache of being across the pond from Jen when she and the Bianchis were still living in New York.

The Irish fans cheered, sang, and danced through the evening, thoroughly enjoying both the American and the hometown band.

Backstage, after Foolish Pleasure's final encore, Greg did not hold back his excitement. "This really worked! Let's see if we can pull it off again tomorrow night." Laura paused, knitting her eyebrows. "By the way, Jon—what did you mean before the show, when you said take no prisoners?"

"Take no prisoners? You know—knock 'em dead... kill 'em! And we did!"

Aidan chuckled and shook his head. "Indeed you did. Now, I think you should all come home to Dublin House and get some rest." He looked directly at Jon.

Jon got up early the next morning to see if there was any mention of their performance in the paper. He found a lot more than he'd expected and couldn't wait to share it. Everyone was gathered at the breakfast table, so Jon walked in, cleared his throat and began to read out loud.

*Incredible Bands, Fantastic Songs and a Perfect Summer Night! The new group Second Wind opened with captivating drama from their talented keyboard player from Dublin, Garrett McCormack. The front man, New Yorker Jon Bianchi, is quite the performer and crowd pleaser with his good looks and charm....*

*Drummer Jen, Jon's little sister, was a joy to watch and she clearly enjoyed herself as she kept the pulse for this high-energy band. Bassist Danny Bailey, from County Tipperary, never missed a beat. At one point he had to signal for more monitor volume due to the overwhelming applause. Lovely Laura Meegan, from County Limerick, danced with perfect rhythm when she wasn't lending her beautiful voice for backups.*

*Liam Delaney, also from County Limerick, delivered his vocals with a passionate intensity that made the show. The band performed song after song in perfect sync. Rarely does an opening act get such a roar of approval from a crowd such as I witnessed last night. This reporter believes that Second Wind will fill its sails to make a smooth voyage into the sea of success.*

The article in the *Irish Times* had been penned by Eoin McKee. He went on to praise Foolish Pleasure as well, again mentioning Liam as having written some of the material.

They were all in astonishment. Jon was the one to finally voice his reaction. "Oh my God! This is a fabulous review. We should call and thank this Eoin."

Molly walked in the front door carrying a stack of the *Irish Times*.

"I'm betting everyone in the family will want a copy," she laughed.

Molly Bailey, one of Danny's two older sisters, had been on staff for Lord Meegan as Laura's night nanny at Montrose Manor since Laura was just eleven. A hairdresser in her twenties, Molly had become a surrogate big sister to Laura and friend to Liam and the others. Aidan valued her enough to employ her as the live-in chaperone to the teens at Dublin House.

As Molly distributed copies of the paper, Aidan was beaming. "I told you I was proud of you. The world agrees with me."

"Hey, Molly Girl, are you coming to see us tonight?" Jon asked.

"After listening to you kids practice endlessly in the basement?" she laughed. "I wouldn't miss it for the world." Jon gave her a hug.

# ᯇ Chapter Five ᯇ

Robert and Catherine Bianchi were flying in later that day for the second night's performance. Jon was a little nervous about the prospect of his parents being in the audience, but Jen was thrilled they were coming.

Peggy, the younger of Laura's two stepsisters, arrived from London with the normally expected luggage—and a rather large box. Jon jumped up to greet her, and she presented it to him. "Hey Cowboy, I brought you a surprise."

His bewilderment was genuine, but he was certainly not one to look a gift horse in the mouth. Jon slowly opened the lid to discover a white straw cowboy hat.

"You can shape it any way you want," she said. "I got you white, for the good guy who always wins." There was special significance in her comment, as the two of them had been recently bonded in a life-or-death struggle during which Jon refused to give up hope and saved them both from freezing in an alpine blizzard.

Jon grinned as he placed the hat on his head. "I love it! Where did you get it?"

"I asked my pilot friend, Chase, to bring it back from California. I thought it would be perfect for you to wear on stage, since everyone calls you The Cowboy."

Jon gave her a hug. "Peggy, you're the greatest. You'll be there tonight?"

"That's what I'm here for. I saw Foolish Pleasure last week in London, and they were great, but I think Wild Spirit is better."

Jon chuckled and corrected, "Ah, we are Second Wind now." Peggy looked confused and Jon shrugged. "It's complicated. And we have a good man on keyboards–Garrett. I'll introduce you to him tonight."

That night's performance was just as exciting and well received as it had been the night before. Jon wore his hat and introduced himself as The Cowboy. The audience loved it, and reporter Eoin McKee latched on to it for his next review. The Cowboy was now Jon's official name.

Peggy and Garrett were introduced by Jon backstage, but it was soon apparent that their paths would have crossed anyway. Peggy, who was quite tall herself, was instantly drawn to the slender keyboardist with the curly blond hair. Ever since her makeover by Molly a couple of years earlier, Peggy carried herself in a manner that was unassuming yet stylish, and her dark hair which was accented with highlights framed her face attractively. She and Garrett were quite taken with each other, and since she was moving home to Montrose for the summer anyway, Peggy now planned to attend all of Second Wind's concerts.

Greg was very pleased with the opening act and the attention it had brought to his own band. After that night's show he took Jon aside.

"You guys have really put together a great performance. We'd like you guys to continue the tour with us after we leave the UK. We're off to Japan and Australia."

"Are you serious? We'd love to!"

"Of course, you'll have talk to your manager."

The reality sank in and Jon's enthusiasm deflated. "Oh, yeah, of course."

Jon found Aidan and presented the offer to him. As he named the cities for the tour, Aidan shook his head. "I don't think we're ready to go so far abroad just yet."

"But the tour would be over before we start classes again. It's perfect timing."

Aidan knitted his eyebrows. "Jon, keep in mind you're only eighteen, and others in the band are younger. I can't be away from Meegan Enterprises to go with you. I think after what happened in St. Moritz you should remember that this is a fast-paced lifestyle, and there's plenty of time before you jump into it with both feet. I'll agree to the additional nights in Scotland."

Liam spoke up. "I think Aidan is right–why burn ourselves out?"

Jon agreed with a deep sigh. He was disappointed but knew they were right.

# Chapter Six

The entire entourage was up early and off to Limerick to set up for that night's concert. Jon had mixed reactions when he found out Kelly and her family were going to be in the audience. The youngest girl in the Bailey family, Kelly was in secondary school and still lived with her parents in County Tipperary. She had played violin in The Siblings, and during that time had developed quite a crush on Jon, the American rock guitarist. Of course he had done nothing to discourage it, and had in fact been involved with her to the point that her older brother Danny had felt compelled to intervene.

Although Jon was a bit nervous, he was also hopeful. That day he spoke to his sister Jen about it.

"Maybe it's a good sign that she's bringing her family to see me perform."

Jen rolled her eyes. "Did it ever occur to you they might be coming to see Danny?"

"Oh… I guess you're right."

The Bailey family, anxious to see Second Wind perform, arrived with their backstage passes well before the concert started. Jon had just stepped out of the dressing room in his new leather pants. He greeted everyone, pausing to give

Kelly his signature charming smile. Kelly blushed and lowered her eyes.

"Hello Jon," she said sweetly.

His heart fluttered at the sight of her lustrous auburn hair. "Can I give you a hug? Your parents just went backstage with Danny."

"Oh Jon, I've really missed you."

He took her reply as a yes and gave her a tender kiss, then whispered to her. "I've missed you more than you know."

Kelly looked into his deep blue eyes. "Please don't say that unless you mean it. I've spent a lot of time trying to get over you."

Jon kissed her again. "Are you over me?"

"You know I'm not. What are we going to do?"

"I don't know, angel, but if Laura and Liam can overcome their odds, there has to be a way for us. I thought it would be best to forget about you and move on. But you keep coming back into my heart."

"Mum still won't let me see you until I'm eighteen. I can't wait another year."

A look of determination came to Jon's face. "Let me think about this for a while. The third song we do tonight is one I wrote for you. It's called *Until Then*. Please keep it in your heart. Now, you'd better join your parents before they miss you."

∞

Before Second Wind went on stage, Jon asked Liam for a favor.

"Hey, Big Guy, would you mind saying a special intro for *Until Then*? Kelly's in the audience and... you know...." Liam grinned and nodded.

The first two songs were well received, and when the audience quieted, Liam stepped up to the mic.

"This next one is written and performed from the heart by The Cowboy himself for a very special young lady. It's called *Until Then*."

As he sang, Jon searched beneath the blinding stage lights until his eyes found Kelly. With renewed purpose his voice took on a greater depth, and soon Kelly's eyes were blinded–by her own tears. She was careful to conceal it.

The entire performance was riveting and the audience demanded two encores. After the show the Baileys went backstage to congratulate Danny and Jen. They didn't notice that Jon and Kelly had slipped behind a curtain for some privacy.

"Jon, that was the most beautiful song I've ever heard," Kelly sighed. "Will you record it for me?"

"Of course–it's your song." He swept her into his arms. "I think I have a plan for us to see each other. Why don't you ask if you can stay with your sister Chloe at Montrose this summer and help her with the babies? Jen and I are going to Italy to be with our parents and Danny's coming, too. What your mum doesn't have to know is that I'm only going for a couple of weeks, and then returning to the manor."

"Jon, you're a genius!" Kelly grinned. "It really won't be lying–I just won't mention that you're coming back sooner than the others."

"After all, it's all for love. Whoa–I think that's the title of my next song."

Kelly looked longingly into his eyes. "Jon, are you saying you love me?"

Tears came to his eyes. "I guess I am. I've never felt this way before. I've seen others in love, but… I never thought it would happen to me."

"Please say the words, Jon."

"Kelly Bailey, I love you. I guess I have for a long time now." They kissed until they heard voices approaching.

The smile never left Jon's face all night, even long after the concert was over. "What's up with my brother?" Jen asked Danny. "I know we were great, but he's still on cloud nine." Danny shrugged. Liam smiled to himself–he had a pretty good idea of what was going on.

Liam found Jon in the studio early the next morning, dubbing from the Tascam master recorder to a cassette deck.

"Hey, we'd better get a move on, Jon. We're almost ready to leave for Cork."

"I'm making a copy of *Until Then* for Kelly."

Liam raised his eyebrows. "Jon, you'd better not be playing with her heart. She's a sweet girl, and maybe a little fragile."

Jon looked up from the mixer. "I wouldn't do that to Kelly. I've fallen in love."

"God help us all!" Liam rolled his eyes.

"Hey man, love isn't just for you guys. I know you think I'm not capable of sticking to one girl, but you're wrong."

"Hey, Cowboy, calm down. I'm just teasing. I know you're a passionate guy and you have a big heart. I just thought you were happy with all the girls hanging on you."

"They're mostly just using me to have a good time," Jon remarked. "They don't really care about me. I like the attention, but the truth is–I'm lonely for the real thing. I want what you and Laura have, and Danny and Jen. I want someone who truly cares about me."

Liam put his arm around his friend. "I'm sorry for teasing. I believe you do love Kelly, and I'll do what I can to help. I know it'll be a tough road with her mum and all."

Jon told Liam about the plans he'd made with Kelly while he put the tape into a mailer and addressed it to her– from Montrose Manor, to disguise the fact that it was from him.

The city of Cork is not nearly as large as Dublin, but is one of many in Ireland where people work hard and play hard–and love good music. The two nights of performances went well with a packed house both nights.

After the dates in Cork, Foolish Pleasure took off to perform in Belfast. As previously decided by Aidan, Second Wind did not accompany the American band to Northern Ireland. They were scheduled to reunite in Glasgow, Scotland, for two concerts, and two more in Edinburgh.

When the young musicians returned to Montrose Manor, there was a message for Laura to call Kelly. She made the call then handed Jon the phone as planned, concealing from Kelly's mum that her young daughter was talking to the older American boy.

"Hello angel, I've missed hearing your voice. Did you get the tape?"

"Yes, and I've already played it many times. I like it so much I'm coming to Scotland to see you perform it live."

"That's a nice dream... I wish!"

"Dreams can come true... and wishes, too. Molly is going to see Brent for a week while he designs a golf course just outside of Glasgow. She asked me if I would like to go with her. It's perfect timing–I can see you at all your concerts in Scotland."

"That's a great plan! Does Molly know about us?"

"Yes, and of course she knows all about Mum's cautious ways. Molly moved out on her own when she turned eighteen. She thinks the world of you, and she's happy for me."

When Jon hung up he danced around the room singing *Until Then.*

"I think he's been bitten by the love bug," Liam chuckled.

Danny shook his head. "He's makin' honey in his heart, all right. I just hope they know what they're doin'"

Second Wind flew off to Glasgow the next morning accompanied by Aidan and Peggy. The band was able to travel light as all their equipment had gone with Foolish Pleasure's roadies.

"Jon, you're sure in a good mood," Peggy commented.

He grinned. "I couldn't be happier, Peggy Girl. And how are things with you?"

Peggy glanced at Garrett, who was smiling at her. "I'd say they're brilliant!"

They arrived at the hotel to find Greg waiting for them at the front desk. He looked worried as he approached Aidan.

"I haven't heard a word from the roadies. They were supposed to be here early this morning. I'm afraid they may have had some trouble getting out of Belfast. Just as our concert was ending, the word got out that another political prisoner had died from the hunger strikes. Rioting broke out." Greg shook his head and looked at Jon.

"Your former drummer, Brian, was a big help to us. With all the roadblocks and police we would've had no way out, but he got a car and driver to take us to the airport. He stayed behind while the roadies got everything loaded, and he was going to show them another route to the ferry."

Jon began to panic. "I knew I should have carried my own guitar!"

"And then what would you do—a solo act?" Liam asked sarcastically. "We all need our equipment."

"I suggest everyone calm down," Aidan said. "I'll make a few calls and find out where they are. Why don't you all go over to the venue; maybe they'll roll up in the lorry while you're there. You can call me here at the hotel later."

Greg agreed and they all headed out to the stadium. Liam did a vocal sound check on the P.A., but without their instruments, there was only so much prep work they could do. After two hours there still was no word from the roadies. There was nothing left to do but return to the hotel.

The look on Aidan's face was not one of encouragement. "I traced them from Belfast. They got on the wrong ferry. I'm afraid they won't make it in time for the concert tonight. I suggest we try to rent equipment."

Jon threw his hands up while Greg muttered something about lunatics in Belfast.

Aidan spoke to Greg. "Consider yourselves fortunate that you got out of there and no one was hurt. Now, I know you want your own instruments, but we have no other choice. Greg, surely you've played other drum sets before?"

"Yes, I have two sets in New York. You're right–we have to make the best of it. Now let's get busy and see what we can rent on short notice."

Greg, Aidan and Jon hit the phone books. They found a music store in Glasgow that welcomed the large volume of business at the last minute. The equipment was delivered and set up, with little time to spare.

Laura smiled as she picked up the cherished tambourine which she had never let the roadies pack. It had once belonged to her maternal grandmother, a mysterious woman who Aidan never spoke of. He had never been comfortable with the fact that Laura's grandmother was an Irish traveler, another name for gypsy. Laura had no qualms about it, and to her the ornate instrument always rang with a brilliant sound that came from a distant age and a faraway land.

The other band members were busy tuning and adjusting, trying to get a feel for the unfamiliar instruments. Jon was not happy with his rented guitar and his mood reflected it.

Just when it seemed like there would be no hope, Jon looked up and saw what he thought was an angel standing before him, all dressed in white with beautiful long hair flowing over bare shoulders. Jon put the guitar down and took Kelly into his arms.

"Everything will be grand, Jon. You're so talented you could play any guitar."

Jon kissed her, feeling a wave of comfort. "Now that you're here I'll be fine."

"Oh, but you already are–a fine *thing*, that is." She winked and gave him a kiss for good luck, then hurried off the stage. It was time for the show to begin.

The Glasgow audience enjoyed both sets as if the musicians were from their own hometown. The concertgoers were, of course, unaware of the equipment problems, and Jon was proud of himself for rising to meet the challenges.

The roadies finally rolled up–after the show was over.

Mark, the lead man and driver, explained. "Brian started giving us directions, but he'd only gotten as far as the ferry terminal before he was interrupted by the police clearing the area. We had to get out of there fast." Greg stood with his arms folded, and the roadie continued sheepishly.

"Things were getting crazy with the rioting. We found the ferry terminal with only a moment to spare. There was just enough room for our truck at the stern and we took our spot– and they pulled up the ramp and left the dock. We were relieved to be aboard. And when the toll taker guy came around, he said something to us–not sure if it was in English– and we just handed him the money. We didn't know we were on the wrong ferry."

Greg sighed, accepting the explanation. "Glad you made it out safely." He patted Mark on the back and the roadie heaved a sigh of relief.

"You guys went through a lot," Jon said. "Thanks for saving my guitar."

Kelly whispered to Jon. "Someday, will I be as important to you as your guitar?"

"Oh, that's my guitar–you're my angel. Without your smiling face I couldn't have played tonight." Kelly was pleased and gave Jon a kiss.

The next night both bands were in much better form with their own instruments, and the enthusiasm of the crowds showed it.

As they prepared to leave for Edinburgh the following morning, Kelly asked Molly if she could go with them.

Molly pursed her lips. "You tell Jon it's time for him and me to have a chat."

Jon cautiously knocked on Molly's door. "Kelly said you wanted to talk to me?"

"As a matter of fact, I do," she said with a wry smile as Jon entered. "I'm trustin' you to be good to my little sister. Don't rush into things best left 'til she's a bit older."

"I'll treat her like fine Waterford crystal–beautiful and very fragile."

"I want to believe your intentions are honorable... but I'll remind Danny to keep an eye on you just the same." Jon frowned but then Molly gave him a wink.

Edinburgh was to be the pinnacle of the four-night engagement in Scotland. The ancient walls of stone seemed to welcome the modern sounds created by the young musicians. Liam instantly felt a kinship with the Scots. He wasn't sure if it had simply come from reading Robert Louis Stevenson or because Liam's own humble beginnings as a horse trainer's son somehow put him in touch with his Celtic roots. As he viewed the benevolent yet lively people in the audience, Liam guessed that many of them had come off a long workday just to hear the bands perform.

On the second day in the storied capital city, Second Wind carved out time for some midday fun, taking a guided tour of Edinburgh Castle. Jon did manage to spend some alone time with Kelly, but they were interrupted when he was recognized by some young girls in the tour group. Jon behaved in a way that was quite respectful of Kelly, introducing her as his girlfriend–much to her delight. Danny reacted with cautious optimism, and he couldn't help wondering if somehow his sister's heart might get broken as it had a couple of years earlier when Jon was involved with a much older girl for a short time.

◗◖◗◖

When the last show ended, it was time to say goodbye to Foolish Pleasure and wish them well on their overseas tour.

"If everything goes well next summer," Greg said, "we'll do another tour to promote our new album. We'd love to have you open for us again. The plan will be to play most of Europe and finish in the US." He smiled at Liam. "That is, if our best songwriter comes up with some more hits real soon."

"I'm working on it."

"I'll talk to Aidan and see if we can do the whole tour this time," Jon said. "As long as we don't miss classes and Aidan can accompany us–or maybe my father–it could work."

"I understand their concerns," Greg smiled. "You're still young."

"Hey!" Jon protested. "Garrett is twenty and Danny and I'll be nineteen soon."

"True, but Laura's only sixteen, right? I know you guys are pretty hip for your age, but you should be thankful you've got Aidan looking out for you. There are plenty of sharks out there in the business."

Liam looked at Jon knowingly. "Oh, we're aware of that. You could say we nearly got devoured in St. Moritz." Jon imitated the snapping jaws of a shark with his arms, his curled fingers as the teeth. They all laughed.

Since it wasn't practical to fly all of Second Wind's equipment home with the group, Jon, Liam and Danny decided to rent a lorry and drive it themselves. Garrett had had gotten word his father was ill, so he would fly back with the girls and Aidan.

Danny drove and Jon was the co-pilot, with Liam busy composing music in his head while staring out the window.

"I know this route well," Jon said. "It's the same way I mapped out for Laura and Liam when they ran off to get married. We'll drive right through Gretna Green."

Danny and Jon looked to Liam for a response, but he was oblivious, lost in his own world. They both laughed.

"What, did I miss something?"

"I guess this is why he can keep the songs rolling off the press," Jon said. "When he's in songwriting mode, he's really out there."

Danny smiled. "Thank God one of us can keep the songs rolling."

A few miles down the road Danny pulled the van over, saying he could use a break. Liam looked around quizzically.

"This place looks familiar." Danny laughed and Jon shook his head.

39

"I'd think you'd remember the place you and Laura almost got hitched."

"Oh my God–Gretna Green! It seems like years ago, like I was just a kid last time I was here."

"Well," Jon said, rubbing his chin, "you kinda *were* just a kid!"

Liam smiled knowingly. "And a really determined one at that."

# Chapter Seven

"I've got a surprise for you," Aidan announced to Laura and Jen when they returned to Montrose. "Actually, two surprises." He smiled, a twinkle in his eye.

"Please tell us!" Laura begged.

"We've got a couple of new horses in the barn that need riders. Jen, do you think you and Danny might be interested?"

"Of course!" she exclaimed. "That's so thoughtful of you—and generous."

"They're geldings from Feyland Stud," Aidan explained. "They're a little small and they won't be runners. I usually sell the ones that don't show race potential, but these two have wonderful dispositions. It's about time we had a couple of extra riding horses around here. Who knows, maybe I'll get to ride again myself."

Laura beamed and threw her arms around her father. "You're the greatest!"

"Welcome home," Patrick greeted when the girls arrived at the barn. A moment later a young man came out of the tack room. "Oh, let me introduce you to Rory, he'll be helpin' out this summer. Rory's been workin' with the new horses from Feyland."

41

"Hello, I'm Laura Meegan and this is Jen Bianchi."

"Rory McClenny at your service," he announced, tipping his cap. He gave Laura a charming smile. "Pleased to meet you." Laura and Jen glanced at each other.

"Rory, why don't you show the girls the new horses while I finish with this colt."

"It'll be a pleasure–right this way." With a tilt of his head and a gesture, Rory indicated the box stalls–called *boxes* in Ireland–where the new geldings were stabled. Rory's natural magnetism had made an impression, and the girls eagerly followed Patrick's tall, slender assistant.

"Cute," Jen mouthed to Laura, making sure the young man didn't see.

Knowing Laura was the boss's daughter, Rory planned to waste no time winning her approval. "They're both bay geldings–Topper has the blaze and Hawk has a star."

While the girls assessed the new horses, Rory was busy assessing Laura.

Jen admired the bay with the blaze. "I like Topper. He reminds me of a horse I used to ride back in Long Island."

Rory flipped his blond hair back. "I'm sure he'll take a likin' to you right away. Why don't you try him out?" Jen nodded and Rory locked his hazel eyes on Laura. "Perhaps you could ride Hawk."

The girls agreed, and Rory moved things along smoothly, tacking up the horses himself and leading them to the arena. He gave each of the girls a leg up into their saddles. Laura and Jen began to ride their horses at a walk while Rory moved to the middle of the arena.

"Jen, give Topper a little more head so he'll relax. Laura, you're doin' great."

"What's Hawk's real name?" Laura asked.

"Soaring Hawk and Topper is Top Win," Rory chuckled. "Neither of them earned their names on the track."

Jen patted her horse on the neck. "I think Topper is a wonderful horse, and he's a winner in my book." Rory smiled politely.

After a few more passes around the ring, the girls felt it was a good first-time ride with the young horses and decided to put them away.

"Let me take care of that for you," Rory offered.

"Rory," Patrick interrupted, coming around a corner. "I need you to bring the horses in from the pastures. It's time to feed."

A flash of annoyance passed over Rory's face, but he just shrugged.

"Oh, we can take care of them ourselves," Laura said.

The girls groomed their horses and rewarded them with some carrots. Laura heard a commotion nearby and looked up to see Sky sidestepping and throwing his head while Rory tried to lead him. Desert Sky was Liam's Arabian gelding that he'd ridden for ten years. Laura knew the horse well, having ridden alongside Liam all that time on her Arabian mare, Desert Rose.

"What's got you all worked up, boy?" Laura took the lead from Rory and Sky immediately settled down. "Now that's more like it." Laura was puzzled. "I'm sorry–this isn't like him. Sky's a little high-strung, but he's never been a problem."

"Well, I've tried with him," Rory said. "He threw a fit this mornin' when I put your mare out, so I made him wait until I put the others out."

"Oh no!" Laura exclaimed. "They always go out together. You only have to lead one and the other will follow. You'll see–Sky is easy. Just don't separate them."

Rory nodded dutifully, but turned away scowling. *Boy, these Arabs are spoiled.*

Jon, Danny and Liam arrived at Dublin House late that evening with the music equipment. Molly and Kelly were there to greet them.

"Liam, there was a message from Garrett. He wanted you to call when you got in. He sounded very... serious."

"Thanks, Molly. I'll call right away. I hope his father is all right."

After he hung up the phone, Liam's face was drawn. "Mr. McCormack passed away–Garrett's in bad shape. I think we should go over and see him."

Liam called Montrose to tell Aidan the sad news. "I'd like to stay here a couple of days to be with Garrett until after the funeral." Aidan agreed, then put Laura on. "Liam, when will you be home? I miss you."

"I know, sweetheart, but Garrett is going through a bad time. He lost his mother just a few years ago. Someone should be here for him."

"I guess you're right... but hurry home. Anyway, I wanted to tell you about what's been happening here at Montrose." Laura chatted on, describing the new horses and meeting Rory, but Liam only half-listened. He had slipped into memories of his own loneliness when his father had died.

Garrett's Aunt Maggie met Liam, Jon and Danny at her door.

"Boys, I'm so glad you're here. Garrett's not takin' this very well. He was very close to his father, and it all happened so sudden. We didn't even know he had heart trouble." She gestured to the stairway. "Please, go right on up to his room."

They found their friend in a chair staring out the window. Liam recognized the familiar look of grief and put a comforting hand on Garrett's shoulder. "I'm so sorry. I know your pain. I wish I could say something to ease it."

Garrett nodded weakly. "Thanks for coming. Maybe you guys could do me a favor–I need to get out of here for a while. The funeral is tomorrow, and I just can't listen to my aunt make any more arrangements."

"Why don't you come and stay with us tonight?" Liam suggested. "When my father died I played my guitar and wrote a song for him. It really helped me get through it. If you want, I'll help you write a song for your father."

Garrett looked up at Liam with tears in his eyes. "Yeah, I would like that." He threw some things into a knapsack and they left for Dublin House.

While Molly showed Garrett to a guest room, the others remained downstairs. "Liam, I just don't know what to say to him," Jon confessed. "I've never been through anything like this."

"If you like, I'll tend to him tonight," Liam sighed. "I've been there, and I know these next few days will be the hardest for him."

Liam and Garrett stayed up most of the night writing a song for Garrett to sing at the funeral. They finally went to bed at four in the morning.

The funeral was late in the afternoon. The boys were there for Garrett, along with his aunt, his cousin Katie, and her best friend Loreena. There were barely a dozen in attendance. Brian didn't come–he was in the hospital for another orthopedic procedure.

Garrett's song was simple and personal, and a much-needed expression of grief.

It was his father's wishes that there be no wake after the funeral, so everyone went their separate ways, but Liam knew his friend shouldn't be alone. In a phone call to Montrose later, Liam recounted the events of the day to Aidan.

"Why don't you invite Garrett to come here with you and stay with us at the manor for a while? It might help him to change his surroundings. I'll tell Laura later when she comes back from the barn."

"Thanks, Aidan. I really appreciate this."

The four boys made the drive from Dublin that night, arriving after everyone else had gone to bed. Liam sensed that Garrett might have difficulty trying to fall sleep alone in a strange room, so he took him into the music studio up in the tower of the large castle-like manor. The two never powered up any instruments but talked well into the night, only dozing for a couple of hours on the couch in the studio.

Once the morning sun began to stream through the windows, Liam's eyes snapped open. He shook his friend awake. "It's a bit later than I usually sleep, but everyone should still be at breakfast. We'll make a stop on the way down–to at least splash our faces."

With the studio being on the top floor, it took the two of them awhile to go down two flights of stairs, stop at their bedroom suites for a few minutes and then descend the grand staircase. Fortunately the family was still seated when they arrived.

Peggy jumped up and gave Garrett a gentle hug. Conversations stopped at the table, and everyone expressed their condolences to Garrett. Jon couldn't think of anything to say but awkward pleasantries, and Danny wasn't much better.

Although he was polite and thanked them all, Garrett soon perceived his own grief as a drain on the others' well-being, and he felt inappropriate sharing it. Only Liam seemed to be able to comfort him.

Laura thought a change of subject was needed, and wanted to show Liam the new horses anyway. She asked him, "How about we go for a ride and get some fresh air?"

"Sorry, sweetheart, I'm really beat. Garrett and I stayed up most of the night."

Laura pouted. "All right, I guess I'll have to ride with Rory, then."

"Who's Rory?" Liam asked, confused.

"I knew you weren't listening to me the other night." Laura tried to explain again, but Garrett suddenly stood up.

"Please forgive my rudeness–your hospitality is appreciated–but I could really use some more sleep."

Liam also stood up. "That sounds like a good idea. I'm going to turn in, too. Laura, maybe you should ride Sky. You know how he is with strangers."

Laura was puzzled by Liam's suggestion. "Well, that's not what I had in mind… but yes. Sky doesn't like Rory very much."

Now Liam was the one confused, but he was too tired to figure it out.

Having slept most of the day, Garrett felt a little more relaxed at dinner. "I really want to thank you all for your support. I know I haven't been very pleasant to be with."

"We all understand," Aidan said. "You are welcome to stay as long as you want."

Laura pouted, wondering if Garrett would take up all of Liam's time. Liam could read her reaction, and he was bothered by her lack of compassion.

Peggy invited Garrett to go for a walk with her around the grounds after dinner. Liam thought it would be a good opportunity to talk to Laura.

"Laura, would you like to go to the barn? You could show me the new horses."

"It's about time," Laura scolded with a smile. "Sky has been acting up. I think he misses you. I know I do."

Along the path Liam stopped to kiss her. "I have missed you, but you know Garrett's been going through a very hard time. Remember, I wasn't alone when my father died. I had you."

"Well, Garrett has Peggy," Laura replied coldly.

Liam searched her eyes. "Sweetheart, this is not like you. What's going on?"

"I'm sorry," Laura said, lowering her head. "I just feel neglected. We've been with the band and traveling so long... I was really looking forward to some private time with you here at Montrose."

Liam responded with a passionate kiss. "Now do you feel better?"

"Much better."

"Sweetheart, what else can I do to show you how much I love you?"

"Just be here for me when I need you."

Laura introduced Liam to the new horses. He decided to check on Sky.

"Hey buddy, I hear you've been acting up lately. What's up with that?" Sky nudged him aggressively as if to tell Liam that something needed his immediate attention. Liam fed his horse a carrot and promised to return soon for a ride. In spite of a nagging feeling that something wasn't right, Liam focused his attention on Laura.

He put his arm around her. "Now, tell me about this... Rory."

"Why, Mr. Delaney, could it be that you're a little jealous?"

"Should I be?"

"Don't neglect me and you won't have any worries."

Liam was bothered by her answer but decided to hold his tongue.

❧

Danny and Jen left early the next morning with Jon for the flight to Italy. Robert and Catherine Bianchi had a long-term lease on a villa on the Tuscan coast while Mr. Bianchi conducted business in Italy. Jon and Jen's parents had generously issued an open invitation to their extended families, the Meegans and the Baileys, to come and stay any time. The summer break from studies was an opportune time.

After wishing Danny and Jen safe travels, Liam decided it would be a good time to go riding with Laura. He voiced his concern to her about his Arabian horse.

49

"Last night Sky seemed unsettled. I think he needs to get out and go for a good ride today."

"Liam, you can ride Sky anytime. You should try out the new horses."

"All right, but let's take Sky and Rose out for a ride to the cave afterwards."

Laura's face lit up. "That sounds like a good plan."

Liam was referring to the cave they had discovered as children when exploring the far reaches of the 850-acre estate. It had served them well in the early days as a secret hideaway, especially during the dark period in Liam's life following the death of his father. In her desperation, Liam's mother had taken up with a religious zealot whose domineering nature–and inclination to violent outbursts–had injured young Liam both physically and mentally. He would not have survived had it not been for Laura.

As the years progressed the bond between Laura and Liam grew in ways they had not predicted, and it wasn't long before their forbidden love became the reason for riding their horses through the woods to the sanctity of the cave.

Rory was already working Hawk in the arena. "Good mornin', Laura," Rory said cheerfully. "You must be Liam."

Liam nodded as he looked the young man over.

"Have you come to ride the new horses?" Rory asked.

"Yes," Laura replied. "I think I'll ride Hawk again–Liam could try Topper."

"Great," Rory said. "I'll go get them ready for you."

"I can get Topper ready myself," Liam said firmly.

Rory raised his eyebrows and smiled at Laura. "Be my guest."

Laura went into the arena while Liam went to tack up the other horse.

"Did I say something wrong to Liam?" Rory asked quietly.

"No," Laura sighed. "He's just a little hard to get to know."

"I guess Sky is a bit like his owner, then."

Laura found this amusing and laughed. Sensing Laura's easy mood, Rory began telling a humorous story about a stubborn horse he had once worked with.

Liam was not happy to hear the laughter when he led Topper to the gate. Unaware of Liam's agitation, Laura trotted off towards the other end of the arena.

Rory started in on Liam the moment he mounted. "Liam, this is not your Arab. You have to show Topper who's the boss. Give him some leg, and give him more contact with the bit. Here, use this crop on him–make him move out."

Liam didn't even dignify Rory's "instruction" with a response, refusing the offered riding crop. Instead, he stroked the young colt's neck and spoke softly to him. "You just need a few minutes to get to know me." Liam gently eased Topper into a walk, moving away from the newcomer.

Laura was busy riding Hawk, oblivious to the tension between the two.

"Laura, you're doing a great job," Rory called out. "You're a very accomplished rider." Laura smiled and Liam rolled his eyes.

Rory refocused his attention on Topper. "I really do think you need to be more forceful, or he'll turn out to be as spoiled as Sky."

Liam set his jaw, glaring at the presumptuous newcomer. Riding to the arena gate, Liam quickly dismounted.

"Liam, where are you going?" Laura called out.

"I've had enough and so has this horse. I'm going to ride my horse my way."

Laura was confused–and a bit upset. "Please wait for me and I'll ride with you."

"All right, then–let's go."

Laura rode up to Rory and dismounted. He shrugged his shoulders, feigning innocence as he took the horse from her.

∞

Liam was silent while he and Laura got Sky and Rose ready. He wasted no time mounting up, and Laura sensed she'd better keep up or get left behind.

A few minutes down the trail Liam finally spoke. "What exactly is it you like about that Rory?"

"Liam, you never like anyone at first. Give him a chance. Rory has a wonderful sense of humor, and he seems like a great horse trainer."

The hair stood up on the back of Liam's neck. "My father was a great horse trainer, but he never used a crop or a whip on a young horse. He would have been patient and watched Topper carefully so he could communicate with him on the right level. That Rory is all flash and hurry-up, with no tolerance or understanding. I won't have anything to do with his methods."

"I think you're just jealous because we get along so well," Laura quipped. Rose broke into a gallop and Laura did not hold her back.

Liam allowed Sky to catch up to the mare. "You're right, I am jealous. Not of him–I think he's arrogant beyond description. But I am bothered that you seem to be taken in by him."

Laura didn't respond and just rode on to the cave.

When they got there she dismounted and turned to face Liam. "I'm not taken in by anyone. He's just a friend. Are you saying I can't have friends?"

"I'm just asking you to use some good judgment."

"And you're using good judgment? You've just met him and only exchanged a few words. I recall how much you disliked Jon when you first met him."

"C'mon–that was a long time ago, and you can't compare Jon to that Rory."

"Will you please quit calling him *that Rory*? He's very nice and he's trying to please. Patrick says he's a hard worker."

"It doesn't help when he keeps putting Sky down."

"If you were here you'd know Sky has been a real challenge. I don't know what's wrong with him."

"Oh, he's trying to tell us–we just haven't been listening. I'll figure it out."

The tension lingered. There was none of the usual warmth between Laura and Liam that they had come to cherish in the cave. But they still had their horses and the lush countryside to insulate them from the world. On the ride back, Sky was relaxed and happy, racing through the trees and across the meadows with the wind flying through his long mane and tail.

As they approached the barn, however, Sky spotted Rory and tensed up.

So did Liam.

He stroked his gelding's neck. "Tell me, boy, I'm listening."

When Laura and Liam led the horses by the feed cart, Sky almost knocked Liam over to snatch a mouthful of hay. Liam was surprised—his horse never did that. He took a good look at the horse's frame and his suspicions were confirmed. Sky had lost weight.

A moment later Patrick came into the barn. "Have a nice ride?"

"Did you notice Sky has lost weight?" Liam asked.

Patrick stood back and took a good look. "Yes, I've noticed. But I haven't cut back on his feed. It probably has to do with all the fussin' he's been doin' lately."

"Keep a close eye on him for me? Something's wrong and he's trying to tell us."

Liam grabbed a handful of grain for Sky and an extra portion of hay. The gelding devoured it as if he hadn't seen food in a week.

Liam waited until Laura went to go for carrots before asking his next question. "Patrick, what do you think about that Rory?"

Patrick smiled. "You don't like all the attention he's givin' Laura?"

Liam shook his head. "No, I don't... but I meant as a trainer."

"Well, he was hired to help out with the horses, but I wouldn't call him a trainer. I guess he wants to be—he's taken on the new geldings himself. I think he tries too hard to impress people. But he shows up to work. With you and Danny away at college—and now Danny off to Italy—I need the help."

Patrick's explanation did nothing to ease Liam's worry. He was in deep thought as he and Laura walked back to the manor.

"Why are you so distracted lately?" she asked

"Sorry–I guess I've been missing my father. I'm sure it's because of Garrett."

"I think it's time for Garrett to go home and get on with his life. You've been a good friend to him, but it's starting to… affect you."

"I can't believe you just said that. How can I turn my back on him now?"

"Well, maybe you should go back to Dublin with him!"

"Laura, what are you saying?"

"I'm saying you're not really here with me anyway. You don't listen to half of what I say, and you've been moody since you got home. You could pull yourself out of it if you would show some interest in the new horses and try to get to know Rory."

Liam clenched his teeth. *I'm so sick of hearing the name Rory.* He decided to ignore his own irritation for the moment and took Laura into his arms. "I'm sorry I've been distant. I promise I'll be here with you. There's no place I'd rather be."

"What about Rory?"

"Okay, I'll do my best to get to know him."

Laura smiled and kissed him. "All right, then."

As they walked, Laura told him about the village fair that was coming up that weekend. The mention of the fair pulled Liam into the memory of a horse training demonstration his father had done when Liam was a small boy. He smiled as he recalled the enthusiasm of the crowd.

Laura paused. "Liam, are you listening to me?"

He looked up with a sheepish smile. "I heard most everything...."

"Good, then. I'm looking forward to having you help me at the fair."

He nodded dutifully. *What did I agree to?*

A few hours later Liam asked Laura if she wanted to go back to the barn with him. "Fiona just gave me a bunch of carrots for Sky and Rose."

Laura looked at her watch. "They'll be feeding, but maybe we can help."

When they got to the barn Rory had already fed the horses.

"He's always one step ahead of me," Patrick shrugged. "I guess I can go and have my dinner now." With that the barn manager strode off towards the cottage that he shared with his wife, Chloe, who was Danny's eldest sister.

Liam approached Sky and instantly noticed there were only a few stems of hay left in his manger. He looked in the nearby mangers and saw that the other horses still had plenty of feed left.

"Sky, I don't think Rory's feeding you enough."

Laura overheard the remark from inside Rose's box. "Sky always eats faster."

Liam ignored her and went to grab an armful of hay for Sky. Liam heard a door close at the end of the barn and walked briskly out to catch up with Rory before he left.

"How much hay did you give Sky?"

"Enough for such a high-strung horse."

"How much have you cut him back?"

"This horse has too much energy and needs to be cut back."

"You're not in charge here!" Liam's face turned red with anger. He grabbed Rory by the collar. "You think you can play God around here? If you ever cut him back again I'll kick your arse first and then have you fired."

Laura came running up. "Liam! What are you doing? Let go of him right now!"

Liam released Rory with a shove and stormed off to find Patrick. He was shaking as he marched towards Patrick's cottage. *I can't believe Laura came to his defense!*

Laura turned to Rory, who was straightening his collar. "I'm sorry about Liam. This has nothing to do with his horse– it's me. Liam gets jealous if anyone even looks my way. Heaven forbid I should have any new friends."

"Forgive me for bein' bold, but why do you put up with that kind of behavior? You've done nothin' wrong. You deserve someone... who trusts you."

"Liam's not like that–the temper, I mean. I'm afraid you've seen his bad side."

"You don't need to apologize for him. I just hope he isn't goin' to get me fired."

"Oh, don't worry about that. I'll put in a good word for you with my father."

When Liam got to Patrick and Chloe's cottage he was shaking. Chloe noticed the moment she opened the door. "Everythin' all right?"

Liam told them about Rory's admitting to cutting Sky's feed down.

Patrick put his hand on Liam's shoulder. "I'll have a talk with him. He's not allowed to make that kind of decision."

"Please watch him," Liam said. "I don't trust that guy."

"Don't you worry, lad. I'll take care of it."

Liam appeared satisfied, so he thanked Patrick and left the cottage.

"I've never seen him like this," Chloe said after the door closed. "That Rory seems to be botherin' him a lot."

Patrick rubbed his chin. "There are two things Liam holds dear to his heart: One of them is Sky and the other is Laura. I think young Rory's been messin' with both."

Chloe nodded. "Ahhhh."

❧

Liam had calmed somewhat as he walked back to the manor. Laura met him at the back door. "You can forget about telling Father and having Rory fired. I've already told Father it was an honest mistake and you were being unreasonable."

Liam shook his head and brushed past her to go wash up.

Dinner was quiet. Finally Garrett cleared his throat. "I'm going back to Dublin tomorrow to meet with my father's attorney. I'll have to settle his affairs."

Aidan thought the young man could use some more help. "Garrett, I'll drive you to Dublin and look over the documents for you if you'd like."

"You would do that for me, Aidan?"

"Of course. And I'm sure Liam will go with us."

Liam glanced at Laura, who turned away. "Sure, I'll go with you to Dublin."

After dinner Laura went to her room. Liam came to her open door, and she spoke right up. "I knew I couldn't count on you. I'll ask Rory to help me at the fair!"

Liam winced. *Rory again.*

The look of puzzlement on Liam's face made matters worse. "You were going to help me take pictures at the fair!" Laura cried.

Liam hung his head. "I guess I wasn't listening. I'm sorry."

"No need to be. You've never really been interested in my photography anyway." Laura slowly crossed her expansive suite with her back to Liam. "When I told Rory about it *he* was interested."

The explosive impulse at the mere mention of Rory's name was almost too much for Liam, but he controlled himself. "Laura, please. I do like your photography, and I want to be with you–more than anything."

Laura wheeled around to face him. "More than anything? How can you be with me if you're going to Dublin with Garrett?"

"I'll talk to him–he'll understand."

"Don't bother! I think we need a break. Go to Dublin."
She walked briskly to the door and held it wide open for Liam.
"Maybe when you come back you'll really want to be with
me. Now go!" Laura slammed the door and locked it.

Liam dragged his weary body across the hall, feeling
completely defeated. Reliving the loss of own his father had
made him depressed and withdrawn, using up all his
emotional reserve. The confrontations with Rory–and the
disagreements with Laura about the brash stranger–had put
Liam right over the edge.

Laura was nowhere to be found the next morning. Iris,
the downstairs maid, told Liam she had gone to the barn
already. As much as he wanted to say goodbye, Liam knew
going to the barn would be a bad idea; he'd see Rory again.
He decided to leave a note instead.

# Chapter Eight

Garrett was thankful for Aidan's business knowledge as they plowed through the dreary details with the attorney.

"I'm afraid the life insurance settlement will only cover the funeral expenses," Aidan said after they left the office. "However, after the sale of your father's house, you should have enough money to finish Trinity."

Aidan and Liam's continued encouragement had Garrett in a better frame of mind when they dropped him off at his aunt's house that evening.

***

Liam was very quiet the next day as they drove back to Montrose.

"I imagine you've been thinking about your father quite a bit these days," Aidan said, breaking the silence.

"Yes, I have; and I'm sure I've been no fun lately."

"Nobody expects you to forget about your father, especially this family."

"Thanks, but Laura's not very happy about the time I've spent with Garrett."

Aidan looked thoughtful. "Well, Laura was only eight when she lost her mother. I think she forgets how deeply it cuts into your soul." Aidan's face filled with sorrow. "I will never forget my Fey–just as you should never forget your father."

Tears came to Liam's eyes. "I couldn't. But Aidan, you've been like a father to me ever since." Liam reached over and squeezed his shoulder, which brought a warm smile to Aidan's face.

When they got back the manor it was late afternoon. Liam knew Laura would be at the fair, and quickly walked to the village. As Liam made his way through the crowds, Laura caught sight of him. She glanced briefly at him but then looked away. "Oh, hello Liam. It was nice of you to make an appearance." Rory was walking alongside her, carrying her camera bag. "Rory's been a big help to me today."

Liam ignored her remark. "Laura, can I talk to you?"

"I'm busy taking pictures. You can talk to me at dinner." Laura turned and walked off with Rory, leaving Liam standing in stunned silence. The noise and bustling activity of the fair seemed a million miles away to him. Devastated, Liam retreated to the manor and the sanctuary of his room for the rest of the night.

"Where's Liam?" Aidan asked at dinner.

Hannah shrugged. "He said he was not hungry and wanted to rest in his room." Aidan studied his daughter, who appeared uninterested. *I suspect there's trouble in paradise. I think I'd better visit Liam after dinner.*

When a knock came to Liam's door, he was eager to open it, thinking it would be Laura. The moment Aidan came into view Liam's head dropped and his shoulders slumped.

"I'm sorry, son, it's just me. Can we talk?"

Liam nodded. Aidan walked in and put his hand on the troubled young man's shoulder.

"Just how bad are things between you and Laura?"

Liam walked to window and stared out. "I really don't know what's going on. She's mad at me for everything I do."

"Does it have to do with the new boy working in the barn?"

Liam sighed. "Yes, she thinks I'm being jealous and unreasonable."

"Are you?"

"Maybe. I don't like anything about him. I hate the way he handles the horses. He's strong handed and goes against everything I was taught by my father."

"Is it possible your judgment is clouded by seeing the attention he gives Laura?"

"Yes, I don't like it one bit. But beyond that, he really doesn't know how to care for horses."

"Don't you think Patrick should be the judge of that?"

Liam sighed. "It really upset me when he cut Sky's feed without asking anyone."

Aidan shrugged. "Laura explained it was an honest mistake. I'm sure it won't happen again. I wish you would work things out with her. I hate to see you so unhappy."

Liam nodded slowly. There was no more to say, and Aidan left the room.

Liam's eyes found the window again. *Sky's been trying to tell everyone.*

❧

Laura opened her door abruptly after Liam knocked.

"Can I come in and talk to you?" Liam asked cautiously.

"I suppose."

"What can I do to make you understand I love you?"

"Maybe that's not the point, Liam. I think you're taking me for granted. You've been shutting me out. Just because you kiss me and say you love me, it doesn't make everything all right again."

Liam tried to put his arms around her but she moved away.

"That's exactly what I mean," complained Laura.

"I'm so sorry you feel this way, Laura. I never meant to shut you out. You're the most important person in my life."

"You say the words, but it's clear you have other things on your mind. Decide where your priorities are. Maybe you need time away to think about where our relationship has been going. Maybe we should break up for a while."

"Laura! You can't mean that! Please tell me you still love me."

"I'm not saying I don't love you. But our relationship is supposed to be more than just hugging and kissing."

"Sweetheart, what's happening to us? I don't understand any of this."

"My point exactly. We need some time to think; I need to be alone for a while."

Liam was enraged. "Alone? Or alone with Rory?"

A flash of fury overtook Laura. "Get out of my room!"

"Laura, think about what you're doing to us!"

"If you don't trust me, there is no *us*. Now get out."

Liam retreated to his room barely able to breathe. He felt as though an enormous boulder was crushing his heart. Unable to make sense of anything that had happened, he spent the night tossing and turning.

Finally Liam decided to get up and pack a bag. He wrote two notes: one to Laura and one to Aidan, telling them he was going to take the train and stay at Dublin House for an undetermined period of time.

It was dawn as he left the manor. Liam stopped at the barn to be with the one who understood. He put his arms around Sky's neck and the gelding gently nuzzled him.

"Sky, you're the only one who really knows. I promise Patrick will look after you. I love you, boy." He hugged his horse's warm neck and left the barn in tears.

Patrick was just coming out of his cottage as Liam approached.

"What's wrong, lad?"

"I have to leave. Will you watch out for Sky? Please don't let Rory touch him."

Patrick put a comforting arm on Liam's shoulder. "Son, you know I'll always look after him. Now, tell me what you're doin' with that bag."

"I'm going to Dublin for a while. I need to write songs… and think about things."

"Do Aidan and Laura know you're goin'?"

"I left them each a note. It's far better that I go before they're up."

"Liam, I'll let Rory go if that'll make things better."

"God forbid! It would only make Laura more upset with me–but thanks anyway. Sorry, I have to catch my train."

"Let me at least give you a ride to the station."

"Thanks, Patrick, but I think the walk in the morning air will do me good." Liam paused a moment, taking in the estate around them. "I love this place... it's my home. But for now, I have to leave." He gave Patrick a hug and hurried down the driveway.

Laura did read the note that morning and went straight down to the barn. "Patrick, have you seen Liam?"

"He's off to Dublin. He said he left you a note."

Tears came to Laura's eyes. "He did–but I didn't want him to leave."

"Perhaps you should tell him that. He was pretty sad when he left this mornin'."

Laura slowly nodded and walked out to Rose and Sky's pasture. The horses trotted over to greet her. She was talking to them through tears when Rory appeared.

"Laura, what's happened?"

"I don't want to talk about it."

"Let me guess: Mr. Hothead has hurt you."

Laura glared at him. "He's not a hothead, and I'm the one who's hurt him."

"I'm sorry–it's none of my business. I just hate to see you so upset. If you want to talk, I'll be here for you."

"No, I'm sorry. You were only trying to help. Lately I seem to be upsetting everyone."

Rory put a hand on her shoulder. "I can't believe that. You're the sweetest and kindest person I know."

Laura smiled. "Thank you for saying that, but I've been unfair to Liam."

"Well, I have my own thoughts about that, but I'll stay out of it."

She stepped back and looked at him curiously. "No, go ahead."

"All I can say is, if I had a girl like you I would do whatever I could to make her happy, and certainly never give her cause to cry."

Laura sighed. "I made Liam feel bad for spending time with his friend Garrett."

"Well, he's nuts to want to spend time with his friend instead of you."

"Thanks for trying to cheer me up, but I did say some things I shouldn't have.

"Well, you can see it anyway you want. But I say if he truly cared for you, there shouldn't be an issue." He turned and walked back to the barn, leaving her to feel the impact of his words.

Laura soon felt embarrassed for the whole drama and returned to the barn.

"Rory, would you like to go for a ride with me?"

"Sure. Later we can take Hawk and Topper out for a trail ride."

Patrick overheard this and shook his head. *No wonder Liam felt like he had to go.*

As Liam stepped off the train at Pearse Station in Dublin, he recalled the thrill of anticipation he'd felt so many times when he'd met Laura there. But now it was just a recollection, replaced by emptiness, as if he was a lost stranger in a faceless city.

Molly gave Liam a warm hug at the door.

"Aidan called and said you were on your way. Is there's anythin' I can do?"

With tears in his eyes, Liam only shook his head and went straight to his room.

Hours had gone by when Molly knocked and asked Liam to join her for dinner. He had no appetite but agreed anyway. They ate in silence at first, but Molly felt compelled to comfort him.

"Liam, I know you're in a lot of pain. I'm all ears if you want to talk."

Liam put his head in his hands. "I don't know what to say. I've let Laura down. She broke up with me. These past few weeks I haven't been myself. I'm afraid I haven't shown her the respect and trust she deserves." He picked his head up. "I feel comfortable here–and in the studio. I'll just dive into my world of songwriting."

Molly smiled and reached over to squeeze his hand. "I think you both just need some time. I'm sure Laura will be callin' soon."

Liam nodded but he wasn't convinced. He thanked Molly for dinner and went down to the studio. He began writing a song with misunderstanding and heartache the key elements. When exhaustion finally overcame him, he crashed on the couch in the studio. He was awakened the next morning by Molly's sweet voice.

"Good mornin', Liam. Could you use some hot coffee and fresh-baked scones?"

He smiled. "You're a lifesaver."

Liam told Molly that he'd made some progress in the studio. He thanked her again and returned to his songwriting.

Days went by as Laura thought about Liam's words– and Rory's.

Liam was not surprised she hadn't called. He phoned Aidan.

"Son, it's so good to hear from you. How are you doing?"

"I'm getting some songs completed. I have two finished and I'm working on two more. I promised Foolish Pleasure I would send them some new material."

"That's great news–but how are you?"

Liam sighed. "I've been better, but I'd be far worse if Molly wasn't taking such good care of me. Can I talk to Laura?"

"I'm afraid she's not here, but I'll tell her you called."

"That's all right. She probably doesn't want to talk to me anyway."

"Son, I'm sure she's going to call you soon. I'll speak to her."

"No, please don't. I'll get back to work–and maybe I'll call later."

Molly watched from the other room as Liam slowly hung up the phone, a look of defeat on his face. She hadn't heard the conversation, but it was clearly not the outcome Liam had hoped for. Her heart ached for him.

∽

Another week had passed while Liam continued to take refuge in Dublin. There were no phone calls from Laura. Aidan did call several times and Peggy once.

One afternoon Garrett came over to visit.

"Peggy called me this morning. We had a nice chat, and then she told me you were in Dublin. Why didn't you let me know you were here?"

Liam lowered his head. "Well... I haven't been very good company. But I have been writing songs for Foolish Pleasure."

Garrett studied Liam for a moment. *Man, he looks like hell.* "Hey, I wasn't very good company when my father died, but you were there for me. Now I'm here for you."

"Thanks, I appreciate that. Do you want to hear my songs?"

"What do you think? Let's go."

In the studio Garrett quietly waited while Liam reviewed his sheet music. Strumming his guitar slowly, Liam did a chord progression which built up to a dramatic sustain, and then he began singing the verse. Garrett was drawn right into the song. Liam projected his emotion with an intensity that continued to build right into the chorus.

Liam moved seamlessly through the next three songs with even greater passion, mesmerizing his one-man audience.

70

"This is your best stuff ever! We should keep these songs for Second Wind."

Liam shook his head. "I promised to get them out to Foolish Pleasure. I'll write more for us. That is, if there's still a band."

"Man, what are you talking about? We have a great band, and we'll be playing as soon as the others get back from Italy."

"What about Laura? I assume Peggy told you everything."

Garrett looked at him with compassion. "Well, not everything, but I know enough. We'll cross that bridge later. As far the band goes, you're the most important member. If Laura chooses not to play, then so be it."

"I don't want to play without her. My heart wouldn't be in it."

Garrett sighed. "Liam, let's get out of here for a while. You've been holed up in here too long. Why don't you get cleaned up and we can catch a movie?"

Liam was unshaven, his was hair a mess, and his clothes were wrinkled.

"I don't know, Garrett. I think I would be a drag."

"Let me be the judge of that," Garrett smiled. "Now come on, let's get going. Can I suggest you go up for a shower first?"

Liam smiled—for the first time in days. "I guess I can take that hint."

When Liam came down the stairs later, Molly smiled broadly when she caught sight of him. "Now you look—and smell—like the dapper young man I'm used to."

"I was that bad, huh?" Liam asked sheepishly.

Molly looked at Garrett and they both laughed. Liam smiled again.

"Now go out and have some fun, for pity's sake!" Molly ordered. She patted Liam on the back, and he actually chuckled as he walked out the door with Garrett.

Molly left soon after to run an errand. The phone rang and the housekeeper answered. "Hello, Dublin House. This is Josie."

"Is Liam there?"

"No, he went out with friends." There was a moment of silence on the other end. "Hello?" Josie asked.

"Sorry, this is Laura. Will you tell him I called?"

"Oh sure, Miss Laura. I'll write it down so I don't forget."

Josie hung up and wrote a note for Liam, which she put into her apron pocket. Just then another call came. It was a friend of hers, and they talked for an hour. When the end of the day came, Josie put her apron into the wash–note and all.

Laura sat by the phone at Montrose, overwhelmed with disappointment. She had so wanted to talk to Liam, but now he was out. *Who are these friends?*

Rory had seized the opportunity to be Laura's constant companion. They rode horses every day and went for long evening walks. He was a good listener and always had words of advice. Rory was twenty-one, and in Laura's mind, full of wisdom.

"I called Liam," Laura confessed to him.

"So how did that go?"

"He wasn't even there. He went out with friends," Laura replied through tears.

Rory put his arm around her. "I told you not to call. I knew he'd just hurt you. He's out havin' fun with someone else, and here you are with a broken heart."

"I couldn't help it–I miss him so much."

"I know, love, but you must try to put him out of your mind. It's not fair that you sit home all alone and wait for him." He gently wiped Laura's tears. "I think I know just what will cheer you up. There's a showin' of photography at the fine arts museum in Limerick this weekend. Why don't we go?"

Laura was surprised. "I don't know... I wouldn't be very good company."

"Let me be the judge of that. Besides, you'll be showin' your own photography in exhibitions someday, and you need to see what it's all about."

"Do you really think so?"

"I think your work is the best I've seen."

"Wow, thank you. I'd like to go, but I'll have to ask Father first."

"Father, would it be all right if I go the Museum of Fine Arts Saturday to see a special photography exhibit?"

Aidan looked up from his morning paper. "By yourself?"

Laura lowered her eyes. "No, Rory has asked me to go."

Aidan put his paper down. "I don't think that's a good idea."

"Why not? It's not a date. We're just going to look at some photography."

Aidan studied his daughter. "What's happening with you and Liam?"

"I called him last night and he was out having fun with friends. Why can't I?"

She looked to Hannah, hoping for support.

"Oh, Aidan," Hannah said, "what harm could there be in going to a museum?"

"I guess I'm out numbered. I suppose... if you promise not to be out late."

Laura kissed her father on the cheek and left the table.

Peggy had been silent during the conversation, guessing that any remarks from her would put Laura more on the defensive. She excused herself from table and called Garrett, wasting no time explaining the situation to him.

"The way I see it, the new stable boy is moving in fast on what he thinks is his new turf. You'd better tell Liam to come home soon."

"I will," Garrett agreed. "I'll convince him we should go to Montrose this weekend. The good part is that I can see you sooner than we planned."

"I'd like that," Peggy replied sweetly.

Garret called Liam as soon as he hung up with Peggy.

"So, I am seeing Peggy Saturday. Will you come with me?"

"I don't think I'm welcome at Montrose anymore."

"That's crazy–it's your home! I'm sure Laura's missed you like crazy."

"All right. But don't tell anyone I'm coming, in case I change my mind."

⸻

Garrett did arrive at Dublin House to pick up Liam Saturday, but much later than expected.

"Sorry, Liam. I had to put a new solenoid in my car. We'll be there before dark."

⸻

Peggy met them at the door and gave Liam a warm hug. "It's good to have you home. But what took you guys so long? Garrett, I hope we don't lose our reservation. We've got to go." Garrett shrugged his shoulders as Peggy whisked him away.

Liam looked around but didn't see Laura. Aidan could see the disappointment on Liam's face from across the room.

"Son, I'm so sorry, but you missed her. We didn't know you were coming."

Just then Hannah walked in. "Liam, I'm so happy to see you. Laura shouldn't be out too late. Rory promised to have her back early."

Aidan winced, and Liam shot him a look of betrayal.

They were both silent while Hannah rambled on about the museum, completely unaware that her words had just pierced Liam's heart. He excused himself and trudged up the stairs. Aidan felt personally responsible for Liam's agony.

Although Liam did come down to dinner, it was awkward with just the three of them. Liam only picked at his meal as Hannah made light conversation about Emily and the baby. Aidan couldn't stand the tension. He put his hand on Liam's arm.

"I'm so sorry, son. Laura said she called you yesterday."

"She hasn't called," Liam replied despondently. "I shouldn't have come. I'll take the train back to Dublin in the morning. There's no point in spoiling Garrett's weekend."

"Son, I wish you would stay. You could talk to Laura tomorrow."

"No, I can't. I hope you understand." Liam left the table with tears in his eyes.

He went to the barn to visit his horse. Liam poured his heart out to the gelding as he fed him carrots. Sky nuzzled him as if he understood. Pleased to see Sky had gained some weight, Liam finally left to return to the manor.

On the way back, Liam saw the headlights of an unfamiliar vehicle approaching. He impulsively stepped behind a tree.

Liam's face flushed with anger at the sight of Rory walking around to open the door for Laura. She stepped out into the moonlight, and Liam's heart skipped a beat as he saw how beautiful she looked. His view of Laura was suddenly blocked as Rory moved in front of her.

Liam couldn't hear the conversation, but Rory's body language told Liam all he needed to know: He was making the moves on Laura.

Suddenly, Rory took Laura into his arms and kissed her. As much as Liam wanted to act, he was frozen in pain. All he could do was turn and retreat into the shadows.

"Rory! What are you doing?" Laura gasped. He had grabbed Laura, holding her so tightly she was unable to pull away until he finally released her.

"I'm sorry, love–I just couldn't help myself. I've had such a wonderful time and… you look so beautiful."

"I thought I made it clear you and I are just friends. I'm in love with Liam."

"You did say that, and again–I'm sorry. Please don't be mad at me."

"Rory, if we are going to remain friends, you will have to respect my wishes."

"I promise. Your friendship means so much to me."

"All right, but I will say goodnight. I can walk to the door myself."

Rory, undaunted, smiled as he watched her walk away. *I'll give it a little more time. This is a sweet deal.*

Laura went straight to her room, deeply disturbed by Rory's behavior. *Maybe Liam's right.*

Unbeknownst to Laura, Liam was just across the hall, lying on top of the bed as he stared at the ceiling. He could almost hear the shattering of the pieces of his broken heart as they scattered to the four winds.

As dawn neared Liam could only focus on one thing: escape.

Laura came down for breakfast and stopped in her tracks when she saw Garrett at the table with Peggy. "I didn't know you were here."

"I guess you didn't know Liam was here, either," Peggy remarked.

"Where is he?" Laura cried. "I need to talk to him!"

Aidan shook his head. "I'm afraid when he heard you were out with Rory he decided to go back to Dublin early this morning."

Laura's eyes welled up with tears. "Oh no, what have I done?"

"That's a good question," Aidan remarked with his eyebrows raised. "I think we need to have a talk in my study, young lady."

Laura was embarrassed, but more than that, she felt ashamed. She knew her father was mad at her, and walked slowly a few paces behind him. Once in the room Aidan stopped, turning to observe his daughter as she slumped into the chair against the wall. He sat behind his desk, and in the long silence, Aidan made a decision to be direct but sympathetic.

"Laura, dear, I want you to think back to when you lost your mother. Do you remember how sad and lonely you felt?" Laura slowly nodded.

Aidan cleared his throat. "I'm ashamed to recall how I ran off to deal with my own grief, leaving you behind. It was Liam who was there to comfort you and help you through it.

"I'm sure you remember how you came to Liam's side when he lost his father, and later his mother. I know he has never forgotten your kindness." Laura was now sobbing, but Aidan persisted, determined to get his point across.

"It seems to me that now, when Liam has turned his kindness to his friend Garrett, you of all people should understand; but instead you punish him for not giving you his undivided attention. And you forget that the death of Garrett's father pulls Liam back into the loss of his own father in that terrible fire."

Laura was beside herself. Aidan paused to pass her his handkerchief.

"To make matters worse, this Rory comes into my barn with his coarse training methods that fly in the face of everything Liam learned from his father, who was the best trainer to ever touch a colt at Montrose." Aidan slammed his hand on the desk. Laura jumped.

"Furthermore, I now believe cutting back on Sky's feed was not an accident. As far as Rory's real motives, I believe the limitless attention he has been paying to my daughter is suspect." Laura looked surprised at his last remark, but then remembered the kiss Rory had forced on her the night before. Aidan went on.

"Regardless of whether you think Rory's motives are pure or not, you would do well to see how your carrying on with him looks to others–and how it affects Liam on all these levels. The belief that he has lost you has devastated him far beyond anything I've seen, including the deaths of both his parents." Laura was sobbing uncontrollably. Aidan was sorry to see his daughter so emotional, but knew he had to finish.

"I'll deal with Rory. By the end of the week he'll be on his way. As for Liam, it will take more than just a quick apology to heal his broken heart."

Laura finally composed herself enough to speak. "I must go to him right now!"

Aidan shook his head. "You should start by calling him. You need to convince him that he has a home here. He needs to know that you still love him."

"I never stopped loving him! I didn't mean to hurt him, I just wanted–"

"It's not always about what Laura Meegan wants. Just remember that and you'll be a stronger person for him."

Laura ran to her father's arms. "I'll call Liam right now." She stepped back and looked deeply into his eyes. "Father, you are the most wonderful person. Mother would be ashamed of me, but she'd be very proud of you."

"Thank you, my dear, but your mother would be proud of you right now."

Laura realized she would have to wait at least another hour until Liam's train came into Dublin. It gave her time to fully absorb what her father had said. Finally she called, and Molly answered.

"Molly, is Liam there?"

"No dear, I thought he went to Montrose with Garrett."

"He did, but he left on an early train for Dublin. Please have him call me."

"I'll tell him the moment he walks in. I hate to see the two of you so unhappy."

"Thank you, Molly. I'm hoping he'll talk to me. I've been... foolish."

"Oh, he'll talk to you–I'll see to it."

Laura thanked her and hung up.

Liam arrived at Pearse Station with no clear idea of what to do next. He got off the train and sat on a bench. Liam pulled his address book out of his bag and placed the call to Italy.

"Jon's villa. What can I do for ya?"

"It's Liam."

Jon could instantly tell something was wrong. "You sound like you need to talk."

"I guess I do. When are you coming back?"

"Next weekend." There was a long silence. "Liam, are you still there?"

"Yeah, I guess I'll see you then."

"Wait! I can try for an earlier flight. Tell me what's going on."

Liam broke down and told his friend the story.

"It can't be that bad," Jon said. "Laura loves you like... nothing I've ever seen."

"Oh, it is that bad. I saw her kissing Rory last night."

Jon was stunned, not believing what he had just heard. Knowing how fragile Liam must be, Jon picked his next words carefully.

"Liam, you're like my brother. I want to be there for you right now. Please wait for me in Dublin. I'll call the airlines and see how soon I can get a flight."

"No. You'll be here at the end of the week. Don't worry about me. I was thinking about going to Belfast to see Brian."

"I don't think that's a good idea," Jon said firmly. "You know how much trouble they've had up there."

"Well, he might need some help. And there's nothing for me here. I feel lost."

"Hey, Big Guy, you'll always have me. And Molly's right there."

"Molly's been great, but I'm tired of everyone's pity. Don't cut your time short in Italy. I'll see you when you get here. I'll be fine. Take care."

Jon was just about to try another approach when he heard the sound of Liam hanging up. He just stood there in the villa, phone in hand, wondering what to do. Jon decided his next call would be to Aidan, the man who was like a second father to him in the few short years their lives had become intertwined.

He told Aidan about Liam's desperation, but decided not to mention Belfast.

"Thank you for contacting me so quickly, Jon. But maybe you should tell this to Laura directly. Let me get her."

Laura ran to phone. "Jon, you talked with Liam?"

"Yes. He called me from Dublin. He's in bad shape. He's headed for Belfast."

"Belfast! Why would he go there?"

"In his mind he has no one. He thought maybe he could be of some help to Brian, and maybe they could talk some. You know, Liam saw you kissing Rory last night."

"Oh my God! Jon, I didn't kiss Rory–please believe me! He forced one on me and I told him off. Oh, it doesn't matter now. The important thing is I've got to find Liam and tell him how much I love him."

Aidan snatched the phone from Laura's hand. "What's going on here, Jon? Why is Liam headed for Belfast?"

"I really don't know," Jon replied. "He's got it in his head he's got to find Brian. Liam thinks there's no one else to talk to. I'll try to get an earlier flight back. I'll call you when I have it booked."

"You do that. I'll get on with tracking him down right now. Time is of the essence."

Aidan firmly hung up and faced his daughter.

"So what else haven't you told me about Rory?"

"Father, please understand that I didn't expect Rory to do anything like that!"

"Well, apparently Liam did."

Laura hung her head. "I'm so ashamed. Do you think Liam can ever forgive me?"

"We have to find him first. Where are Garrett and Peggy?"

Laura led her father to the living room where he walked right up to Garrett.

"We need your help. Where does Brian live?"

"Well, he was living with his uncle. Until the man got thrown in jail."

"Jail!" Aidan and Laura responded at the same time.

Garrett lowered his head. "I'm afraid I haven't told you everything about Brian. He's involved with some guys who… well, they're IRA sympathizers. One of them has a brother who's been imprisoned, and that's why they've all been demonstrating in Belfast. It usually turns into a riot when the Garda arrive, and Brian's been arrested several times." Garrett paused and wiped his brow. All eyes were upon him.

"Anyway, during the last riot Brian broke his arm in the skirmish. It's no place to be for someone like Liam." There was an uncomfortable silence before Aidan spoke.

"Garrett, I've always supported the belief in the unification of Ireland, but I've never condoned the violence—from either side. Right now I have to focus my concerns on Liam. Has he been aware of Brian's involvement in all of this?"

Garrett hesitated. "I'm afraid I've kept that from Liam, too."

Aidan shook his head. "Your answer does not surprise me–otherwise he wouldn't have headed up there. Liam has his own problems to deal with, and I'm quite certain he wouldn't be taking them to Belfast if you'd been straight up with him."

Garrett put his head in his hands. "I'm so sorry, sir. Brian asked me not to tell anyone. I never thought it would...."

Aidan put his hand on the young man's shoulder. "You must understand that we're a family here. We know that no good can come of it when we keep secrets from each other." Aidan looked directly at Laura, who was sobbing.

"Father, please! We have to find Liam before he gets hurt."

"Garrett, how can we find Brian?"

"I know Brian called Liam just before we started our tour with Foolish Pleasure. He may have given him his phone number, but I don't have it."

"Maybe Liam will call and let us know where he is, but we can't count on that," Aidan said. "I'm making some calls to Belfast right now."

Laura crumpled into a chair. *How could I have been so wrong? Rory is the complete opposite of sweet, gentle Liam.*

# Chapter Nine

It had been hours since Jon's phone call, but there was no news from Molly. Conversation was minimal at dinner, with each person lost in thought about Liam and where he could be. Everyone jumped when the phone rang. Aidan answered.

"Hello? Oh yes, Emily, I'll put your mother on." Even Hannah looked disappointed. Aidan's second wife was not easily given to showing her emotions, but she did care about Liam. Her eldest daughter, calling about the grandbaby, drew her attention, so Hannah took the call in the other room.

Aidan's eyebrows were furrowed when he returned to the table. "I was hoping it was Liam, or at least someone calling from Belfast. I just wish he would let us know he's all right."

"This is all my fault," Laura sighed. "There must be something I can do to help."

Aidan folded his arms. "You can start by keeping away from Rory—and that means not going to the barn. As far as Liam goes, just keep him in your prayers." Laura nodded and hung her head in shame.

"Maybe I should drive up to Belfast and look for him," Garrett suggested. "I've been up there a couple of times."

"I don't think that's a good idea," Aidan said. "The hunger strikes are still going on, and rioting could break out at any time. If anyone goes, it will be me."

"Sir, I know some of the places Brian hangs out. You'll have a much better chance of finding him with me."

Aidan eyed the young man for a moment while he weighed the risk against the measure of hope it could add. "All right then. If we don't hear anything tonight, we'll try to leave sometime tomorrow. But I've got a conference call midday with business partners. I hope it won't keep me too long."

Hannah returned to the room. "I'm going to meet Emily and the baby in Dublin Wednesday. She's going to shop for new clothes now that she has her figure back, and then we will come to Montrose together."

No one responded—or cared. Aidan went to his study and placed some calls.

All eyes were on him when he returned. "I've spoken with the captain at the Belfast main Garda station. They've got their hands full up there, but I faxed a photo of Liam to them and they'll keep an eye out. Regarding Brian, I'm afraid the news isn't good. He's in jail again." Garrett winced while Peggy let out a long breath she'd been holding. Laura just bit her lip, still feeling ashamed for her behavior.

Liam had sat alone on the bench at Pearse Station for quite a while after talking to Jon. Thoughts of Laura, and how they'd gotten to this point, swirled through his mind. He was snapped into the present by the announcement that the train to Belfast was now boarding. Grabbing his bag, Liam hopped aboard with no clear idea of why he was going, let alone how to find Brian.

With his gaze to the window as the train took him northward, all Liam could see were reflections of Laura's face telling him they should break up. He silently prayed that every leg of the journey would take him further from his pain.

Liam got off at the first station in Belfast and again tried Brian's number. There was still no answer. He guessed that maybe he'd had some more surgery done on his arm. It was already past nightfall, and Liam's exhaustion left him with little imagination on what to do next. He found a small hotel at the edge of the city and rented a room. Sleep never came–partly from the sirens that wailed through the night, but mostly from the turmoil in his soul.

When morning broke Liam was so choked with emotion he could barely breathe. Without Laura's love, his future was uncertain and devoid of hope.

He asked at the front desk for directions to the hospital.

"We have eight hospitals," the clerk answered. "Which one do you want?"

"I'm looking for a friend that may have had bone surgery done on his arm."

The man narrowed it down to four and wrote the names on a scrap of paper.

Liam spent the day checking each one, to no avail.

Aidan's conference call didn't come until late Monday and went on for a lot longer than he'd expected. He was fairly exhausted afterwards, and there was still no news about Liam. Aidan considered heading out that night with Garrett but then remembered one more important task he hadn't yet handled. It would be best to stay at Montrose one more night.

Early Tuesday morning Aidan called Patrick with his decision to fire Rory. "Don't tell him why, just give him two weeks' severance pay and send him on his way. That should be the end of it."

"It's the right move to let him go," Patrick said, "but I need to keep him through tomorrow, if it's all right. I'm takin' two colts to Feyland and I'll need someone to feed. There's nobody else in the barn on Wednesday afternoon, and Chloe and the little ones are goin' with me."

"That's fine," Aidan agreed. "But don't dismiss him until you come back. I don't want any trouble."

"I understand. I'll take care of it."

Aidan's worries about Liam grew deeper as the day wore on. There was still no word on his whereabouts. It was time for decisive action. He told Hannah he was leaving that evening for Dublin.

"I will go with you," Hannah said. "I can meet Emily and the baby there tomorrow." Aidan agreed and went to find Garrett.

"Garrett, we're leaving for Dublin in a couple hours. Why don't you ride with Hannah and me, and then you and I can leave for Belfast first thing in the morning." Garrett agreed and Aidan nodded in appreciation, but then rubbed his temples. "God, I can't believe tomorrow's Wednesday already."

❧

"Hello?" Peggy answered anxiously.

"It's Jon. Have you heard anything from Liam?"

She sighed. "No, not a word since he left Sunday… and we're going crazy around here. Aidan and Garrett are on their way to Belfast to look for him."

"It's going to be hard to do in such a big city. My prayers are with them. I'll see you at the airport in the morning. Thanks for meeting me, you're a sweetheart."

Although it was late when the three arrived at Dublin House, Molly met them in the entryway, giving each of them a hug. "I wish Liam would've come home, or at least called me here. I feel terrible."

"We'll find him," Aidan said, trying to convince himself as much as the others. "He is troubled right now, but I have faith in that keen mind of his."

They all agreed a good night's sleep was needed and went right to bed.

Molly got up before dawn the next morning to make coffee and scones for Aidan and Garrett. They ate in silence and then Aidan stood up.

"Thanks for breakfast," he said. "Hannah's still sleeping. Tell her we needed to get an early start. I'll call you from the road later to let you know where we are, and to see if you've heard from Liam."

Molly was wringing her hands. "I've been so worried about him with the riots and all up there. My prayers are with you."

"I trust that all of our prayers will be heard," Aidan replied. "We'll need a light from heaven to guide our search."

After they tackled the morning chores, Rory helped Patrick get the colts ready and loaded into the lorry. Patrick quickly went over some instructions. "I'm goin' back to help Chloe with the little ones. Oh! I forgot to check the oil."

"I'll take care of it for you," Rory offered. Patrick thanked him and headed up to the cottage. Rory soon discovered the oil level was low, and went to the tractor shed to find some. After searching unsuccessfully, he headed up to the cottage to tell Patrick.

Chloe handed her husband yet another baby bag. He shook his head. "You'd think we were goin' for a week with all this stuff. I don't know what I'm goin' to do for help tomorrow after I let Rory go."

"Well, it's best he does go," Chloe said firmly. "He's rubbed several people the wrong way around here. Now they've all gone to look for Liam. It's a shame he felt the need to leave just because of this newcomer. It's obvious Rory's got eyes for Laura. I'll bet that's the reason Lord Meegan's lettin' him go."

A gentle morning breeze came in through the open window, and Chloe wrapped the baby in an extra blanket. Little did she know that Rory stood just outside, listening to every word.

Infuriated, he quickly retreated to the barn, stopping at the lorry to slam the bonnet down.

"Let him run out of oil—to hell with him! To hell with them all!"

Earlier Peggy had asked Laura if she wanted to go with her to the airport to pick up Jon.

"No, thank you. I need to ask God to watch over Liam. I'm going to church."

"I understand," Peggy said. "I've been praying too. I'll drop you off on my way out."

Laura entered the church in the local village where she and Liam had sung in the choir as children; where they had prayed together so many times. She slowly walked down the aisle to the front pew. She knelt and closed her eyes. *Dear God, please let him come home to me.*

Liam, in his own search for guidance, was knelt in prayer in a small Catholic church in Belfast, the city in which he had spent two full days searching for Brian. With the midmorning sun igniting an array of colors from the stained glass window, Liam felt the strong presence of Laura–and that she was calling out to him.

Laura suddenly had the most overwhelming feeling that Liam was right there with her. She found herself saying his name aloud. "Liam… Liam… please come home!"

Wanting only to prolong the connection she had felt, Laura remained in the church for quite some time.

She carried renewed hope in her heart as she walked back to Montrose in the gentle breeze of the late morning. Looking into the sun, Laura could see some kind of motion. It was Patrick pulling away from the barn in the lorry van. The silhouette of someone in the passenger's seat came briefly into view. *Good. Rory is going with him–it's all right for me to go to the barn.* Laura went straight to the tack room for carrots. As she fed the horses their treats, the horses' rhythmic munching soothed her. Stroking Rose's neck, she thought about Liam and the many hours they'd spent bonding with the horses and each other. *I wish he would come walking in right now.* She was pulled out of her solitude by the sound of a door closing at the other end of the barn. Laura impulsively walked in that direction.

Garrett had suggested that Aidan drive to a few different pubs in Belfast where they might find Brian. At the second one there was a group of young men immersed in loud and raucous conversation. Garrett recognized one of them as a protester who had been arrested with Brian once before.

"Maybe we should just leave them be," Garrett said to Aidan. "They're talking about the hunger strike–they seem pretty riled up."

"Nonsense," Aidan replied. "We've come all this way. We have to at least ask him when he last saw Brian, and if Liam was with him." Aidan paused thoughtfully. "How about we buy them a round?"

Garrett agreed and placed the order. The barmaid delivered the pints and pointed to the two men who had been so generous. Aidan nodded, and Garrett stepped forward into the light where he hoped to be recognized.

"Thanks, mates," a short, wiry man in the group said. "Hey! I know you... Brian's mate from Trinity. I'm Devon. What's your name again?"

"Garrett's my name. I play in the band with Brian. This is our manager, Aidan."

"Good to meet you," Devon said with an extended hand. "But if you've come to see Brian, you know you'll be visitin' him at the jail downtown."

"Yeah, I heard," Garrett said. "Actually, we're looking for another bandmate who came here a few days ago to find Brian." Aidan pulled out a picture of Liam. There was a sudden silence.

Devon looked at Aidan suspiciously. "And why might ya be lookin' for him?"

"He's my son."

"Okay, sorry. It's just that we can't be too careful these days." Devon looked at the picture, and then flashed it at the others who shook their heads. "Well, we haven't seen him, but it doesn't mean he didn't see Brian sometime anyway. If Brian was lookin' out for him, he probably told him to head back south. Things are gettin' pretty hot up here... And they're gonna get hotter tonight, if you catch my meanin'."

Devon folded his arms and studied Aidan thoughtfully. "I'll give you some advice. If you haven't found your son before nightfall, I'd leave the city."

❧

Laura rounded the corner of the barn in anticipation. She stopped in her tracks and gasped. There stood Rory.

"Well, look who's come to say goodbye to me," he said, a smirk on his face.

"You surprised me. I thought you went with Patrick."

"No, love, it's just you and me." Rory moved towards her. Laura instinctively backed up, but he lunged forward and firmly grabbed her arm.

"Don't be rushin' off—we have some unsettled business. Let's see... I think you owe me for goin' to Daddy and gettin' me fired."

"Rory, let me go! I didn't get you fired!"

Ignoring her pleas, Rory pulled Laura to his chest and grabbed her hair. He yanked Laura's head back and aggressively kissed her on the lips. The more she struggled to get free, the tighter he gripped.

"Now, let's see what's under these fancy, expensive clothes." With that he shoved Laura into the feed room, ripping her blouse.

"Please, Rory! Don't do this!"

"Go ahead and cry, little princess. No one can hear you."

Laura bolted for the open door, but Rory easily moved to block her path. Her attempt to escape only fueled his anger—he grabbed her forcefully by the throat.

"Typical spoiled rich bitch," he sneered. "You think you can tease me to make your boyfriend jealous, and then toss me away like garbage?"

Rory threw Laura toward the sacks of feed by the wall. She stumbled, hitting her head on the side of a bin, rendering her nearly unconscious.

As she tried to regain her senses Laura realized Rory was on top of her. He had torn off her skirt. She kneed him in the groin. Rory cursed and backhanded her across the face. Fighting to stay conscious, Laura struggled to her feet, only to be thrown back to the floor with even greater force. She landed sideways on her arm. The sudden excruciating pain caused her to scream.

Again he came at her, and her efforts to roll away were futile. The pain from her arm was unbearable. She shrieked hysterically in agony and terror, until Rory gripped her in a choke hold. Laura drew on all she had to save herself from what she now felt could be her death. With her good arm, she dug her fingernails into her attacker's cheek. One finger at a time she climbed his face until she found his eye. She jabbed at him with full force. Rory cried out and released his grip on her throat.

Jon and Peggy had arrived at Montrose only minutes after Laura had first stepped into the barn.

Fiona, the cook, lit up the moment she saw Jon. "Look who's here, just in time for lunch!"

94

Jon gave her a hug, and then looked around the room. "Will Laura be joining us?"

Fiona looked puzzled. "I'm not sure where she is."

"I dropped her off at the church," Peggy said, "but that was awhile ago."

"You think she's at the barn with the horses?"

"I wouldn't think so," Peggy replied. "Aidan warned her not to go down there until after Rory was out of here for good."

A sudden chill ran down Jon's spine. "We need to find her!" With no further explanation he bolted out the back door, driven by an unknown force. Peggy followed, but had to quicken her pace just to keep Jon in view.

Just as the two crossed the bridge, a piercing scream could be heard coming from the barn.

"That's Laura!" Peggy cried.

Jon had never slowed his pace, but now took off sprinting like a gazelle. He followed the sound of Laura's cries to the feed room.

The horror of the scene unfolding before him became the fire that propelled Jon into Rory, sending him to the wall and down into a heap. Rory, partially blinded already from Laura's fingernails, was now cowering from Jon's repeated blows to his face. His larger frame was no match for the street fighting skills Jon had mastered years before to fend off bullies on Long Island.

Peggy ran to Laura, who was covered in blood. She was moaning, her arm limp at her side, obviously broken.

"It's all right now, Laura, we're here. We'll get help— just don't move." Laura nodded weakly and reached for Peggy with her good arm.

Peggy looked in the direction of the skirmish. "Jon! Stop! Now! You're going to kill him! He's not worth it!"

Jon pulled back. "You're right. I think I'll leave something for Liam." He turned to Rory and kicked his limp but still conscious form. "Now get out of Laura's sight before I change my mind." Rory attempted to get up but stumbled. "Need a little help?" Jon rushed at the scoundrel sideways, driving his shoulder squarely into the back of the assailant. The sheer momentum sent Rory flying twenty feet outside the barn and down into a tumble. Jon was ready to advance again as he saw Rory stagger to his feet.

"Enough with him!" Peggy cried. "Laura needs us! Call an ambulance! I'm sure her arm is broken–and who knows what else."

"You stay with her. I'll call." With that Jon quickly ran for the only phone in the barn.

Laura tried to speak, but her throat was too swollen to get the words out.

Peggy reached for Laura's torn skirt, placing it over her bare legs. "Laura, did he... rape you?"

Laura passed out before she could answer. Her breathing was shallow, and the swelling around her face and neck was increasing. Peggy was frantic.

Jon returned to confirm that an ambulance was coming, and then he began gently blotting Laura's facial wounds with clean cloths he had dampened in the tack room. Every few moments, though, Jon glanced around just to be sure the attacker was nowhere in sight.

❧

It seemed an eternity until the ambulance arrived. Peggy rode with Laura to the hospital while Jon stayed at Montrose, trying to contact Aidan, Liam–or anyone.

He finally reached Molly at Dublin House, shaking as he described the ordeal. "Oh my God!" Molly gasped as she nearly dropped the phone. "Of course I'll tell Aidan the minute I hear from him, and Liam–if he would only call."

Fiona, who had listened to it all, was beside herself. Jon gave her a reassuring hug, even though he was distraught with worry himself.

"Laura's going to be fine," he said, trying to sound convincing. "I'm going to the hospital. Stay by the phone." Fiona promised and Jon grabbed the keys to Peggy's car.

The moment Jon arrived at the hospital, Peggy jumped up and threw her arms around him. "I'm so frightened! They've been in there with Laura for so long."

"I should have finished off the punk–or at least had him arrested."

"I gave the Garda a report and a description of him," Peggy said.

"Did you call the Garda?"

"No, I think it's something the hospital does in… rape cases."

Jon lost any composure that he had. "No… he didn't…" Tears filled his eyes.

"I'm not sure. I tried to ask Laura but she passed out."

Jon clenched his fists. "I've got to find Liam. I've got to be the one to tell him."

Finally the doctor came out, looking exhausted. "She's still unconscious; she will be for a while. We had to set her arm, it was broken in two places. She has a badly bruised larynx and a concussion. I had to suture her lip."

Peggy looked fearfully at the doctor. "Was she...."

"No, thank God. She put up a good fight. She has bruises on the inside of her thighs, though. Have you been able to reach Lord Meegan yet?"

Peggy shook her head. "No, we've left messages for him."

The doctor's attention was drawn to Jon's hands. "I think you could use a few sutures yourself, young man."

Jon became suddenly aware of the throbbing in his knuckles. The doctor asked him to hold up the left hand. It was deeply cut, bruised and swollen.

"Man, that's my fretting hand–on the guitar. I guess I'd better let you stitch it."

It was after six when Jon and Peggy returned to Montrose. Jon stepped out of the car, and then stopped in his tracks. "What about feeding the horses? Fiona said Patrick wouldn't be back until late. It's safe to say Rory's not going be doing it."

Peggy shook her head. "I know nothing about horses, and I have hay fever."

Jon smiled. "What a pair we are! I can't use my left hand and you can't breathe. Well, someone has to feed them. Let's do the best we can."

They were greeted by a symphony of equine voices as they arrived at the barn.

"Wow," Jon said. "I think they're happy to see us."

Peggy shook her head. "I think that means, 'it's about time'!"

Jon headed for the hayloft. "I guess this would be the right stuff. Oh, that's right. They have doors above the mangers and you just drop the hay down."

Peggy sneezed and Jon threw his hands up. "Don't start that now, you have to help."

To Peggy it seemed as if it took hours to feed. The two were exhausted when they returned to the manor. Peggy headed straight for her room and a shower.

Sometime later Jon was nodding off in a chair when the phone rang.

"Hello, Montrose Manor."

"Jon, is that you?"

"Oh my God! Liam! You have to come home right now–Laura needs you."

"Jon, I just called to let everyone know I'm all right. But I'm not coming home."

"The hell you're not! Laura's in the hospital. You have to come home!"

"What happened?"

"It's a long story. I think she's going to be all right, but she really needs you."

"Did she ask for me? Tell me what happened. Is Aidan with her?"

"No! He's out looking for you in Belfast—and God knows where else! And Laura can't ask for anyone, she can't even talk. Trust me–she needs you right now!"

"Jon, please. Tell me what happened." Liam's voice was shaky.

"It was Rory. He attacked her... and beat her."

"Oh, my God! I'm going to kill the bastard!"

"Don't worry, I almost did, and Laura got him pretty good before I showed up. Where are you anyway?"

Liam didn't answer right away. His head was spinning with anger. He looked up at the board in the train station. "I'm in Drogheda. It's not far out of Dublin."

"Go to Dublin House and call me when you get there. Aidan may be there soon and he can bring you home."

"Jon, is Laura really going to be all right?"

"She will be when you get here. She's been so worried about you."

"Tell her I love her."

"You get here and tell her yourself. By the way—we all love you."

"Thanks, Jon. And thanks for being there when I wasn't."

Jon hung up and called Dublin House again.

Molly's relief in hearing that Liam had called was only momentary. "Oh, God, he must be beside himself with worry now. Oh—wait, Jon—Garrett and Aidan are back. I can't even begin... I'll put Aidan on."

As he took the phone the concern on Aidan's face was plain to see; but nothing compared to how it darkened as Jon told him the nightmarish tale about Laura.

When Aidan finally spoke his voice was broken, barely a murmur.

"Dear God, please let her be all right."

"They're taking good care of her. And Liam finally called. He'll be at Pearse Station soon."

Aidan began to regain his composure. "I'll call the hospital right away. Then we'll drive to the station to wait for Liam. We'll be home late tonight." He paused. "Jon... you saved her. The gratitude I have in my heart will never fade."

Jon held back his tears. "Just drive safely."

Aidan greeted Liam with open arms when he stepped off the train. "Son, we've been so worried about you. Please don't ever scare us like that again."

Liam stepped back and hung his head. "I feel so guilty that I wasn't there."

"Son, you mustn't blame yourself. This Rory put one over on us."

Aidan gestured towards the car, where Garrett had moved to the back seat, knowing Aidan and Liam would need to draw strength from one another.

"You're sure you're okay to drive?" Garrett asked.

Aidan nodded. "Yes, thank you. Let's get going. Maybe we'll be able to see Laura as soon as she wakes."

# ⊂↶Chapter Ten↷⊃

Knowing that he and Liam would not rest until they saw Laura, Aidan drove straight to the hospital in Limerick. Images out of the past flooded both their minds during the drive back, all associated with the hospital that was miles from Montrose Manor, but the closest with emergency services. The most recent incident involved serious injuries Danny sustained in a harrowing battle with a felon who was on the run after burglarizing the manor–and attacking Jen. The image penetrating Aidan's thoughts now, however, was of Laura at age nine when she nearly drowned trying to save Liam in the River Maigue.

⊂↶↷⊃

When they arrived, the night nurse didn't even look up from her paperwork as she began her speech on how visiting hours were over and would resume the next morning.

"Ahem."

"Oh! I'm sorry, Lord Meegan! Your daughter is right this way, in Critical Care. She's sleeping, so perhaps one at a time would be best. Please keep it brief."

Aidan went first, trying to prepare himself as best he could. What he saw was shocking beyond belief. His daughter's beautiful face was so swollen and cut up she was almost unrecognizable. Aidan touched her hair.

"Laura, dear," he whispered in a quivering voice, "I'm here now and I'll take care of you." Her motionless form was almost too much to bear, but Aidan held back his tears as he retreated to the waiting room. Liam jumped to his feet but Aidan stopped him.

"Son, remember, she's been badly beaten."

Liam swayed at Aidan's words and had to steady himself before entering the dimly lit room. He slowly walked towards the bed. Laura's face gradually came into view, and he cried out her name before he could stop himself. Laura murmured something inaudible, and Liam rushed to her side. He tried to control his own horror as he carefully stroked Laura's hair away from her face.

"Sweetheart, I'm so sorry I wasn't here. I'll never leave again. I'll always love you." He gently kissed her on the forehead and remained at her side until Aidan came in and touched him on the shoulder.

"The nurse says we should let her rest. We'll come back first thing in the morning."

When they finally arrived at the manor it was after midnight. Aidan had called from the hospital, and Jon and Peggy were still waiting up. Aidan noticed Jon's hand.

"You didn't tell me you got injured. I hope that hand's not broken."

Jon grinned. "Oh no, just cuts. It'll heal a helluva lot faster than Rory's face!"

"Jon was a real hero," Peggy declared.

Liam gave him a hug. "Thank you so much for being there."

"I'm thankful God put me there before…"

"Amen," Aidan agreed solemnly.

"Mother called from Dublin," Peggy said. "Molly told her everything. She said to give Laura her love." Aidan gave Peggy's hand a squeeze.

Jon put his arm around Liam. "It's good to have you home, Big Guy!"

They all went upstairs for some much needed rest. Aidan kicked off his shoes, loosened his belt and fell on the bed in sheer exhaustion.

Right after dawn Liam was downstairs and ready to leave for the hospital before most of the others were even up— except Fiona, whose shock at Liam's appearance caused her to speak her mind freely.

"You've lost so much weight! You must eat some breakfast."

"Just coffee and a scone. I have to see Laura."

Aidan crossed the floor towards the coffee urn. "She's right, eat something. We'll leave soon enough. I've already spoken to her doctor, and Laura's doing a lot better. There's a chance she may be able to come home today."

A nurse on the floor guided them to a private room where Laura had been moved. Aidan paused at her door. "Son, let me go in first, then you can spend some time alone with her."

Aidan entered the room and kissed his daughter on top of the head. "Laura dear, I'm so sorry about all this."

"Father." Laura's swollen throat constricted her voice. "Did you find Liam?"

"Yes, dear, he's here and very anxious to see you." Aidan motioned for Liam to come in, and then left the room.

Laura reached out and Liam tearfully kissed her hand. "Sweetheart...."

"Liam, I love you," she whispered weakly. "Please don't cry."

"Sweetheart, I love you so much. This is all my fault for leaving."

Laura shook her head. "No, it was my fault."

"Laura, I want to hold you and kiss you all over, but I'm afraid I'll hurt you."

Aidan returned. "I have good news. The doctor will let you go home if you promise to rest and let us take care of you."

Laura managed a weak smile with her sutured lip.

Although relieved to finally be in her own bed at Montrose, Laura's swelling and bruising had increased, and the pain was almost unbearable. She struggled to speak, asking for a few minutes alone with Liam. Aidan and Iris agreed and left the room.

"Liam, I'm so sorry. Please forgive me."

He shook his head and put his finger to his lips. "Shhh—we'll talk later when you're stronger. Don't worry about anything now."

"Thank you." Laura braved a smile as her eyes closed.

"There are some people anxious to see you," Liam said when she awoke. "Are you up for visitors?" Laura nodded and Liam helped her take a sip of water before turning to wave the others in. Jon, Peggy and Garrett moved cautiously into the room, masking their shock at Laura's appearance.

Although she'd been unconscious during the last part of the ordeal with Rory, Laura had been told of Jon and Peggy's intervention and rescue. She reached her good arm out to Jon. "How did you... find me?"

"We had a little help," he replied, pointing straight up.

They took turns wishing her a speedy recovery, leaving after a few minutes.

Liam was Laura's constant companion all day, driven by a feeling of duty to protect her fragile frame from simply disappearing if he were to slack off. He held her hand, and when it was time for sustenance he carefully fed her Fiona's potato leek soup, and then read to her until she was ready to fell asleep again. Suddenly Laura jarred herself awake.

"Liam," she whispered. "I have to tell you something."

"It's all right. I told you we could talk later."

Laura shook her head. "No... he grabbed me... I didn't kiss him."

"I know. Jon caught him attacking you."

"No, the other night... you were there. He forced me...."

Liam was silent. He realized Laura meant the night Rory had brought her home from Limerick. He looked straight into her eyes. "That was the night I decided to leave."

She nodded and squeezed his hand when she saw that he finally understood.

"I never stopped loving you," she whispered, and drifted off to a peaceful sleep.

Hours later Aidan peeked into Laura's room. His daughter was asleep and Liam was nodding off in his chair. Aidan spoke quietly. "Son, I'll stay with her for a while. Go get some rest. I know you didn't sleep last night."

Liam reluctantly released Laura's hand, knowing Aidan was right. He went to his suite across the hall, but left the double doors open.

Hours later Liam was awakened by the sound of Laura's moaning. He jumped up and ran to her. "Sweetheart, I'm here."

Laura opened her eyes, looking fearful. "I had a bad dream about–"

"Shhh, don't worry. I won't let anything happen to you." Liam lay on the bed next to her, softly singing until she returned to sleep. He gently stroked her hair and soon dozed off himself.

Aidan stopped in to say goodnight and smiled when he saw the two of them. He decided to let them be and covered Liam with a quilt.

The next day Laura again tried to apologize to Liam for her behavior, but he shook his head. "Laura, we'll have our time to talk, but not until you're stronger. Please be patient, I'm not going anywhere."

It took several more days of rest and eating in bed before Laura was able to come downstairs and visit everyone. The swelling in her face had reduced significantly and her bruises had begun to fade, but the stitches in her lip were still quite prominent. The lingering soreness of her thighs and the awkwardness of having her arm in a cast made getting around a major chore.

In spite of the challenges, her spirits were good—because of Liam's loving care.

"Today we'll have some visitors," Aidan announced. "Emily and Olivia are coming home with Hannah."

"I can't wait to see Olivia," Laura smiled. "Liam, will you braid my hair so it won't be in the way when I hold the baby?"

"I'd like nothing better." Liam was pleased to see Laura's spirits lifted, but concealed his dread at the thought of seeing Emily. In marked contrast to her sister Peggy, Emily was egocentric to the point of viewing herself and her husband as aristocracy. Her earliest transgressions against her mother's newfound family had included trying to seduce Liam when he was just fourteen.

❧

From the moment Emily arrived there was tension in the manor. She barked orders to all of the servants, spewing remarks about how conditions were unsuitable for her precious child.

Liam was helping Laura downstairs to greet them, and the sight of the baby lit up Laura's face. "Emily, she's so beautiful!"

"Yes, she is," Emily replied smugly. She removed the French lace bonnet from her infant daughter. "Olivia is the best baby in the world." Emily looked up at Laura for the first time and gasped.

"You look frightful–you're going to scare my child!"

"Emily," Hannah scolded. "That is an unkind thing to say to Laura. She has been through a very difficult time."

"Sorry, I'm just trying to protect my child."

"May I hold her?" Laura asked innocently.

Emily stepped back. "I should say not. Your arm– you'll drop her."

"I can help Laura hold her," Liam offered.

Emily frowned. "Laura is too immature to hold my baby. Look at the mess she has gotten herself into."

Liam's jaw dropped in disbelief at Emily's cruel remark. Tears came to Laura's eyes as she turned and left. Liam followed her while Aidan just stood in shock.

Peggy looked at Emily in disgust. "You're just as hateful as you've always been. I'm so glad I have a loving sister like Laura. I'm ashamed to even call you my sister." With that, Peggy stormed out of the room.

Hannah was actually embarrassed and had nothing to say in Emily's defense. Aidan took a long look at his older stepdaughter. *She's already been here too long.*

◦❧◦

"Why does she hate me?" Laura whimpered. Liam took her into his arms.

"Emily's jealous of you and always has been. She thinks that putting you down will elevate her to an even higher status. But no one likes to be around her, and she's going to ruin her daughter. Laura, you have so much love to give to children. It's a shame little Olivia will miss out. However, I know two little ones who can't wait to see you. Do you feel up to going to Chloe's?"

Laura's face brightened. "You always know what to say. Let's go see Beth and Little Philip."

Just then Aidan walked in and put his arm around his daughter. "I'm sorry Emily is being so hateful."

"It's okay," Liam said. "I'm taking Laura to see two babies who love her."

A smile came to Aidan's face, and he pulled a set of keys out of his pocket. "Liam, I don't think Laura should walk all the way to the cottage. Why don't you take the Mercedes coupe and drive there."

"Wow! You trust me with your baby?"

"I've trusted you with my most precious baby." Aidan smiled at his daughter.

"Let's go, Monkey Boy–before he changes his mind!"

Aidan laughed. "Put the top down, it's a beautiful day."

Liam didn't need any more encouragement and went straight to the garage. Soon he pulled up in the classic convertible and jumped out to help Laura get in.

"You two look grand in her," Aidan remarked. "Drive around as long as you want, just stay within the gates of Montrose."

Liam revved the motor and they were off. The sun was out, and a gentle breeze blew through the air. Liam took the long way around, circling the estate several times. Laura turned the radio on; naturally it was Aidan's favorite classical station. She instantly dialed in some rock 'n' roll, hearing the familiar announcer's voice.

"This next song, from Foolish Pleasure, was written by one of Ireland's own, Liam Delaney." It was *Remember When*, the song Liam had written about his childhood memories with Laura. For a short time they were both able to set aside the recent trauma.

Laura admired Liam. "You look really handsome driving this beautiful car."

"Oh, but it's the beautiful lady in the car that paints the pretty picture."

She tried to smile, but winced in pain and touched her lip.

Little Philip opened the door the moment they got to the cottage. He jumped into Liam's arms and gave him a hug.

"Now," Liam cautioned, "Laura has some owies, and we have to be careful."

The child leaned over and gently touched Laura's chin. "Owie," he said.

Chloe, stunned at the sight of Laura's battered face, forced a smile. Liam nodded his head at Beth and then towards Laura. Chloe picked up the cue and gently placed the baby in the crook of Laura's arm. Beth looked right into Laura's eyes and smiled at her, to Laura's delight–and relief.

"She still knows who I am, and I'm not scaring her."

Chloe smiled. "You're a natural when it comes to holdin' the little ones. We all love you and feel so bad about what happened."

"Me too," Laura replied. "I know it was mostly my fault for trusting that Rory."

Patrick walked in. "Oh Laura, I'm so happy to see you're up and about." He looked around the room. "I thought maybe Aidan was here. I saw the car out front."

Liam beamed. "No, he's let me escort this lovely lady out on a drive."

"There isn't a young man more worthy of carin' for Lord Meegan's most precious things." Patrick's face suddenly darkened. "I'm so sorry I hired that con man, Rory. He turned out to be a monster. With Danny bein' gone and all... well, I was desperate for some help." He looked right at Liam. "The hoodlum never showed me any of the natural skills you have with the horses. He sure wasn't taught by anyone as good as your father."

Liam put his hand on Patrick's shoulder. "I should have gone to Aidan the first day I met Rory. He said some things to me, and I saw some things, that I don't think anyone else was aware of. Except Sky." Liam looked at Laura. "A horse will always tell the truth–you just have to listen. It was more my fault than anyone's."

"Enough of this talk about takin' the blame," Chloe scolded cheerfully. "You all know that Rory was connin' everyone. The best part is that he's gone now, and Laura's goin' to be all right, and Liam's back home where he belongs."

"Oh, by the way," Patrick added, "in the confusion that night, we had some emergency barn help–to do the feedin'." Liam looked at him quizzically. "They left me a note. I want you to thank Jon and Peggy for me."

Liam looked surprised. "Jon? And Peggy? She's got hay fever!"

Patrick shrugged. "They did just fine, and I'm sure the horses appreciated it."

The weekend came with a wave of peace over Montrose Manor as Emily and child departed for the airport.

Jon began spending most of his time with Kelly from the moment she arrived for her summer visit. They went for longs walks around the estate with Beth in her pram, Little Philip sometimes running along, sometimes riding on Jon's shoulders.

Jon laughed. "If only the boys back home in Long Island could see me now–pushing a baby buggy."

Kelly smiled. "I think it's a wonderful picture: a very loving and caring Jon."

Peggy had made Garrett feel like he belonged to a family, and he made her feel like the beautiful and compassionate young lady she had become.

Aidan was at peace with his family–minus Emily, of course. He approached Liam the next day.

"Liam, I would like to go riding and see how the new horses are working out."

"I'd be honored to ride with you. When Laura takes her nap we'll go to the barn."

Laura sighed. "I'll be fine. You don't have to be with me every moment. Go riding with Father."

Liam agreed, and soon the two were walking along the river path.

"Liam, I'd like to talk to you about Laura." Liam looked at him with concern. "Don't worry, son, it's not a lecture, just some fatherly advice." Liam took a deep breath as Aidan continued.

"I'm afraid you and I have spoiled Laura. This whole thing with Rory was a direct result of her insecurities. It's time she learned to appreciate how much she is loved."

"Don't blame it on her," Liam said. "I shut her out with my self-pity."

Aidan shook his head. "Laura should have been sensitive to your needs. It seems you always give in to her demands, just as I do. She's not mature enough yet to realize that the world doesn't revolve around her."

"I don't see it that way," Liam said defensively. "She's a very loving and considerate person. I can understand her insecurities. Losing her mother at such a young age, she fears the ones she loves the most will leave her."

Aidan hung his head. "I know it was a terrible thing for me to run off and leave her with strangers when she was so young. I've spent most of my life since that time trying to make it up to her. And that's the point, maybe we're both going overboard."

"Remember, Aidan, I was one of the strangers you left her to grow up with. I see it very differently."

"You have been there for her all along. I do respect your feelings."

"I owe everything that I am to Laura because she loved me. When I first met her she was very lonely, but she went out of her way to make me feel comfortable. I gave her a hard time, but she persisted." Liam's voice softened as he continued.

"Laura hasn't had a mother to help her grow up. With all due respect, remember that when Hannah came into her life things were traumatic. Even though Laura forgave her, Hannah has never really been someone she could go to with questions about life. Then there was Emily and Peggy, initially both of them cruel stepsisters; they were certainly no help.

And my own mother, even though she was Laura's nanny, when she became ill she withdrew from all of us. Molly was the closest thing to a mother for Laura as she became a young woman. Now, even Molly has moved on."

Aidan had been studying Liam as he spoke. *This young man is more perceptive than most people three times his age.*

Liam continued. "I've always tried to be there for Laura. She grew to be dependent on me, and then we had to be separated for school. When I went on to Trinity she felt the need to be reassured that I was not leaving her for good. That's when she wanted the *total* commitment from me."

Aidan raised his eyebrows. "And that's when you … made love."

"Yes, sir," Liam replied. "And here we are today. I should have realized how much Laura needed me to come back home to Montrose after the tour in Scotland. She wanted us to go riding together. She wanted everything to be like it was when we were growing up. The fast life on the road with the band gives us very little time to ourselves, and it can make anyone feel insecure. We needed to come home to Montrose."

Aidan put his arm on Liam's shoulder. "I'm so happy you feel the need to come home. I was worried that the glamorous life on the road would take you both away."

"Not a chance! Laura and I will always return to Montrose." Liam's face suddenly darkened. "About this Rory–I'm more to blame than Laura is. When I finally did come home after being with Garrett, I was deep into my own self-pity, thinking about my father. I wasn't really here for her. I didn't show any enthusiasm for the new horses because I didn't like Rory. I'm afraid it was a bad combination of all those things."

"Liam, you're a very perceptive person, but I disagree with your taking the blame. Laura should have stood by you in your time of grief. It can't always be about her."

"I love her so much... I can forgive her when she makes any mistake."

"My point exactly. That's unconditional love, but it should go both ways."

"I know she feels bad about hurting me, but she's been punished enough."

"I'm not talking about punishment; she's definitely had enough of that. But I think you should let her know how seriously she hurt you. This could be a turning point for her. She should realize she has no reason to feel insecure anymore."

Aidan's last remark really struck a chord in Liam.

They were quiet as they rode, Aidan concentrating on his riding skills. Back in the day he was an accomplished equestrian, but he hadn't ridden in years. After Aidan and Hawk settled into a comfortable trot, he looked over to see Liam break into a canter, gently encouraging Topper as he changed gait. *Liam's a natural.*

Enjoying the diversion, the two rode quietly in the arena for an hour. Then Aidan trotted over to where Liam and Topper had just finished a cooldown walk.

"Liam, I would like you to continue to work with both horses until you go back to school. They have a good disposition but need some of the fine Delaney training."

Liam smiled proudly. "I would be honored to work with them every day I'm here. Maybe you and I could go for a ride on the grounds soon."

"That would be nice."

They untacked, groomed and put the horses away, and then walked back to the manor, mostly in silence, just enjoying the peace of the estate.

Liam waited a few days until he felt Laura was ready.

"Sweetheart, let's go for a ride in the sports car. It's time for us to have our talk."

She looked up at him with her big brown eyes. "I know. Thanks for waiting."

They drove to a quiet place and parked.

"Liam, I want to tell you how sorry I am and what a fool I was."

"I know you're sorry, but please let me say what I have to say now." She looked at him with uncertainty. "Sweetheart, please don't be frightened. I love you and I always will. I just don't want us to ever go through anything like this again."

Laura took his hand, preparing herself. "Go ahead. I expect you to be mad at me, and I deserve a lecture."

"I guess you really don't know me after all. I'm not mad at you, I love you, unconditionally. I want you to feel the same."

"Oh Liam, I do. As a matter of fact, I trust your love so much that I was sure you wouldn't leave me, even when I told you to go back to Dublin." She lowered her head in shame. "And by doing that *I* took *your* love for granted; not the other way around." Laura was in tears as she looked into his eyes. "Liam Delaney, you are the deepest and truest part of me. I'll never lie to you, and I'll never hurt you again."

# ⊂ℐ⊃Chapter Eleven⊂℧⊃

The next few weeks were peaceful, and Laura's wounds seemed to be healing. Liam now viewed the emotional turmoil as a bumpy road behind them, and the way ahead was clear and unobstructed. He had given Laura the chance to show him how much she truly loved him. For her it was a giant step forward in growing up, in moving past naiveté. She was determined never to let her insecurities get the best of her again.

Laura was enjoying the cool breeze coming off the Maigue River as she sat on the back patio brushing her hair. Her thoughts turned to a future that once again felt secure and bright. *I'm looking forward to going back to St. Andrews with Jen.* Suddenly she found herself quietly laughing. *It was just two years ago I was terrified of that private school.*

Liam was walking up the path from the barn after another morning of working with the geldings. He heard Laura's gentle laughter and caught sight of her with the sun glistening in her hair. *Her beauty is surreal.*

He came up behind Laura and kissed her on the top of her head. "How's the most beautiful girl in the world?"

"Very happy, because I have the most wonderful guy in the world."

Iris came to the patio. "Excuse me, Miss Laura, you have a call from Italy."

Liam helped her up and they went to the phone.

"Jen! When are you and Danny coming home? We miss you both so much."

"We'll be back next week," Jen replied. "How are you doing?"

"I'm getting better with all of Liam's help."

Liam whispered in Laura's ear. "Tell her we need Danny's help in the barn."

Jen laughed. "I heard that, and no, I won't tell him. He already feels guilty enough for being gone so long. Father has been wonderful to Danny. They're getting along so well, I hate to spoil it."

"I'm very happy for you," Laura said warmly. "It's a wonderful thing when the men you love get along."

Liam returned to the barn after a short break so that he and Patrick could move on to their next task, working with two yearling stud colts. Although they made progress, the two trainers were nearly exhausted by noon.

"I'll be happy to see this pair go off to the auction next weekend," Patrick grumbled.

"They definitely need more work," Liam agreed. "But we've started them well. Hopefully they'll go to someone who can keep working with them."

When he returned from the barn Liam came into the library and saw Laura sitting at the desk rubbing her temples. Her eyes were shut and tears were streaming down her cheeks.

"Sweetheart, what's wrong?"

She looked up with a pained expression. "I didn't want to make anything of it, but I've been having these dreadful headaches… and now my eyes… I can't seem to focus."

He came to her side and gently messaged her neck. "How long has this been going on?"

"A few days with the headaches. But today's the first time I've had trouble with my eyesight."

"We must get you to the doctor. I'll get Aidan."

"Please, let's wait and see if gets better."

Liam shook his head. "I'm sorry, but you need to be seen by a doctor right away. I can't let anything happen to you because we waited too long. Remember Italy." Laura slowly nodded. He kissed her on the cheek and left.

❧

It wasn't long before they were on the way to the hospital, with Aidan driving and Liam gently holding Laura's hand in the back seat. Before too long her headache subsided, and she sat up straight.

"You know, Father, I really think I'm going to be fine."

"Laura, darling, we'll let the doctor decide that."

Liam gently squeezed her hand. "Remember, you had a concussion. We need to have you checked out."

❧

Laura's regular doctor had already ordered a consult by the hospital ophthalmologist, Dr. Mullins. The nurse brought Laura into his exam room the moment they arrived. Aidan followed but remained respectfully silent while the lengthy initial examination was underway. The doctor then asked Aidan to join him in his private office.

"Lord Meegan, I think the blow young Laura took to her head may have caused pressure to build on the optical nerve. I've ordered several tests to be run, and we need to get additional x-rays as well."

Aidan's eyebrows furrowed. "Is the nerve damaged?"

"We'll know more after her tests are completed."

The doctor's response was no comfort to Aidan, but he thanked the doctor and returned to the waiting room. Once again he and Liam would find themselves sitting around, feeling helpless and praying for Laura. Aidan began to relive the nightmare of being stuck in London when Laura was undergoing emergency surgery in Italy.

Almost two hours passed before the nurse finally brought Laura out to the waiting room.

Liam jumped up. "Are you all right?"

"I suppose, but I can't strain my eyes and I'll have to wear glasses for a while."

The nurse turned to Aidan. "Lord Meegan, Dr. Mullins would like to see you in his office."

Aidan left with the nurse and Liam took Laura into his arms. "Sweetheart, you're going to be fine. I'll take care of you."

"The tests confirm that there's pressure on the optical nerve," Dr. Mullins said from behind his desk. "I've seen this kind of thing heal with rest and care, but–"

Aidan interrupted. "Anything else you feel is necessary, just say the word."

"Absolutely. I'll consult with Dr. Stanton in London. He's the best–we were in medical school together–and his clinic is state-of-the-art. I'm sure he'll concur with me on the need for rest, but of course he'll want to see her. I'll call you as soon as I've spoken with him."

Aidan returned to the waiting room feeling powerless, except he knew to put on his best face for Laura. "They're consulting another specialist; we'll know more soon. In the meantime, Dr. Mullins says you need rest and quiet, and no bright lights."

On the way home everyone was quiet, lost in thought. Aidan struggled to control his temper as he thought about what he would do to Rory if their paths ever crossed. *I mustn't feed my own anger–it won't help Laura. I'd better leave that bastard to the authorities.*

Liam held Laura's hand and massaged the back of her neck, concealing his own rage. *I'll kill him if I ever get my hands on him.*

Laura began to worry about the outcome of everything. *What will my life be like if I'm blind? I know Liam would still love me–but would it be fair to him?*

As expected, Liam watched over Laura carefully at home. He read to her and played his guitar, sometimes accompanied by Jon. Liam had recently completed a new song, *That Smile*, and he performed it for Laura during a time when the two of them were alone.

"I love it!" Laura exclaimed. "It means so much to me." Then she looked away, the smile fading from her face. "I hope you'll always feel that way about me."

"You know I will."

"Liam, my vision isn't getting any better, even with my glasses. What if...." He interrupted her with a kiss.

"Laura Lye, we'll get through this together. Now I want you to push all the negative thoughts out of your pretty head."

Patrick appeared at the door. "My apologies for interruptin'." Liam waved him in. "Laura, I hope you're feelin' better. We sure miss your cheerful smile."

"Thanks, Patrick. I'll be down at the barn pestering you before you know it."

"You could never be a pest."

She thanked him and asked how Rose and Sky were doing.

"Well, they miss you, but as long as they're together they're always happy. There's a couple of other horses that need some help, though, and I need to ask a favor."

Laura looked at him quizzically. "Of course, Patrick. Whatever I can do."

"Well, you could loan me Liam for a day. I need to take two yearlings to Clonmel for the auction tomorrow."

Liam looked surprised. "I forgot it was tomorrow. I can't leave Laura."

"I wouldn't ask, but I can't handle the both of them, and you're the man I put my trust in."

"Please go with Patrick," Laura said. "I'll be fine here with Father and Hannah, and Jon and Peggy will entertain me. Besides, you need to get outside and get some fresh air."

Just then Aidan walked in. "I agree. Liam, you need a break, and I do need to get those colts to the sale tomorrow."

Worry clouded Liam's eyes as he looked at Laura. "Are you sure you'll be all right?"

"Yes, I'll be fine. As a matter of fact, I'll be busy. Molly is coming tomorrow to do my hair."

Liam forced a smile for Laura's sake and turned to Patrick. "What time do you want to leave tomorrow?"

"Right after the mornin' feedin' is done. We'll be home before dinner."

Liam nodded. "I'll be at the barn early to help you feed."

Patrick smiled and turned to Laura. "I'll have him home before you know it."

Laura was peacefully sleeping the next morning when Liam quietly entered her room to check on her. He gently kissed her on the cheek and stayed for a moment to simply gaze at her, seeing all the beauty that still shined despite the persistent injuries. *Why should Laura have to endure all of this pain? Why should that Rory go free? Will he avoid punishment for his crimes? Or will I somehow get the chance to even the score and make him curse the day he ever set foot on Montrose Estate?*

Once the trip to Clonmel was underway, it turned out to be an enjoyable break for Liam. He gave his undivided attention as Patrick fondly told stories about the days when he and Liam's father, Philip Delaney, had gone to auctions together.

"One time there was this horse trader name of O'Sullivan–we all called him Sully. He was the unsavory kind, you know. Anyways, this Sully had a reputation for druggin' his lame horses to get them through the auction lookin' sound. Your father and I knew about his tricks and wanted no part of him. Well, Sully had left a young kid in charge of his horses that day while he went to the pub. This kid knew nothin' about druggin' horses. He asked us if this bottle was what he should use on the colt, and we said yep! And he gave the lame colt a big dose of tranquilizer instead of bute.

"We knew the tranquilizer wouldn't hurt him none, but the colt was so dopey he could barely stumble into the arena. Of course no one bid on him. The inspector pulled the colt from the sale and fined Sully. He wasn't allowed to sell from that auction again. Ol' Sully suspected Philip and I had somethin' to do with it, but couldn't prove it. We were glad to see that shady excuse for a horseman get caught." Liam shook his head in disbelief while he laughed.

∽

After they unloaded the colts, Patrick introduced Liam to several old friends as the two walked around the auction grounds.

Everyone had loved and respected Philip Delaney, and Liam was treated like a celebrity. Kevin McCully, one of the old timers, was especially impressed.

"I coulda guessed he was Philip's son without you tellin' me. He's the spittin' image of the dapper lad." Liam smiled with pride.

Patrick looked at his watch. "Our colts are up in about two hours. I think I'll go over to the office and use the phone to check in with Chloe—and Aidan, of course. Liam, why don't you go watch how they run the horses through the auction. I'll meet you back at the barn."

Liam agreed and wandered over towards the arena. Passing through the chaos of nervous young horses and impatient handlers, he heard a whip crack. Liam shuddered and turned to see a frightened filly rearing straight up in the air.

At the arena gate a man was struggling with a frisky young colt. The handler was short-tempered and continually tugged on the shank, which caused the horse to pull back and rear instead of moving forward. It was obvious to Liam the handler was inexperienced. *It seems there are so few real horsemen like my father was.*

Just then his attention was drawn to a tall, thin young man wearing a cap and sunglasses walking along on the rail at the far side. *He seems familiar somehow.* Liam kept watching, but it was hard to see his face through the crowd, so he decided to move in for a closer look. He made his way around several grooms leading horses and soon found the young man was directly in his path. Liam's spine began to tingle as the figure turned to look squarely at him. They both stopped in their tracks. *Rory!*

Liam sprang forward as Rory spun around and headed through the crowd.

# Chapter Twelve

Kevin McCully was in his late sixties and quite agile for a man who had been thrown from many a "green" horse in training. He was not without his share of aches and pains, but he was not one to complain, and got around quite well with his lean, wiry frame. When he was a much younger man, McCully had ridden in a tight race during which three horses collided and went down in a tangle of reins, legs and jockeys. Being the first to emerge from the pile unscathed, he was dubbed *Kevin the Cat*.

Kevin walked by himself back to the barn where his colts were kept, still reliving some of the good times he had spent with Philip Delaney only a few years back. He smiled as he remembered Philip's special way with the young colts, always able to calm them with ease.

Suddenly Kevin's attention was drawn to the corner of the next barn. A tall young man with a cap stood there motionless with a pitchfork in his hands. *What the–?*

Someone rounded the corner and the character lunged with the pitchfork–but missed. Even from a distance Kevin recognized Liam as the one who was being attacked.

"Hey!" he yelled out. "What's goin' on here?"

Liam took advantage of the distraction, kicking the pitchfork out of Rory's hands. The wooden handle caught Rory under the jaw as it left his grasp. He was thrown off balance, but snapped back fast enough to retaliate, throwing a right hook that almost found its mark.

Liam pulled back to avoid the punch, as if the movement had been rehearsed. In a way it had–in Liam's mind. Ever since that phone call when Jon had told him of Laura's beating at the hands of Rory, Liam had been visualizing a scene in which Rory would be on the receiving end of Liam's own fury.

Liam focused his rage into his fists and began his surgical attack on Rory, delivering repeated blows into the face and body in rapid-fire succession. Rory fell back against the barn as astonished as he was weakened. He knew that Liam already had the upper hand. With a broken nose and blood streaming into his mouth, he could taste Liam's rage: unleashed and unrelenting.

Rory slumped to the ground, and Liam stopped his attack to yell between breaths.

"It's not so easy for you now, is it?... This time... you attacked someone big enough to fight back... instead of a helpless girl half your size!"

Kevin had now reached them. "Liam, are you all right?"

Liam answered with his eyes fixed on the squirming assailant. "I'm fine. Call the Garda! There's a warrant out for this criminal."

"Is this the hoodlum from County Limerick I heard about?"

"Yes, and he's more than a hoodlum. He almost killed Laura Meegan."

At the mention of Laura's name Rory spat at Liam's feet. Liam responded by kicking dirt at him. "This one is finally going to get what he deserves."

Kevin shook his head in disgust. "I'll get to the office right now and call."

Rory knew he would have to escape, and realized his lorry was just behind the next barn. He slowly started to push himself up, raising his left hand in a gesture of surrender. The fingers of his right hand began to grasp a fistful of loose dirt and straw.

"Just stay right where you are," Liam warned. He stepped forward, and Rory's right hand flung its contents straight into Liam's eyes.

"Ahhhh!" Liam fell back, temporarily blinded.

With all the strength he could muster, Rory jumped up, grabbed the pitchfork and swung it, aiming right for Liam's head. Liam felt the blow coming in time to duck–but not completely out of the way. The flat of the tines caught him on the top of the head, giving Liam a sharp jolt of pain that sent him to his knees.

Rory bolted off in the direction of his lorry.

⚬

Kevin stumbled into the office, out of breath, nearly falling on top of one of the men at the counter. Patrick, a few feet away, rushed to catch him.

"Kevin! What in God's name is goin' on?"

"It's Liam... that hoodlum... he tried to kill him... call the Garda!"

"Slow down, mate. What are you talkin' about?"

"Rory–call the Garda!"

The office clerk dialed the number as Patrick headed for the door. "Kevin, where are they?"

"By the second barn!"

129

Several of the men in the office followed Patrick.

Liam forced himself to stand up. When he got to his feet everything was spinning and he needed a moment to steady himself. His eyes felt like sandpaper. With blurred vision Liam saw Rory running around the corner of the barn.

Dizzy and half-blind, Liam stumbled in pursuit, pausing to dunk his head in a water trough in an effort to clear his vision.

Rory, his face cut and bleeding, ran past several people on his way to his old flatbed. He pulled himself in and attempted to start the engine, but the aging motor did not come to life.

Liam rounded the corner of the barn and headed towards the only vehicle that had someone in the driver's seat.

Rory was beginning to think his escape would have to be on foot when the starter finally kicked in, turning the engine over and bringing the lorry to life. He jammed it into reverse, and then caught sight of Liam approaching. *Jesus! This guy's unstoppable!*

He backed up but Liam came right at him, jumping on the running board on the driver's side. Rory jammed the transmission into first gear and peeled out in an unsuccessful attempt to knock the aggressor off.

The tires squealed as Rory made a hard turn and headed towards the main road, flying past the office and scattering those who were walking about. Patrick and several others were nearly run over. As he jumped back, Patrick was stunned to see Rory driving with Liam hanging onto his throat. The lorry swerved wildly and gained even more speed as it approached the highway.

Rory somehow managed to get his vehicle to the main road. In another effort to knock Liam off, he steered sharply towards a patch of thick bushes on the edge of the road. Liam saw the approaching brambles and jumped free in the nick of time. Rory turned to see Liam rolling in the dirt as the side of the lorry scraped against the brush.

In his moment of triumph, Rory cracked a crooked smile and thrust his arm out the window in a gesture of victory. But victory was not his. As gravel pelted the undercarriage, the steering wheel jerked out of his hands and the lorry plunged down the embankment at high speed. The vehicle flipped over and rolled several times before coming to rest upside down in a ditch.

❦

Patrick and several other men had jumped onto a flatbed which had gained ground in pursuit, and they were close enough to witness the last few seconds of the ordeal. Liam had hit the ground hard, rolling several times to a motionless stop. Patrick leaped off the lorry and raced to Liam's side.

"Liam! Are you all right?"

"I... I think I'm..." Liam's eyes fluttered and he passed out.

The other men ran over to the crash site where the motor was now billowing smoke. They could see Rory's limp body covered in blood and rushed to pull him out. Moments later, a small fire erupted and quickly grew to engulf the old lorry in flames.

The emergency vehicles had just arrived at the auction yard, having come in from the main road. Several men pointed towards the back road where the black smoke was coming into view. Paramedics, fire brigade and Garda all rushed to the scene, one of the officers staying behind to take statements. A man stepped forward to tell his story.

"The poor boy was tryin' to drive out–to get away from the other one who was on his runnin' board. He was chokin' the driver!"

The paramedics began CPR on the crash victim, but one of the attendants, assessing the vitals, looked at his partner and shook his head.

The Garda continued their procedure of barricading the road and directing traffic elsewhere so the brigade could work safely. Officers were taking statements from the other nearby witnesses, who pointed in Liam's direction. The lieutenant in charge was taking a call on his radio. He hung up with a grave look on his face. He approached the dazed young man who pressed a blood-soaked handkerchief to his head.

"Are you the lad that was on the runnin' board of the vehicle while it was proceedin' down this road?" Liam nodded weakly.

"Then I'm afraid I'm goin' to have to place you under arrest."

"What's the charge?" Patrick asked in astonishment.

"Reckless endangerment… and manslaughter." The final word engulfed Liam in a blur of horror and disbelief. The next sound came to him as if out of a dense fog. "Put your hands behind your back and do not resist."

Another officer slapped the handcuffs on and Liam was led away. Patrick could barely contain his fury. "Don't worry, Liam–I'll be callin' Lord Meegan–we'll get you out of this!"

Patrick got a ride back to the auction yard and grabbed the nearest phone in the office, feverishly dialing the manor. He did not mince words when he described the harrowing events to Aidan.

"They're chargin' Liam with manslaughter! I don't see how they could charge him with anythin.' Rory attacked *him!* And he ran his lorry off the road all by himself."

Aidan's blood boiled with anger as he listened. "I'll be there as soon as I can. Go to the Garda station and stay with him. Tell him not to speak to anyone until my attorney arrives. I'll let Chloe know."

"I'll go right now."

Aidan hung up, then immediately placed a call John MacDonald, who agreed to cancel the rest of his day's appointments to accompany him to Clonmel.

Giving Hannah only a vague description of the situation, Aidan then asked her to call Chloe for him. "Do not say anything to Laura."

"But what if she asks where Liam is, and where you are?"

"Tell her there was trouble with the lorry and we'll all be home in the morning."

Although she was not entirely comfortable with the plan, Hannah agreed.

∞

Aidan rushed out the door and sped off in his Jaguar. His mind was racing. *Liam has always been so mild mannered. But I can't blame him–I wanted to kill Rory myself!*

John MacDonald was waiting on his office doorstep when Aidan arrived.

"John, I can't thank you enough for dropping everything and…"

The attorney waved his hand. "This is family."

"Thank you, John. How can they charge him with manslaughter?"

"Adequate provocation," the attorney answered flatly.

"But there were witnesses who saw Rory McClenny drive the lorry off the road and flip it after Liam jumped off."

"Aidan, let's talk to Liam and the witnesses before we plan our defense. The fact that this McClenny had a warrant for his arrest is in our favor. But it also gives Liam a motive for attacking him. I'm afraid this is not just going to go away."

Aidan felt a chill come over him. He was silent for the rest of the trip to the jail.

The Garda were taking Liam's fingerprints and booking him when Patrick arrived at the station. They would not let Patrick see him for over an hour, and then it was behind a screened partition.

"Liam, has anyone looked at your wounds?" Liam shook his head. "I'll tell one of the officers to take care of it." Patrick bit his lip, holding back his rage. "Lad, I'm so sorry it all turned out this way. I would have gone after him myself after what he did to our sweet Laura. I can't believe God will let them punish you for this."

Liam looked at Patrick through tears. "I'm so worried about Laura. She doesn't need this upset after everything else. I need to be with her."

Patrick could feel Liam's angst. He put his hand against the screen and Liam did the same. "Aidan is on his way, and he'll take care of this. In the meantime, don't give them a statement. The lawyer is comin' with him."

Liam slowly nodded then closed his eyes, grimacing with pain. Patrick found himself looking up. *Philip, if you're lookin' down on your son, he could sure use some help right now.*

The duty officer came up to Patrick. "Excuse me, sir. I'm sorry, but your time is up here. Mr. Delaney will have to be placed in his cell now."

"The lad needs medical attention–you can't put him in a cell!"

"You have to leave now, sir. We'll take care of him."

Patrick stifled his anger and turned back to face Liam.

"Don't you worry," he said with a quivering voice. "We'll have you back home before you know it."

The officer impassively escorted Liam down the cold hallway, through another locked double door to the row of cells beyond. Each small, dim, windowless cubicle was identical to the next, with colorless concrete block walls and heavy steel bars across the front. A single cot-like bed hung off the wall, topped with a stained bare mattress. The scene was complete with an old discolored sink and a rusty toilet to match.

As the jail door slammed behind Liam, the deep sound of finality echoed through his head. Loneliness and despair overwhelmed him as he sat on the edge of the lumpy bed. *How did this happen? I was only trying to stop him, not kill him.*

It was only when Liam attempted to lie back on the lumpy cot that he became acutely aware of his physical pain. The pounding in his head was almost unbearable. His right shoulder was bruised and swollen, and abrasions and cuts covered his body.

Like a wild animal that had been trapped and caged, Liam began to shiver–from the primeval chill of pure fear.

With his swollen, stinging eyes closed, Liam saw the image of Laura trying to find him. The need for sleep finally engulfed him, but then the image in his mind's eye turned into a nightmare. Rory was attacking Laura in a scene that zigzagged between crystal clarity and muddled confusion. Liam's efforts to help her were futile. He was completely powerless, forced to stand and watch. The sound of laughter began to take over the nightmare, and everything suddenly came into focus: It was the Deacon, laughing and holding a whip as he stood over Laura's limp body. Liam bolted upright, shaking and soaked with perspiration. A cold chill racked his body as the nightmare was replaced by the reality of where he was.

The excruciating pain from sitting up so fast gave him a wave of nausea. The shivering intensified, and Liam began to wonder if he was in shock. He stumbled over to the toilet bowl and vomited. Too weak to stand, he remained there on his knees.

There was some noise down the hall–the squeak of a doorway followed by the sounds of footsteps and keys jingling. Liam struggled to his feet. Just as people came into view outside his cell, he staggered and fell against the sink.

"Oh my God!" Aidan exclaimed. "Open this door immediately!"

The officer didn't move any faster, having seen many times before what he viewed as just another sloppy drunk behind bars.

John MacDonald was furious. "This is an outrage! This boy needs immediate medical attention. I demand to see your captain, now!"

The officer stepped aside as the two men rushed past him to aid the broken boy.

Aidan could not control his emotions as he saw the dried blood on Liam's face and the torn and filthy clothes clinging to his body. He looked into Liam's red and swollen eyes and blinked back his own tears.

"I didn't mean for Rory to die," Liam murmured. "It was an accident."

"I know that, son. We all know that." Aidan put his arm around Liam and hugged him as gently as he could, but Liam winced in pain.

MacDonald touched Aidan on the shoulder. "I'll have us out of here soon."

The officer let the attorney back into the hallway. "Sorry, sir, but I'll have to lock the cell before we go. Regulations, you know."

"All right, but let's move it along, please." They disappeared down the hallway. "What about Laura?" Liam said sadly. "She's doesn't need to worry about me."

"She doesn't know anything," Aidan assured him. "I told Hannah to tell her there was a problem with the lorry and that we'd have to spend the night. Right now let's concentrate on getting you some help."

MacDonald had arranged for the County Tipperary judge to call and have Liam released on bail. While he waited, he looked scornfully at the captain.

"I would have expected a little better treatment for the seventeen-year-old son of Lord Meegan."

"Meegan?" The captain asked, beginning to squirm. "I thought the boy's name was Delaney."

"Oh sure, the boy's name is Delaney. But Lord Meegan is his legal guardian, and he's like a father to him. He's quite upset about his son's treatment–or the lack of it!"

"Well, I'm sorry, sir. I suppose we could have tended to his wounds a bit more. You must keep in mind that the boy's been charged with a very serious crime."

MacDonald wasn't impressed. Just then the phone rang and the captain answered. "Yes, Judge Finnegan. Yes, sir, he's right here." He handed the phone to the attorney, who already had a satisfied smile on his face.

"Hello, Paul, this John MacDonald." The captain raised his eyebrows at the familiarity. "How's Paul junior? I saw the game against Cork on the telly. He was lookin' good!"

"He's doing fine, thanks," the judge replied. "A bit bruised from the game but nothing serious. So, I hear that Aidan Meegan's son has been arrested?"

"Yes, he has. My immediate concern is the poor condition he's in after his stay in this... jail facility." He shot the captain a glance and the man looked away. "The boy has some serious injuries from a traffic accident, and his wounds have not been treated."

The judge said, "I think that can be prioritized. I'll see he gets transported to a hospital as soon as possible. Now, what is the basis for the manslaughter charge?"

"Well, unfounded, of course. But we will answer the charge effectively at the hearing. For now, I would like the young man released to Lord Meegan's custody."

"John, you know I can't do that on a manslaughter charge. However, since it is his first offense... and there are other circumstances, I will set the bail accordingly and you can take him to the hospital yourself, if you like. However, I must follow protocol regarding his release. You'll have to submit his passport to the court within twenty-four hours, and I'll require that he remain in Ireland until the hearing."

"Thank you, Paul. I'll see to it the bail is taken care of immediately. The boy will finally get the medical attention he should have received hours ago. I'll put the captain back on the phone so you can give him the directions he'll need to expedite the process." With a smug look, MacDonald handed the phone back to the captain.

The man nodded repeatedly and uttered–several times– "Yes, sir," and "Right away, sir," and hung up. He reached in the desk drawer and pulled out the necessary forms.

"If you'll sign here, sir, we'll have you on your way."

"Thank you, Captain. Now, can we get the boy out of that godforsaken cell?"

# Chapter Thirteen

"**I** have one of those feelings," Jon said. "You know, in my gut. I should have gone with Patrick and Liam when they went off to that auction." The living room window reflected his worried expression in the morning sun as he scanned the driveway.

"They really should be back by now," Peggy agreed. "Besides, it doesn't make sense that Aidan went to help them with the lorry. Why didn't he send his mechanic?"

"Well, we don't know that it's bad news," Jon remarked as he stepped away from the window. "I'm sure everything will be fine, so we should stop worrying."

When the phone rang Hannah quickly answered it. Everyone stood motionless in anticipation, searching for any expression, any gesture that might reveal something. Unfortunately, the woman's reserved character was on point, as always. Her voice was no different than usual: even-toned, polite, and anything but agitated.

"Yes, dear… yes… all right. Yes, they're all here, anxious to see you. Yes… all right, dear, I'll tell them. Hurry home. Goodbye."

Hannah gently hung up and turned to the concerned faces. "They're going to be home in a few hours."

"Are they all right?" Laura blurted out. "What's taking them so long?"

Hannah remained calm, as Aidan had reminded her to say nothing. "I'm sure your father will explain everything when they get home." The woman hurried off in a clear dismissal of any further questions.

Laura looked at Jon in disbelief. "I think she knows more than she's telling us."

In an attempt to de-escalate their concerns, Peggy took Laura's hand and led her to the kitchen. "I think we should get a nice hot cup of tea."

Jon gazed out the window again. *I know there's more to this story... Chloe! She'll know something!*

Aidan stood at the hospital pay phone after talking to his wife. He sighed and returned down the hall.

Liam had stayed the night in a private room after having his wounds treated. As Aidan entered, the nurse was handing Liam some neatly folded clothes to put on. They were not his.

"Thank you. Where did they come from?"

She smiled. "Well, we couldn't have you goin' home in those tattered rags you were wearin' when you checked in last night. My nephew is about the same size as you, though maybe not quite as tall. These should be good enough to get you home."

"I think they will be perfect, and it's greatly appreciated," Aidan said. "I'll replace them, of course." Aidan pulled out his wallet.

"Oh no, sir, that won't be necessary. But thank you."

Aidan shook his head as he pulled out two large bills. "Surely there must be something your nephew needs."

The nurse tilted her head slightly. "Well, he has had his eye on some boots."

"Well then, I insist."

"Very generous of you, sr. Thank you."

"Well, son, how about you get changed and we head for home?"

"Sounds like the best idea I've heard yet," Liam replied with a painful smile.

Liam had sustained a concussion, which explained his earlier nausea and shock. There was nothing broken, but his shoulder, arm, and hip were badly bruised when he jumped from the moving vehicle.

The contusions were hidden beneath clothing now, but the facial abrasions and stitches were quite visible. He looked in the mirror with dismay. "How are we ever going to explain this to Laura?"

Aidan looked at his own disheveled reflection and shook his head. "Well, we've got a two-hour drive back to the manor. I'm sure we'll think of something."

"You know we can't lie to her."

Aidan raised his eyebrows. "Oh, I know that. But maybe we can figure out a way to soften the story a bit."

The attorney met them in the lobby of the hospital, looking fresh and dapper, after having spent the night in a local bed and breakfast.

"Well," Aidan said, "I'm glad someone got some sleep last night."

MacDonald put up his hand. "Not as much as you might think. I spent quite a few hours last night interviewing witnesses. One of them saw McClenny attack Liam with a pitchfork. His name is Kevin McCully, and he just may be our star witness. Anyway, I've got a list of others who will help us a great deal."

As they approached Aidan's Jaguar sedan, MacDonald studied his exhausted client. "If you're all right to drive, Aidan, I could use the time to ask Liam some questions."

"I'll be fine. You use the time we have–as long Liam's up to it. The sooner we act on this, the sooner we can put it behind us." Aidan looked to Liam, who nodded.

Once they were on the road, MacDonald reviewed his notes as he prepared to take Liam's statement.

"Now Liam, I'd like you to recount everything from the time you arrived at the auction yard. Don't leave anything out, even if you think it is insignificant. It could be important. Tell me about every person you came in contact with and what time of day–everything you can remember."

Liam leaned into the pillow they had brought for him. He stretched out in the back seat of the car, looking thoughtfully out the window as he began recounting the events of the day before.

❧

Jon hurried down the path towards the cottage, speculating on the various possibilities of what might have happened to Liam, Patrick and Aidan. *Peggy's right, Aidan wouldn't go if it was only a problem with the lorry. Wait... What?* Jon caught sight of the blue lorry parked in front of the barn. He got closer and it appeared fine–and the engine hood was cold.

Jon turned off the main path and quickly ran up to the cottage, knocking rapidly on the door. Much to his surprise, Patrick answered. Jon's mouth dropped open.

"When did you get back? Where is everybody?"

Patrick leaned out the door, looking both directions to make sure Jon was alone. "Come in, lad." He offered Jon a chair. "I'll explain everythin' to you, but you must promise not to say anythin' to Laura just now. Lord Meegan wants to tell her himself. I promised, so don't you go gettin' me in trouble."

Jon quickly agreed, and Patrick recounted the events. Liam's best friend was shaken by the end of the harrowing tale.

"Good God, I thought we'd seen the last of that bas–" Jon bit off a profanity, realizing Chloe and the children were listening.

"Well," Patrick mused, "I guess we've seen the last of him now."

"Poor Liam," Jon said. "What can I do to help him?"

"Just be the good friend that you are," Chloe said from the rocking chair.

"I'll always be there for Liam. Thank you, Patrick, Chloe. I should go."

Patrick put his hand on the young man's shoulder. "He'll be fine, you'll see. Liam's wounds will heal, and Lord Meegan's lawyer will fix everythin'. We'll know somethin' real soon. They should be home anytime."

❧

Jon walked slowly back to the manor, wiping away his tears. *Why do these things always happen to Liam? And Laura?*

His thoughts were interrupted by the sound of a car pulling up the driveway. It was the Jaguar, and he ran to meet it in front of the manor. When Jon pulled open the door, Liam lowered his head in an attempt to hide his face.

"Don't worry, Big Guy, I just heard the whole story. Laura doesn't know anything. Aidan, don't be mad at Patrick. I was walking to the barn and I saw the lorry. I made him tell me."

Liam could barely stand up straight. Aidan looked towards the manor to see if anyone had come out.

"Jon, why don't you stay with him and help him up the steps. I'll go in and call the family into the living room. I'm sure I won't be able to hold Laura back for long, but I'll do my best." Jon agreed and offered Liam his shoulder.

Hannah met Aidan in the entry. "Aidan, you are a sight." She looked behind him. "Where is Liam?"

"Jon's helping him out of the car." Just then Iris appeared and took Aidan's coat.

"Thank you, Iris, and would you please ask the girls to come to the living room?"

Iris turned, but Laura and Peggy were already approaching.

"Oh Father, I'm so glad you're all right. Where's Liam?"

Aidan embraced his daughter. "Everything will be fine. I'll tell you the whole story. Now, let's go into the living room."

Laura followed her father and anxiously seated herself on the edge of the couch.

Aidan began in a gentle tone. "Now, Liam's been in an accident." Laura jumped to her feet, but Peggy took her hand and urged her to sit. Aidan continued. "Dear, he's going to be all right. He's sore, and he has some cuts and bruises, but he's already been treated. Jon's helping him in now."

As the front door opened, Laura pulled away from Peggy and ran into the entryway. The moment she got close enough to see Liam's face she burst into tears. Liam reached for her with his good arm and pulled her in, closing his eyes and burying his face into her hair.

"God, it's good to be home."

The three moved slowly towards the living room, Laura doing her best to support Liam on one side, Jon flanking him on the other.

A few steps later, Liam stopped abruptly.

"What's wrong?" Laura asked.

"It's just that… I don't think I want to sit down again for a while."

"Of course not," Aidan said. "You've been in the car for over two hours. Maybe you should just go to bed."

"I'll help you up to your room," Jon offered.

Laura clung to Liam, not quite ready to give him up.

"Laura, let Jon go with Liam," Aidan gently suggested. "He'll need help taking his shoes and trousers off. I'll tell you all what happened, and then you can go visit him."

Laura gave Liam a quick kiss on the cheek. "I'll be up soon."

Jon turned to Liam with a wry grin. "I'll race you up the stairs!"

Laura hit him. "No funny business."

"Yes, Nurse Laura."

Jon and Liam had barely started up the stairs when Peggy begged Aidan to tell the story. Aidan did his best to

146

tone down the events, intentionally leaving out the more graphic details of the chase. In spite of his efforts, Laura was still upset.

"Why would they arrest Liam? It wasn't his fault Rory died."

Aidan took his daughter's hand. "I know, dear. It's a misunderstanding by the Garda. I'll take care of everything. Now go check in on Liam."

Laura quietly entered Liam's room and sat down next to him on the bed. She gently stroked his hair.

"I'm so sorry this happened to you. Father will take care of everything, and soon this will all be behind us."

"Please lie next to me for a while."

Laura snuggled up close to Liam and he closed his eyes.

Aidan and Hannah came up to check on Liam and found him with Laura in the crook of his arm, the two of them sound asleep.

Hannah reacted with a gasp. "It is not proper for a young lady to be lying on a young man's bed–especially with him in it."

Aidan put a finger to his lips. "Shhh... let them be. They're just comforting each other. They have been through so much–and there's more to face before it's over."

Less than a week had passed since the traumatic events at the horse auction. Jon and Aidan were on their way to the Shannon Airport to pick up Jen and Danny, who had returned from their stay at the villa in Italy.

"Jon, now that it's just the two of us, I wanted to talk. I got a call from Dr. Stanton in London this morning. He wants to examine Laura as soon as possible to see if she's a candidate for surgery."

Jon raised his eyebrows. "So you haven't told Laura and Liam yet?"

"No, and I'll need your help on this. Liam will want to go with us."

"You bet he will. Are you saying he can't?"

"He can't leave the country–it's a condition of his bail."

"Liam is not going to be happy about this."

"I know. It's going to be hard on both of them. I'm counting on you to help Liam get through this. I'm hoping Jen will go with us to London. I think she could be great support for Laura."

"You know my sister and I will do anything to help."

Aidan reached over and patted Jon on the shoulder. "I appreciate this more than you know."

Soon after arriving at the airport Jon spotted a young woman who he recognized as his sister. Sneaking up from behind, he gave her a bear hug; but her response was not what he expected. In one quick motion, Jen broke free and spun around to face her perceived assailant.

"Jon! That's a good way to get flattened."

"Wow!" Jon replied with a grin. "From the looks of you, I guess you could do just that. You're so buffed! What have you been doing, pumping iron?"

Jen flexed a bicep. "I've been drumming a lot, building up my stamina and power. I've also been swimming and sailing every day."

Danny gave her a hug. "She's hot and ready to take on any song you can throw at us. As a matter of fact, I'm not sure if I can keep up."

"Very cool!" Jon exclaimed. "You two are both ready to be on an album cover with those suntans."

"The Tuscan sun has certainly done you well," Aidan agreed. "But I'm glad you're back in Ireland."

"And so are we," Danny replied, but then his smile vanished. "How's Laura doing? And Liam, for God's sake?"

Aidan put a hand on his shoulder and gestured to the car. "We'll fill you in on the way back."

Once they were on the road Aidan began to recount the details of the entire ordeal. Danny shook his head in disbelief several times during the story, clenching his fists whenever Rory's name was mentioned.

"I can't believe poor Liam is being charged with manslaughter," Jen said.

Jon hit his own hand with his fist. "I should have finished off Rory...."

Aidan frowned. "Now Jon, you know that's not right. If you had done that, then you'd have been the one thrown in jail instead of Liam. I trust you boys realize by now that it's best if you stand back and let the Garda do their job." Jon grunted.

"Unfortunately, Liam's situation is not all we have to worry about," Aidan continued. He explained about the injuries Laura sustained from Rory's attack, and her possible need for surgery in London. "And Liam can't leave the country," he finished solemnly.

Jen reached forward from the back seat, putting a hand on Aidan's shoulder. "I'd like to go with you to London so I can be there for her."

"You can count on me to be there for Liam," Danny added.

"I thank you for being such good friends to both of them," Aidan said. "I only hope we can get through all of this quickly."

Jen and Danny were pleased to see that Laura and Liam were waiting for them in the grand entry of the manor, and hugged them both very carefully.

Fiona announced lunch was ready, and everyone took their seats in the dining room. Jen and Danny helped to keep the conversation light with a description of some unusual culinary delights they had tried in Tuscany.

"Don't even ask me how to pronounce the names of these things," Danny added.

Aidan smiled often but he was mostly quiet during the meal, deep in thought over bringing Laura to London for surgery.

"Laura and Liam," Aidan said when the table was cleared, "would you please join me in the study?" Not waiting for an answer, Aidan stood up and glanced at the others. Jon nodded, knowing full well it was not any time to add his two cents. Laura and Liam looked at each other inquisitively and then followed Aidan down the hall.

"I have some good news," Aidan announced as he sat behind his desk. "Laura, Dr. Stanton wants to see you as soon as possible. He's very hopeful he can help with your eyesight." Laura looked fearfully at Liam and he took her hand.

"When do we go?" Liam asked.

Aidan hesitated. "I've booked a flight for tomorrow morning. Jen and I will go with you, dear." Laura didn't reply, trying to be brave but holding back tears.

Liam put his arm around her. "Don't be frightened. I'll be right there with you."

Aidan sighed. "Son, I'm afraid you can't go with us."

"Why not?" Laura cried.

"Liam can't leave Ireland. I'm sorry, but it's a condition of his bail."

Liam jumped up. "This isn't fair! I have to be with Laura–she needs me."

"Father, please! You have to call someone and get permission for Liam to go."

"I'm sorry, dear, I've already tried everything. I had to surrender his passport. Liam is out on bail, and for now he cannot leave the country. "

Laura broke down in tears and Liam held her. "Please be brave, Laura Lye. I'm so sorry I've let you down. You must go and take care of your eyes."

"No. I won't go without you."

"Laura," Aidan cautioned, "Dr. Stanton insists you need to get on with your treatment now."

"Aidan, do you mind if I talk to Laura alone?"

Aidan nodded and left the room, unable to say another word. Even with all his money and power, and friends in high places, he was unable to have the court order lifted. His frustration was immeasurable.

Liam kissed Laura tenderly and wiped her tears with his fingertips.

"Sweetheart, we must believe our love for each other will get us through this. I promise you I'll be there, if only in your heart."

"I'm so frightened," Laura sobbed.

"I know you are. I want more than anything to be there with you. Remember how frightened you were when you went off to St. Andrews and we were separated for the first time? We got through it by believing in our love."

She kissed him. "I do believe in our love, and it will make me strong." They held each other in silence for a moment.

Liam gently lifted Laura's chin, looking deeply into her eyes. "Laura Lye, let's go tell Aidan you're ready to go to London and have your beautiful eyes treated. We have a lot of this big world to see together."

"Liam, you always know just what to say to me. I love you so much."

"Sweetheart, you have truly grown into an extraordinary, strong woman. I'm proud of you."

They walked down the hall together and into the living room where Danny and Jen continued to tell stories about their time in Italy. The conversation halted and all eyes were on Laura.

"I'm ready to go London."

Aidan heaved a sigh of relief. *Liam is a miracle worker. I don't know what he said, but he sure has the gift when it comes to my daughter.* He rose to embrace his daughter. "I think that's a very wise decision." He turned and winked at Liam.

"Right on, Laura!" Jon exclaimed, jumping up. "I just know everything's going to work out. Now, how about some local entertainment?" He looked at Jen. "I'm anxious to hear my buffed sister play the drums."

"You got my vote," Danny said.

Jen was eager to show off, so they all went to the studio. Laura and Liam were happy to just be spectators.

Danny began thumping a rhythm on the bass which Jen picked up quickly. They built up to a crescendo, and Jon came in with a power chord. It was improvised, but the three were in sync. They jammed for twenty minutes, ending with a thundering solo by Jen. With smooth rolls up and down the toms, driven by a strong, steady kicking of the bass drum, she clearly demonstrated her increase in power and speed. She finished with a series of loud cymbal crashes.

"You're dynamite, sis! I think you're ready to take on the biggest stadium we can find."

Jen glowed with pride, finally having her brother's critical approval. "Rock drumming has been dominated by guys, but I'm going to change that."

Liam felt compelled to compliment her. "Jen, you're a living example of how practice makes perfect!" She smiled and took a bow.

Laura suddenly put a hand to her forehead, which Liam noticed. "I think you should rest for a while, maybe take a nap. You have a big day tomorrow. I'll walk you to your room." He turned to the others. "You guys play on and I'll catch you later."

They waved to Laura and resumed jamming.

"Liam, you can always just sing with them until your shoulder gets better."

He smiled. "Trying to get rid of me?"

"You know better. I always want you with me."

"Well then, I'm staying where I want to be. Besides, I can sing to *you*." Liam did just that until Laura fell asleep, and then said a silent prayer.

*Dear God, please let her eyesight get back to normal. She has so many beautiful things to see in this world.* He gently kissed Laura on the cheek and left the room.

# C꙰Chapter Fourteen꙰

After dinner Jen helped Laura pack a bag and get ready for the trip to London.

"I know you would rather have Liam with you, but I'll be there to help you get through this."

"Jen, you're the best girlfriend anyone could have. Thank you."

Liam knocked on the half-open door. "Can I come in?"

"No secrets here," Jen said. "Well, I'll leave you two. Besides, I'd better go and spend some time with Danny so he won't forget me."

Liam laughed. "Sure, like that would happen."

The next morning brought the inevitable goodbyes at the airport. In spite of his vow not to upset her, Liam clung to Laura until the last possible moment. The final boarding call came over the loudspeaker, and Laura couldn't hold back the tears any longer.

"I promised myself I would be strong and not cry anymore."

"You are strong," Liam reassured. "Nobody said it would be easy."

Jen took Laura's arm and promised Liam she'd call.

"We've got to board," Aidan said. "We'll keep you posted."

After boarding the plane, Laura hesitantly took her seat between Jen and her father. Unable to see the latch, she fumbled with her seat belt.

"Here, Laura, let me do that for you," Jen said. "Why don't you just close your eyes, and I'm going to tell you all about our summer in Italy."

Laura smiled as she sat back, placing her hand on Jen's. "Thank you. I'd like that very much."

Jen began her story with a soothing yet captivating quality to her voice, drawing both Aidan and Laura fully into her Tuscan adventure.

"We sailed into the beautiful deep blue Genoa Bay. All the white yachts were gently bobbing on the peaceful water. The pastel buildings decorate the hillsides. It's like a picture-perfect postcard. We were completely engaged with the breathtaking view, and Danny took a step backwards. Unfortunately, he was at the edge of the deck and fell right into the bay. Everyone on the boats around us broke into laughter. We even heard a few Italian comments, like *stupido!* When poor, embarrassed Danny climbed back aboard, dripping wet in all his clothes, he took a bow–like he'd just finished a Broadway production. He got a big round of applause."

Laura laughed easily, picturing shy Danny hamming it up. Aidan also laughed, but it was more from relief that Jen doing such a great job of distracting his daughter from her fears.

Once they were checked into their London hotel, Aidan called Dr. Stanton's office to confirm the afternoon appointment. When he hung up, Aidan reminded Laura they were leaving soon.

"Do I have to stay in the hospital?"

"Possibly, but we won't know until we see the doctor. Whatever he recommends is what we should do."

"Remember," Jen said, "the faster you get treatment, the faster we can go home."

Dr. Stanton was tall, blond and had sparkling blue eyes. He greeted everyone with a warm smile and made Laura feel at ease right away. Aidan was a bit uncertain; he'd imagined the head ophthalmologist as a much older man.

The preliminary eye examination took only a few minutes. Dr. Stanton left the room with a promise that he would return shortly. Jen took Laura's trembling hand.

"Isn't he cute?" she asked. Aidan smiled at Jen's ploy.

The doctor returned about ten minutes later, but to Laura it had seemed an eternity. Dr. Stanton noticed the look of concern on her face.

"Laura, I'm very encouraged," he began. "I feel you're a good candidate for a new procedure that we've been very successful with. It's called Argon Laser Surgery."

"Surgery!" Laura gasped.

The doctor took her hand. "No need to worry, Laura, this is done with a laser. There is no incision, and the healing time is just a matter of days." When Laura did not look convinced, he continued. "I think you'll feel more comfortable if I explain the procedure.

"Argon Laser Surgery is used to reduce intraocular pressure. The pressure is causing damage to the optic nerve fibers, and that is what is causing your progressive vision loss. Once the pressure is relieved, the optic nerve fibers will start to heal. It's very important we do not delay any longer so we can avoid any more damage."

"I'm sure we all agree," Aidan said. "It must be done right away."

All eyes were on Laura as she slowly nodded her head. Everything was happening so fast she didn't have time to object.

"Good," Dr. Stanton said. "I'll make arrangements for surgery first thing tomorrow morning."

❧

"Wow," Jen said, once inside Laura's private hospital room, "this looks like a hotel suite. I wonder if they have room service."

"Yeah, but look at the awful lingerie," Laura remarked, holding up a hospital gown. They both giggled. Satisfied that Laura was settling in, Aidan slipped out to call home.

Liam listened intently to Aidan's description, repeating the words *laser surgery* aloud. He had obvious concerns about a new technique being used on Laura.

"Don't worry," Aidan reassured. "Dr. Stanton is very confident about the procedure, and there should be very little discomfort. And thanks to Jen, our patient is in good spirits. Laura seems to like Dr. Stanton. But a call from you would be just the thing to ease her mind."

"Can't I talk to her now?"

"I'm not actually in her room. Jen's helping her change. I'll give you the number and you can call later."

Naturally curious, Jon was hovering over Liam, demanding the news the instant Liam hung up. "Tell me about this laser surgery. It sounds really far out, like Star Wars or something."

Liam described the details to Jon as best he could, but doubt riddled his face.

"Liam, she's getting the latest treatment from the best people. She'll heal fast and there won't be any scars."

"I know you're right, but I should be there. I'm going to call her right now."

Jen answered the phone in Laura's room. "Laura Meegan's suite, may I help you?"

"Jen, it's Liam. How is she doing–I mean *really* doing?"

"Fine, *really*... but she wants to talk to you."

"I want to talk to her, too, but first, I've got a favor to ask. Will you find a gardenia to give to her from me after the surgery?"

"Sure; now, talk to Laura. She's pulling this phone right out of my hand."

"Liam! I miss you and I wish you were here."

"I know, sweetheart. Aidan tells me you're in the best place for this, and you could be home in a few days."

"Well, I do like Dr. Stanton, and he does seem encouraged."

"Everything will go just fine."

"Oh, Liam–Dr. Stanton is here. I think I have to get off the phone."

"Okay. Please have your father call me right after your surgery. I love you so much, Laura Lye."

Dr. Stanton came to Laura's bedside and took her hand.

"I don't want you to worry about a thing, Laura Meegan." His tone was warm and reassuring. "This will be a smooth and quick procedure. I'll see you first thing in the morning. Now, get a good night's rest." He squeezed her hand and smiled.

"Thank you, Doctor. Goodnight."

The handsome young doctor turned to Jen. "Good night, ladies." Jen's eyes followed him as he left the room. Laura tilted her head, noticing Jen's expression.

"Jen... don't forget about Danny."

"Oh, I know. But did you notice the way Dr. Stanton smiled at me? I wonder what he'd be like to–"

"Dr. Stanton?" Laura said with surprise. "He's way too old for you!"

"He's not *that* old. What do you think... late twenties?"

"I guess. He does look a little young to be such a famous ophthalmologist."

A playful look crossed Jen's face. "You have to admit he's gorgeous... those incredible blue eyes. And his smile...."

Laura laughed. "Okay, you're right, he is gorgeous. And... he has a nice *bedside* manner."

The girls were both laughing when the nurse came in.

"Well, I'm glad to see the sad faces are gone."

"I have a question about Dr. Stanton," Jen said coyly.

The nurse smiled knowingly. "He's older than you think. And yes, he's married with two children. All the young girls ask."

Jen blushed.

The nurse looked at Laura's chart. "We all agree he's very good-looking. But most importantly," she added, looking up at Laura, "he's very talented." The nurse turned to Jen with a smile. "Now, behave yourself. He *is* the doctor!" She left the room with the girls laughing again.

Just then Aidan walked in. "I guess Liam called and cheered things up a bit?" The girls nodded and laughed even harder.

"Yes," Laura replied. "Liam always cheers me up."

Back at Montrose, Jon was already working on his own plan to distract Liam. He went to the barn where he found Danny doing the evening chores with Patrick.

"Hey you guys, Laura's having surgery in the morning. They say it will go well, but you know Liam's going to worry anyway. We need to give him something else to think about. Garrett is on his way here, he's staying for a few days. I think we should have an all-night jam session."

Danny looked to Patrick for approval.

"Go ahead and enjoy yourselves, I can take care of everythin' myself. Liam needs his friends and his music."

They thanked him, and Jon hurried back to the manor to tell Hannah his plan.

"Jon, that sounds like a nice idea, but make sure you do not wear him out. Remember, he is still healing from his recent injuries. I will ask Fiona to make some snacks for you. Is there anything else you would like?"

"Well... maybe we could have some beer. Just a couple each–it will help Liam relax."

Hannah hesitated, but before she could say no, Peggy answered from the doorway.

"Mother, they're all old enough to drink; except Liam, and he'll be eighteen in the spring. It won't hurt anything, no one is driving anywhere."

Hannah threw her hands up. "All right then, but only two beers each." She walked off in a clear demonstration that she didn't want to have any part of it.

∞

When Garrett arrived, he found Peggy right away. "Thanks for understanding about the all-night guy thing. I owe Liam a lot for helping me through the hard times when my dad passed." He gave her a kiss.

Peggy smiled seductively. "I know you'll make it up to me."

"All right, get a room, you guys. But not tonight," Jon said. "Let's go find Liam."

The two hardly knocked on Liam's door before they barged in.

Momentarily startled, he nearly dropped the book he was reading. "What's up?"

Jon grinned. "You'd be much better off drowning yourself in rock 'n' roll than in a book."

"I don't know, guys. I wouldn't be much fun."

Jon held up a beer. "Maybe you could drown yourself in this."

"Or this!" Garrett added, pulling out a pint of Bushmills from his jacket.

Liam shook his head. "What are guys trying to do to me?"

"Anesthetize you," Jon quipped, and they all laughed. "C'mon, let's go to the studio." Liam gave in with a smile.

Danny was already warming up on his bass when they walked into the studio. Jon grabbed his guitar and ripped out a screaming solo right off the bat. His enthusiasm was contagious, and it was just what Liam needed. Although thoughts of Laura were with him, he allowed himself to enjoy the camaraderie. After two beers and a couple of shots Liam was totally relaxed–and feeling no pain from his shoulder.

Sometime after three in the morning, Liam finally put up his hands. "I think I've run out of steam. We should call it a night. Thanks, guys, you've been great. You're the best."

It was hardly dawn in London, and Laura was prepped and ready to go into surgery. Jen held her hand and Aidan kissed her on the forehead.

Dr. Stanton smiled at his patient. "Now, let's fix those beautiful eyes. We'll have you as good as new and headed back to Ireland before you know it."

Jen smiled and winked at Laura. "You're in good hands now."

After the nurse rolled Laura away, Jen squeezed Aidan's arm. "I think I'll go to the chapel for a while." She was fighting back tears.

"I'll join you," Aidan replied in a shaky voice.

Laura closed her eyes to block out the endless grid of lights on the ceiling as the gurney squeaked down the long corridor. She began to see a dreamlike image of sunlight flickering through the trees by the Maigue River as she and Liam galloped their horses towards the cave. Sky's mane was flying in the wind, and Liam's hair danced in the same rhythm as they flew forward. Rose quickened her pace, and Laura could feel her own heart racing as they rode up even with Liam and Sky. She looked over at Liam and their eyes met. His were the bluest of blue, deep and soulful.

All at once Laura knew she would see everything again as clearly as she had before. *I'll be fine. This is going to work. I'm ready.*

The procedure didn't take long, and Dr. Stanton was pleased that it went smoothly.

He found Aidan and Jen in the chapel. "Well, your girl came through it just fine. We'll have to wait until tomorrow to see how much she's improved, however. She'll be back in her room in about an hour."

Aidan thanked him repeatedly and went to the nearest phone to call home.

"Hannah, everything went well. The doctor is very optimistic. We'll know more in the morning."

"Thank God. We have all been saying prayers."

"We've been praying here, too. Now, can I talk to Liam?"

"Liam is still sleeping. Should I wake him?"

"Let him sleep for a while. Laura won't be back in her room for an hour, anyway. He can call her later."

Liam woke with a jolt, the sun shining brightly through his window. *What time is it? Oh my God, I've slept in. Laura must have had her surgery by now.* He dressed and hurried downstairs.

"Hannah, have they called?"

"Yes dear, you were sleeping."

"Why didn't you wake me? How is she? When can I talk to her?"

"Liam, calm down. Everything is fine. You can call Laura after you have your breakfast."

"Please, Hannah–I need to talk to her now!"

"You will have to wait until she is back in her room, so you may as well eat."

Liam suddenly realized he had a hangover. "Maybe some coffee and a scone."

Jon and Garrett stumbled in, looking as if they'd slept in their clothes. They joined Liam at the table, but there was no attempt at conversation.

Peggy came into the room and shook her head as she surveyed the motley crew. "Good afternoon, guys! You all look like something the cat dragged in."

Liam glanced at the others and smiled. "I guess it's the price you pay for having such good friends."

Danny came in the back door, having finished his morning chores. He looked like his normal energetic self. Peggy looked at him with surprise.

"Weren't you at the same jam session as these... hooligans?"

"Yeah," he laughed as he looked them over. "But I only had one pint. Any word from London?"

"Hannah said Laura came through the surgery just fine," Liam replied. "I'm going to call right now." They all cheered and Danny patted Liam on the shoulder.

◎◝◞

"Hello, Laura, is that you?"

"Yes, Monkey Boy. Thank you for my gardenia."

"Oh, sweetheart, I'm so happy to hear your voice. How do you feel?"

"I'm tired, but I feel good. Dr. Stanton said everything went well. I should be home in a few days."

"Thank God–and Dr. Stanton. Now please get the rest you need and hurry home to me. I love you."

"I love you, too. Thank you for giving me the courage to go through this. Oh, the nurse just came in to check on me. I'll call you later. Goodbye."

Liam felt the weight of the world lifted from his shoulders as he hung up the phone.

# Chapter Fifteen

With the changing season came a renewed feeling of confidence for Laura, now ready to resume studies with her regained eyesight. But she would no longer be within the confines of St. Andrews; the time had finally arrived for Laura and Jen to join the boys at Trinity.

The air of excitement at the manor was not entirely shared by Hannah, who expressed her concerns to Aidan about the co-ed living situation at Dublin House.

"Molly cannot possibly keep an eye on all of them."

"My dear, if we can't trust them by now, we'll never be able to. Besides, if they were to sneak around, they could do it here just as easily. They're all responsible young adults, and Molly has their respect. And don't forget, Peggy will be there as well."

"Yes, Peggy is older and she is sensible, although I still cannot understand why she transferred to Trinity. The law program in London would have been just fine."

Aidan chuckled. "Oh, I think a certain young keyboard player may have had something to do with that. But I am pleased she's going for a law degree. Peggy has a sharp mind. She can argue a case to anyone."

"Aidan, do you really think she is serious about that Garrett? He has no breeding or social status."

Aidan sighed. "Now Hannah, Garrett is a fine young man. He clearly cares a great deal for Peggy. I think we should stay out of it." Aidan was trying his best to conceal it, but he was bothered that his wife was once again allowing her issues with social class to prevail.

Unaware of his discontent, Hannah added another remark. "I suppose it is too much to hope Peggy will marry as well as Emily did." With that she turned and left the room. Aidan only shook his head.

Soon after settling in at Dublin House, the students were ready to begin the first day of the fall session at Trinity. Near the campanile, Liam and Danny were pointing at the campus directory, showing Laura and Jen where their classes would be. Danny looked away from the map and noticed several guys in the bustling crowd eyeing Jen and Laura.

He nudged Liam. "I'm afraid I'll have to escort Jen to each of her classes."

"I see what you mean." A husky blond rugby player flashed a smile at Laura.

Laura blushed, but Jen laughed. "Now you know how we felt, with all the pretty girls here."

"You girls had nothing to worry about," Danny replied.

"And you guys have nothing to worry about," Laura said.

After the girls promised they were clear on the campus layout, they all agreed to meet again at noon and went their separate ways.

When they met up later at the campanile, Jen was excited about her first morning.

"I've already met so many nice people! They know me from the band."

⁂

As the days progressed, Jen was becoming very popular at school and enjoying it. For the first time in her life she seemed to have more friends than her brother Jon. As a "chick drummer" in really good shape, she was being noticed– by a lot of guys. The focus that used to be on Laura the Gypsy was now on Jen the Drummer. The fact that she was so taken with all of it was really starting to bother Danny.

"Jen darlin', we need to talk. I'm getting the feeling you like the attention from all the guys too much. I'm not looking for a problem, but it's in my face now."

Jen laughed. "Oh Danny Boy, you're so cute when you're jealous." She ran her fingers through his hair. "You have nothing to worry about. Now, I have to get to class."

Her quick dismissal of the problem was little consolation to Danny. He was hurt that she was insensitive to his feelings, but now he felt foolish for even bringing it up.

Liam was the first to notice Danny's withdrawal from the gatherings around Jen that were becoming all too regular on campus. One morning he watched as Danny patiently waited to talk to Jen while she was surrounded by a half dozen guys. Danny just shook his head and walked away.

⁂

A few days later Jon announced that Molly had approved his request for having a small party in the basement studio for his birthday.

"That sounds great," Liam agreed. "Of course you'll clear it with Aidan."

"Of course," Jon said. "I'll get on it right away."

When he told his sister the next day, she asked if she could invite a few friends.

"I guess a few more wouldn't hurt. Garrett's coming, and Peggy's inviting a couple of girls from class, and they'll probably bring dates." *This party's getting a little bigger than I planned.*

Jon approached his sister the morning of the party.

"I'm going for supplies; I need a head count. How many people did you invite?"

"Oh, I think it'll be about... six."

"Wow! Like three more couples, huh?"

"Well, not exactly," she replied. "It's actually... six guys."

"Guys? Who are these guys? Are they going to bring dates?"

"No, they're coming alone. They're just friends of mine."

Jon looked at her in shock. "I'm not sure I know you anymore. What's happened to you? What's going on with you and Danny?"

"Danny doesn't have a problem," Jen snapped. "He trusts me. He knows I'm just being outgoing and friendly, like you, The Cowboy. Maybe you have the problem because it's my time to shine now. Danny's fine with my popularity."

"I'm not so sure. He doesn't seem happy lately to me. He is your fiancé, remember? Maybe your ego is too inflated for you to see how he's been."

Jen stormed out of room, slamming the door. Jon shook his head. He got busy making music tapes, running to the store, and anything else he could think of. He didn't see his sister all day.

The party was well under way when Jen finally showed up–with the six guys she'd invited. All of them were in succession behind her like groupies following a rock star. They filed noisily down the stairs to the studio, where Jen turned to see the look of shock on her brother's face.

"Lighten up, Jon. They brought their own beer." He stood speechless until someone asked if he was the birthday boy. He only nodded as he watched the beer bottles being opened. Somebody cheered, and the level of noise in the room doubled.

"Hey Jen!" one of the partiers hollered. "Are you going to play drums for us tonight?" There were shouts of encouragement.

Liam walked over to Jon. "Who are all these guys?"

"I don't know… friends of Jen's."

Liam frowned. "Wait till Danny gets home from his rugby match. He's not going to like this." Their attention was quickly drawn to Laura, who was suddenly surrounded by several young men.

"I think I'd better save my own girl, first." Liam remarked.

Peggy had a déjà vu memory of the wild party in the St. Moritz hotel suite. "Garrett? What can we do to reduce the noise level here? It's a safe bet the neighbors will be calling the Garda before too long."

Garrett shrugged, and then he had to yell his answer. "I think pulling the plug might make things worse!"

∽

"Danny, I'm so glad you're here," Molly said when he finally arrived. "The noise from the studio is horrible. I'm afraid the neighbors are going to start complainin'."

"I'll see what I can do," Danny said.

With each step down the stairs came a huge increase in the cacophony of sounds. A cloud of smoke–of several varieties–came wafting up, along with the pungent smell of beer. The hairs on the back of Danny's neck bristled as he felt the sanctity of the studio in Aidan's Dublin House being violated.

Jon's party was in full swing, with dancing and drinking in abundance. Danny recognized no one at first, and his stomach tightened into a knot as he made his way over to the stereo to turn it down. Suddenly Jen appeared, cranking it back up. "Not too low!"

"Who are all these people?" Danny asked. "Did Jon invite them?"

"Well," Jen answered, "I invited some of them."

"Is that so?" Danny's anger was building.

"Danny, aren't you glad to see me?" She grabbed his arm. "Dance with me?"

He pulled away. "I think I need something to drink."

Just then one of Jen's "friends" took her by the arm and led her to the dance floor. Danny narrowed his eyes and went to grab a pint of Guinness. He slammed down the first one and started on the second before surveying the crowd again. He caught sight of Jon, Liam and Laura, all laughing together. *I guess it doesn't bother them that our studio's been invaded. Why do I feel like I'm the outsider?*

By the time Liam found him, Danny had chugged three pints and was slumped on the couch. The hair hanging over his eyes masked Danny's expression as he watched Jen dance with the other guys.

Liam sat down next to him. "Danny, are you all right?"

"Sure… it's a grand party."

Laura came over a moment later and exchanged a worried glance with Liam. She put a hand on Danny's shoulder. "Would you like to dance?"

Danny shook his head. "Thanks, but I'm fine. You and Liam go ahead."

Liam stood up and took Laura aside. "I hate to see Danny hurting like this."

"Me too, and I'm upset with Jen. How could she do this to Danny?" Laura looked into Liam's eyes. "I guess coming from me that sounds pretty stupid."

Liam pulled her close. "Sweetheart, we've both made mistakes, and we've learned from them. I think Jen's caught up in the moment. I don't think she can see how upset Danny is. We need to stand by them and help them get through this."

Danny continued to drown his sorrows, watching Jen spin around on the dance floor, oblivious to his pain. The music changed to a slower pace, and most of the people left the floor to get drinks. Jen began to approach Danny, but stopped when someone grabbed her arm.

"Jen! Remember me? Quinn?" He pulled her close and they began slow dancing. She looked to Danny, hoping he would cut in, but he wouldn't meet her eye. Jen could now clearly see the wounded look on his face, and she tried to pull away from her aggressive dance partner. Instead, Quinn held her tighter, moving his hands down her back.

That's the moment Danny looked up. In an instant his rage erupted like a volcano. He jumped to his feet, knocking over the table, sending drinks crashing to the floor. In one swift motion Danny yanked Jen's dance partner away from her and threw him to the floor. The young man stood up, but Danny was right on him, attacking with all the fury that had been building inside him for days. The long-haired skinny student was no match for the seasoned rugby player. Jon jumped in to break up the fight, but Danny was out of control, swinging at anyone in the way. One of Danny's punches caught Jon squarely in the jaw, and he dropped to the floor.

Liam and Garrett were there in seconds. Quinn's friends were also in the mix, and now it was a free-for-all, complete with girls screaming and bottles flying. Someone was pushed backwards, falling into Jen's cymbals, which went crashing to the floor.

Molly was not about to venture down the stairs, but stood at the top screaming. She didn't even hear the sirens as the Garda arrived. Every girl at the party had begun to clamber up the stairs.

The Garda let the first group pass by without incident, knowing there was still brawling in progress below. With nightsticks in hand, the officers rushed down to the basement and began shouting orders to break it up. All but three complied–and Danny was among them. They were hauled out in handcuffs.

With his long hair hanging over his eyes and blood running down his chin, Danny turned to face Jen as he was being led out by the Garda. "Nice party," was all he said.

Jen hung her head in guilt, but then raised her chin defiantly to everyone. "I'm not taking the blame for all this."

"Do you live here, young lady?" an officer interrupted.

"Well, yes, but–"

"Then you and the other residents of this house wait over there. The rest of you leave quietly and go home, or risk arrest."

"What about my brother?" Molly asked.

"If you mean one of them in restraints, they're goin' to the jailhouse now."

Molly paled, but offered no protest as the officer took her statement. It took a long while before the last of the Garda left. Molly whipped around to face Jon.

"I can't believe you let this party get so out of hand– with my brother gettin' arrested! Aidan will have my head when he hears about this, although he's probably already been called by some of the neighbors. I'm ashamed of all of you! This is not the behavior I would have expected."

Jon's shoulders were slumped, his head hanging. "Molly, I'm so sorry. I'm not even sure how the fight happened. Danny was sitting in the corner by himself, then the next thing I know he's grabbing this guy."

"Jon, the truth is, there were too many people here," Liam said.

Jon glared at his sister. "I think I know how that happened."

"What, you think this was all my fault?" she snapped. "Danny was drunk. He wouldn't dance with me, so I danced with other guys."

"Well they wouldn't have been here if you hadn't invited them."

Liam put up his hands. "Enough! We have to bail Danny out. We can't let him spend the night in jail."

"It might do him some good," Molly disagreed.

"No!" Liam said firmly. "I'm not going to let that happen. I've been there. Besides, Danny is a peaceful and easygoing guy. Something provoked him."

All eyes turned to Jen and she looked away.

"Jon, will you drive me down to the Garda station?" Liam asked.

"I'll drive," Peggy volunteered. "You've all been drinking. Besides, I know the law on this, and they have nothing to hold him on."

"Let's go," Jon said. Peggy grabbed her keys, and the three headed out the door.

"We're all sorry for our part in this, Molly," Laura said. "We'll clean up the mess tomorrow morning."

"You bet you will. Now off to bed with you, girls. I have to figure out how to explain this to Aidan."

Laura walked Jen to her room. "It's probably a good time to tell me what's going on with you and Danny. I'm not sure you can see what you're doing to him."

"He was drunk, and he had no cause to start a fight," Jen protested.

"Jen, I've gone down that road, making Liam jealous, and it's the worst mistake I've ever made."

"I wasn't trying to make Danny jealous. He's just so… sensitive," Jen sighed. "But maybe I didn't know those guys so well. I thought they were my friends. I really do feel bad that it got out of control."

Peggy marched into the Garda station. "You have no grounds to hold Danny Bailey. If necessary, I will call Lord Meegan; although I'm sure he might be a little upset at being awakened at two in the morning."

The duty officer looked over his glasses at the young lady with the attitude. "And who might you be, missy?"

"Peggy Morann, if you must know. I'm Lord Meegan's stepdaughter."

The officer wasn't in the mood to pursue any arguments. "You can save your call to Lord Meegan for the mornin', when you'll be explainin' to him how your little party got out of hand. I'll release the boy to you. You'll have to sign some papers. I advise you to take him straight home and let him sleep it off."

On the drive home, Jon suddenly realized how sore his jaw was. "Danny Boy, you pack a helluva punch."

Danny put his head in his hands. "I'm sorry. I guess it was the Guinness talking. I don't know what's wrong with me."

Liam put his hand on Danny's shoulder. "It's all right, we understand. I've gone a bit too far myself defending Laura."

"My sister caused all this," Jon said. "But it's not really her fault. Jen's never had this kind of popularity before. Back on Long Island she was only invited to parties because she was my sister. She was always the skinny, plain little girl. I even had to ask a guy to take her out once. But after this summer in Italy she came home looking really hot, and now she's in the limelight drumming for a popular band. I think it's gone to her head. I know I shouldn't make excuses for her, but I think she'll come back to being the Jen we all know and love."

"Jon's right," Peggy said, "but we have a bigger problem now–Aidan. We're all going to have some explaining to do."

The reality of that statement hit Danny like a ton of bricks. "Aidan will probably throw me out."

Molly finally got up the nerve to call to Aidan the next morning. As expected, he was not happy with the news about the party.

"I know you're doing your best, but maybe having all of them there is too much."

"Well, it was all a shock to me, but I really don't think it was their fault. These outsiders came to Jon's party. He didn't even know them. Anyway, I've I told them no more parties. That should keep things under control."

"All right, Molly, I'll leave things as they are for now, but it's time I have a talk with all of our young students–face to face. I think I'll come up Monday."

Jen agreed to go for a walk with Danny in Merrion Square Park where they could be alone for a while.

"Jen, darlin', can you forgive me for my behavior last night?"

"You can't be flying off in a rage because some guy is dancing with me."

"True, but his hands were all over you."

"And you saw me trying to break free, didn't you?"

He nodded. "Yes, and that's when I went nuts. I was trying to help you."

Jen gave him a kiss. "I'm wearing your ring, and I intend to marry you as soon as we can. Please trust me. I'm just having fun and enjoying college life. You don't want me to be unfriendly and have people think I'm a snob, do you?"

"No, but I don't want you to give them the wrong idea, either. You're so beautiful... and I know guys. When a girl is friendly, they're going to take it as an invitation. I don't strike up conversations with every girl that smiles at me. It doesn't mean I'm a snob, it just means I'm always thinking about you."

Jen smiled. "I get what you're saying. You know I'll always love you."

As each of the students returned to Dublin House after classes Monday, they shared a sinking feeling at the sight of Aidan's car parked in front. Molly met them at the door with a look of foreboding on her face.

"Aidan's waiting for you all in the living room." They walked quietly through the entryway as if they might wake a sleeping giant.

"I knew we'd have to face Aidan soon," Jon whispered, "but I thought it wouldn't be until next weekend."

"I'll talk to him," Danny said bravely. "It was my fault."

Liam put his hand on Danny's shoulder. "We all had a part in this. We're not going to let you take the heat alone."

Aidan heard the last remark. "Do you think someone should take heat over this?"

Liam lowered his head. "Yes, sir."

Aidan surveyed the group. "First I want to say a few words to all of you together, and then I want to see the boys alone." Everyone squirmed but Peggy, who stood up tall as if she were about to present her case in court.

"Aidan, this was not intended to be a wild party–although there may have been a bit of Guinness involved." A slight smile came to Aidan's face, and Peggy continued.

"We were all having fun and enjoying the music when a young man–name of Quinn–proceeded to get fresh with Jen. Now Danny, being the gentleman that he is, took it upon himself to defend her honor. Then Jon stepped in with an honest attempt to put a stop to the skirmish. Unfortunately, Quinn's friends perceived this as an invitation to join in.

"Subsequently Liam and Garrett were compelled to intervene to save their mates and put an end to the altercation. Now, no one was hurt and only minor damage was done to the studio, which is private property; uh, yours, of course. I've consulted a barrister, my professor, Aaron McAlester, retired, and he has assured me that no charges should be filed."

"Peggy," Aidan remarked, "someday you'll make a fine solicitor. You have pleaded their case well, but that doesn't excuse this fiasco. I cannot have any activity here that will lead to this kind of behavior. There will be no more parties." Aidan scanned the roomful of guilty faces. "Quite frankly, I'm very disappointed in all of you."

Danny's feeling of guilt was compounded by the long history of opportunities given to him by Lord Meegan. Danny had worked hard and shown his appreciation all along, but last night's actions now seemed to erase all of it. *How could I have been so foolish and let Aidan down?*

When no one spoke, Aidan continued. "Hannah expressed her concern to me that it would be too much responsibility for Molly with all of you living at Dublin House. I hate to admit that she may have been right."

Suddenly arguments from the group began coming at him from all directions.

"Silence!" Aidan commanded. "I will speak to the boys alone in the study now. Whatever my decision, I will let you know right away, and there will be no argument. In the past I've considered you to be sensible young adults, and I have respected your judgment. In this instance you have acted irresponsibly and made poor choices. Therefore I shall make any and all decisions myself. Is that understood?"

Everyone nodded silently, and the boys followed him out.

Tears filled Jen's eyes. "Oh, Laura! I hope he doesn't make us live apart. This is all my fault! I invited those guys to the party. I guess I let celebrity go to my head. I've hurt everyone–but mostly Danny."

Laura put her arms around her friend. "We all love you. Don't worry about Danny. He has a forgiving heart, like Liam. But I've learned the hard way you can't take that for granted."

The boys each took a chair across the desk from Aidan. Jon started to speak, but Aidan put up his hand. "I will speak first." Jon slumped in his seat.

"I'm well aware of the circumstances and all the events that took place. But I don't think you realize the consequences of the resulting brawl." They all sunk a little deeper into their chairs.

"First of all, Jon, you called and asked if you could have a small get-together in the studio for your birthday. It's clear you deceived me, and Molly. Thirty or more young people, some of whom you didn't even know, is not a small get-together." Aidan paused to let Jon respond.

"I'm so sorry–it just got out of hand. I promise it will never happen again."

"You got that one right. Now Danny, I can understand your feelings about this fellow making advances on your fiancée. But don't you think there might have been a better way to handle it? Taking of the drink is not an excuse. And you all know very well what can happen when you react with your fists." He glanced at Liam before he continued.

"Danny, what's going to happen if the scholarship department at Trinity hears about this? And how would your parents react? You're the first in the family to get a college education."

Blinking away tears of shame, Danny spoke. "I'm so sorry I have disappointed everyone. I have no excuses. It was bad judgment on my part. I promise I will use my head in the future. If you want, I'll move out." Aidan didn't answer but turned to Liam.

"Son, I am shocked most of all by your behavior." Liam put his head in his hands and Aidan continued. "We haven't begun the court proceedings over your last encounter. How do you think it will go if they get wind of this brawl? You're still on probation. One thing I can tell you: I spoke to our solicitor, and he is not happy about this. Your good character is the central theme of his defense. You jumped right into the thick of it, from what I've heard. What were you thinking?"

"I didn't think–I just reacted. Can this really hurt my chances in court?"

Aidan nodded. "I'm afraid you've done a very foolish thing. I'm trying my best to get you out of the mess in Clonmel, and you have to help. I had to call in a lot of favors just to get you back at Trinity. Everything depends on the outcome of your trial. You are not to be around any hint of trouble. Period." Aidan folded his arms.

"I think until the trial is over things are going to be different around here. No music, no social activities and no outside friends in this house. You will all give your studies full attention. If this order is not followed, you will be separated. I will have you boys move into a dorm at university. Do you understand how important this is to Liam's trial?" Everyone nodded without protest.

They were dismissed, but Liam hung back. "What have I done?" His voice was quivering. "What's going to happen to me?"

Aidan closed the door, then put his arms around the shaken young man. "Son, I will fight until the end for you. You still have a bright future ahead of you. We will get out of this mess. I just need your help."

# ᴄᔆ∘Chapter Sixteenᙋᒼ

The weather had turned unusually chilly for late fall, and most agreed it was the first sign of a long cold winter to come. The feeling of gloom in the manor, however, was not just due to the weather: Liam's trial date had been set for early January.

The more time Liam spent with his solicitor, John MacDonald, the more depressed he became. With the fear of going to prison and being separated from Laura constantly on his mind, Liam could not escape the dark cloud that hung over him.

The gravity of the upcoming trial was dramatized by articles in the *Dublin Times*.

### Trial Date Set for Heartthrob Singer

*Will Fame and Fortune allow him to Get Away with Murder?*

### Rock and Roll Royalty to Face the Music

*Dublin Trial has all Eyes on Local Lord and Musician Son*

Even walking through the halls at Trinity, Liam could hear the whispers and feel the burning eyes of accusation. He became so withdrawn he hardly spoke to anyone, and it seemed his only solace might be Christmas break.

Still in Italy, Robert and Catherine Bianchi could only imagine how difficult it would be for their extended family at Montrose to get into the Christmas spirit. Knowing Liam was not allowed to leave the country, they decided they would come to Ireland in an effort to bring some holiday cheer.

Once Aidan heard the news, he called Dublin House to tell Laura.

"We will all be here over the holidays, including the Bianchis, to give Liam the love and support he needs to get through this. I suggest when you come home to Montrose you plan for another family concert. Maybe music will pull him back to life."

Laura asked Jon later about the concert idea. He shook his head.

"I'll bet money he won't go for it. Liam never likes to perform, or even rehearse, unless he's feeling good about himself. The truth is, this is all pretty scary–especially the way the newspapers are jumping on it."

Laura started to cry, and Jon put his arm around her. "Don't do that. We need to be strong for Liam. I'll figure out something. I have faith that God will help."

Later Jon walked into the kitchen to find Molly pleading with her brother to go with the Bailey family to Scotland for the holidays. Danny was shaking his head.

"Please, Danny," Molly implored. "It's part of Brent's bonus for gettin' the golf resort completed before schedule. He's invited the entire family, all expenses paid."

"I'm sorry–I just can't leave Liam over the holidays with the trial coming up."

"Are Chloe and Patrick going, too?" Jon asked.

"I want them to," Molly sighed. "But Patrick said there's no one to take over running things in the barn."

"That's all the more reason for me to stay," Danny said firmly. "Chloe and Patrick should definitely go to Scotland. They've never even had a honeymoon."

"I've got a better idea," Jon smiled. "What if Liam takes over the barn duties? It would make him really feel needed–and it just might keep his mind off the trial. And then you guys can all be together in Scotland for Christmas."

"That's a good idea," Danny said, "but I think we should get Patrick to ask him. Liam shouldn't know we were involved. But he'd do anything for Patrick." Then Danny took a step towards his sister, putting an arm around her. "Of course, I'll want to include my fiancée on the trip to Scotland."

Molly smiled. "You know she's welcome to come. Her family had you for Christmas in Tuscany last year. Now it's our turn–in Scotland."

"Who's going to Scotland?" Jen asked at the kitchen door.

"You, darlin'… that's if you will accompany me and my family to the finest golf resort and spa in Scotland over Christmas–compliments of Brent and Molly."

"I'd love to!"

Danny filled her in on the plan and explained how it would help Liam. Jon went right to work, calling Aidan at Montrose.

"Brilliant idea, Jon. I'll make the arrangements with Patrick and have him talk to Liam as soon as you all come home from Dublin. I think this may work."

After the students had returned to Montrose Manor and everyone was settled in, Liam wanted to go to the barn to see Sky. Laura was busy decorating the Christmas tree, so Liam went by himself. He absorbed all the sights, smells and sounds as he walked along the river, not knowing how much longer he would be able to. His heart was filled with fond memories, but his fears kept creeping back in. Sky nickered to Liam as he approached.

"Oh, I have missed you, buddy. What will I do if I can't see you again?"

Sky nuzzled his companion. Patrick tactfully waited, giving Liam his time with Sky before approaching.

"Good to have you home again, lad. We've all missed you."

"There is no place I'd rather be than right here in this barn."

Patrick tilted his head. "Do you really mean that?"

"You know I do."

"Well then, it would be a great personal favor to me if you took over in the barn for the holidays. That way I can go with Chloe and the family to Scotland."

"Patrick, you know I would do anything for you and Chloe. Don't worry about a thing. I'd be happy take care of the barn. Besides, I want to spend more time with Sky."

Patrick gave him a hug. "Bless you—and I mean it from the bottom of my heart."

⁕

Jon met his parents at the Shannon Airport. Catherine gave him a hug and stepped back with tears in her eyes. "I will only get to spend a few days with Jennifer before they leave for Scotland. Well, I suppose it's only fair. Danny did spend the holidays with us last year. And we'll be helping support Liam."

Robert agreed. "I'm also worried about Aidan. He's been really stressed over this trial; and now the heart condition." He winced the moment he uttered the words, and Catherine glared scornfully at him.

Jon saw the look. "Wait–what heart condition? He hasn't said anything to us."

Looking somewhat sheepish, Robert explained. "Oh boy. I wasn't supposed to let on, so please keep this to yourself, son. I'm not sure if Aidan has even said anything to Hannah. He's been waking up in the middle of the night with his heart pounding and finding it hard to breathe. He went to a specialist and they're running tests; supposed to have the results back next week. I'm sure there's no cause for worry."

But worry is just what Jon did. *Good God, where would we all be if something happened to Aidan?*

Jen was thrilled to see her parents again, but felt a bit guilty. "Mother, I'm sorry I'll be leaving so soon, and I hope you can forgive me."

Catherine smiled. "We understand, dear."

Fiona had prepared a special dinner, and of course Danny and Kelly were invited. Robert tried to bring cheer to the table by involving everyone in conversation.

"Kelly, Jon tells me you're in flight attendants' school in Shannon. That's sounds like an adventurous career."

Kelly lit up with excitement. "Yes, I think it will be. And I have all of you to thank for it. My first flight ever was when I came to your villa in Tuscany. It was so thrilling. I knew right away that somehow I would be a part of the world of travel."

Laura turned to Liam, but noticed the distant look on his face. It seemed as if he hadn't even heard a word.

Aidan, too, had been withdrawn, but he was hiding it well.

After dinner the adults retired to the living room for drinks. When Catherine asked Hannah about her daughters, she began with the usual boasting about Emily and the baby. Then her expression changed to a frown.

"Now Peggy, on the other hand, is a mystery to me. I do not understand her attraction to that Garrett. She is insisting he come here for the holidays, even though he has an aunt and a cousin he could spend Christmas with."

Aidan slammed his drink down on the coffee table. The room went dead silent, and all eyes were on him as his face turned red with anger and his hands began to shake.

"Enough about Garrett! As long as Peggy wants to be with him, he's welcome. Hannah, for once you should think about your daughter's happiness and forget about your precious image!" Aidan collected himself after the outburst. "If you will all excuse me, I'm not feeling well."

Hannah was humiliated and embarrassed, but waited for Aidan to leave the room to apologize. "I'm so sorry about Aidan's behavior. We do not agree about Garrett. Please excuse him."

Robert nodded politely, but his thoughts were really with Aidan. "We're all a little tense about the trial, and it's been a long day. We should turn in now."

Aidan apologized to Robert and Catherine the next morning–but not to Hannah. There was an unmistakable chill between them at breakfast. Thankfully the tension was forgotten during tearful goodbyes as Jen, Danny and Kelly left for Scotland.

Liam became completely immersed in his duties running the barn. Laura knew that the hard work was a welcome diversion for him, but she had been pleading with him to take a break and go riding with her. Finally he agreed to take the horses to the cave after the morning's chores were done.

Even with the familiar exhilaration of the wind in his face as they galloped, Liam was still plagued by worries.

Once inside Laura gently took his hand, and the gesture eased him enough to put his arms around her and speak his mind. "Why is everything so turned upside down? I feel like I'm a kite blowing in the wind–first up, then crashing down. I've disappointed everyone–you, Aidan, the band."

Even after the passage of several years the cave still afforded certain comforts, like the scented candles along the rock wall. Laura slipped out of his arms to light some of them and then returned to take his hand, leading him over to the side. She placed his hand on the wall where he had carved his pledge of love years before.

"Do you remember how you felt when you wrote this?"

Liam couldn't help but smile. "It seems like it was a lifetime ago. Whatever happened to those young, carefree children?"

"We're still here, and our love is even stronger now. Liam, we can get through anything together. I know this for a fact. Someone very wise told me this, and I have always believed it. My Monkey Boy has never let me down." The term of endearment was something she coined years before when Liam had scrambled up a tree to get honey from a hive. She could always rely on the nickname to warm his heart.

Liam buried his face in her hair before he spoke. "Sweetheart, without your love I would have given up a long time ago. As long as you believe in me, I'll be all right."

"The magistrate will also believe in you, and this will all be over soon. I would like us to pray together, right here."

They kneeled, holding hands tightly with heads lowered. As they prayed there was a sudden gust of wind, blowing out the candles and bringing a chill to the cave. Then came an ethereal sound... like a whispered voice.

"What was that?" Laura asked fearfully.

"I don't know—it was like someone... calling out."

"Yes, it sounded like... *a victory.*"

"No, it was more like... a *vic-mo-ree*"

Hearing nervous calls from Rose and Sky, they hurried from the cave. The horses were uneasy, anxious to leave.

Laura and Liam galloped swiftly through the trees to the safety of the barn.

The haunting voice was on their minds, but Laura did not want to talk about it anymore. Liam went about his work and she returned to the manor.

After dinner Liam was seated in the library studying an old Gaelic book when Aidan came in.

"Are you looking for something in particular, son?"

Liam shared the experience of the whispered voice with Aidan, who listened with great interest. Aidan rubbed his chin thoughtfully.

"You know, it could have been *A Vic Mo Cree*. It means *son of my heart.*"

A strange feeling come over Liam as he repeated the words several times. "Yes, that was it. Do you think it was… my father? Speaking to me?"

Aidan put his arm on Liam's shoulder. "I know Philip is with you all the time. He will help you get through this trial."

"Do you really believe that?" A glimmer of hope came to Liam's eyes.

Aidan nodded. "I know my Fey comes to me in times of need. I believe the spirits of our loved ones are always with us."

"Thank you, Aidan. I will hold on to that belief."

Liam went straight to his room, and a feeling of comfort began to envelope him. For the first time in a long while he slept peacefully, believing his father was by his side.

At breakfast, Aidan noticed the color had returned to Liam's face. "Good morning. How did you sleep?"

"Very well, thank you." Liam walked to the window, gazing out. "It looks as though the dreary skies have gone and the sun has returned."

Aidan smiled and joined Liam at the window. "It is remarkably good to see the sunshine again." They enjoyed the view for a moment before Aidan spoke.

"I'm planning on taking the Bianchis to Limerick today, and then maybe a drive up the coast to see the Cliffs of Moher. Would you like to join us?"

Liam shook his head. "I've got too much to do with the horses."

"Why don't you ask one of the barn boys Patrick hired to come back and feed this evening? You've been working so hard. Take a break."

Jon had overheard before he walked into the kitchen. "I'll help you get things done this morning. C'mon, go with us. I know Laura would love it."

"Sure, why not?" Liam smiled. "I know I've been no fun to be around, but today I might be tolerable."

⁂

A few hours later the limousine arrived and everyone was ready, except for Peggy and Garrett, who decided not to go so they could spend some time alone.

On the way to Limerick, Laura noticed a Celtic fair near the road. A caravan of traveling craftspeople was lined up, selling their wares.

"Could we stop here for a while?" Laura asked.

"I do not care to wander around with gypsies," Hannah stated. "I would prefer to do my shopping in Limerick."

Aidan, always mindful of Laura's maternal connection to Irish travelers, was going to agree with Hannah, but suddenly changed his mind. "I don't see any harm in it. We'll pick you up later."

Laura hugged her father. "Thank you."

"Now stay together, and we'll be back in a while."

Hannah frowned but did not comment any further as the three teenagers got out.

Laura headed right for the caravan, with Liam and Jon not far behind. An old gypsy woman was watching Laura with great interest. Drawn to her, Laura found herself admiring the woman's gold coin bracelet.

"What's your name, girl?" the woman asked in a soft deep voice.

"Laura. What's your name?"

The old woman took no notice of the two young men and looked deep into the girl's eyes. "I'm Eliza from the Claddagh of Galway." Her tone was mysterious.

"The Claddagh," Liam repeated. "I've read about them somewhere...."

"I'm sure you've read no truths," the gypsy snapped.

"It was the clan's music in an old book from Laura's grandmother," Liam said.

Eliza studied Liam for a moment then turned back to Laura. "And your grandmother's name would be...."

"Maura."

"Of course, Maura. You look just like her. You must be Fey's daughter."

Laura gasped. "Yes! I am! Please tell me about my grandmother. Do you know where she is?"

Eliza shook her head. "No, she left Ireland years ago. I got word she settled in New York City with some dance troupe. I never heard from her after that."

"Can you remember what part of New York?" Jon asked.

"No! Enough questions. I must get back to selling my goods."

"I must know about my grandmother," Laura pleaded. "I'll buy something."

The woman opened a weathered case and showed Laura some cheap jewelry. "Now, what would you like?"

The only thing that held Laura's gaze was the gold coin bracelet on Eliza's wrist. The woman pulled her arm back.

"That is not for sale. Only women of the Claddagh have them."

Eliza took Laura's hand, placing one of the costume bracelets on her wrist. The old woman got a faraway look in her eyes. "Maura was a beauty... her hair was like spun gold. She danced like her feet never touched the ground. And her love for horses... she could ride like the wind. Maura was a wild spirit, always chasin' her dreams."

Suddenly Eliza looked up as if awakened from a dream. "Now—that's all I know. Do you want the bracelet or not? I must wait on other customers." Liam paid for the cheap trinket and thanked the woman.

As they walked away, Laura looked pensive. "I can't believe I finally found someone who could tell me about my grandmother."

"I know it means a lot to you, sweetheart. The world moves in mysterious ways."

"Did you run into any trouble with those gypsies?" Hannah asked when the three got back into the limo.

"Oh, I just bought a fun little bracelet," Laura replied. She didn't want to let on about her encounter with the Claddagh woman.

Hannah shook her head. "Why would you want something worthless from those people? You have so much fine jewelry of your own."

"Oh, you don't think it's real?" Laura said with feigned innocence, holding the bracelet up to Hannah. She glanced at Jon and Liam, who restrained their laughter.

The drive up the coast was enjoyable. When they got to the Cliffs of Moher everyone walked up the steps to O'Brien's Tower, the old lookout built in 1835. The cold day was redeemed by the sunshine and the spectacular panoramic view. Aidan pointed out the Aran Islands, Galway Bay and Connemara.

Laura and Liam hiked down the trail to the other end and stood at the edge of the breathtaking cliffs, which drop dramatically 700 feet into the pounding Atlantic below. The strong winds sweeping up from the sea made a soft rhythmic sound.

"Do you hear that?" Laura asked.

"Yes, I do. It sounds like... monks chanting."

"It's so spiritual."

"This is truly God's country, Laura. We're surrounded by Mother Nature in all her glory." Liam embraced her and told her what Aidan had said about the voice they'd heard in the cave.

"Yes!" Laura exclaimed. "That's what it was: A Vic Mo Cree. Son of my heart. It was your father calling to you." She kissed him. "Liam, you are *my* heart."

# Chapter Seventeen

Christmas morning had arrived with a dusting of snow. The winter wonderland of Montrose Manor was a glorious sight for Laura, who gazed through the living room window room while sitting by the warm fire waiting for Liam to join the family.

Liam had a slightly different experience of the frozen grounds. When he came in from the morning chores, he was chilled to the bone. Laura greeted him with a hot cup of coffee and wrapped a woolen throw around his shoulders.

"Come sit by the fire with me."

"Merry Christmas!" Aidan said, offering Liam a splash of Irish whiskey for his coffee. "This will warm you right up."

Liam smiled. "I bet it would, but I think I'll pass."

"Aidan, he is still under age," Hannah scolded.

Aidan chuckled. "Nonsense. He's a hardworking man I would be proud to drink with, especially on Christmas Day."

Aidan had been making a special effort to maintain the Christmas spirit, hoping to divert everyone's focus away from Liam's impending trial. However, Hannah saw this as yet another sign of Aidan's weakening authority as head of the manor. She had voiced her opinion on several occasions, to no avail. To her it seemed as though "the children," as she called them, were making all the decisions, including, of course,

Peggy, whose choice of a boyfriend was Hannah's constant source of irritation.

Peggy was well aware of her mother's disapproval of Garrett, but she didn't care. She was so tired of living in the shadow of her "perfect" sister, Emily.

Now that Liam had joined them, it was time to open gifts, and Garrett began by placing a small jewelry box in Peggy's hand.

Hannah cringed. *Dear God, do not let it be an engagement ring.*

"Garrett! Gold earrings!" Peggy exclaimed. "They're so beautiful."

She kissed him and her mother looked the other way.

Liam handed Laura a present, and she looked up at him with surprise as she began to open it. *When did he even find time to go shopping?* Tears came to her eyes when the flickering firelight revealed a brilliant gold coin bracelet–which Laura recognized.

"Liam, this is a real treasure. How did you get this?"

He smiled triumphantly. "I went back to see Eliza while you and Jon were getting coffee at the fair. I knew she would barter for the right ransom."

"You're amazing," Laura beamed. "Now I have something for you."

Liam opened the gift box to find an ornate gold crucifix and chain which he proudly held up for everyone to see. Laura gently placed it around his neck.

No one had noticed that Aidan had slipped out of the room, but when he reappeared, all eyes turned to him.

"Aidan, your cheeks are so rosy," Hannah remarked. "Have you been outside?"

Without answering, Aidan handed a plain envelope to Liam. "Go ahead, son."

Puzzled, Liam opened it to find a Saint Christopher's medal attached to a key by a silver chain.

"Thank you," he said, looking baffled. "But… what's it for?"

"The Saint Christopher is for safe traveling," Aidan replied. "Now, as for the key… go look out the front door." He beckoned to everyone to follow.

Liam could not believe his eyes. Parked out front in the snow, with the top down, was Aidan's Mercedes coupe.

Aidan smiled proudly. "She's all yours, son!"

"Oh my God!" Liam exclaimed, hugging Aidan. "Are you sure?"

"I've never been surer. I've had some of the best times of my life with this car, and now you and Laura will. But remember, you can't drive off the estate until April, when you turn eighteen."

Hannah was incredulous. *The best times of his life? Why, I have never even sat in that car. I cannot believe Aidan's indulgence.*

Everyone shared in Liam's excitement, oblivious to Hannah's reaction. Jon admired the Mercedes with envy.

"I'll bet I could spin some serious doughnuts in that fresh snow."

"And that's why you're not driving!" Liam retorted as he grabbed a couple of jackets. He and Laura hurried out the door for a drive around the estate.

Robert smiled. "It's sure good to see Liam happy again. Aidan, you did well."

"It's a small diversion. I want him to feel he has something to look forward to in the spring. He needs all the encouragement we can give him."

"Catherine and I agree. We talked last night, and we'd like to stay on until after his trial. We'll do anything we can to help."

"Thank you both. You're great friends."

Hannah cleared her throat. "Aidan, you know I had planned to go to York to spend the rest of the holiday with Emily and the baby. I suppose I could cancel."

Catherine shook her head. "Oh no–please go ahead. You need to spend time with your granddaughter. We'll be just fine. We can spend more time with Jennifer when she comes back from Scotland."

Aidan swiftly agreed. "You don't need to change your plans. Go ahead, and please give Emily and Elliott our best."

The holidays were soon over, and the trial was about to begin. Laura had convinced her father that missing a few days at university to attend the proceedings would be justified. To her surprise, he agreed.

With everyone back from Scotland and Patrick resuming his duties in the barn, Liam was now forced to focus on the trial. The attorney had scheduled an appointment to brief him on the procedures.

"As the solicitor," MacDonald began, "I gather all of the pertinent information, interview the witnesses and work on the defense strategy. I am not the one who presents the case to the court, however. That is the role of the barrister."

"He does not normally deal directly with the public. It is said that the result is a more… unbiased presentation to the judge and jury. Roen Dennehey is our barrister. He is a specialist in litigation and advocacy. He's one of the best.

"The prosecutor is also a barrister. He will present the charges against you to the court. I've gone against this one before–Stephen Collins. He can be tricky: He's an Englishman. But don't let that intimidate you. Just take a moment to think before answering any of his questions, and answer them truthfully, and briefly."

Liam nodded as if he was following, but MacDonald could see the young man was nervous and unsure of himself.

"Now Liam," MacDonald continued, "we do have a few tricks of our own. For example, the way you present yourself to the court when you're on the stand. Don't look at me or anyone else but the barrister when you're being questioned, or it'll look like you're being coached. Take your time; count to three before answering every question. If he asks you anything confusing, just tell him you don't understand. He'll rephrase.

"Barrister Dennehey is one of the best. He feels we have a strong defense and several good witnesses."

"Will Patrick be called to testify?" Aidan asked.

MacDonald frowned. "It's likely the prosecutor will want to call him, in spite of Patrick's potential for bias in Liam's favor. You see, his testimony could end up hurting us. Remember, he did not see Rory attack Liam. What Patrick actually saw was Liam on the running board of the truck hanging onto Rory's throat."

MacDonald paused, noticing the look of dismay on their faces.

"Hmmm," he said with a sly grin. "I think we'll just call Patrick to the stand first. Think of it as... damage control. We'll present his testimony in an environment of our choosing. Then we can be sure he'll be the best character witness for Liam."

Aidan rubbed his chin thoughtfully as he considered MacDonald's words. "Liam, don't look so downhearted. This sounds like a good strategy."

The solicitor sat back in his chair. "I'm certain that Kevin McCully will be our best eyewitness. He clearly saw Rory attack Liam with the pitchfork." Liam's expression remained drawn, but MacDonald remained on point.

"Liam, you must keep a positive attitude. If you look defeated in the courtroom, people will assume it's because you're guilty. I know it won't be easy, but it is very important that you look confident."

Liam nodded slowly. He knew there was no choice but to put his trust in John MacDonald and his faith in God.

While the others busied themselves packing the night before the trip to Dublin, Robert took the opportunity to speak to Aidan alone.

"Are your test results back yet?"

Aidan sighed. "My doctor said I have high blood pressure, and he's prescribed some medication. He thinks the other symptoms are the result of anxiety. They've scheduled some follow-up exams."

Robert patted him on the shoulder. "You must take care of yourself. I know the strain you've been under, and we may have some rough sailing ahead."

Liam and Laura went down to the barn the next morning to say goodbye to the horses. Patrick greeted Liam with a hug. "Lad, I'll do my best when I testify. And I know Philip will be watchin' over you."

"Thank you. Sometimes I do feel he's with me."

Liam whistled for Sky and Rose, who ran to the fence to greet them. Sky put his head over Liam's shoulder, pulling him in as if giving him a hug. Liam fed them each a carrot, and then walked away. Tears ran down his face as he heard the gelding call to him.

Laura caught up to Liam and took his hand. "Please don't be so upset. You'll be home riding Sky soon." He took Laura in his arms.

"I want to believe that so much. I'm frightened. I feel like I have no control over my fate. It's in the hands of the court."

"No, my love, it's in God's hands now. I have faith the truth will be told and you will be acquitted."

Liam was silent on the trip to Dublin. He held Laura's hand as if it might be the last time. She stayed close to him all evening at Dublin House until they turned in.

Later, Jon knocked on Liam's door. "Hey Big Guy, I know you've got a lot on your mind, but I wanted to tell you…" Jon's voice was shaky and he paused to regain his composure. "I think you're the greatest. You've been my inspiration, my guidance, my best friend and my brother. I love you, man, and I'll be there for you."

Liam was overcome with emotion. They embraced.

The night seemed endless to Liam as a torrent of worries prevented any possibility of sleep. He found himself softly knocking at Laura's door.

She was not surprised to see Liam standing there, but the look of despair on his face nearly broke her heart. No words were spoken as she took his hand, leading him to the bed where she held him in silence.

The comfort of her arms drew Liam back to the time his father died, when she had held him all night in the cave. Laura was *the someone* he'd desperately needed. Here she was again with a love more profound than he could have imagined. He finally drifted off into a sound sleep.

Laura gently kissed Liam until he woke. "Oh my God! Was I here all night?"

She smiled. "Yes, and you'd better go to your room before anyone finds us."

"Thank you for comforting me last night. I needed–"

She interrupted him with another kiss. "Remember, I will be there for you."

When Liam came down the stairway he was wearing his new dark blue suit, which accented his deep blue eyes. Laura gave him *that smile*, a unique and wondrous allure that defied description but warmed his heart a she unveiled it to him. With her head slightly tilted, Laura's brown eyes sparkled through long dark lashes, disarming any worry he had for a long moment. He could always stretch that moment by carrying it with him.

"You look fabulous, Monkey Boy."

After breakfast Aidan gave a pep talk. "Remember, we are all here to support Liam. No matter what we hear in court today, everyone must remain silent and let the barrister speak for Liam. I have every confidence in our barrister, Roen Dennehey. He is well respected and will get the job done." Aidan looked directly at Laura. "If this will be too emotional for any of you, I suggest you not attend."

"I will be strong," Laura proclaimed. "I believe justice will prevail." She turned to Liam and took his hand. "We're ready to go to court now."

# ⊂⟡Chapter Eighteen⟡⊃

Arriving at the Four Courts building in Dublin, Liam and Aidan met with MacDonald for another briefing. The rest of the group waited anxiously outside.

"Where's Peggy?" Aidan asked. "I thought she'd be here."

"She's doing some research for me and will join us tomorrow." A few weeks earlier MacDonald had asked Peggy if she would like to be part of the legal team as a student solicitor. Honored, she had thanked him and eagerly began her assignment of doing background work on the witnesses.

⟡⟐⟡

The proceedings of the High Court of the Republic of Ireland began with the prosecutor, Barrister Collins, reading the charges of reckless endangerment and manslaughter. Liam's plea of not guilty was also read aloud. The judge asked the jury directly if they understood the charges and the plea. They did.

The prosecution wasted no time in calling the first witness, a groom who said he had seen Rory running for his lorry with Liam in pursuit.

"The poor boy was just tryin' to get away from the big guy." He pointed to Liam.

There were several more witnesses who provided similar testimony, all painting a picture of Liam as the aggressor and Rory as the victim. One of them was Ryan Mullins, who was working in the sales office at the auction yard on the day of the events.

"Mr. Mullins," Collins directed, "please describe to the court anything out of the ordinary that you witnessed on that day."

"Kevin McCully came runnin' into the office out of breath. He said, 'Call the Garda! It's that hoodlum Liam! He tried to kill Rory!'"

"Objection! Hearsay!" Dennehey called out over the sudden uproar in the courtroom.

"Sustained," the judge replied. "Mr. Collins, please direct your witness to restate his response."

Collins complied with the order, but smiled slightly, knowing the intended damage had already been done. The turmoil escalated, with reporters jumping up to call their newspapers.

"Order!" the judge called, pounding his gavel repeatedly. The noise diminished, but the judge decided he'd had enough. "We will adjourn until tomorrow at ten a.m."

Dennehey was annoyed that the judge hadn't allowed him to cross-examine this witness, ending the day on such a sour note.

"John," Dennehey whispered, "I'm concerned that this judge might be biased. He seems to be giving the prosecution a wide latitude."

"You may be right, but it's still early yet."

Knowing their clients were watching, MacDonald decided to end their conversation.

"Liam, don't look discouraged! We'll have the opportunity to present our side."

❦

The second day of trial began with Dennehey's cross-examination of the prosecution's witness, Ryan Mullins. Focusing on the fact that there was noise and commotion surrounding Kevin McCully's dramatic entry into the office, Dennehey left the jury with some doubt about what Mullins had actually heard.

Unfortunately, the prosecutor brought even more witnesses with testimony focusing on Liam's aggression towards Rory. Most of Dennehey's objections were overruled by the judge. At this point, Dennehey's strategy in cross could only establish that none of the witnesses had actually seen anything prior to Rory's escape in the lorry. It was a good effort, but didn't really gain any ground.

Aidan was unhappy with the direction the trial was taking. He was immensely frustrated with the judge's rulings, and his confidence in the defense team was wavering. Peggy was still absent from court. *Where is she?* Aidan did his best to remain calm for Liam–and for the sake of his own health.

❦

On day three the prosecutor rested his case, and at last it was time for Barrister Roen Dennehey to present the defense.

Although it was his option not to, Dennehey felt it was necessary to put Liam on the stand. In spite of the risk that Collins could undermine Liam's testimony, Dennehey wanted to establish the facts of the case as they actually occurred: that Rory had initiated the attack and that there was just cause for Liam to stop Rory's flight.

In the beginning of his testimony, Liam nervously stumbled over his own words. He was asked several times by the judge to speak up. But Dennehey, through carefully crafted questioning, began to guide Liam through the events of the confrontation.

"Mr. Delaney, would you please describe, in your own words, the circumstances of your initial encounter with Rory McClenny in the auction yard?"

"Yes, sir." Liam paused to gather his thoughts. There was a hush in the courtroom as he began. "We saw each other at the same time, and Rory ran. I felt I should stop him until the Garda could be called."

"And why did you feel the Garda should be called?"

"There was a warrant for his arrest."

"Thank you. What happened next?"

"When I came around the corner of the barn, Rory attacked me with a pitchfork."

An outbreak in the courtroom caused the judge to pound his gavel repeatedly. When order was restored, Dennehey continued.

"Mr. Delaney, was anyone else present during Mr. McClenny's attack on you?"

"Kevin McCully saw Rory attack me, and I asked him to call the Garda."

"Were you able to detain Mr. McClenny until the Garda arrived?"

"I tried, sir, but Rory threw dirt in my eyes and escaped. When I caught up to him, he was taking off in his lorry. I jumped on the running board and stayed until he drove into the bushes to knock me off."

"Objection!" Collins commanded. "The witness cannot testify to the victim's intent."

"Sustained," the judge ruled. "Mr. Delaney, please confine your testimony to your own experience."

"Yes, sir."

Dennehey continued. "Mr. Delaney, would you please tell the court if it appeared to you that Mr. McClenny was in control of the vehicle?"

"Yes, sir. He was laughing when I had to jump off the truck because of the bushes." There was a murmur in the courtroom.

"Thank you," Dennehey said. "I have no further questions, my lord."

Liam took a drink of water while Collins rose to begin his cross-examination.

"Mr. Delaney, is it not true that you wanted revenge on Rory McClenny for what he had done to your girlfriend?"

"Objection, my lord!" Dennehey jumped up.

"Overruled. The witness will answer." Collins repeated the question.

Before Liam answered, he looked at Laura, against Dennehey's explicit instructions. Laura shook her head almost imperceptibly.

Liam immediately refocused on the prosecutor. "There was a warrant for his arrest. I felt he should be captured and brought to justice." Liam was scared but his tone was steady.

Collins was not impressed. "Do I take that as a yes?"

Liam hesitated before responding. "I felt he was a danger to society and should be stopped."

Collins faced the judge. "If you please, my lord, this witness must be directed to answer the question with a simple yes or no answer."

The judge agreed, and Collins restated the question about Liam's revenge.

Liam hung his head. "Yes."

"Thank you. That will be all."

Laura's heart was breaking for Liam as she watched the look of frustration on his face. She found it difficult to control the anger that welled up inside her, seeing how the prosecutor had twisted Liam's statement to make him look guilty.

With a profound look of defeat, Liam stepped down from the witness stand. MacDonald tried to reassure him when he returned to the defense table.

"You did fine. Don't worry. Patrick's up next."

Dennehey called Patrick O'Brogan to the stand, and began to establish the long history of Liam's hard work at Montrose, his diligence with his studies, and the simple fact that he had accompanied Patrick to the auction yard for the express purpose of helping him sell horses.

"Mr. O'Brogan," Dennehey continued, "how would you describe young Mr. Delaney's state of mind that day, prior to the events in question?"

"Well, he was in a good mood, I'd say–laughin' right along, as I was tellin' him stories of the old days when I used to go with his father, Philip, to the auctions."

Dennehey nodded. "Mr. O'Brogan, prior to the events in question, have you ever seen Liam Delaney engaged in fisticuffs or other forms of altercation?"

"Objection!" Collins declared. "What is the relevance here?"

"Goes to character, my lord," Dennehey stated.

"Overruled. The witness will answer."

"Altercations? Liam? Heavens, no," Patrick replied. "He's as levelheaded a man as I've ever known, just like his father."

Dennehey was satisfied and thanked Patrick, who started to get up from the stand.

"Not so fast, Mr. O'Brogan," Collins said. "I have just a few questions for you."

Patrick eased back into the witness chair, heaving a sigh of disgust. Collins began.

"That was quite a glowing testimony you gave regarding Liam Delaney. Now, several times you've mentioned Liam's father, Philip Delaney. Would you say that you and Philip were rather close?"

"Yes, sir."

"And would you say that you've looked after Liam since his father's death?"

"Well, yes... of course."

"So would it be fair to say that you would do anything for Liam Delaney?"

"Yes! No! I wouldn't lie under oath, if that's what you mean."

"Fine, then. Please describe for the jury what you actually saw Liam doing when he was on the running board of Rory McClenny's vehicle."

Patrick's face was red with anger. "He was tryin' to stop the hooligan!"

"And what method, exactly, was Mr. Delaney using to accomplish this?"

"He was… hangin' on to him."

"And where, exactly, were Mr. Delaney's hands?"

Patrick's rage flared. "Around his scrawny neck!"

There was an outburst in the courtroom, and Dennehey took leave of his usual composure, lowering his head into his hand. MacDonald cursed under his breath, Aidan clenched his fists, and Liam sank deeper into his chair.

Collins stood smugly, waiting until the noise died down.

"My lord, the prosecution has no further questions for this witness."

A short recess was called by the judge. "Thank God," Dennehey muttered.

Kevin McCully was the next witness called for the defense when court reconvened. Dennehey and McDonald were counting on his testimony, which they felt could be pivotal in turning things around. Dennehey had carefully selected his questions for McCully, whose answers would establish what he had actually said when he ran into the auction office.

McCully gave his account of the events, affirming Liam's testimony about how Rory had hidden with a pitchfork, waiting to attack Liam.

"Liam could've died on the spot right there!"

"Objection!" Collins cried out. "My lord, the witness should refrain from conjecture."

"Sustained."

McCully glared at Collins, and Dennehey decided to move things along.

"Mr. McCully, please tell the court what happened next."

"Well, Rory came after Liam with the pitchfork, but Liam managed to knock it away. Then there was a scuffle and Liam got the upper hand, and then he asked me to call the Garda, so I ran to the office."

"Go on, Mr. McCully."

"Well, I was out of breath, you know, runnin' all the way from the barns. It's a long way from those barns to the office, and I'm not a young man anymore."

"My lord, is there a point to this story?" Collins asked.

"Mr. Dennehey, please instruct your witness to be brief and to the point," the judge said.

"Yes, my lord. Mr. McCully, will you please repeat what you said when you entered the auction office?"

"Yes, sir. Now, what I actually said was, 'It's Liam. That hoodlum,' meanin' Rory, 'tried to kill him,' meanin' Liam. And then I said, 'call the Garda.'"

There was another outbreak in the courtroom. The judge pounded his gavel. "I'm warning you–I will close the court to all outsiders."

Dennehey was satisfied that his strategy had worked, and announced to the judge that he had no further questions.

Collins stood up and folded his hands before addressing the witness.

"Mr. McCully, were you close friends with the defendant's father, Philip Delaney?"

McCully was insulted. "Well, yes, but it doesn't mean I'd lie in court."

The prosecutor rolled his eyes, but continued. "Mr. McCully, is it true your eyesight is weak with respect to distance?"

"I guess, but I know what I saw, and it was Rory with the pitchfork!"

Collins looked over the rim of his glasses at the witness. "Can you tell me what the sign above the main doorway says?"

The elderly man squinted his eyes, but the words would not come into focus. He lowered his head. "No, I can't read it from here."

The prosecutor wheeled around dramatically, facing the jury, but still addressing McCully. "And you claim you could see clearly who was attacking from an even greater distance?" There were chuckles from the crowd, and the judge pounded his gavel again. Collins faced the judge. "I have no further questions for this witness."

"Mr. Dennehey," the judge asked, "do you have any redirect?"

Dennehey hesitated, weighing his options. "I have no further questions at this time, my lord, but the defense reserves the right to recall this witness."

"In that event, court is adjourned for the day."

Another day of trial had ended with Liam in a bad light.

When they exited the courtroom Aidan was relieved to see Peggy waiting for them. She summoned the defense team, along with Aidan and Liam, into the briefing room, shutting the reporters out. She pulled the attorneys aside, leaving Aidan and Liam to sit in suspense as they watched the intense conversation at the other end of the room. Aidan couldn't help but notice Peggy's air of confidence. A spark of hope welled up in him for the first time in four days.

The conversation halted, and the three walked towards their clients. MacDonald looked strangely calm.

"Peggy has some new information." He gestured towards her.

"I went back to the accident site and discovered who owns the land where Rory's vehicle went off the road. I found out it belongs to a Jimmy O'Doole, a farmer who just happened to be plowing his field when the lorry rolled." Aidan and Liam sat up in their chairs. Peggy continued. "O'Doole has been reluctant to come forward. He doesn't want to get involved. He has a farm to run, you know–all the usual reasons."

MacDonald nodded. "Go on, Peggy."

"Well, when I explained how a young man's future was hanging on the outcome of this trial, O'Doole started to open up. I soon realized his testimony was vital."

"So that's where you've been," Aidan said. "Great job, Peggy."

She nodded her thanks and turned to MacDonald. "I think if you come with me right now to Clonmel, O'Doole just might be convinced to testify voluntarily."

"We have no time to waste," Dennehey said decisively. "Get going."

The next morning Aidan's optimism was elevated when MacDonald and Peggy walked into the courtroom with their surprise witness. The opposing barristers approached the bench, and Aidan watched closely as an animated conversation with the judge ensued. Liam just closed his eyes.

When the barristers stepped back, Roen Dennehey made his formal request to the court to introduce the new witness, which the judge approved. Aidan released a breath he was unaware he'd been holding, and Liam released his grip on his crucifix.

"My lord, the defense would like to call Jimmy O'Doole to the stand."

Jimmy O'Doole was a rather scruffy old man who looked like he'd just crawled off his tractor. He was short, with rounded features, and unshaven with wiry gray hair that would have been better left covered up by his cap.

"Mr. O'Doole," Dennehey began, "when you are plowing your fields, can you see the main road clearly?"

"I can see the road, I can see who's drivin', I can see with me own eyes damn well!" O'Doole spoke with a strong brogue but got right to the point.

"Thank you, Mr. O'Doole," Dennehey said with a slight smile. "Now, will you please tell the court what you saw at half two in the afternoon on the day in question?"

"I saw a lad drivin' a lorry reckless down that road. He tried to kill this lad here." O'Doole pointed to Liam.

"Objection! Objection!"

"Oh Mr. Collins, sit down!" the judge ordered. "Let the man speak. You'll have your turn with this witness."

O'Doole continued without prompting.

"It was the lad drivin' who knocked this lad off the runnin' board by steerin' into the bushes on the wrong side of the road. After this lad fell off the truck, the driver was lookin' back laughin'! The arse took one hand off the wheel and leaned way out the window to give him the finger!" O'Doole put his hand up in a demonstration of the gesture, sending the courtroom into raucous laughter.

The judge pounded his gavel. "Mr. O'Doole, you are in a court of law. Now please go on without your hand gestures."

"Oh! Sorry, m'lord. Well, when the driver finally looked back to the road he was now headed for the ditch. He turned the wheel sharp and it flipped his lorry right over. If he'd 'ave been watchin' where he was goin' he'd be alive today!" Some members of the jury were nodding their heads. A few were still smiling.

Collins was shaken, and he began his cross aggressively. "Mr. O'Doole, why did you come forward with this story now and not months ago?"

O'Doole threw his hands up. "No one asked me! ' Twas this pretty young lass came 'round askin' if I'd seen anythin'." He pointed to Peggy. "She explained about this young lad, about how he was wrongly accused and he could go to prison. Well, that's just not right. The lad behind the wheel was clearly to blame for his own reckless drivin', and I rest my case!" Again there was an outburst in the courtroom.

The judge pounded his gavel, demanding order. As things quieted down, Collins stood motionless in his realization that this witness was the only one who had actually seen the events play out at the end.

"Mr. Collins?" the judge demanded. "Mr. Collins! Are you ready to proceed?"

The prosecutor collected himself and resumed his cross. He continued with any and every attempt to discredit the witness, if only in an effort to save face as a respected barrister. Try as he might, he could not find a hole in the farmer's testimony. The old man's story was solid. As good as Collins was, he could recognize his own defeat, and announced he had no further questions.

After the judge dismissed O'Doole, he made the formal inquiry to the defense as to their need for more testimony. Dennehey replied with a hint of smugness on his face.

"My lord, the defense rests."

The judge announced that closing arguments would be heard the following day.

⁂

Collins began his closing as expected, with a review of the key points of fact as he saw them: Liam's history with Rory established clear motive. After a review of testimonies of his selected witnesses, the prosecutor dramatically delivered his summation as he faced the accused.

"The forceful pursuit by Liam Delaney clearly resulted in the death of Rory McClenny, which otherwise may not have occurred, had the defendant left the process of capturing young McClenny up to the proper authorities."

An uneasy murmur swept through the courtroom. Collins suddenly turned on his heels, throwing his hands forward to the jury in a posture of melodramatic command.

"You, ladies and gentleman, as the voice of the High Court of the Republic of Ireland, must find the defendant guilty as charged."

All eyes turned to the defense table. Liam used every fiber of his being to appear strong, but the impact of Collins' words had drained the color from his face. Laura, sitting four rows back as instructed, felt powerless, knowing Liam needed her now more than ever. She could feel Liam's pain in her own heart. A sob escaping from her lips, Laura lost control for a moment. Jon tried to comfort her with an arm around her shoulder, while Jen squeezed her hand tightly.

"Mr. Dennehey, are you prepared to deliver your closing arguments?"

"Yes, my lord." Roen Dennehey confidently approached the jury box, where he took the time to make eye contact with each and every juror. He nodded decisively.

"In the final analysis, we have only two actual eyewitnesses. Kevin McCully was the only person to observe McClenny's initial assault on young Liam. Jimmy O'Doole was the only person to observe the attempt by McClenny to inflict serious harm to Liam with a moving vehicle. Let us not forget that Mr. O'Doole observed McClenny actually laugh triumphantly at what he thought was a successful escape. Rory McClenny's own behavior was clearly the singular factor resulting in his death."

Dennehey drew a deep breath, deliberately pausing. He stepped back, his outstretched hand inviting the jury to look directly at Liam.

"Young Liam was only defending himself, ladies and gentlemen. He did not initiate any violence. In fact, he was protecting others in the direct path of a man who was wanted by the Garda for brutal assault." He turned back to the jury.

"You, the members of this jury, were selected after a lengthy process to determine your intelligence and your sense of justice. You know in your hearts that in God's own country of Ireland, every citizen has the clear right to defend himself. In fact, our history in this land dictates that self-defense is one's duty, lest he and his brothers be overrun by assailants.

"Ladies and gentlemen of the jury, you have heard the facts in evidence. You hold in your hands and in your hearts the sacred principles of justice. It is time now for you to draw upon those principles and reach the only conclusion possible: Liam Delaney is innocent of all charges. I thank you all."

The judge waited for the reaction in the courtroom to die down before giving the formal instructions to the jury. He reminded them to uphold the law and give fair consideration to all the evidence and testimony. They were dismissed for deliberation, and the court recessed with instructions to reconvene when summoned.

MacDonald gestured to the briefing room. "Aidan, Liam—we can wait here."

"Can Laura come with me?" Liam asked. Before MacDonald could answer, Peggy intervened.

"It would be a great comfort to Liam." MacDonald glanced at Dennehey, who nodded his approval. The group entered the side door, avoiding the reporters.

Once inside the sanctity of the room, Liam took Laura into his arms and held her as if she would slip away. The others seated themselves at the far end of the room.

With tears in his eyes, Liam spoke softly. "Sweetheart, my greatest fear is being without you."

"My darling Liam, please have the faith that I have. You will never be alone."

Liam felt Laura's heart beat like the ticking clock on the wall. Time seemed to drag endlessly, but less than an hour had actually passed when there was a knock on the door. Both Laura and Liam jumped. It was the court officer.

"The jury is ready to return."

With the door now open, Jon took the opportunity to slip into the room. He put his arms around Liam. "Remember the wind: We may not be able to direct it, but God will help us to adjust the sails."

Dennehey approached. "Liam, are you ready?"

Liam kissed Laura on top of her head, and then turned to reply. "I'm ready."

Aidan put his hands firmly on Liam's shoulders, looking deeply into his eyes. "A Vic Mo Cree," he whispered. A tear came to Liam's eye, and he felt his spirit lift as he walked back into the courtroom.

Peggy observed the body language of the jurors as they returned to their seats, hoping for a clue as to the verdict–to no avail. Collins seemed to be just as confident as Dennehey. Aidan looked to Peggy for any sign, but she could only shrug.

The judge made his inquiry to the jury foreman. "Has the jury reached a verdict?"

"Yes, my lord, we have, with no dissentions."

"Thank you," the judge replied. "Will the defendant please rise." Liam, Dennehey and MacDonald all stood to face the jury, and the judge instructed the foreman to read the verdict.

"On the charge of reckless endangerment, we, the jury, find the defendant not guilty." The courtroom began to buzz with excitement, and the judge put his hand up.

"Please continue, Mr. Foreman."

"Yes, my lord. On the charge of manslaughter, we, the jury, find the defendant… not guilty!" The courtroom erupted with commotion, and a drove of reporters began to scramble for the phone booths.

The judge pounded his gavel again. "Order! Order! This court is still in session. I have not yet made my ruling." The noise quieted and the judge cleared his throat.

"The court hereby finds in favor of the defendant, and the charges are dismissed." A loud cheer erupted from the fourth row behind Liam, with Jon's "Way to go, man!" the loudest of all. The judge faced Liam directly and waited for the court to calm.

"Mr. Delaney, although you are free to go, your victory comes with a strong word of caution: Do not let your temper make your decisions for you. Furthermore, under no circumstances should you ever engage in any activity which could be construed as taking the law into your own hands. In the future, let the Garda do their duty without your help."

"Yes, my lord, I understand."

"Very well. This court is adjourned."

Everyone jumped up. Liam took a moment to formally thank both Roen Dennehey and John McDonald, and then turned to Peggy, giving her a tearful hug. "Peggy, you got me out of this mess. How can I ever repay you?"

"You already have—you're my family."

Aidan put his arms around both of them, and Laura squeezed in.

"Peggy, you're a genius!" Aidan proclaimed. "Thank you from the bottom of my heart."

Aidan decided a celebratory dinner was in order. He invited Dennehey and MacDonald to join the family.

"I'm afraid I will have to decline," Dennehey said. "Previous engagement. But my best wishes to you and your family." He turned to Peggy. "Miss Morann, I was most impressed with your work. When you get your law degree, I would like my firm to be the first one you contact."

Peggy gave him a glowing smile. "Thank you! I'll make point of it."

The barrister smiled back at her. "You know, your last name, Morann, is the same as the legendary judge of ancient Ireland who never gave a wrong verdict. I think there is more than a coincidence here."

She cocked her head and raised her eyebrows. "Hmmm… Judge Morann. Who's to say what the future may hold for me?"

At dinner everyone was ready to party. Jon stood up, beaming at the student solicitor. "A toast to our Peggy Girl! We're all so proud of you!"

*May the sound of happy music*

*And the lilt of Irish laughter*

*Fill your heart with gladness*

*That stays forever after.*

Peggy embraced him warmly. "Thank you for always being in my camp. Thank you everyone, but the truth was on Liam's side, and he was innocent."

"But you were the one who found Jimmy O'Doole," Jon pointed out.

Aidan smiled. "I believe Peggy is on to a brilliant career in law. As for Jimmy O'Doole... I've made some phone calls. I believe he may be taking delivery on a brand new tractor in a couple of days." Everyone cheered.

# ᴄᴥᴑChapter Nineteenᴄᴥᴑ

With the prospect of a career in law, Peggy was eager to pursue her studies. For the others, the routine of classes at Trinity felt like a lifetime ago. Compared to manslaughter charges and the threat of prison, college seemed trivial.

Jon answered the ringing phone in the hall. "Dublin House, Lord Jon speaking."

A laugh came from the other end. "I take it Aidan isn't there?"

"Oh! Hi, Greg! You got that one right. What's new with you?"

"We've had a few problems with the band. We may have to cancel our tour."

"You've got to be kidding! You guys are on top of the charts."

"Yeah, the timing is bad. Our keyboard man, Mike, is in the hospital. He won't be going on the road with us—or playing with us anymore. And Brad, our bass player, has got some... family problems. He doesn't want to go on tour."

"Can't you replace them before you go on the road?"

Greg sighed. "I wish we could, but we start in Paris in less than six weeks. I really don't want to replace half the band with guys that don't know our material. What I'd like is to borrow Garrett and Danny. They know almost all of our stuff."

"So you think you can steal half our band just like that?" Jon laughed.

"Just for a little while… I'd return them."

"Sure you would," Jon scoffed.

"C'mon, you guys will be touring with us this summer anyway. They could play for both bands."

"No way. You guys start the tour before the semester ends."

"At least ask them," Greg pleaded. "If we don't get someone soon, we'll have to cancel. You know that would mean canceling the opening act–that's you guys."

"Okay, okay! I get the point. I'll get back to you as soon as I can."

That evening Second Wind assembled in the basement studio. Jon explained Foolish Pleasure's dilemma and presented Greg's offer to Danny and Garrett.

Danny was already shaking his head as he wrapped his arm around Jen, pulling her in. "You know there's no way I'd leave Jen. And what about Trinity?"

All eyes turned to Garrett, who hesitated. "I guess I could help them out. I know I could use the money." He looked right at Danny. "I'm sure you could use it too."

Jen gave Danny a squeeze and he looked at Garrett. "No. I have commitments. My scholarship would be taken away."

"So, Garrett, you're in?" Jon asked. "Do you want me to call Aidan and let him know? He is our manager."

"Yeah, go ahead," Garrett replied. "I'm sure he'll have something to say about my leaving Trinity, but tell him I'm planning to finish up in the fall."

"How do you think Peggy will take this?" Danny asked.

Garrett lowered his head. "Probably not well." He looked up hopefully. "Hey! Maybe she'll join me. We can come back in the fall together."

"Dream on!" Jon said, rolling his eyes. "She's determined to get that law degree as soon as possible. You should know that." Garrett only shrugged.

∽

The next day Garrett told Peggy of his plans. As predicted, she was upset.

"Garrett! You know how important my education is to me–and it should be to you. You can't go–you've only got three months till graduation."

"I'm sorry, but music is my career, and this is my big break. I'll be playing with a band that's number one on the charts in America. C'mon, Peg, you could join me when school's out." Tears came to Peggy's eyes, and Garrett took her into his arms. "I can see why you need to stay, but please try to understand, this is my golden opportunity."

Jon played out the whole scenario of personnel changes in his mind as he stared out his bedroom window that evening at the city lights. It didn't take long for him to realize that Foolish Pleasure's gain on the keyboards was Second Wind's loss. As if his answer was coming from the heavens, the sound of the Steinway grand piano being played suddenly filled the living room of Dublin House. He descended the stairs to find Laura practicing a classical piece she had learned as a child when she and Liam took private music lessons together. She was playing it flawlessly.

Jon decided to approach her about playing keyboards for Second Wind. "There's no way Garrett would be able to play for both bands. Laura, you have a softer touch than Garrett, and I like your embellishments. But sometimes we need those power chords. Can you give us more attack when we need it?"

Laura glanced at Jon with an air of confidence. She took a deep breath and rose from the bench, dramatically tossing her hair back as she raised her arms. In one fluid motion, she lunged at the keyboard, her cascading blonde locks veiling a dynamic progression of chords that Jon felt to his very soul. He unconsciously took a step back.

"Whoa! I don't think we'll be needing Garrett anymore."

As expected, Aidan was not happy with Garrett's decision, but he knew the temptation was just too much for the young man. When he called Robert in Italy to tell him of the developments, Aidan made a point of mentioning that Danny had been offered the same opportunity, but had turned it down.

"I'm pleased that Danny is committed to finishing college," Robert said. "I know it's not easy for him. The promise of a good paycheck was probably hard to pass up. Danny's got a lot of determination, and his devotion to Jennifer is obvious. We're lucky our daughters have chosen such responsible young men."

"I couldn't agree more," Aidan replied.

"Anyway, the timing of your call is perfect. I've been working on a great idea for Easter vacation. A client of mine has offered to let me have his villa in St. Tropez for a few weeks. There's room for all of us. What do you think?"

"I think a holiday in the sun is just what the family needs after what we've all been through this winter. We have plenty to celebrate, with the legal problems behind us and three upcoming birthdays."

"Great! I'll make the arrangements for the villa. Talk to you in a few days."

❧

When Aidan announced the trip there were cheers from everyone, with the notable exception of Danny, which Aidan was quick to see.

"Now Danny," Aidan said, "I know what you're going to say, and I'll have no protesting. This is a reward for your wise decision to remain in college. We all know you could have gone off with Garrett and made lots of money. Robert and I feel you deserve this trip. So, if you turn us down we will be offended."

Danny looked at Jen, who smiled with feigned innocence. He figured his fiancée had something to do with the friendly coercion.

"Well, I guess I'd better not offend my future father-in-law. Or my manager, either. Thank you very much."

Jon noticed Peggy's lack of enthusiasm. "Hey, Peggy Girl, why the long face?"

"We're going to such a romantic place, and once again I'll be without someone."

Jon looked hurt. "What about me? We could check out all the clubs together."

"I'd assumed Kelly would be going with you."

"I'll invite her, but she won't be out of flight attendant program until the end of our vacation." Jon sighed. "There's always something to keep us apart. First it was her mum and now her school. So I think you're stuck with me."

"No, I think you're stuck with me! I'll have to watch you around all those French girls; they'll probably be drawn to you like a magnet."

Jon grinned at the compliment, but then Peggy's smile began to fade before she spoke again. "As for me, Garrett is the first guy to really care about me... and now he's off on a concert tour."

A thoughtful expression came to Jon's face. "You know, Foolish Pleasure opens the tour in Paris over Easter break. I think it's only a few hours by train from St. Tropez to Paris."

Peggy's eyes lit up. "Oh, Aidan, can we? Please?"

"I'm sure we could take a couple of days for a side trip to the City of Lights."

He smiled and she threw her arms around him. "And Jon, you're always thinking! You really are my best friend."

❦

Easter break finally arrived with everyone packed and ready to go to St. Tropez. The magnificent villa, actually a large Moroccan-style castle, was located on the Mediterranean region of the French Cote d'Azur. It was set in a private park overlooking the spectacular beaches of the French Riviera.

Catherine and Hannah were thrilled with the enormous size of the four master suites downstairs, but they were immensely pleased to see that a maid and cook were included. Robert and Aidan appreciated the fact that the upper floor had six bedrooms, each with a private bath–perfect for the teenagers. Four terraces overlooked the coastline, the largest of them complete with a sparkling swimming pool and waterfall.

Even before unpacking, the girls were anxious to go to the beach.

"You know, in France they sunbathe in the nude," Jon mused.

"Are you serious?" Laura gasped.

Aidan chuckled. "Only at certain beaches. I'm sure Jon knows which ones."

"Yep, Plage de l'Escale, here I come," Jon laughed.

Robert shook his head. "Jon, I think that might be a little more than you can handle. I suggest you stay right here at our beach."

"That's okay. It's tradition for the women to go topless all over the Riviera."

Jen hit her brother. "That doesn't mean we're going to. And I don't think Kelly would approve of you watching topless women."

Jon smirked. "Don't you girls want to get a feel for the local culture?"

"No!"

～

The next few mornings were spent sunbathing and swimming. The afternoons became breezy at times, perfect for flying kites on the beach. The locals had made it a regular pastime, with a friendly group showing up daily to practice their craft.

"That's really cool," Jon said to a tanned young man skillfully guiding his kite.

"Thank you," the young Frenchman responded with an accent. "There is a shop in town that specializes in these fliers. You can build your own."

It wasn't long before Jon, Danny and Liam were competing with each other on the workbench and the beach for the best kite. Liam was spending extra time alone in the boathouse laboring on his own special design. Laura and Jen thought it was all a little silly, choosing instead to work on their suntans.

Aidan made arrangements to have Laura's birthday party at a fine restaurant in St. Tropez. That day the girls spent hours in town pampering themselves with manicures, pedicures, facials and hairstyles.

Laura had picked out an elegant white lace, off-the-shoulders dress. With her hair up and long sparkling earrings she looked stunning, and couldn't wait for Liam to see her. But to her disappointment, only her father was there when she came downstairs.

"Where is everyone?"

"I guess they're all still getting ready," Aidan replied offhandedly. He smiled. "By the way, you look lovely, dear."

"Thank you, Father." Laura's eyes darted back to the stairs. "I can't believe Liam is taking so long to get dressed."

Aidan rubbed his chin. "You know, I think Liam and Jon are still on the beach trying to fly that big kite Liam made."

"Good Lord! Are they still doing that? They'd better come and get cleaned up or they'll be late for my birthday dinner."

"Hmmm–maybe you should go and get them."

"Father! I'm all dressed." Laura frowned, looking down at her new high heels. "I can't go walking on the beach."

Aidan glanced at his watch. "Sorry. I've got an important phone call to make, and everyone else is busy. You can slip off your shoes and walk out there. A little sand won't hurt you."

"I can't believe Liam would get so caught up in that silly kite," Laura pouted. "Did he forget it's my birthday?"

Aidan shrugged and turned away, leaving his daughter with her frustration. Laura kicked off her high heels and marched down the path.

As she approached the beach, Laura heard Liam yelling.

"Faster, Jon, faster!" Liam and Jon were running with the kite, trying to get some lift. The usual afternoon winds had died down.

Laura appeared at the crest of the sand dune just as a sudden breeze pulled the big blue kite up and away. The boys, gasping for breath, were intent on the flier and didn't even notice her standing there.

"Well, happy birthday to me!" Laura yelled. "I guess this is more important than our dinner plans."

Liam turned and waved at her to come join them. Laura threw her hands up in frustration and reluctantly started down the dune.

"Do you have to fly that thing now?"

Liam grinned. "Yes, Laura Lye, this is very important. Now come here and help me reel it in safely."

"Can't Jon help you?"

"No, I'm afraid not! He's gone."

She looked around. Jon seemed to have vanished into thin air. Laura, taken aback by Liam's insistence, nevertheless took control of the kite. Liam stood behind with his arms around her.

"Now she's really blowing in the breeze. Who's to say which way she'll go?"

He slowly helped Laura reel the kite in. "Nice and easy now–for a soft landing."

The big blue kite dove towards her with the last rays of the afternoon sun glistening off its face and where bright gold lettering was now visible. As the words came into focus, Laura was completely stunned.

The shiny letters spelled out *Will You Marry Me?*

When Laura turned around, she was surprised to find Liam right behind her, down on one knee with a small open box revealing a spectacular engagement ring.

"Oh my God! Liam!"

"Is that a yes?"

"Yes! Yes! You know it's yes!"

He stepped forward, placing the ring on her finger. "True love never leaves the heart. Wear my ring and we will never part." He kissed her tenderly. "By the way… you look breathtaking."

Laura held up her hand, admiring the dazzling ring as it caught the light.

They embraced as the sunset broke into glorious colors. In the distance Jon and Danny played guitar and harmonica. Liam began to sing That Smile to Laura. Tears flooded her eyes.

They returned to the villa to be greeted by everyone with cheers. After the noise died down Laura smiled sweetly at the group.

"Are you all sure I said yes?"

Liam answered the question by gently raising Laura's left hand to reveal the spectacular marquise diamond in an antique-gold setting. The others had known about Liam's secret plan, but he'd kept the unveiling for her eyes only.

There were oohs and ahhs, and Jen stepped forward, anxious to view it up close. "Oh my! It's beautiful."

Peggy gave Liam a hug. "I didn't think you'd be able to pull this off."

Laura laughed. "I can't believe everyone knew about this but me." She patted her father on the arm. "Now I know why you made me go to the beach."

Jon dramatically put his hand to his heart. "Thank God you came when you did! Liam was about to kill me, making me run back and forth to get that big kite airborne."

They all laughed as Laura touched Jon's cheek. "But it was worth it."

Aidan smiled. "I promised Liam he could give you an engagement ring after your seventeenth birthday. He obviously wasted no time. Now remember, he also promised me you would wait to get married–at least until he graduates."

"Thank you for giving us your blessing, Father. We promise to wait."

The celebration continued through the dinner party, which in itself would have been an event with the exceptional French cuisine.

Robert was enjoying himself. "Aidan, I can't put into words how much it warms my heart to see all our children living life again, without any worries."

"I'll drink to that!"

⟪⟫

The following morning the entire group embarked on their next adventure, the journey to Paris. The luxury high-speed train, TGV, raced through the countryside, leaving little villages a blur behind. Laura was quite content mesmerizing herself with the sparkling diamond as she held her hand up to the light coming through the window. Liam gave her other hand a squeeze, and she turned to give him *that smile*.

The fears that had plagued Liam at the trial only a few months earlier were now a forgotten nightmare. To him the ring symbolized far more than the promise of marriage. He looked at his fiancée dreamily. "Everything you are is everything to me."

The announcement came to prepare for the arrival into Paris. Laura jumped up in anticipation of finally seeing the colorful city she had read so much about.

Soon they were checked into the hotel, and Aidan turned to everyone in the lobby.

"I've got your passes for Foolish Pleasure tonight. Peggy has already joined Garrett at the band rehearsal. How about we all do some sightseeing before you young people go off to the concert?"

Laura nodded enthusiastically. "I've got to see the Eiffel Tower!"

Jon sighed. "Go ahead. I'm waiting for Kelly to come in."

"You won't have to wait for me," Kelly smiled as she walked into the hotel lobby. To Jon she looked more beautiful than ever, and he ran to kiss her.

"Wow!" Kelly beamed. "I guess you missed me."

"Ahem," Robert said. "The metro subway is just a few steps out. Let's get to the Eiffel Tower."

To no one's surprise, Jon was prepared with his own tour guide-styled dissertation, a routine he had established years before during their travels to Italy.

"The magnificent Eiffel Tower, standing at 1,052 feet to the top of the antennas, can be easily seen from everywhere in Paris—" He was silenced by a kiss from Kelly and everyone laughed.

"That's one way to shut him up!" Jen said.

At the second level above the massive arched base of the tower, Laura took photographs before they sat down to lunch at the Le Jules Verne Restaurant. The large windows offered a panoramic view of the city, thrilling to most and dizzying to some.

Danny groaned. "After this lunch I'm not sure I can handle going up to the top."

"Oh c'mon!" Jen laughed. "You can't be the only one to chicken out!"

Danny was reluctant until Jon began clucking like a chicken.

"All right! But no funny business when we get up there."

It was a spectacular ascent to heights that towered over Paris. The cars below looked like tiny ants crawling about, and the river a ribbon of blue weaving its way through the city.

Next was a dinner cruise along the Seine River. As they slowly passed museums and monuments, Liam was mesmerized by the magic of the balmy twilight.

"This could be the romantic night that tops them all," he whispered to Laura. She smiled but shook her head.

"*Au contraire, mon cher.* I think there was one that flew higher... my kite."

"You're right, but I was too worried that it would all come crashing down."

She laughed easily.

They arrived at the large stadium to find Foolish Pleasure doing a sound check.

"Not bad for an American band!" Jon yelled out. "Oh– but I see you've got an Irishman!" The band stopped playing, and Greg signaled the soundman for a break.

Aidan and Robert remained just long enough to go over the summer tour plans with Greg. They reviewed the list of cities on the schedule.

"Looks good," Aidan said. "Second Wind can open for you the middle of June in Dublin. I'll accompany the band in the UK and Germany. Robert will then take over for the American tour. Then they'll have to return to Ireland to get ready for fall classes."

Greg agreed and thanked them. "You know, our producer is going to mix a live album from the tour. I could arrange for them to do the same for Second Wind."

Aidan looked thoughtful. "We'll consider that idea."

"An album!" Jon jumped in. "Aidan, what's there to consider?"

Aidan ignored his outburst. "Greg, send me a proposal and we'll get back to you." Knowing his son would continue to protest, Robert shot Jon a glance.

The two men wished Greg and the band a good tour and left to rejoin their wives back at the hotel. Greg and Garrett took the opportunity to speak to Danny alone.

"I'm unhappy with our new bass player," Greg grumbled. "Danny, your rock-steady playing is just what we need. You'd only miss six weeks at Trinity."

"You're at the top of your class," Garrett added. "You can miss some."

Danny shook his head. "I'm at the top of my class because I don't miss any. I appreciate your confidence in me, but I'm at Trinity because of my rugby scholarship. We have playoffs coming up. Besides, I'm only solid because Jen and I work so well together. We're a team and I intend to keep it that way!"

⁂

That night's concert was somewhat of a disappointment. Danny could see what Greg meant about the bass player, but it didn't change his mind.

When the show was over Aidan and Robert were waiting for them in a limousine. Before she got in, Peggy asked Aidan if she could speak to him for a moment.

Robert nodded. "I'll get out for minute. I hardly get to see my son anyway."

"Aidan, I've thought it over, and I want to stay on with the band." She looked away nervously. "I know what you're going to say, but I promise I'll come back and make up my classes in the fall. I'm twenty-one now, and I can make my own decisions. Please try to explain it to Mother for me."

Aidan folded his arms but looked at her sympathetically. "Peggy, you're thinking with your heart, not your head. As far as telling your mother, you're on your own."

Jon had figured out what was going on and motioned to Peggy to step out. He waited until his father got back into the limo before speaking to her.

"Garrett shouldn't even be asking you to stay. Think about your career."

"Jon, he loves me. He wants me to be with him and I want that, too."

"Peggy, you know I'm your friend. Will you please just think about this? Garrett's caught up in all the fame and fortune. He'll never come back to Trinity. "

"You're wrong!" Peggy cried. "He promised. We'll both come back in the fall."

Jon shook his head, but gave her a hug. "We care about you, Peggy Girl."

"I know that. But I also know what I'm doing."

The two joined the others in the limo. Peggy was silent on the drive back to the hotel, dreading the thought of facing her mother.

Hannah was furious with her daughter. Their argument escalated until Peggy grabbed her overnight bag and stormed out of the hotel. Hannah, in a rage, immediately went to confront Aidan, who was in the cocktail lounge with Robert. It took only one look at the woman's face for Robert to excuse himself.

"Thanks a lot, friend," Aidan muttered under his breath. Robert was already heading to the far door.

Hannah got right to the point with her unique ability to yell in a whisper.

"Aidan, once again you have let the children make all the decisions. Just because you let your daughter get engaged at seventeen does not mean you can give my daughter permission to go off with her boyfriend and abandon her education."

"Hannah, I know you're upset, and you can blame me if you want," Aidan said in an even tone. "Peggy is of age and has made up her own mind. I could not influence her." He downed his glass of whiskey.

"If anything happens… I'm holding you responsible," Hannah retorted. With her head held high she marched out of the lounge. Aidan ordered another drink.

Without Peggy, they all left Paris in the morning, returning to St. Tropez.

Jon and Kelly only had a few days together, so they enjoyed every moment to the fullest. When it was time for Kelly to leave for the airport, Jon decided to go with her.

After her flight departed Jon started thinking about Peggy again. He hopped into a taxi, and the driver naturally asked him for his destination.

Jon impulsively answered, "The train station."

As they rolled up Jon paid the man and hopped out, not even sure what he was doing. He could hear announcements over the PA, and one of them mentioned a train leaving for Lyon. He quickly ran to the window and bought a ticket. Foolish Pleasure would be performing their last show in Lyon before moving on to Spain. And Peggy would be with them.

When Jon arrived the concert was nearly over, but the roadies let him backstage.

"Jon!" Peggy exclaimed. "I'm happy to see you, but what are you doing here?"

"Just in the neighborhood and thought I'd drop in."

She tilted her head. "Is that so?"

After the show Jon asked Garrett and Peggy to have a drink with him. They agreed, but in the short time it took to walk there, Peggy figured out that Jon wasn't there for small talk.

"Jon, I've made up my mind to stay with Garrett on the tour."

"I know, Peggy Girl, but hear me out. Garrett, have you been completely honest with her? She believes you plan to come back to finish college."

Garrett lowered his head. "I know what I said... but I can't give this up." He looked at Peggy. "Greg's asked me to stay with the band. It's the chance of a lifetime."

"Hey, I don't blame you," Jon said. "But what about Peggy's career? What about *her* chance? You didn't see how great she was in that courtroom a few months ago."

Garrett downed his cognac, and then took his girlfriend's hand. "Peg, he's right about one thing. I don't know much about your career. It's important to you, isn't it?"

Her eyes were filled with tears and she nodded. "Yes, it is important to me." Peggy turned to Jon. "Can you give us a moment alone?"

Jon stood up. "The train to St. Tropez leaves in half an hour—and I'll be on it."

Garrett turned to Peggy after Jon left. "Wow, that sounds like an ultimatum or something. I thought you were a woman of the world—a free thinker."

"No one's telling me what to do, Garrett, but I do need time to think. I need to just go for walk. Alone."

Garrett wasn't mad, but maybe a bit shocked. "Fine, whatever you need. I'll be back at the hotel." He gave her a quick kiss and she stood up.

❧

The din of the city crowds was nothing but white noise to Peggy as she went down the boulevard with a thousand thoughts in her mind. *Should I listen to my heart and stay? Or should I jump right back into my career and turn my back on Garrett? If I leave him... will I ever find love again?*

Suddenly Peggy recalled a moment when she felt like giving up and Jon had pulled her through: in the Italian Alps in the middle of a blizzard. She was giving in to the elements and could see no hope of survival. Jon had picked her up out of the snow and promised they would make it. He had told her to trust him. *Should I listen to Jon now? God knows what would have happened if I hadn't trusted him then.*

❧

Jon paced at the train station: back and forth, looking around, hoping Peggy would come. He recalled how vulnerable she'd been with the con artist boyfriend from Spain who turned out to be a wanted fugitive. *She was so starved for love then... but she's come so far since then. It's her time to shine now.*

His thoughts were interrupted by an announcement that the train to St. Tropez was now boarding. It took only a few minutes before the platform was empty of those who had been waiting. The conductor motioned to Jon to join the others, and he glanced around once more before he reluctantly went up the steps.

After shuffling down the aisle Jon was about to take a seat, but he heard some kind of commotion outside. There was a woman running on the platform, waving her ticket at the conductor and pleading for him to hold the train.

It was Peggy.

Jon ran to meet her as she boarded and they embraced.

"Jon, I haven't left him for good–but I'm not dropping out of classes. Thank you for coming to my rescue again. You are one of a kind."

"Good God, I hope so. I can't imagine another me!"

Peggy laughed, but Jon could see she had been crying. They spoke no more words as she laid her head on his shoulder. Within a minute she was asleep.

# C/Chapter Twenty✎

"Ah, life can be grand," Molly sighed as she gazed through the front window of Dublin House towards the park. "I feel as though the veil of sorrow that hung over the family a few months ago has been lifted, and all the troubles have been left behind. Now the trees are sweetly bloomin', love is in the air and we have an abundance of happiness."

Brent smiled at his wife. "It's been many a day since I've seen you so happy."

She laughed. "It's been many a day since my husband has been home."

"I know, my love, and I intend on making it up to you. How would you like to accompany me this summer to America?" Molly looked skeptical, having seen his usual whirlwind of meetings and jobsite visits. He took her hand.

"I promise it will not be all work. We'll have a second honeymoon."

She threw her arms around him. "Brilliant idea! I won't need to be here anyway. Dublin House will be empty with everyone off on their concert tour."

In spite of the pressure of upcoming final exams, Jon still insisted the band give every spare moment to rehearsals.

"Please don't come up with a new song list," Danny grumbled.

Jon grinned. "Liam does have two new ones, but I think we're good to go on the rest. Second Wind will be ready to rock any audience!"

Peggy was focusing all her energy at Trinity, determined to finish at the top of her class. John MacDonald, aware of her dedication, had offered Peggy an apprenticeship with him over summer vacation. She had declined, jumping at the opportunity to spend that time with Garrett as he toured with Foolish Pleasure.

Aidan was not entirely pleased with Peggy's decision, but he decided to put her talents to good use on the recording contract sent by Foolish Pleasure's manager.

She began skimming the contract as soon as Aidan handed it to her. She looked up a few moments later. "It looks like there's no mention of royalties from future sales."

"I didn't find any," Aidan replied. "I know Second Wind is a relatively unknown band, but this language seems pretty one-sided in favor of the record company."

Peggy looked up. "For starters, I'll ask Garrett–quietly, of course–to see if he can get his hands on Foolish Pleasure's recording contract."

"Sounds like a good plan," Aidan said, admiring his stepdaughter's astuteness.

Within a few weeks Peggy had a new contract of her own drawn up. She presented it to Aidan in his study.

"I believe this is fair to all parties," she explained. "Second Wind will not get paid anything until after sales of the album exceed the expenses. They will receive a percentage on a sliding scale, getting a larger royalty as sales progress. This way the record company will not be taking a risk on an unknown band. They're more likely to approve the new terms. I've also included some other things for our band: artistic license for song selection, album cover and promotional photos."

"This document is impressive, very professional," Aidan remarked. "Did you draft this on your own?"

Peggy beamed. "Yes, I did write it myself, but Professor McAlester reviewed it for me. In fact, I used it for my final grade–withholding the names, of course. I got the top score in my class."

"I'm proud of you."

Aidan made a point of coming to Dublin House to give everyone the news that Peggy's contract had been accepted. Jon was beside himself with exhilaration.

"I've been working on ideas for an album cover, and we need a great photo of the band. I want our fans to put a face to the songs. None of that weird cover art."

Danny looked thoughtful. "We really want to say that our roots as a band are in Ireland. How about a photo shoot somewhere on the grounds of Montrose?"

"Brilliant idea," Aidan said. "We'll need pictures for promotion of the tour, too. We'll have to hire a photographer. Laura, you're going to be in these pictures."

She smiled. "But I can help compose the shots. I think the band should set up, instruments and all, in the garden with the manor and the River Maigue in the background."

"That sounds perfect," Liam said. "Let's put footnotes inside the album about our studio in the tower. After all, Montrose is the place that brought us all together."

Summer break from Trinity finally arrived, and Second Wind was almost ready for the tour opening in Dublin. A few weeks before the show they were tossing around ideas for a stage set that could be uniquely theirs.

"Would you mind," Robert asked, "if I had a hands-on involvement with this project?" Jen looked at her father in surprise.

"What do mean, hands-on?" she asked.

"I mean everything from sketching the layout to driving the nails," he replied.

He could see his eighteen-year-old daughter was unconvinced. "You might not know this, but I minored in architectural design in college. I haven't had a chance since then to really put my skills into action."

Jon grinned. "Aidan, you're the manager. Can we afford this guy?"

Aidan chuckled. "Oh, we're not paying him. We might mention him in the album credits–if he's any good."

Robert's participation was accepted by unanimous approval, and they launched right into discussing the design for the backdrop of the stage. It would be a natural extension of the Montrose Manor theme, complete with a castle set in the rolling green hills of Ireland. Once Robert got to work on the sketches, the dramatic scene began to unfold, to the amazement of his son and daughter, as well as the others.

Three days before the mid-June concert date, the creation began to take shape, and included a platform for Jen's drums and a walkway for Liam jutting out from the stage. The night before the show, the custom lighting was tested and the final touch-ups were added to the paint.

Robert smiled as he stood back to take it all in. "We did a great job, if I do say so myself. And believe it or not, it won't be hard to tear down and set up in the next city."

"I'm impressed, Father," Jon remarked. "And, I'm really glad we've gotten to do something creative together. It feels great!"

⌒〜○

The Dublin stage went dark and Second Wind took their places, with Liam waiting in the wings. They began playing softly, building gradually in volume and intensity, with the musicians still in the dark. Light began to emerge from several points that soon took shape as leaded windows, giving life to the manor. Next came the illusion of dawn breaking from the background, with the full outline of the castle coming into view. Laura played broken chords in a run up the piano, tastefully ringing in the colors of a new day. Liam's offstage voice now came to life while the emerald green hills of Ireland were bathed in full morning light.

Suddenly Liam burst on the stage, and the concert hall erupted in applause. He pushed his voice to hit the highest notes, and his delivery was the catalyst that sparked the entire group. Jen's steady percussion melded perfectly with Danny's rock-solid bass lines, providing Laura with a rich footing for launching the song into full motion with her dramatic keystrokes. Jon's amazing guitar solo followed, rounding out the thrilling experience.

The energy never paled during the entire set, and the audience went berserk.

It was literally a hard act to follow, and Foolish Pleasure was clearly a letdown as reflected in the crowd's subdued applause for the American band.

The next morning the reviews were out, with Eoin McKee once again writing the column in the *Irish Times*.

### Opening Act Rocks Dublin Concert Hall

*Second Wind Blows Away American Act*

*The Dublin crowd was in a frenzy the moment frontman "The Cowboy" Jon Bianchi hit his first power cord. He was nothing short of supercharged, jumping around the stage while delivering spellbinding riffs from the fret board. Liam Delaney confidently delivered his unmistakable lyrics with an honest passion that went well beyond what this reporter heard last year. The really pleasant surprise was the dynamic keyboard playing by beautiful Laura Meegan, who continues to provide entrancing backup vocals. Danny Bailey and Jen Bianchi wield a magically powerful beat with their bass and drums, driving the band to create an exhilarating rock 'n' roll experience.*

### Headlining Act Appears Foolish

*The once-professional sound of Foolish Pleasure appears to be lost now that they've replaced half their band, which happened only weeks before the tour began. At times the four musicians appeared to be more of a four-ring circus as they spun off in their own directions, soloing with no cohesiveness.*

Greg was so furious he didn't even finish reading the review before calling Jon at Dublin House.

"I'm afraid to show my face in this hotel!" Greg shouted. "This is crap! I know the Irish are always behind their own, but we're number one in America."

"I'm sure the reviews won't be so one-sided once we leave Ireland." Jon was trying his best to be diplomatic, keeping his real opinion to himself: In his mind Foolish Pleasure was on a downward spiral, and Second Wind was soaring.

After the phone call, Jon gathered the band, praising them for their performance and the review. "But Greg is feeling pretty burned. There could be problems."

"Hey!" Danny exclaimed. "It's not our fault they can't get it together!"

"I know," Jon agreed. "But I really don't want any trouble."

"I think we've already got trouble of another kind," Liam remarked. "Doesn't it bother anyone else that Katie and Loreena are hanging around?" Garrett's cousin, Katie, was the first one who met Jon and Liam when they were new students at Trinity. Her best friend Loreena had taken to Liam, pursuing him romantically over the course of several weeks to the point that he nearly quit the band.

"Relax," Jon said. "We're only in Dublin for two more nights, then it's off to Germany. They'll be history."

To everyone's surprise, however, Katie and Loreena showed up at the airport, announcing they were traveling with Foolish Pleasure.

Liam took Jon aside. "Please tell me I'm going to wake up from this nightmare."

"Hey, I don't like it any more than you do, but they're with Garrett and those guys. We can't call the shots on who's hanging with their band. I know Peggy's not happy–she wants her time with Garrett. But Katie is his cousin."

Liam sighed and Laura put her arm around his waist. "Don't you worry, Loreena won't be bothering you while I'm around."

Once they were all seated on the plane, Peggy cuddled up next to Garrett.

"Why are Katie and Loreena traveling with the band?"

"Well, Katie's hooked up with the new bass player, Ron. And you know wherever Katie goes, Loreena's not far behind. Besides, Greg's got them doing all sorts of errands. They're pretty useful."

"I bet they are," Peggy said sarcastically.

Both bands were well received by the German audiences. Second Wind had delivered the better show, but the crowds in Frankfurt were accustomed to avant-garde rock at loud volumes–just what Foolish Pleasure gave them. Greg was happy again.

During one of his usual after-show critiques, Aidan praised his group. "I can't even begin to describe how pleased I am with all of you. But Foolish Pleasure–why do they have to play so dreadfully loud?"

"Well," Jon mused, "when a band is weak, they turn up the volume to drown out the flaws. Their original keyboard player, Mike, was the one that used to arrange most of their songs. He was pretty tasteful, and he kept the live material closer to what their fans were used to hearing on the radio. Garrett is a good keyboard player, but he tends to get indulgent with the soloing, and he kind of goes off on an ego trip."

"Brad, their bassist, was always in sync with Greg," Danny added. "This new guy Ron is all over the place."

Jon looked thoughtful. "I've learned a lot about what it takes to be a great band. I believe we can be one of the best. We're more than just five good musicians; we're a family that cares about the end result. Sure we all have egos, but we never try to outshine one another." He turned to Laura. "I remember a time when you and Jen both stepped down to let us move on with Garrett and Brian. Looking back, it was wrong of me to bring outsiders into what we had. I've learned from my mistakes, and we'll always be together as a group and a family."

Laura threw her arms around Jon. "Thank you! I'll work hard to keep up."

"Keep up?" Danny exclaimed. "It's us that have to keep up with you!"

Laura beamed and Liam gave her a hug. "Not to mention she is my inspiration."

The tour continued through Germany. The heavy schedule of rehearsals and shows left little time for sightseeing or anything else. Before long it was time to pack up for the trip to America.

Peggy was disappointed that she and Garrett could hardly find time alone. She decided to make a change.

"Garrett, there's no point in my going with you to America. We never have any time together. I'm going home with Aidan to see if John MacDonald will still have me."

Garrett protested, to no avail. Peggy was determined.

Robert had a sly smile as he welcomed the group at La Guardia. "I have a surprise for you."

Jon was looking at his father quizzically when Kelly sneaked up from behind and threw her arms around him. He swooped her up with delight, kissing her repeatedly.

"Why didn't you tell me you were coming to New York?"

"My schedule got changed," Kelly beamed. "Surprise!"

"I suggest," Robert said, "that tonight everyone get a good night's sleep. Tomorrow we have a free day. We could spend it on Long Island."

Everyone except Laura liked the idea. "Tomorrow I think I'd like to rest in the hotel, if it's all right with everyone. I'm fine–just a little jet lagged."

Liam sensed she wasn't revealing her real purpose. "I'll stay with you."

❧

He waited until the next morning after the others had left for Long Island.

"Okay, Laura Lye, confess. What's going on in that pretty head of yours?"

Laura looked at him innocently. "Whatever do you mean?"

"Nice try. Now give it to me straight on."

"Well," she answered sheepishly, "I was hoping we might look up some dance companies to see if we could find my grandmother. This may be my only chance. Who's to say when we'll get back here again? Besides, Father's not here to object."

"Sweetheart, you know I'll help you, but I don't want you to get your hopes up. New York is a big place, and we don't even know if she's still here."

254

Laura gazed wistfully out the window. "I've got to at least try."

Liam called half a dozen dance companies with no luck, until he came across one with a possible lead: the owner of a studio who said his grandfather had known some gypsy dancers. The man was reluctant to give any details over the phone and asked Liam to see him in person. They took a taxi to the small studio in Greenwich Village.

"Hello, I'm Anthony. Please come and have a seat. You say you're from Ireland. What is it you want to know about the gypsy dancers?"

"My name is Laura, and this is Liam. I'm the one who's looking for my Grandmother Maura. I believe she could be here in New York."

Anthony looked carefully at the young Irish girl before he spoke. "My grandfather did speak of a gypsy dancer from Ireland, but I never met her. She could be your grandmother. The others were from Hungary."

"Sir," Laura pleaded, "if there's any way you can help me find her…."

He shrugged. "I'm not sure I can. I think she left the Village years ago. I can't ask my grandfather, he passed away last year. I suppose I could look through some of his things. Maybe he had an address or phone number."

Tears came to Laura's eyes. "Please, I need to know about my grandmother."

"I'll have to dig through some boxes in storage. I can't make any promises, but leave me your address in Ireland. It may take awhile, but I'll do my best."

They thanked the man and left, but Laura was disappointed.

"Now that we've come so far with our music, I feel an even stronger connection to my grandmother."

"Sweetheart, all we can do is try. And speaking of music, we'd better get back for our sound check."

Jon and Jen spent the day visiting old friends from Long Island, giving them passes to the show and, of course, introducing Kelly and Danny.

Tonight would be special for Jon on many levels. He was to perform at Brown's Beach, the very stage where he'd seen so many rock stars. Now it was his time to shine. And Kelly was right there to see it all.

Strobe lights followed the Irish castle and countryside set opener, creating a frenzied thrill for the Long Islanders, especially Jon and Jen's friends.

Soulfully Liam worked the crowd with his voice. Laura was particularly animated in her keyboard technique, her long sleeves and flowing hair suggesting the dance of a gypsy. Jon was on a special high, looking like he would never come down, and his guitar solos reflected that.

Wearing a sparkling tank top, Jen looked sizzling hot, showing off her buffed body to all who remembered her as Jon's skinny little sister. Her drumming was innovative and progressive. As usual, Danny played off Jen's energy, enhancing his own style with embellishments that came easily.

The emotionally charged performance by Second Wind would long be remembered as one of the greatest ever at Brown's Beach.

Unfortunately, Foolish Pleasure's set did not command the same enthusiasm from the crowd, but the loyal American fans did give respectful applause.

$$\infty$$

At breakfast the reviews were out, and Robert read them aloud to the young group.

### Local Teens Return to Play Brown's Beach Concert

*Siblings Jon and Jen Bianchi, originally from Long Island, returned last night to open the show with their Irish rock band, Second Wind.*

*Acrobatic frontman Jon played his guitar with vibrant intensity. Drummer Jen never missed a beat, syncopating rhythms of the drums with the bass. Bassist Danny Bailey also did a bluesy vamp on the harmonica. The youngest of the group, seventeen-year-old Laura Meegan, added tasty backup vocals while her fingers caressed the keys with great skill. The vocals were pure, the chords perfect and the melody moving. Songwriter and lead vocalist Liam Delaney completed the picture for this outstanding young group.*

*This fine blend of American and Irish musicians should collect quite a fan base as they complete their multi-city North American tour.*

Everybody was thrilled, but Jon shook his head. "I'm afraid to ask, but… the review for Foolish Pleasure?" Robert read on.

### Loyal Fans Come Out to See Foolish Pleasure

*Promoting their chart-busting album by touring with new members may not have been the best call for this American band. Greg Watts, lead singer and drummer, seemed to have strained his voice after many months of touring. Overall the group wasn't as tight as the loyal fans have come to expect. Nevertheless, they cheered the familiar*

257

*tunes, even though the band was using the old trick of cranking up the volume to cover their shortcomings. It wouldn't be foolish to say this loyal fan didn't get quite as much pleasure as he has in the past.*

Robert saw his son wincing when he finished reading. "Jon, you know you can't be responsible for the reviews. If Greg gets upset, have him talk to me. I'm proud of the great job you're doing, and you should be, too. By the way, last night the sound engineer was recording for your live album."

The mere mention of Second Wind's debut album brought smiles to everyone. But their enthusiasm was guarded, knowing how Greg was going to react to the review.

As predicted, there was a phone message for Jon when he returned to his hotel room. It was from Greg, indicating there were going to be "some changes."

Reluctantly, Jon went to Greg's hotel room.

Greg opened the door and assumed a rigid stance, folding his arms. "I want you to drop some songs from your set. Second Wind's time on stage is being cut in half."

"Why, Greg? We're just trying to be our best. We're not competing with you."

"This is business and we're all competing. I asked you before to tone it down, but you just turned it on instead! I have the say, and I'm cutting down your opening act."

"Look, I'm sorry, man. I guess playing for my hometown got us a little fired up. We'll figure out a way to control things from here on out."

Greg shrugged. "It's your call. Back off, or you're cut to three songs."

"I'll talk to the others."

Jon gathered the band and his father together for a meeting. "Tonight is a really special concert–it's Madison Square Garden. There's likely to be some big guys from the recording business there in the audience. This could be our big break, but Greg said the opening act shouldn't be grabbing all the attention. He wants us to 'tone it down.'"

"How are we supposed to do that?" Liam asked.

"We don't have a choice. If we don't, he'll cut our set down to nothing."

"He can't do that!" Danny protested.

Robert shook his head. "It certainly doesn't seem right, but I think he can."

"I sure wish Peggy was here," Jon said. "We need some legal advice."

"I'll call my attorney," Robert said. He left the room and Jen looked at her brother with tears of anger in her eyes.

"You're asking me to cool it after all the work I've put into building my stamina!"

"How can we not be true to ourselves?" Laura asked. "We're good because we put our very souls into it."

"I can't sing half-heartedly," Liam agreed. "I'd rather not sing at all."

"I'm with all of you," Jon said. "But Greg's going to cut us off."

"Let him cut us off!" Danny shouted, standing tall with his head up high. "I say tonight we give it our very best and go out with a concert everyone will remember!"

A wicked smile came across Jon's face. "You're right–to hell with Greg! Let's go out there tonight and kick some *arse*!"

"We'll take no prisoners," Laura said, with an evil grin.

"I'm sorry I didn't get back to you sooner," Robert's attorney said. "I've been tied up in court all day. I'm afraid my answer to your question is not going to make you very happy. Unless there's something in the contract that states the length of the opening act, technically your band could be restricted to just one song. It's still an opening act."

Robert thanked him and hung up the phone, wondering how he was going to break the news to the band. He met up with them in the dressing room prior to the show and told them what the attorney had said.

Jon listened politely before responding. "It's okay, Father, we've made our decision. Second Wind will not play second fiddle. We do it right or not at all!"

Robert smiled. "Bravo! I admire your integrity. Now go out there tonight and give the Garden a show they'll never forget!"

The fired-up feeling stayed with them all the way to the concert stage. As the stage director signaled them to go out, Jon turned to the others.

"Are we ready?"

"Let's go out in a blaze of glory!" Danny cried. They had a quick group hug and then took their places at their instruments.

Danny smiled at Jen. "Darlin', show the world what a powerhouse you are!"

The stage was dark with only a blue light on Liam as he began to sing. With the dancing of Jen's sticks on the ride cymbal, the stage seemed to awaken with flickering multi-colored lights. Then the rhythm section of Danny and Jen started a steady pulse, a slow tempo at first, escalating to a frenzy, like the heartbeat of a racehorse.

Jon's guitar screamed a progression of power chords as he strutted down the runway towards the shrieking fans. Laura pounded out a succession of runs up and down the keyboard while tossing her hair. Liam's vocals cut through it all, his sprit seemingly on a winged flight.

Carla Antonelli, an entertainment columnist for the *New York Times,* was seated in the front row, focused on Liam. The complexity of his deep blue eyes mesmerized her, and the sweat dripping from his brow validated the passion in his performance.

Second Wind left the stage after their eighth song, the crowd deafening with their applause. Greg was livid as he waited in the wings.

"That's it! You blew it! You guys are out!"

Jon grinned. "Then we're going out in a blaze of glory!" He turned to the others. "C'mon guys–they're calling for an encore!"

Second Wind's encore left the audience begging for more.

The young musicians did not stick around for Foolish Pleasure's performance. Returning to the hotel, they collectively tasted the bittersweet of success. Although they knew Greg was going to drop them out of the rest of the tour, they felt they had delivered their best performance yet.

Antonelli wasted no time getting her review ready for the morning paper.

### Ireland Rocks the Garden

*Unique Experience in the Big Apple!*

*The five teenagers from Ireland–two actually from Long Island–performed all original songs, riveting the New York crowd. This reporter is blown away by Second Wind, who is sure to become one of the greatest bands of our time.*

She went on to describe each member of the band, stating that they possessed skill and showmanship "far beyond their years."

Curiously, Antonelli had nothing to say about Foolish Pleasure, which was a statement in itself.

Around noon, Jon decided he'd better tie up any loose ends with Greg.

"I guess we'll make arrangements to have our gear sent back to Ireland," Jon said. Greg only nodded. "What about the live recordings–and the album?"

"Not a chance," Greg said firmly.

"Well, we're at least going to get the tapes, right?"

"'Fraid not."

"C'mon, Greg! You can't do that. You know how hard we've worked for this."

Greg threw his hands up. "Hey, this is the real world. You kids aren't back in Ireland playing a gig for your college. I'm looking out for my band. This is business."

Feeling disillusioned, Jon left to find the others. They all shared his gloom by the time he finished the story. "I'm calling Peggy to see if they can really do this to us."

After talking to Jon, Peggy called Garrett, hoping she could get him to persuade Greg to release the tapes. "Tell him all the costs would be met, the sound engineers paid, so no one is out-of-pocket."

"Peg, I really don't want to get involved."

It was a copout, and it was obvious to Peggy where his loyalties were. She persisted, but Garrett only accused her of putting him on the spot.

"Will you at least have Greg call me?" she asked.

"Yeah, whatever." Garrett hung up.

Greg never returned her call.

"It doesn't look promising," Peggy said to Jon on the phone. "I'm sorry. I tried."

"You did your best and we appreciate it," Jon sighed. "I'm getting a rude awakening to this cutthroat business."

Jon hung up and told the others the news. Liam shook his head in disbelief. "How can Greg be this way after all the songs I've written for them? I hope he doesn't think I'm doing any more."

"I'm with you," Danny agreed. "I want nothing more to do with those *eejits*."

"I agree," Jon said. "And they're not worth getting bummed out over. We've been doing great. Last night was a rush! We'll get our own recording contract."

Jon had said the words, but inside he felt he had let them down as bandleader.

For him, the flight back to Ireland was long and depressing, even though Kelly was right there by his side. She tried to be understanding, but Jon continued to be preoccupied, much to her disappointment. Kelly's new career as a flight attendant had already given her the thrill of life in several cities on two continents, and the adventure of all that was fast becoming a kind of expectation for her. She now wondered if Jon's personal struggles were going to come between them.

The rest of the group just wanted to get home. The fast pace of touring, along with the cutthroat competition in the business, was more than they could handle.

"I don't care if I ever leave Ireland again," Danny said.

"I hear you," Liam agreed. "I like the music, but I don't like the business."

Peggy met them at the airport with a positive attitude.

"This is just a stumbling block. We've all learned from it. Whatever the next step is for Second Wind, you can be sure it'll be lots of fun, lots of work, and there will be lots of contracts!"

Jon raised an eyebrow. "Are you offering to take the job, Peggy Girl?"

She winked at him. "Who's to say how it will all turn out?"

# Chapter Twenty-One

A couple weeks of country air and the surroundings of Montrose Manor were all the young musicians needed to feel rejuvenated. Laura and Liam always felt grounded here, whether they were gazing out their windows at the perfectly manicured gardens below or washing Rose and Sky outside the barn after an exhilarating ride to the cave and back.

Danny also felt a profound sense of home, whether he was in the cottage provided for him by Aidan, or visiting the house next door where Patrick and Chloe were raising their children, his niece and nephew. And then there was his work in the barn and on the grounds, where Danny knew he was really earning his keep. Although not skilled as a trainer like Liam, Danny had grown up on a farm and had an affinity for the equine spirit. He could already ride with good balance, and was now becoming more confident as Jen guided him in the arena.

Back when the Bianchi family was living full-time in Long Island, Jen had become quite the equestrian at a training stable there. She was now demonstrating to Danny how you could simply "ask" your horse to change its gait by making subtle changes in your leg pressure. Danny thoroughly enjoyed the whole process, and got to see the results immediately when he and Jen took the horses out on the trail together.

Jon had his own agenda, and asked to speak to Aidan privately one morning.

"I want to propose to Kelly, and I'd like to do it at Dublin House. Would it be all right with you if I go there this weekend?"

At first Aidan raised his eyebrows, but then shook Jon's hand. "I expect congratulations are in order, and I wish you two the best. But I must ask if you've spoken to your parents about this."

Jon had expected the question. "Yes I have, and I did make them the same promise Liam made to you about him and Laura–and Danny made, too, about him and Jen–that the wedding will not happen until after I graduate Trinity."

Aidan felt a sense of fulfillment knowing that the guidance he'd been giving them through the years was working. But then a look of concern came to his face.

"Jon, I just remembered that Molly is still gone with Brent and she won't be back until Monday. I want your word that you won't do anything I wouldn't approve of."

Jon stood up straight and answered, "I promise!"

Aidan nodded with satisfaction and Jon thanked him, giving him a hug.

Peggy got a call from Garrett, who apologized for being insensitive–about the contract dispute, her career–everything. Guarded at first, she soon softened as he played on her sympathies by making references to his loneliness. He persuaded her to come to London, where Foolish Pleasure was doing a benefit concert.

Preoccupied with romantic thoughts, Peggy was floating down the hallway when she literally ran into Jon.

"Sorry, Jon! Garrett called to apologize, and I'm meeting him in London."

"And I was thinking about Kelly. Look at the two of us, love-struck fools."

"I know Garrett and I are going to work things out. I do love him very much."

"I wish you the best, Peggy Girl."

"Jon, you're like a big brother to me." Then she laughed. "Except you're two years younger and two inches shorter."

"Hey, it's just that you always see me next to Danny and Liam, the giants."

"I love you just the way you are; you've got a big heart. Kelly's a lucky girl."

The others were excited for Jon. Laura and Jen showed up to his room, offering to help him pack for his trip and hoping he would tell the details of his plan.

"I'll have champagne on ice and the ring ready to put on her finger."

"Can we see the ring?" Jen asked.

"Not a chance! I'll let Kelly have the pleasure of showing it off."

Peggy was pleased to see Garrett waiting for her at Heathrow Airport. He welcomed her with a passionate kiss.

"Peg, I've really missed you. I've been so miserable. Please forgive me."

She kissed him. "I already have."

Garrett took her to a romantic dinner at the hotel, during which they went through two bottles of champagne. An hour later they were in his room.

He took her into his arms. "Peg, I want us to be together all the time. The road is a lonely place, and I need you here with me."

She sighed. "I want that too, but Trinity starts in a week."

"You can't leave me again! Baby, you're my inspiration–my world."

Garrett was playing her emotions like they were a keyboard. Before the night was over, Peggy had agreed to take a leave of absence to help Garrett follow his dream.

Late-morning sunlight streamed into the hotel room, waking Peggy with a start.

She slipped out of bed and into the shower. The fog began to clear from her mind while the water ran down her body. As she dried herself with a towel in front of the mirror, Peggy realized she was looking at the same insecure girl once again, the one she had left behind so long ago. She tried to shrug off the feeling of self-doubt.

Realizing her overnight bag was in the other room, Peggy decided not to disturb Garrett and opened the bathroom cabinet in hopes of finding a hairbrush. Instead, she discovered a makeup bag and other items that clearly belonged to a female.

Anger ripped through her as she marched into the room clutching the makeup bag. *The shame... the betrayal... the bloody bastard!* She launched the bag at his head.

Garrett's eyes shot open. "What the—"

"You lied to me, Mr. Lonely!"

"Peg! Give me a chance to explain," he pleaded, rubbing his head.

"You've got until I'm packed to talk your way out of this!" Peggy began stuffing clothes into her suitcase.

Garrett jumped out of bed. "Baby, you know I only love you."

"Don't touch me. And don't try to tell me these things belong to the maid."

"It's not what you think. Loreena needed a place to stay, and..."

"Loreena! Needed a place to stay? Okay—let's see... you let Loreena have the bed and you slept on the floor?"

Garrett lowered his head. "No. I won't lie to you. I was... lonely... and I'd been... drinking." She turned her back to him, not wanting to hear another word.

"Please, Peg! It didn't mean a thing! That's why I wanted you to come to London. I need you to be here with me."

"I see!" Peggy spun around. "If I give up my career and follow you around the world, you'll be faithful. And if I don't, you'll let Loreena—or whoever—take my place!"

"You don't understand how lonely I get."

"Oh, I understand completely. What I don't understand is how I could have been so ready to give up everything for someone as shallow as you!"

Peggy held back her tears until she got into the cab for Heathrow Airport. She was not sure where she was running to, but very sure of what she was running from.

~

At Dublin House, Jon had everything in place but kept nervously rearranging the flowers and candles.

Kelly had agreed to meet him as soon as she could, but as a flight attendant she was never sure exactly when she'd get in. Jon paced the floor and repeatedly looked out the window. He was beginning to feel doubtful that she would even show up.

Finally a taxi pulled up in front of the house. Jon ran to light the candles and turn on the music. He raced to open the front door.

There stood Kelly–and she took Jon's breath away. To him she looked more beautiful than ever, and he impulsively took her into his arms and kissed her tenderly. "Angel, I've missed you so much. Come in. I have a surprise for you."

Kelly walked into the living room and stopped in her tracks, stunned by the romantic setting: a heart-shaped arrangement of red roses and candles. Their song *Until Then* was playing softly in the background.

"It's all so wonderful!" she exclaimed. "What's the occasion?"

Jon couldn't wait a moment longer. He led her to the center of the heart. Slowly descending to one knee, he gazed up into her eyes and presented her with a ring.

Her reaction was unexpected. Kelly gasped and turned away, tears in her eyes.

"Kelly, will you marry me?" She didn't respond. "Angel–why are you crying?" Jon stood up and put his arms around her, but Kelly wouldn't look at him.

"Jon, I didn't expect this. You know I care about you. But... I can't marry you."

Kelly's words echoed profoundly through Jon's soul, in a surreal syncopation with the intense pounding of his heart.

"I'm sorry, Jon. I want to have my own career. I can't be the wife of a rock star, always waiting in the wings, or waiting at home, wondering how many girls are chasing after you. Even if you're faithful, you're so committed to your music I would always come second."

Jon sank down on the sofa, his head in his hands. "I thought you loved me."

"I do love you, and I'm sorry if I've hurt you. I just can't sacrifice my life–not after it took me so long to earn my independence."

"I just thought... we could still be together." Jon's words came through tears. "I don't understand."

Kelly slowly turned and left.

Jon was lost in numbed silence as he sat watching the candles flicker and while his heart crumbled. *I can't believe this is happening.*

Opening the bottle of Dom Perignon, he poured himself one glass after another, trying to drown his sorrows. But nothing could calm the waves of pain Jon was feeling from the storm of rejection.

∽

By midday, Peggy found herself at the doorstep of Dublin House. *I don't know why I've come here.*

Just when Peggy was sure she'd left misery behind, she came through the entryway to find Jon lying on the floor in the middle of a large heart made of wilted red roses and burnt-out candles. Beside him were two empty champagne bottles.

"Jon, Jon…" She gently shook him.

He slowly opened his eyes, disoriented. "Kelly… you've come back."

"No Jon, it's me, Peggy. Please sit up. What's going on?"

"Leave me alone. I can't talk now."

Peggy went to the kitchen and made a pot of strong coffee. She returned with a cup for Jon. "Now tell me what happened. Or, should I say, what didn't happen."

Jon drank half the cup before he spoke. "She doesn't want to marry me." Tears ran down his cheeks. He looked to her like a lost little boy. Peggy took him into her arms. She knew exactly how he was feeling–wasted and wounded.

Peggy decided Jon just needed to tell his story, and to lean on her for a while. There would be plenty of time later to tell him about Garrett.

Finally she suggested Jon take a shower and they go get something to eat. There was little fight left in him and he agreed. They found a nearby pub that was relatively quiet, and Jon's attention turned to the meal, which he really needed. When his plate was clean Peggy became optimistic that he was regaining his strength.

"How are you feeling now?"

Jon sighed. "Humiliated, hurt and hung over."

"I know what you're going through, and I'm here for you."

Jon looked at her quizzically. "Wait a minute–I thought you were spending the weekend with Garrett. What are you doing here?"

"It's a long story," Peggy said. "Let's stop at the market and pick up a few things, and we'll go back to the house to talk."

Jon rubbed his head. "As long as there's some kind of anesthetic on your shopping list."

"Yeah, I could go for some Bushmills myself."

Jon looked closely into Peggy's eyes, seeing her pain for the first time. He put his arm around her. "They say every fool has a reason for feeling sorry for himself. I'm inviting you to a pity party tonight."

She chuckled sarcastically. "I accept!" Just then there was a distant crack of thunder. "We'd better get moving before the heavens open up!"

After a hurried trip to the corner store they barely beat the rainfall back to Dublin House. The two were soon sharing tales, tears, and whiskey into the wee hours, with heavy rain pelting the windows and a good fire crackling to warm their bones.

Jon raised his glass. "To the best pity party in Dublin!" Peggy sighed and they clinked glasses, and then Jon suddenly put a hand on Peggy's shoulder and pulled her in for a kiss–on the lips–which she allowed to linger.

But then Peggy pulled back. "Jon! We may be drunk, but we're not stupid."

Jon shrugged his shoulders. "We can hurt together… or we can hurt alone. It's up to you."

He poured them each another glass, and Peggy contemplated her loneliness–and his suggestion. Jon gently stroked her hair then softly touched her lips. It wasn't long before his deep blue eyes and tender persuasion broke down Peggy's defenses. She needed to be loved–and held. She took his hand and stood, and together they staggered up to Jon's room.

In the morning Peggy slipped out of Jon's room and went down the hall to her own. It didn't take long before she was showered and dressed. And then she heard the front door open. It was Molly and Brent returning from their trip. She could hear Molly shaking rain off her umbrella while making a remark about the storm.

Peggy hurried down the stairs to greet them–but not in time to cover up the evidence of the pity party.

Brent figured it was best for him not to get involved and took their bags upstairs. Molly remained and wasted no time questioning Peggy.

"What's goin' on? You look... off somehow. Is everythin' all right?"

Peggy told her own dismal tale, and then Jon's, and it wasn't long before Molly's natural compassion took over.

"Oh dear, what can I do to help?"

"I'll be all right, but I'm worried about Jon. He's taking this very hard."

Molly sighed. "I can't believe my little sister would hurt dear Jon like that. I'll call her and give her a piece of my mind."

"He'll probably be sleeping most of the day. I think when he's up we should head back to Montrose together."

"You're welcome to stay here, of course, but do what you think is best."

"Thanks, Molly. I'm going to call Aidan now to tell him we're coming home."

Aidan was sympathetic. "I'm really sorry about Jon. I know how disappointed he must be. Peggy, you sound a little down yourself. How did it go in London?"

"I'm afraid it didn't go at all. Garrett and I are history. Please don't say anything to Mother, she'll just say I told you so."

"Don't worry about your mother. I'll talk to her. Remember we love you. Of course we love Jon, too. So bring him home and I'll let the others know."

❦

Molly gave Jon a hug when he finally came downstairs. "Jon, Peggy told me about Kelly. I don't understand my little sister, but I'm going to have a talk with her."

"Forget about it. She doesn't want to marry me. I understand she wants her career, but I thought if we loved each other enough we could make it work. I guess it's better that she's honest with me."

Molly made him some breakfast and coffee. "Now, please have something to eat before you two head on to Montrose."

Peggy appeared at the kitchen door. "Are you ready to face everyone?"

"We've got to do it sometime… better we do it together."

❦

Jon was deep in thought as they started the drive. Peggy was hoping he would say something–anything–about their night together. He never did, so she began.

"Jon, about last night." She waited until he looked at her before continuing. "I needed you... and you were there. I can't thank you enough."

He reached for Peggy's hand, squeezing it gently. "Hey, you were there for me. I don't remember how I even got to bed. I was so wasted. But I do remember you made me feel that I wasn't all alone. I love you, Peggy Girl." He gave her a big smile.

Peggy smiled back but suddenly felt like she and Jon were miles apart. His words "I love you," didn't exactly have any passion behind them. The phrase sounded more like friend-to-a-friend. Peggy took a deep breath. *Oh my God–he doesn't even remember!*

Everyone at Montrose showed great compassion for Jon and Peggy. They were sincere and Peggy knew it, with the exception of her mother. Hannah did go through the motions of hugging her daughter, saying she was sorry, but Peggy knew the truth, that her mother was pleased that the relationship with Garrett was over.

Danny didn't hold back the disappointment in his little sister. "I don't understand her. I thought she wanted you to propose. I'm really sorry, Jon."

"Hey, don't blame her. I should never have sprung it on her like that. I was so excited I didn't think it through."

Jen gave her brother a hug. "I feel so bad for you."

Laura put a comforting arm on Peggy's shoulder. "Are you going to be all right?"

"I feel like I have a hole in my heart, but I'm sure it will mend. I think I'll go to my room for a while."

"I'll walk with you," Hannah offered. Peggy accepted but hoped it wouldn't turn into another argument. She really didn't need that right now.

Jen waited until they left the room. "How could Garrett be unfaithful to her?"

"Well, it was Loreena," Liam said. "She's always been trouble."

Jon made a fist. "If I ever run into Garrett again I'll make him sorry he ever broke Peggy's heart. Besides, I've got some other scores to settle with him."

Aidan spoke up. "Now, haven't we all learned we can't settle things with our fists?"

"I just hate to see anyone in my family hurt," Jon replied. "But you're right. I'll stay out of it. I'm sure he'll get what's coming to him."

Liam chuckled. "Loreena should be punishment enough."

∞

The last week of summer vacation was spent at Montrose, and the recent wounds had begun to heal. Jon and Peggy were both looking forward to returning to studies. They had never mentioned their pity party to anyone. In fact, in the days following the return to Montrose, they had never mentioned it to each other.

# ᏟᎷᎧ Chapter Twenty-Two ᎧᏜᎧ

Returning to Trinity was good therapy for both Jon and Peggy. Jon, caught up in the celebrity of the concert tour, was never alone, surrounded by fellow students who had become fans. The attention helped to ease the pain of Kelly's rejection.

For Peggy, involving herself with a group of young law students was a perfect way to blend her focus on career with social interaction. Peggy was particularly drawn to Mick Carlton, a young man whose sharp mind and quick British wit always had her laughing. He was tall and thin with blond hair accented by pale blue eyes, and it was easy to see why he had so many friends. Peggy's spirit was lifted each time they spoke.

It was in the dining commons that Jon happened to meet Mick when he heard Peggy's laughter in a crowd and walked over. The introductions were friendly but brief, and the law students resumed their conversation. Jon could soon see how entertaining Mick was to Peggy, but for some reason he just couldn't take a liking to the young Brit.

A week later Peggy surprised Jon with an announcement that she was going to bring Mick home to Montrose to meet her mother and Aidan. Jon masked his doubt–and shock–with a smile and a nod of approval. *Wow, I guess he's more than just a friend.*

Peggy knew exactly what she was doing–using her head instead of her heart. Her mother would certainly be pleased with Mick's credentials: His father was a well-known barrister in London, and the Carlton family came from old money.

Hannah waited anxiously in the living room for their arrival that Saturday. "Aidan, Mick Carlton is from a proper family of means. I only hope Peggy can keep him interested."

Aidan rolled his eyes. "She's bringing him to meet us and show him the manor, nothing more. Let's not be hasty."

❧

Upon their arrival, Mick walked politely behind Peggy as she entered the front door and then stopped in his tracks on the marble floor of the grand entryway. His eyes moved from the grand staircase up to the Waterford crystal chandeliers and back down again. Just then Hannah entered and Peggy introduced them.

Mick bowed slightly and said, "Lady Meegan, it is a distinct honor to be a guest in this luxurious manor."

"Please, call me Hannah. Aidan will be joining us before long. Shall we retire to the living room?"

Laura and Liam soon came down as well, and as Peggy had expected, Mick was entertaining them–and several of the staff–with a humorous story about life in London.

Jon only appeared briefly to greet Mick and then headed to the kitchen. He was preoccupied with thoughts of Kelly, who had surprised him with a phone call earlier to say she was coming for Little Philip's third birthday party. Jon was trying not to get his hopes up, and Peggy took notice of the concern on his face. She excused herself from the others and followed him.

Jon explained the situation, and Peggy did her best to encourage Jon. After a few minutes it seemed to be working.

"I believe with every breath I take she's worth the fight. I'm going to see her."

"Then do," Peggy said. "Follow your heart. I wish you the best."

A myriad of thoughts went through Jon's mind as he walked down the path by the River Maigue which led to Chloe and Patrick's cottage. It seemed like only yesterday that Kelly was a sweet young girl just beginning to learn who she was–while hanging on Jon's every word–and hoping he would come back to her from his travels. *How did everything get so turned around?*

Jon knocked on the front door, his heart pounding so loudly he was sure everyone inside could hear it.

Kelly answered, a glowing smile on her face. "Would you like to go for a walk?"

Jon only nodded and Kelly took his hand, leading him to the river path.

"Please say something, Jon."

He took a deep breath. "Kelly, I love you even more than ever. What can I do or say to have you come back to me?"

"I do still love you, Jon, and I'm sorry I hurt you. You must understand that I'm out on my own for the first time in my life. I'm not ready to get married yet. I like making my own money... and my own decisions. You completely surprised me with the ring and everything. Please understand I need time to find the real me."

"If I have to, I'll wait for you."

"Then can we go back to being a couple, but not engaged?"

"Anyway you want it, Kelly."

"Thank you for understanding."

Jon was elated. He kissed her tenderly, then stopped. "Hey, my birthday is in a few weeks! Aidan said I could have a small party here at the manor. Do you think you could work it out to come? It would mean so much to me, Angel."

Kelly did not look hopeful. "I've qualified for the overseas flight program. I only have a few days a month in Dublin, and I'm never sure when it's going to be. But maybe I can trade with someone."

The answer seemed good enough to him, and they returned to Little Philip's party. Jon was back to feeling like his good-natured self again, and he helped the three-year-old race his new cars on the floor.

The next few weeks at Trinity were busy, but Jon still felt lonely without Kelly. He decided to invite a few selected friends to Montrose for his party. Peggy had invited Mick and asked Jon if she could include Mick's roommate, Stephan.

Jon folded his arms. "All right, but I hope you know this guy. I can't have anything happen like the brawl here last year."

"Stephan is as gentle as a lamb. I know him well; he's always with us."

Jon didn't quite know how to respond to the odd remark but agreed to have the roommate come along. *Peggy and Mick's relationship is strange.*

Jen and Danny returned to Dublin House one evening after one of Danny's rugby matches. Molly ran to meet them at the door, with Laura and Liam not far behind.

"Jen! I have exciting news! Aidan called–there's a reporter from *Rock n Roll* magazine who wants to interview you for an article on drummers!"

"Are you kidding?" Jen asked. "Why me?"

"Because you're so hot!" Danny exclaimed.

Laura gave Jen a hug. "Why not you? You're one of the best drummers out there, not to mention one of the only females."

"And guess what else?" Molly added. "It's not just the article, they're going to put your picture on the cover! One they took from a concert, I think."

"Wow!" Liam cried. "What an honor. We're all proud of you, Jen. Wait till Jon hears about this, he's going to flip out."

The telephone interview took place the next day at Dublin House. Danny held her hand, and she only began to relax when it was over.

"Well, how'd I do?"

"Darlin', you were brilliant!"

With the arrival of everyone for Jon's twentieth birthday party, Montrose Manor was once again bustling with the high energy of youth. Stephan and Mick got a tour of the manor and then joined Aidan and Hannah in the living room where Jon and some of the others had gathered.

"Lord Meegan," Stephan remarked, "I simply love your tennis courts."

"Oh, thank you. Do you play?"

Mick chuckled. "Does he play? I used to beat this chap at tennis, but now he's going pro and can't be bothered to even lob a ball at me anymore." They both laughed.

"So you've been friends for a long time?" Hannah asked.

"Good Lord! We've been mates since our early teens." He smiled at Stephan.

Jon had heard the last part of the conversation and for some reason took an instance dislike to Mick's friend.

After dinner they went to the ballroom where Danny was starting the music tapes. Kelly still hadn't arrived, and Jon was becoming doubtful. *Why can't she at least call?*

"Hey buddy, why the long face?" Liam asked. "Come on, it's your birthday."

"I know. I just wish Kelly was here. But I'm happy you guys are here."

"Birthday boy, I insist you dance with me," Peggy said.

"Where's your date?" Jon asked.

"He went out with Stephan to have a smoke."

As they turned to the dance floor, Peggy tried to conceal her mood with a smile, but Jon was not fooled.

"Peggy Girl, I see sadness in your eyes. Is there trouble in paradise?"

The music changed to a slow song and Peggy put her head on Jon's shoulder, not giving him a direct answer. "Just dance with me."

The fragrance of Peggy's hair made Jon even more aware of his own loneliness. He watched Danny gracefully spin Jen around, while Liam gently lifted Laura's face to kiss her. *Here we are again, Peggy and me, outcasts from the circle of love.*

Kelly never called and never showed up.

❧

The next morning, Jon was only picking at a scone in silence when Chloe came up the back stairs into the kitchen. "There you are, Jon! Kelly called late last night to say she had a long layover and wouldn't be able to make your party. She said she'd called the manor, but there was no answer."

"Thanks," Jon replied, somewhat relieved. "I guess the music was too loud. I was worried something had happened to her."

Chloe could see his disappointment. "She'll call again as soon as she can."

Jon retreated to his room, only wanting to be alone. His solitude was interrupted when Jen came bouncing in.

"Look! I'm on the cover!" She jumped up and down, waving the new issue of *Rock n Roll* magazine. Jon grabbed it from her.

"Wow! This is a hot picture of you. It's from Madison Square Garden. I didn't even know they took this." He gave her a hug and read the article aloud.

### Little Dynamo Drummer!

*They say good things come in small packages, and they certainly do when it comes to Jen Bianchi, drummer for the young Irish rock band, Second Wind. She can keep the beat with any of the macho boys and out-drum most of them—and*

284

*all that power coming from a gorgeous, petite eighteen-year-old. She's also very modest and gives credit to her older brother, Jon, for insisting she play the drums when she was only thirteen.*

*"He needed someone to keep time while he played his guitar. Jon and I are very close, only sixteen months apart. He's always wanted to be a rock star, and I went along for the ride. But it was my fiancé, Danny Bailey–our bass player–who gave me the real focus to kick the rhythms. We play off each other's energy. Our band is a family, and everyone does their part to make it the best. Jon's the lead guitarist, Laura Meegan does keyboards and backup vocals, and our songwriter, lead vocalist and rhythm guitarist is Liam Delaney. He's the soul of our group."*

*"Where did you get your unique style and technique?"*

*"Jon arranges most of our songs. He loves to put a dramatic edge on them. He's a showman and believes we need to connect with our audience. I follow his lead."*

*"What's next for Second Wind?"*

*"Well, we're all students at Trinity College, so we devote most of our time to studies. But we love the music and plan to continue performing."*

*"Jen, are you saying you're not signed to a record label yet?"*

*"At this time we're keeping our options open."*

*I'd say, after seeing the young group perform at The Garden last summer, there must be some record scouts lost in the woods. I've seen lots of young artists, but Second Wind has all the components to make it big!*

Jon hugged her, the magazine still in hand. "This is the best birthday present."

"Let's go show it to the others, Jon. They're waiting in the living room, but I wanted you to see it first."

Jon, his spirits finally lifted, rushed downstairs, holding up the magazine so everyone could see the cover picture of Jen.

"Fantastic!" Peggy exclaimed. "The photo really captures your spirit, Jen."

"Wait till you read the article," Jon said.

Peggy read the article aloud to the anxious group, who cheered at the end while Jen took a bow. When everyone quieted down, Peggy flipped to another page.

"Oh–here's something about Foolish Pleasure," she said, a curious look on her face. "Although the band's been on a whirlwind tour," she read, "keyboardist Garrett–" Peggy suddenly quit reading and put the magazine down. Her eyes filled with tears and she left the room.

Hannah reached for the magazine and scanned the article before looking up. "It mentions that Garrett has married somebody named Loreena."

Jon looked around for any sign of Mick, but he and his mate, Stephan, were nowhere to be found. He got up to follow Peggy, but from the patio Jon only caught a glimpse of her running towards the bridge.

She was sobbing by the time he caught up to her.

"Peggy Girl, I'm so sorry."

"Jon, I did love him so. I can't believe that what we had meant so little to him."

"I know, he's a disappointment. I'm certain he loved you, but Garrett's not a strong person. When his father died he was left without anyone but an aunt and his crazy cousin

Katie. You and the band became his family. After Garrett left to join Foolish Pleasure he got... lost. I guess he turned to the closest comfort he could find–Loreena. He's a fool, but I do think he loved you."

Peggy searched Jon's eyes. "Do you really believe that?"

"Yes, I do. But what about Mick? I thought you two were... an item."

Peggy wiped her eyes and stepped back. "It's complicated. Mick and I do get on well, and I have fun with him. He says I'm smart and tells me he's proud of me."

Jon raised his eyebrows. "And that's grounds for a relationship?"

"It's different than what Garrett and I had, but for now... it works for me."

"Peggy, you deserve to be loved. Are you just settling for someone to fill the void?"

Her reply was not really an answer. "Thank you, but I'll be fine. I have great friends, and there's none better than you, Jon."

It was over two weeks before Kelly finally called Jon at Dublin House.

"Hello, Jon. Are you mad at me?"

"Yes, but I'm also glad to hear from you."

"I've been so busy. We've been making all these long transatlantic flights."

"And you couldn't find a phone?"

"With all the time changes it's difficult. I never seem to be at a phone when it's not the middle of the night in Ireland. I'll be home next week. I've got to go."

Jon stood there unsure of how he felt, excited to hear her voice, but disappointed she was gone again. He was deep in thought when Peggy came in the door with Mick.

She looked at him quizzically. "Jon, are you all right?"

"I'm fine," he smiled.

"Okay. Anyway, I'm going to London this weekend to meet Mick's parents."

"That's great. You two have a good time." Jon watched as the couple went up the stairs to Peggy's room. *I guess this is serious now.*

A few days later, Laura and Liam came home from class to find the Jaguar parked in front of Dublin House. The rest of the group was already gathered in the living room.

"Hurry in!" Jon motioned to them. "Aidan has some news for us and wouldn't even drop a hint until we were all here."

Laura gave her father a hug. "Please tell us it's good news."

"I think you may consider it good," Aidan teased. "Now, I know how disappointed you were when the record deal fell apart. But remember, everything happens for a reason. I've been contacted by the biggest record label in Great Britain. They want to meet with Second Wind over the holidays and have you cut a demo."

"I can't believe it!" Jon yelled. "Someone out there wants us!"

"Hold on," Aidan cautioned. "We'll have Peggy go over all the conditions of the contract before we commit. So far it looks good."

"I guess that means we won't be going to Italy for Christmas?" Jen asked.

"I've talked to Robert, and he knows how much this means to you," Aidan replied. "So the Bianchis will come here for Christmas. The demo will be done right here in Dublin at the River Front Studios."

There were many questions, which Aidan answered as best he could.

"I know you're anxious to work on your music, but remember you have finals coming up. You need to devote time to your studies."

"It'll be easy," Jon said. "We already have enough material for at least two albums. All we have to do is practice."

"That's a relief," Danny sighed. "There's no way I'd have time for new songs."

"Twice a week is about all I can do," Liam added.

"No worries, mates!" Jon chuckled. "We are Second Wind... and it'll be a breeze!"

Liam laughed with the others, but wondered if it really would be a breeze.

When Kelly finally called again, Jon shared the news with her about the recording agenda. Her response was not what Jon had expected; it was almost as if she hadn't really been listening.

"Hmmm–you don't seem happy for me."

"Sorry, I am happy for you and the band. But I've got some exciting news of my own. We've been invited to Greece for five wonderful days over the holidays. One of the pilots I know has a vacation home right on the water. He's invited several of the flight attendants and their boyfriends."

"Kelly, didn't you hear what I said? We're making the demo over the holidays."

"Oh, Jon, don't tell me it's going to take up all your time."

"Well, we do have to rehearse, and I'm sure we'll be in the studio for several days. I really can't go with you."

"You can't go, or you won't go?"

"Angel, please understand how important this is to me."

"Oh, I understand all right. This is one of the reasons I don't see us getting married. I'll never be number one to you. I intend to go to Greece, and I would like you to join me. I suggest you get your priorities straight. Goodbye."

Jon slowly hung up and then buried his face in his hands. He picked up his head when Danny walked in the room. "I just got off the phone with Kelly. We can't even talk without fighting. Kelly wants me to go to Greece with her, but it's at the same time we'll be doing our demo. Danny, I just can't seem to please her."

"It's not you, Jon. I can't talk to her anymore either. She has some new high and mighty friends that travel in big circles. I'm a bit worried about her, she's gotten so independent. She has to do it her way."

"Well, I'm not giving up the demo. She'll have to go without me."

Peggy returned from her weekend with the Carltons and ran to find Jon. He was in his room studying.

"Jon, I have some news!"

He looked up. "I hope it's good–I'm full up to here with bad news."

"Well, I think it's good. I'm getting married."

"That's the good news? Peggy Girl, are you sure you know what you're doing?"

"It will make Mother very happy. Mick's parents are already making plans."

"I don't care what makes everyone else happy. I want to know if it will make you happy. Peggy, tell me you love him and he loves you."

"Jon, that's insulting!"

"I don't care. I want to hear you say the words."

Peggy turned away. "I do love Mick… in a way. I know you can't understand, but someday you will."

Jon faced her and put his hands on her shoulders. "Not good enough. I want to know why you're doing this. Is it to get back at Garrett?" Peggy started to cry.

Jon quickly apologized. "I'm sorry, I didn't mean to upset you. Tell me what's going on."

"Jon, I'm pregnant."

"Dear God, how did this happen?" He smirked. "Well, I know how it happens, but why? And with someone you don't love."

"Please believe me, this is not the way I planned my life." Peggy searched Jon's eyes while considering her next words. "I really want this baby, Jon, and my career. I know it can work for me."

Jon gently stroked her hair. "I'll be there for you and the little bambino. Let's see… Uncle Jon. Yeah, that sounds good."

"Please let me tell everyone when I'm ready. You're the first to know."

"What about Mick?"

"Why do you think he proposed?"

"I guess I had him figured wrong. I'm glad he's stepping up to the plate."

"Jon, he really is a great guy. Give him a chance."

"He'd better be a great guy–to you and the bambino–or Uncle Jon will step in."

Hannah was thrilled when Peggy told her of the engagement. Aidan was silent as his wife launched into wedding plans.

"Now, Peggy, dear, we must start planning immediately. A summer wedding in the rose garden would be perfect. We can accommodate both families and all our friends. I'm sure the Carltons will have a large guest list."

"Mother, please! We don't want a big wedding. Mick and I would like a small ceremony with just family."

"Dear, you do not have to worry about a thing. I will take care of all the arrangements. Aidan will pay for whatever you like." Aidan raised his eyebrows.

"We intend to marry over Christmas break," Peggy stated firmly.

"That is not enough time. We cannot have a gown made for you by then."

"Mother, forget the big wedding–it just won't work."

Before Hannah could protest, Aidan put a hand up.

"Please, Hannah, let Peggy decide what she wants."

"Thank you, Aidan," Peggy said. "Now, I know you'll both be... disappointed, but I have something else to tell you." She faced her mother. "I'm pregnant."

Hannah gasped. "Oh, dear God!"

Aidan hugged Peggy warmly. "A baby is always a blessing and we welcome yours. Make whatever plans you want, and we'll be there for you."

Hannah couldn't say another word. She turned and left the room.

"Thank you for everything, Aidan. You've been the best father."

"Thank you. And don't worry about your mother. She'll get over the shock." Aidan stood back for a moment and studied his stepdaughter. "I hope this doesn't mean you're giving up on your law degree."

"Not a chance!"

# Chapter Twenty-Three

Late December that year brought a whirlwind of unusual events. Peggy and Mick decided on a wedding date. They chose that month, the weekend before Christmas. Hannah, under protest, arranged a simple midday wedding ceremony at Montrose with only family. To Jon, it seemed like watching a second-rate play, where the actors were putting on their best faces but not really convincing the audience.

Only hours afterwards, the newlyweds left with the Carltons to spend the rest of the holidays in London.

Kelly did not come home over the holidays, and only called Jon once to wish him a Merry Christmas. It only confirmed his suspicions that she was fading away from his life. It was painful, but Jon knew he had to face reality.

The recording sessions at River Front Studios took up most of the time the young musicians had off from studies. As much as they had rehearsed, the days in the studio were still long and drawn out. Jen and Danny complained when they were asked to play individually, and Liam was uncomfortable with the way the recording engineers dissected their songs, putting the tracks together one at a time.

To the pleasant surprise of the group, the demo came together nicely. The record company was pleased, wanting Second Wind to return to the studio as soon as possible, with a complete album in the works as the goal. With John

MacDonald's guidance, Peggy put together a tight contract specifying that the members of Second Wind would not take any time off from college classes for recording, promoting or touring. Thankfully, four songs from the demo were ready for the album, but the agreement asked for six more, to be recorded during Easter break.

∽

Mr. and Mrs. Carlton had been told about the pregnancy and were happy about the prospects of Mick being a father. They were pleased to see their younger son finally falling into step with the family's expectations. For a wedding present they bought the newlyweds a townhouse close to Trinity campus. Mick would graduate in the spring, and after passing the bar, he would join his father's firm like his brother had.

Peggy was not sure where she fit into the picture with the Carltons, but her main focus was keeping up with studies during her pregnancy. It wasn't easy, but being more than halfway through the law program was a solid motivator. She spent a lot of time studying alone, and Jon made a point of stopping by her place as often as he could. Mick was never around.

"Peggy, I know it's none of my business, but why is your husband always gone?"

"He's Mick–you know, Mr. Social. He's out with his friends."

"He should be home with his wife."

"I don't blame him. I'm afraid I'm a bore these days. I can't drink or dance, and I'm tired all the time."

"If you were my wife, I'd be here with you."

"I know you would. But Mick's… different." Suddenly Peggy started to cry. "I'm sorry. My emotions are like a roller coaster these days. You know, hormones."

"I don't buy that, Peggy Girl. Now tell me what's really going on."

"Oh, Jon… I thought this could work out with Mick. But I'm lonely, and I want to come home to my family." She leaned into Jon and began to sob. "I guess I'm a fool."

"I don't think you're a fool. But tell me, has he hurt you?"

Peggy smiled through her tears. "No, Mick has been a good friend. But he doesn't love me, and I never loved him. It's a marriage of convenience for both of us."

Jon nodded his head. "I figured something like that. You didn't have to marry him just to give your baby a father."

"Jon… Mick is not the father of my baby."

Jon's jaw dropped. "Please tell me this is not Garrett's child."

"All right then. This is not Garrett's child," she said sarcastically.

"Very funny, Peggy. Do you intend to tell Garrett?"

"Garrett is no longer part of my life and certainly not part of my baby's life."

"Does Mick know this is not his child?"

"Jon, Mick has never made love to me. He's… gay."

Jon threw his hands up. "Now it all makes sense! I knew there was something weird about him. Let me guess… Stephan's the boyfriend?"

"You got it! Mick's father threatened to cut him off if he didn't give the impression he was living the straight life. The Carltons only want me around for appearances. They were anxious for us to marry, and my pregnancy is a bonus."

"Why didn't you tell me this a long time ago?"

"I'm sorry. Pregnant and no husband? I couldn't face Mother."

"If you needed a husband, I would have married you. I really mean that."

"Yes, I believe you. But you love Kelly, and I wasn't going to ruin your life, too."

Jon slumped in a chair and rubbed his forehead. "You know, lots of young marriages don't work out. Why don't you just leave Mick and come home to Dublin House–and your family?"

"Sure, after three months of marriage? I think that would be a record."

"Look, you both can save face. You won't be an unwed mother, and Mick will appear to be straight. I think it's time you started thinking about yourself and the baby. An unhappy mother can't possibly be a healthy mother, and you need to be healthy–and happy."

"That's very sweet and I'm sure you're right. I'll talk to Mick whenever he comes home, and we can work it out for the both of us."

Jon put his hand on her belly, just as the baby kicked.

"I guess you're due sooner than we all thought," Jon smiled. "You know he's going to be a musician, don't you? He's already got good rhythm."

Peggy laughed. "I have a strong feeling it's going to be a boy."

"Have you got a name for him yet?"

"Well, the Carltons want him to be Michael Blake Carlton III. But he's not their child. I like the name Michael Jon Morann–I'd like to call him Mickey."

"That's a good name. Did you know my name is Jon Michael?"

"Is that so?" She smiled at him. "Thanks for all your support, Jon. You are truly the best person I know. Once again you've come to my rescue."

He smiled. "I'll come by tomorrow and help you move your stuff over to Dublin House. I'll tell the others."

Everyone was happy to see Peggy move back in, and they gave her much-needed encouragement. Laura was like a nursemaid, ready to help her stepsister in any way.

Hannah's reaction to her daughter's separation was predictable.

"Aidan, how could she walk out on their marriage after only three months? She will never find a more suitable husband, and what will the Carltons think of her... of us?"

"Hannah, your daughter needs our support and understanding. I, for one, think that if Peggy has decided to leave Mick, she must have a good reason. Isn't it time for you to think about her and the baby and not worry about appearances? I'm looking forward to having a little one running around the manor, and you should, too. Emily never brings her child here. I suggest you take the opportunity to be close with your younger daughter and grandchild."

"I guess you are right," Hannah said, momentarily humbled. "I do want to be a grandmother. Emily has isolated me from Olivia."

By the first day of Easter break, Jon made sure the band was ready to go back to River Front Studios. This time they knew what to expect, the process was easier, and the recording was completed in less than two weeks. The producer and engineers would then apply their skills to mixdown and mastering, with the album targeted for a summer release.

"We need a name for our first album," Jon said. "We could call it Number One!"

Liam groaned. "Come on, we can do better than that."

"Remember how Jon said it would be a breeze?" Laura smiled. "So how about... Breeze. It ties in with our name, and one of the songs."

Everyone liked the idea, even the producer. The band selected their favorite from the outdoor photo shoot that Aidan had set up at Montrose: sunlight glinting off their instruments and Montrose Manor in the background. There was nothing left to do but wait for the album's release.

Being tall and thin, Peggy hadn't shown her pregnancy for a long time, but now her belly had grown quite a bit. She was having an increasingly difficult time getting around school. *I hope I can finish the year. I feel like I'm going to pop any day.*

Jon guessed that Peggy was much closer to her due date than the others believed and began driving her to and from Trinity, even though the campus was only a few blocks away. The fact that Peggy needed and appreciated him helped to make up for the growing realization that he and Kelly were now living in two different worlds.

One Friday in mid-May, Kelly called unexpectedly and asked Jon to join her and her friends for a weekend in the English countryside. He agreed to fly over and meet her there, feeling that maybe some time together might make a difference. Jon only had one nagging concern: Everyone else had gone to Montrose, and Peggy would be alone at Dublin House all weekend.

Jon found her in the library studying. "Peggy Girl, are you sure you'll be all right without me this weekend?"

"Sure, I'm fine. Go ahead and have fun. It's about time you and Kelly had a weekend together."

"Here's the number where I'll be–call me anytime. I'm worried about leaving you alone, though. No one realizes how far along you are."

"Don't worry, Jon. I need to be alone so I can study. Besides, Molly and Brent will be back Sunday."

Jon put his hand on her belly, something he'd done a couple of times before when Peggy had felt the baby kick. "Hmmm... the little one is quiet today."

"Get going, Jon, you'll miss your flight!"

He gave her a quick kiss on the cheek and headed out.

Twenty minutes later Jon realized that even though his car was heading towards the airport, his mind was back at Dublin House. A haunting feeling came over him, like he wasn't supposed to go for some reason. With no logical explanation, Jon turned the car around.

Peggy put her book down and stood up. *Oh... the pressure seems unbearable today.* She had only begun to climb the stairs when a sharp pain hit. *Oh! My God! No, it's just false labor.* Peggy sat down on the steps to rest. But each time she attempted to stand, another pain stabbed through her body.

*Dear God, I think the baby is coming! Please don't let me deliver here... alone!*

Suddenly the door flew open and there stood Jon.

"Peggy! I knew it! We're going to have a baby!"

"Jon—thank God it's you!"

He rushed to Peggy's side and gently brushed the hair from her eyes.

"Don't worry about a thing, I'm here. I'm going to help you."

"Thank you," she answered with a grimace. "We'd better hurry...."

Jon sprang into action, helping Peggy to the car as quickly as they could. He jumped in and raced to the hospital as swiftly as traffic would allow.

It didn't take long before the nurse had Peggy prepped in the labor room.

"The doctor will be here momentarily," the nurse reassured.

"Will you get Jon?" Peggy groaned.

The nurse agreed and opened the door to find him anxiously standing there. "Peggy Girl, what can I do to help?"

"Stay with me, Jon—I'm scared."

"Wild horses couldn't drag me away." He smiled and stroked her hair. "Do you want me to call Montrose... or anyone else ... Mick?"

"No! All I need is you." Peggy took his hand and squeezed it.

The nurse soon returned, followed by the doctor, and Jon was asked to leave. He paced nervously in the hallway.

The doors burst open, and Peggy was wheeled towards the delivery room. The nurse nodded at Jon and he rushed to keep up with the moving gurney.

"Peggy Girl, I'll be right here waiting for the both of you."

She smiled and found his hand, pulling it to her lips. "Bless you."

The doctor came out into the hallway twenty minutes later and pulled down his mask to reveal a smile.

"Congratulations! You have a healthy six-pound baby boy."

"Thank God–how's Peggy?"

"She's doing fine. The nurse will come get you in a few minutes."

"Thank you, Doctor." He heaved a sigh of relief and slumped into a chair.

When the nurse came to get him Jon followed cautiously, but a big grin came to his face at the sight of the tiny bundle in Peggy's arms.

"Peggy Girl, you did it–a handsome boy with long fingers… five on each hand." Peggy smiled and Jon kissed her on the forehead. "Can I call the manor and let them know Little Mickey has arrived safely?"

"Yes, and tell them it was thanks to you. You've rescued me again."

"Just call me Superman!"

Jon made the call using the phone at Peggy's bedside. He spoke to Hannah first.

"Hey Grandma, there's a cute little guy waiting to meet you. Peggy just delivered a six-pound baby boy."

"Dear God–is she all right? The baby is so early! Is he all right?"

"He may be tiny, but he's strong and has a good set of lungs. Listen." Jon held the phone to Mickey, who was announcing he was hungry.

"As soon as Peggy calms him down I'll put her on. By the way, she did a great job." Peggy took the phone a minute later.

"Hello, Grandmother. I can't wait for you see my son. He's so beautiful."

Hannah was now in tears. "I am so relieved you and the baby are both well. Now, you need to get your rest. We will be there in the morning. I am looking forward to seeing my grandson. Have you named him yet?"

"Michael Jon, but I'll call him Mickey."

"Of course–you named him after his father. Is Mick there with you?"

"No. But I'm sure he'll come by later. I've got to go now, the baby needs me. I love you, Mother."

"Yes, dear. I'll see you tomorrow."

Mick and Stephan arrived that evening, presenting a large bouquet of flowers.

"Well done, Peggy! We saw the baby in the nursery. He's a good-looking tyke." He glanced at his Rolex. "Sorry we can't stay, but Stephan has a tennis match. Take care."

Jon rolled his eyes as the door closed. "He'll never win Father of the Year."

"Come on, Jon, at least he came to the hospital. I'm sure he doesn't feel very comfortable here."

"I couldn't care less about Mick's comfort. But enough about him. I'll let you rest while Mickey is napping."

⌒∽⌒

Peggy awoke later to a room full of flowers. Most were from everyone at Montrose, but there were a few surprises. A colorful bouquet had come from John MacDonald and an elaborate arrangement from the Carltons.

Jon poked his head in the door. "Wow, you're sure popular! Well, I have something for you, too." Jon handed Peggy a small gift-wrapped box. "This is for the beautiful mother from her son."

Peggy's eyes lit up when she lifted the lid to see a gold heart-shaped locket with *Mother* engraved on the outside. Inside the locket she read *Michael Jon "Mickey" May 15th 1984*. The other side of the locket had a place for his picture. Peggy began to cry.

"Jon, I love this. You and Mickey are the world to me."

A wave of emotion swept over him. "I...." Jon wiped his tears away. "I'm going to check up on Little Mickey. I'll be back."

Jon was surprised at his own reaction as he went down the hall. Then a smile came to his face the moment he reached the viewing window. Watching the nurses busying themselves with the newborns, it only took Jon a moment to recognize Mickey.

"Which one is yours?" a nurse asked from the door.

"Oh, I'm just the uncle," he replied as he pointed.

The nurse smiled. "With all those blond curls we call him Golden Boy."

The family arrived the next day anxious to see Peggy and the baby.

"I think we should let the grandmother go in first," Aidan declared. "Then we can take turns." Hannah smiled at him.

She entered the room to find Peggy nursing the baby. Jon motioned to the chair alongside the bed then slipped out of the room. Hannah waited for the door to close before she spoke.

"Peggy, dear, it is not proper for Jon to be here while you are nursing."

"Oh Mother, it's 1984, for pity's sake. Besides, if it wasn't for Jon, we wouldn't have made it to the hospital."

"Yes, of course." Hannah, moved by the tiny newborn, dropped the subject.

"Want to hold him, Grandmother?"

"I do not want to wake him. He looks so peaceful."

Peggy ignored her and placed the baby in her arms. "I think it's time you two met. Mickey, this is Grandmother."

Hannah beamed at the infant as he opened his blues eyes to look at her.

"Peggy, he's absolutely beautiful. I think he has your mouth."

Aidan came in with Laura, who snapped a photo of Hannah holding her grandson with Peggy looking on.

"My, that is a grand picture," Aidan said with pride.

"Would you like to hold Little Mickey?" Hannah asked.

Aidan backed away. "I might drop him–better let Laura."

"Nonsense, sit here." She placed the tiny bundle in her husband's arms.

Aidan's expression was warm. "Hello, Mickey. Welcome to the family."

Peggy was thrilled with the outpouring of love and acceptance, Mickey at the center of attention. Aidan gently handed the newborn to Laura.

"Hi, Mickey, I'm your Auntie Laura. Your Uncle Liam and I are going to spend a lot of time with you." A moment later Jen carefully took the baby.

Jon smiled. "He sure was in a hurry to see this big world. We almost didn't make it to the hospital."

"Thank God you came home when you did," Peggy sighed. "I would have had him on the stairs, all alone." A puzzled look came to her face. "Wait–Jon, I thought you were on your way to see Kelly."

"Kelly! Oh no!" Jon put a hand to his forehead. "I didn't even think to call her."

"She'll understand," Danny remarked. "After all, with the rest of us gone to Montrose, you were the only one around to help."

As the baby was finally passed back to his mother, Hannah looked around the room. "Where is Mick? He should be here with you."

"Mick has already been here, Mother, but don't expect him to come around much. Remember, he and I are going our separate ways."

Peggy looked lovingly at Mickey, snuggled in her arms. "You are my son, and I'll give you everything you need."

# ᚳ⟎Chapter Twenty-Fourᚲ⟎

Hannah spared no expense in welcoming her grandson to Montrose, with the nursery suite on the second floor newly decorated by the time mother and child arrived. They settled right in with Hannah's help.

"Peggy," Hannah remarked while rocking the baby, "you know I enjoy helping with this lovely child, but I still think he should have a nanny. You are not getting enough rest."

"Mother, we're fine. I want to take care of Mickey myself." Peggy placed the baby into his bassinet.

"Then I assume you are not going back to Trinity in the fall?"

"No, I am going back. My professors have allowed me to miss finals this year on the conditions that I make them up and then return to finish the last year of the law program. I've made arrangements with Molly to take care of Mickey while I'm in class." Peggy smiled at her son, sleeping peacefully. "I'm going to work my schedule around this little one. It may take longer to graduate, but he's worth it."

Jon poked his head into the nursery. "Lunch is ready," he whispered. "Do you want me to watch Mickey?"

"Thanks, Jon. How about if you bring me a tray and we can watch him together?"

"I guess I am not needed," Hannah remarked. "My daughter has it all figured out."

Peggy put her arm around her mother. "Nonsense; you're a very important part of our life. Mickey is already quite attached to you."

Hannah had tears in her eyes. "But you will be taking him away from us."

"We'll be home on weekends," Peggy said in a comforting tone. "Dublin House is not the end of the Earth."

Hannah nodded but left the room still feeling unsure of her future role.

"I'd be upset if you took him away from me," Jon remarked. "Go easy on her."

Peggy watched Jon thoughtfully as he left to get their lunch.

He soon returned with sandwiches and tea. They stepped over to the far side of the suite and spoke softly.

"Jon, isn't your album supposed to hit the record stores tomorrow?"

"Yeah, and I think it's going to do really well. Liam and Danny are less optimistic, but that's just them. Laura and Jen are pretty excited–they actually want to go to Limerick to see how many copies sell. I think Aidan put a stop to that idea. Maybe he thinks they'll get mobbed or something, I don't know."

"Well, I'm with you. I think *Breeze* is going to be a big hit."

"Thanks, Peggy Girl. Now, why don't you take a nap while the baby sleeps? I'll come back to check in on him." He paused to gaze into the bassinet. "I can't believe how attached I've gotten to this little guy."

"You should be attached to him," Peggy said. "You helped bring him into the world." Jon smiled proudly and left the room.

The record company had planned Second Wind's entire summer, beginning with several local concerts followed by a tour of Great Britain for four weeks. The pressures of touring with Foolish Pleasure were a distant memory. The young musicians were now enjoying themselves, playing to packed houses at night with plenty of time for sightseeing during the day. And to top it off, *Breeze* was climbing the charts.

Jon made time to call Peggy regularly from the road, and it always warmed his heart to hear news about Little Mickey. Jon found himself missing Kelly less each day, especially since their last conversation, which was the day after Mickey's birth.

Setting aside a special time with no distractions, Jon had called Kelly with the news, and figured she would forgive his no-show for their date in England. But with her lack of interest in the blessed event, coupled with her lack of forgiveness … Jon took it personally and was sorry he'd even called.

After all that had happened, Jon was truly surprised when Kelly appeared in his dressing room after one of the London concerts.

"Hello, Jon. Are you happy to see me?" She smiled seductively at him.

"Uh, yeah… hello." He gave her a quick hug.

"I've brought some friends," Kelly said. "They'd like to meet you and the band."

Jon politely agreed, but it didn't take him long to realize that she was only there to impress her companions.

For the first time Jon was seeing Kelly in a different light. She was still beautiful, but she no longer made his heart stop. Even her laugh seemed unfamiliar. At that moment Jon somehow knew Kelly would no longer be part of his life; but it was okay with him. *It's been a heavy load to carry, all of the heartache and none of the love.* She suddenly broke his train of thought. "Jon, we're going out on the town tonight. Will you join us?"

He shook his head. "No… it's been a long day and we leave in the morning."

She pouted. "Oh, c'mon–a party boy like you?" One of her friends giggled and Jon shook his head again.

Kelly shrugged. "Oh well, it was good to see you again. I'll be at the Ambassador for a couple of days. Will you call me?"

Jon looked thoughtful before he spoke. "Kelly, I'm leaving tomorrow for Scotland. You know how hard it is to get to a phone when you're on the road."

A look of disbelief came to her face.

"You know The Cowboy–my music comes first!" With a satisfied smile, Jon turned and walked away.

The tour was exciting, as well as profitable. Album sales were skyrocketing, with regular airplay happening all over Great Britain. The producer was so pleased that he approached Jon after the show in Edinburgh to propose a three-record deal for Second Wind.

Jon was ecstatic but kept his cool. "It sounds good, but naturally I'll have to have my people in Ireland go over the proposal first."

"If you mean Miss Morann, I'm sure she wouldn't have it any other way. We can always count on her to dot the i's and cross the t's."

Jon smiled. The truth was, although he couldn't wait to begin recording their next album, he missed Peggy and Mickey more than he could have imagined. Jon had bought a special Paddington Bear for Mickey while they were in London.

Paddington had gone on tour with the band, and everyone was amused with how Jon set up the stuffed animal in a chair in each hotel room, as if it were a special guest.

Jen studied that bear for a moment and then looked back at Jon with a perceptive grin.

"Hey, didn't you have one like this when you were little?"

"Yep! Paddy, I called him. He was a good friend... until the neighbor's dog got to him. I logged years of good times with my Paddy. I sure hope Mickey will like his."

"I'm sure he'll love him eventually, but don't you think he's a bit young?"

"Nonsense! You're never too young to have a faithful friend." Jon patted the bear on top of the head.

"Well, I think it's very sweet of you," Laura remarked.

Liam chuckled. "This is hardly the wild Cowboy we're used to." Everyone nodded in agreement, even Jon.

Suddenly Jon looked at his watch. "Oh—I think the afternoon paper is out. Maybe there's a review of last night's show." He left the room to head for the lobby.

Danny was still looking at the Paddington Bear. "I've never seen this side of Jon. He's so taken with the baby, always talking about him. We all love Mickey, but Jon seems to have a special connection to him."

"Hmmm..." Jen said. "I think it's not only Mickey. He's always right there for Peggy, too."

"I like this Jon," Liam smiled. "If being close to Peggy and the baby helps to fill the void in his life, I'm all for it."

"Well," Danny said, brushing his hair back, "I do think he feels needed, after everything he went through with Kelly. I'm disappointed in her. She never even comes around to see Mum and Dad."

Jen gave him a kiss. "I know how important family is. Our parents will always be in our lives."

"Jen, darlin', this is one of the many reasons I love you so much."

The tour ended successfully, and everyone was happy when they returned to Montrose. Peggy and Mickey were waiting downstairs, and Jon immediately presented the Paddington Bear to the baby, whose sparkling blue eyes came alive with wonder.

"See–he likes him!"

Peggy hugged Jon and held onto him for a long moment. "You are so thoughtful. We've really missed you." She suddenly stepped back, blushing. "All of you."

Later that day Iris presented Laura with a large brown envelope. "You have a post from America."

Laura waited until Iris left the room and she was alone with Liam. "It's from Anthony in New York," she said softly. "I hope it's news about my grandmother."

Liam put his arms around her. "Sweetheart, promise me you won't get your hopes up. It's been a long time since we talked to him."

Laura bit her lip. "I'll try... but I think I should wait until later to read it. I don't want any interruptions."

"We can read it together. We still have time to ride to the cave and get back before dusk."

Laura tucked the envelope in her backpack. "Let's go!"

Sky and Rose had missed their friends and galloped eagerly through the trees to the destination they'd enjoyed as much as their riders. Once the horses were in the corral he and Laura had built years before, Liam took Laura by the hand, leading her to the field where the late afternoon light was still good. They sat on the grass together and she leaned back into his arms, carefully opening the large envelope. There were two letters inside, the first from Anthony.

*Dear Laura,*

*I'm sorry it has taken me so long to write to you. When I went through Grandfather's belongings I could not find anything that might help you. It wasn't until we did some remodeling that I came across this letter hidden behind an old mirror. I can see why he didn't want it to be found. It's from your grandmother, and I'm sure you'll want to read it. I'm sorry there was no return address. Take care.*

*Sincerely, Anthony*

Laura picked up the second letter with apprehension and excitement, her hand trembling. Liam placed his hand on top of hers as she brought the faded script into view.

*My Dearest Mario,*

*I know you must be unhappy with me for disappearing. It is hard for me to explain my behavior. You know I have always been a wanderer and have followed my heart. This time, I feel I have left my heart behind. I have been with you longer than anyone and I have found it is so difficult to leave you. I think of you with loving thoughts and I can only hope you will think of me the same way.*

*You always wondered about my mysterious ways and I told you nothing. Why I kept so many secrets from you I'll never know, except that I am a gypsy and will always be a gypsy.*

*Years ago they tried to tame my wanderlust when I was married to a good man in Ireland. We had a beautiful daughter named Fey–it means "fairy." She was the light of my day and I regret leaving her behind. But my heart wanted more. I felt trapped and confined living life as a Royal. One day I walked out and left my husband and daughter behind and I followed my spirit to America where I met you.*

*You gave me the freedom to be myself, to dance and to love you without question. I will always hold your love close to my heart.*

*You'll remember years ago when we toured Ireland with the dance company, I left for a short time. I went to see my grown daughter, Fey. She met me in Dublin and brought my granddaughter Laura to meet me.*

*Fey turned out to be a very loving and confident young woman. She was well educated and married to one of the richest men in Ireland. My granddaughter was the very image of Fey. Laura was only three years old at the time but I could see she had my spirit. Fey played the piano and Laura and I danced around the studio. I'm sure the girl has my gift for music and dance. There was a song in my heart that day and I vowed I would always carry the memory with me.*

*I knew if I stayed I would only bring unhappiness to them. We said our farewells and I returned to New York, never to see them again.*

*For years I have carried the guilt of leaving my husband and daughter. I have always been careless and selfish. I know you love me, but you have a family who needs you. I know you will stay at your wife's side, especially now that she is ill. You have a son and a grandson who think the world of you. I cannot destroy another life. I need to move on to where my spirit calls.*

*Please know you will always have a special place in my soul along with my daughter Fey and granddaughter Laura. I ask you please do not try to find me. Remember, when a gypsy disappears... it's into thin air.*

*Wishing you all the best life has to offer,*

*Your Gypsy Dancer*

Tears were streaming down Laura's cheeks. Liam gently wiped them with his fingertips, and then kissed her tenderly. "Sweetheart, your grandmother loved you and your mother very much. She gave you her gift of music and dance." Laura nodded but couldn't speak. Liam continued. "Maura has made a lot of sacrifices to be a free spirit. She wants no ties. You have to respect her wishes."

"I know... I just wanted to see her again," Laura whimpered. "I don't know where she is, or even if she's...."

"She will always be with you, just as your mother is." Liam softly kissed her forehead. "You are my gypsy heart."

# ⟡Chapter Twenty-Five⟡

Hannah shook her head as she gazed out the front window of Montrose Manor at what appeared to be a moving caravan. Jon was driving Liam's truck, which was loaded down with all of Mickey's things: crib, pram, toys, you name it. Following him was Danny, behind the wheel of the Mercedes sedan, with Liam heading up the rear in the Mercedes sports car Aidan had given him. With them were Peggy and the baby, Jen, and Laura. They were headed to Dublin House, with the fall session soon to begin.

Hannah sighed. "The manor seems so empty now. I wish Peggy would wait to go back to college until Mickey is a bit older."

"She's made her decision and they'll be fine," Aidan said. "Peggy has all the help she could possibly need. Laura and Jen are always fighting over who gets to take care of the baby, and now Molly will be fussing over him as well. And don't forget Jon–he's always doting over Mickey. Peggy is lucky to have so many caring babysitters."

"I know, but I will miss him terribly." Hannah wiped her tears.

"How about we drive up next week? I have a meeting and you can visit with your grandson." Aidan kissed his wife on the cheek and she smiled.

"That would be lovely."

It was the last year at Trinity for Liam, Danny, Jon and Peggy. They would all be facing a heavy load of studies, but each of them was determined to graduate with high grades. Liam's goal was to finish at the top of his class, in his desire to show his appreciation for Aidan's help and support through the years.

Jen and Laura had other things on their minds.

"Laura, Danny and I are thinking of a June wedding, but I don't want to conflict with yours. Have you and Liam set a date?"

"No, and it bothers me that it's been awhile since he's even talked about us getting married." Laura frowned. "I hope he didn't ... forget."

Jen laughed. "Oh, sure—Liam forget about marrying the love of his life? I think you just need to bring it up to him. I told Danny what kind of wedding I wanted and he said, 'Whatever you want, darlin'. I'll just show up with the travel tickets for a honeymoon!'"

"Jen, that's so sweet. But I'm not going to remind Liam."

"Maybe when he hears Danny and I have set our date...."

Laura sighed. "We'll see."

In spite of everyone's hectic schedules, Jon had Second Wind working on the new album. They were recording one song at a time at River Front Studios on the weekends.

By late November the finishing touches were being done on the album, called *Storm*. New photos were taken and the hype had begun. The record company, pleased with the sales of *Breeze*, targeted early December for the release of the new album in Europe and America.

Just in time for the Christmas shopping season, *Storm* was on the shelves, the publicity was enormous, and sales took off like a rocket. The last week of classes before Christmas break was a blur for the young musicians, with final exams competing with feverish periods of signing record albums for fellow students.

Liam and Danny were not happy about the fame. It was hard enough to focus on studying, and making it to classes on time was a challenge when fans on campus would stop them to deliver a compliment about the new album. Rudeness was not an option, so a conversation would always unfold, consuming precious time.

Danny particularly felt he was being singled out for attack on the rugby field by jealous players from the opposing team. He had taken a good beating in the last match and ended up with a couple of cracked ribs.

Jen told Danny he should drop out of rugby. "I can't stand to see you getting beaten up like this."

"Jen darlin', I can't! Remember, the scholarship comes with a required commitment, and you know me–I'm not a quitter. Besides, I only have a few more months of matches. All my mates will watch my back from here on out. Don't you worry."

She accepted his response with a sigh. "I can't wait until we all go to the Tuscan villa this Christmas. Once I told Mother we wanted a June wedding, she immediately got busy making plans. I'm getting fitted for my gown in Milan. You're sure it's okay with you that we get married there?"

"Darlin', we made plenty of money on our last album and tour, so I can afford to fly my family there. I feel good that we are well on our way to financial security."

∞

As with so many college students, reserve energy comes when you really need it, and that seemed to give new meaning to the name *Second Wind*. Each of the five students was pleased with their results at the end of term, and packing for the trip to Italy was a real joy instead of just another chore.

Danny's relief that his ribs had healed made a simple task like carrying bags through the airport a sheer joy to him.

"Finally I can pull my weight again."

∞

Catherine and Robert were thrilled when everyone arrived in Tuscany for Christmas, and Little Mickey was a bonus. At seven months old he was a cheerful and adorable baby, and had learned how to capture the spotlight with his cute personality. With his blond curly hair, twinkling blue eyes and contagious laugh, Mickey was irresistible.

Jon's parents were continually amused at the way he was so taken with the child, but they were no more immune to the little one's charms than anyone else. One afternoon, Robert found Catherine completely entranced by Little Mickey. He waved his hand in front of his wife's face.

"What's got you so mesmerized?"

"Robert, doesn't Mickey remind you of Jon?"

He shrugged. "Well, he has the same twinkle in his blue eyes. I think he's just a little entertainer; but most kids are at this age."

320

Catherine nodded her head slowly, but something inside her was becoming... unsettled. She couldn't put her finger on it.

The villa was laid out perfectly for the Bianchis to enjoy having so many guests. With ten bedrooms and a large terrace with a pool, nobody ever had the feeling of being on top of one another. The six downstairs bedrooms were perfect for the young adults, and the large common room had been set up by Jon as a music studio. When taking a break from composing, practicing, or for no particular reason at all, any of them found the terrace to be quite a relaxing place to hang out.

Laura found Liam out on there alone just enjoying the view of the bay below. She sneaked up and slid her arms around his waist.

"Make a wish, my love," she said softly.

"A wish... hmmm." Liam rubbed his chin thoughtfully. "Let's see...."

Laura pouted. "C'mon, don't tease me."

He spun around. "My wish is to have the most beautiful girl in the world marry me this summer."

"Oh Liam, I was wondering if you'd forgotten."

"Laura Lye, how could I forget about the most important thing in our lives? I want our day to be everything you have ever dreamed about. I don't want to squeeze a wedding and honeymoon in-between tours. I want to take my wife on a long honeymoon... to America."

"America! You mean we'll get to see more than New York City?"

"I'd like to start at the east coast and go clear across country to the west." A gleam came to Liam's eye. "Let's just say… for the first month I want you all to myself."

Jon opened the terrace doors. "Hey, it's cold out there. Come on in–let's jam."

"Sweetheart, this is just what I'm talking about." Liam waved Jon away.

"You're right," Laura laughed. A thoughtful look came to her face. "You know, I'm going to Milan tomorrow with Jen. She's being fitted for her wedding gown. Maybe I'll look around for myself."

Liam took her into her arms and held her close. "Sweetheart, I want you to find the gown of your dreams. Our day is coming soon, I promise." They kissed and held each other in silence.

That evening Laura and Liam chose a date in August for their nuptials.

And then Hannah got her wish: Laura asked her to coordinate everything. Now Hannah would be in her element as Lady of the Manor. *My wedding is going to be the social event of Ireland.*

Catherine, Hannah, Jen and Laura were off to Milan the next morning, alive with anticipation about their appointed private showing of wedding gowns at Angelo's, the most sought-after designer shop in Europe. Angelo himself had agreed to personally oversee the entire process, from the fitting to the finishing touches.

From the moment the ladies were greeted in front of the lavish boutique, they knew this would be a memorable experience. They were ushered to the private viewing room, where they were seated in velvet chairs arranged behind a marble coffee table that would afford them a perfect view. After they were served tea and biscuits from an elegant silver set, Angelo made his entrance, introducing himself, and assuring his guests that anything they desired for their personal comfort was at their beck and call.

"Mrs. Bianchi, ladies, I cannot begin to describe the thrill among my staff when they found out that we were to have both the Bianchi and the Meegan families grace our establishment."

Angelo continued. "In a few moments, our models will present my creations. These were, of course, selected for your viewing based on your preferences. First, for Miss Bianchi, we will present the more traditional lace gowns, and then, for Miss Meegan, the more contemporary fitted styles."

Jen easily made her choice, a delicate lace gown with a sweetheart neckline.

"Now," Angelo said, "for your veil, may I suggest this–the chapel length?" He gently positioned it on Jen's head and lowered the blush veil over her face. "Ahhhh, this is just the right touch."

Jen smiled. "Perfect!"

Laura chose a strapless satin dress with an elegant long train.

Angelo was pleased. "Miss Meegan, you have the perfect figure for the fitted gown you have chosen, and I have several embellishments in mind. May I suggest this lovely veil?" He reached for one similar to Jen's, but Laura had her eye elsewhere.

"I like this one–without the blush veil."

Angelo looked concerned. "Well, my dear, there are certain... traditions...." He seemed to be at a loss for words as he looked to his assistant.

"Please, let me tell her," Isabella suggested. Angelo, now genuinely embarrassed, suddenly left the room. The lady spoke softly. "It is tradition in Italy for a virgin to have the veil cover her face."

"Well, I'm not...." Laura paused when she noticed Hannah's horrified look. "I'm not... getting married in Italy."

Hannah sighed in relief. "Whatever she wants."

The excitement about the upcoming nuptials stayed with everyone right through Christmas, with most of the talk focused on Jen and Danny's wedding, set for early June.

On Christmas Eve, Jen remembered a holiday from several years before that had been particularly fun–from a sibling's point of view.

"Hey Jon, why don't you tell Peggy about your gift from *La Befana* a few years ago?"

Peggy looked curious and Jon smirked at his sister.

"La Befana," Jon began, "is a kind of a female version of Santa Claus. She's an old woman who flies around on a broom and brings treats to good children."

"And coal to bad ones," Jen added. "So what did you get that year, Jon? I can't seem to remember."

Jon rubbed his chin, mocking her. "I can't seem to remember either."

"I think I can guess," Peggy said. As she started laughing Jon stuck his tongue out at his sister first, and then her.

Little Mickey saw this and laughed out loud, to the delight of everyone. Jon repeated the gesture to the baby and he laughed even harder.

"Now Jon," Catherine cautioned, "don't teach the child bad habits."

Everyone was in stitches by then. The holiday joy was well underway, soon to be enhanced by Little Mickey's fascination with the ornaments and packages.

⟨∽⟩

The Christmas break was over too soon, and it was back to reality for the students at Trinity. Peggy was eager to move on with things, starting with her marital status. In January 1985 she called Roen Dennehey's office and arranged to meet with him.

"Miss Morann!" he said, pleased to see her again. "My door is always open to you, particularly when you get your law degree."

"Thank you, Mr. Dennehey. I'm working on it. Today, though, I have another matter I need some advice on."

"Please, you can call me Roen. Now, tell me what I can do for you."

Peggy explained the circumstance of her marital separation from Mick Carlton. The barrister listened carefully before he spoke.

"Peggy, I'm sure you're aware of the fact that divorce is not recognized by the state or the church in Ireland. However, there could be special grounds for an annulment if both parties agree."

"I know Mick will agree, but his father may not. He wants Mick married, you know. Appearances for the Carlton family are paramount."

Dennehey nodded and rubbed his chin. "Another way this could be approached is to have Mick file for divorce in England. But my guess is that the Carlton family would prefer a quiet annulment. Why don't you let me call Michael Carlton senior and present the options? We can go from there."

"Thank you, Roen. I really want to resolve this without complication. I want to focus on my career. I hope to pass the bar exam later this year."

A few weeks passed before Dennehey was able to call Peggy with an update.

"I have some good news for you. With a little persuasion Michael Carlton agreed to the quiet annulment for you and his son. As I predicted, he wanted no publicity. I think he wants everyone to think his son is still married; although I don't know how long he can pull that off. But that, of course, is his concern, not ours."

"You are wonderful! How can I ever thank you?"

He laughed. "Oh, I have plans for you after you pass the bar. But there is one thing about the annulment you should know: Mick wants to make sure he will not have any responsibility for your son."

"Roen, I am caring for my son myself. As I told you, Mick is not the father. That's why I gave the baby my last name."

"Of course. I'll file the papers, and you should be a free woman in a few weeks."

Peggy thanked him and sighed with relief as she hung up the phone.

Before long, midterms were over and the students were all looking forward to Easter break at Montrose. Catherine and Robert arrived at the manor the day before everyone else.

One afternoon, Peggy and Mickey were in the nursery alone and Catherine went in for a visit. Mickey was now eleven months old and walking. He loved attention, and, happy to see Catherine, he toddled to her with open arms.

"My, he has grown so much!" Catherine gushed as she picked up the child. "Peggy, he is such a beautiful baby–and a very happy one."

"Thank you! I think he's very handsome. But then, I am his mother, so perhaps I'm a bit biased. I'm so pleased he's not shy. He loves people and they all love him."

"I've noticed how devoted Jon is to him," Catherine said deliberately. "I would have never guessed he'd be so taken with a baby."

Peggy replied with no hesitation. "Well, I know Jon was really hurt by Kelly, and I believe this is part of his need to *feel* needed. He's been wonderful to both Mickey and me. I don't know what we would have done without Jon." Peggy smiled at her son.

Catherine looked at Peggy cautiously. "Do you mind if I ask you something… personal?"

"If you're wondering about Jon and me, don't worry. We're just good friends, and we've always been there for each other."

Catherine toyed with Mickey's blond curls. "I feel like there is a… special bond between you and Jon. As a mother I can see the love in his eyes when he looks at this baby–and at you, too, Peggy."

Peggy looked away. "It's a… brotherly love he feels for us."

Catherine slipped two photos out of her pocket and placed them on the table.

Peggy looked at them curiously. "When did you take these pictures of Mickey?"

"Look again, dear." Catherine had a coy smile on her face. "These pictures were taken of Jon when he was about eleven months."

Peggy blushed. "Oh! With the Paddington Bear and everything, it looks like Mickey."

Catherine tilted her head slightly. "Yes, the resemblance between Mickey and Jon is remarkable. And they have the same precocious personality."

Tears came to Peggy's eyes and Catherine put an arm around her. "You don't have to say anything to me if you don't want to. And if you do, I'll keep it between us."

"I'm so sorry... I don't know what to say. It's not what you think. Jon and I were never... involved; it was only one night. He was so upset about Kelly's rejection, and I had just found out Garrett was cheating on me. We ended up at Dublin House alone... together, having a pity party. We drank a lot, and Jon was so drunk he has no memory of that night. And I never told him what happened. Please–he has no idea Mickey is his child!"

Catherine embraced Peggy, then stepped back and offered her a hankie. "Don't you think Jon has the right to know?"

Peggy wiped her tears and thought for a moment. "I can't ruin his life. Jon and I are best friends. If I tell him it could change everything."

"Yes, I imagine it would change things. But it could be for the best. Jon thinks the world of you and Mickey, and that will never change."

"I can't tell him right now. Please promise me you won't say anything."

"Well, I have to tell Robert, but he'll keep it to himself. You have my word on that. But, we are the grandparents, and we'll want to be part of Mickey's life." Catherine kissed the baby on the head and Peggy took her hand.

"Thank you for understanding. Mickey is so blessed to have you for grandparents. I promise I'll tell Jon when the time is right–after Jen and Danny's wedding. I don't want to spoil their big day."

Catherine nodded, picking up the photos. She gave Peggy's hand a squeeze and left the room, suddenly realizing she had tears in her eyes. Her instincts had been right, and now she could finally embrace the joy of being a grandmother.

Several weeks later at Dublin House, Peggy and Jon decided to take time out from studies to go to the park with Mickey. Peggy had just gotten some good news.

"Jon, I just heard from Roen Dennehey; my annulment is completed. I feel like the weight of the world has lifted. I'm now a free woman and I can go on with my life."

"Peggy Girl, I'm so happy for you!" Jon threw his arms around her. "I'm sorry you ever got into that mess. If you would have come to me in the first place, I would have stopped you from marrying Mick."

Peggy felt warm and safe in Jon's embrace. *Maybe I should tell him now. No!* "Jon, when are your parents coming for graduation?"

"They'll be here in a few days. You know, my father said he would buy me a Porsche for graduation. But I've decided I don't want one anymore." Jon looked at Peggy with a twinkle in his eye.

"What? Oh, I suppose you want a Ferrari or Lamborghini instead?"

"No, I think I need a family car, one you can put a baby seat in."

"Jon Bianchi, you don't need to spend all your time with us, and you certainly don't need to drive a family car around," Peggy scolded.

Jon put his arm around her. "But I want to spend my time with the two most important people in my life."

Peggy's heart was pounding. "Jon, you're very important to us. But you have a life, and I don't want to get in the way."

"Peggy Girl, why don't you let me decide who I want to spend my life with?" Jon suddenly kissed her, on the lips, and she didn't pull away–at first.

"I think we should take this one day at a time, Jon. We've both been through some heartbreak, and we need to think about graduation, and your sister's wedding." Jon interrupted her with another kiss–one that lingered a bit longer.

"Honey, I know what I'm doing. I love you and Mickey. You make me feel important and loved. I can't imagine my life without you two in it."

Tears streamed down Peggy's cheeks. "I do love you, too. But we need time to think this through."

"I'll give you all the time you need." Jon held her tightly.

Mickey's fussing brought them back to reality, and Peggy reached for him.

"He has to be the center of attention or he's not happy."

Jon put Mickey up on his shoulders, and the child laughed with delight.

# ᐸᔌᐳChapter Twenty-Sixᐸᔌᐳ

Graduation day at Trinity College of the University of Dublin was a proud one for the Bianchis, Baileys and Meegans. Second Wind had achieved so much notoriety on campus that the audience cheered loudly for Jon, Danny and Liam when they lined up for commencement. The Dean of the School of Liberal Arts took his place at the podium and opened with a word of thanks to the faculty.

"Before we move on," the dean announced, "I would like to acknowledge a certain member of the graduation class. I know many of you recognize this young man from seeing his face on another kind of stage." Liam approached the podium to an outburst of applause, and the dean shook his hand before continuing. "It appears that most of you know the talented Liam Delaney, who has been busy with far more than his music. I would now like to recognize Mr. Delaney for another accomplishment." He turned to face Liam. "I am proud to present you with this special award for Academic Excellence in Literary Achievement."

Aidan was beside himself with joy, and Laura gave her father a tearful hug.

"Liam always wanted to prove to you that he was worthy of your respect."

"I've always believed in him," Aidan replied with conviction.

Liam took the podium and the crowd quieted, with the exception of a fellow student, who yelled out a song request. "*I Remember When!*" Many in the crowd laughed, and Liam smiled.

"It's funny you should request that song, because I can *Remember When* all of this was an intangible dream in the head of a stable boy in County Limerick. In a stroke of luck–fueled by divine destiny–Aidan and Laura Meegan came into my life, and the dream began to take hold, becoming a vision in the mind of a young artist."

The crowd was now listening intently, and Laura's tears could not be stilled.

"Today I look to so many special faces and heavenly places to give thanks for all that this young artist has created." Liam gazed skyward. "To my mother and father, who gave me the brush and palette, may they rest in peace. To Aidan Meegan, who gave me the easel and canvas, and the guidance to face the task. To Laura Meegan, the love of my life, who gave me the inspiration to take the first strokes, creating the brilliant spectrum of colors. To the Bianchi and Bailey families, who have given me strength and encouragement, lest I grow weary of holding the brush. And last, but certainly not least, to my professors at Trinity College, who have not only provided the frame in which to display the landscape of my life, but the light to shine upon it. I thank you all, from the bottom of my heart."

The crowd cheered wildly: a reaction much like Liam had heard before from music fans, but one which he never took for granted.

Hannah had arranged for a catered party at Dublin House for the graduates. Spirits were high, with everyone congratulating each other, including Peggy, who had earned high honors from the School of Law. The festivities were in full swing when Jon heard the doorbell rang and went to answer it.

"Congratulations!" Kelly cried as she stepped in and threw her arms around him.

Jon was taken by surprise. "I didn't know you were coming."

"I couldn't miss the graduation party for Danny–and Liam–and you."

"Peggy graduated too, you know."

"Oh, right. Anyway, haven't you missed me? Aren't you going to give me a real welcome?" She smiled seductively.

Jon gave her a quick hug but she suddenly kissed him– passionately.

Just starting to descend the stairs after checking on the baby, Peggy looked down to see Jon and Kelly in the moment. *I knew Jon wasn't over her.* Quickly retreating to the nursery, Peggy put her back to the door, shutting out the world. *How could I be so stupid to think he could love me the way he loves her?* Tears streamed down Peggy's cheeks.

Jon pulled back, stunned by Kelly's kiss.

"This won't work, Kelly. We can't go back to what we had. I've moved on."

She looked deeply into his eyes. "I know I've been foolish, and I'm here to apologize. Please try to remember how you felt. I still see desire in your eyes."

Jon looked away, stunned and confused, and then faced her again.

"Kelly, why are you doing this? It's taken me months to get over you."

She flashed an inviting smile at him, then lowered her eyes. "I could never get over you, my first love."

Danny came to the entryway. "Sis! I'm so glad you could make it." He gave Kelly a hug and led her into the living room. She looked back over her shoulder to see Jon still standing in disbelief.

A few minutes later Jon joined the others, but he felt disconnected from the party. The lively conversation and laughing seemed to be off in the distance.

"Jon... Earth to Jon." Jen laughed as she waved her hand in front of his face. "What's wrong with the life of the party? Are you still in shock that you graduated?"

"Oh no, it's not that. I've got... some other things on my mind."

Jen looked across the room at Kelly and then back at her brother. "Uh huh. I bet you do." She squeezed his hand and gave it a tug. "C'mon–it's your party, too."

Jon tipped his head to the side. "Yeah, maybe I'll get a beer."

After filling a mug he went to the center of the room. "Excuse me! Could I have everyone's attention, please?"

Liam looked a little tipsy as he turned around. "Oh! So you really are here."

"Laura," Jon teased, "would you please silence this hooligan so I can make a toast?" Laura laughed while she reached up to put her hand over Liam's mouth.

"This may be a little... unconventional," Jon began, "but I'd like you to raise your glasses to The Three Musketeers." Aidan and Robert looked at each other in bewilderment. Jon continued. "Liam, Danny, and myself, who fought the battles–sometimes with each other–but who emerged victorious against the odds." There were cheers and laughter, but Jon raised his hand.

"We must also remember the Fourth Musketeer, Peggy, who fought the most courageous battles." He looked around the room, as did the others. "Where is she?"

Hannah answered. "She went upstairs earlier to tend to the baby."

Jon looked disappointed. "Well, I'd better finish this now, while we're all still standing. To The Four Musketeers!"

"Here, here!" Liam cried. "Especially to The Fourth Musketeer, whose wizardry in court saved my *arse!*" Everyone cheered and lifted their glasses.

Before too long everyone was going to bed–except Kelly, who had waited to catch Jon alone.

"Jon, you've avoided me all evening. Are you mad at me?"

"I'm not sure how I feel."

"Well, I have a flight out tonight, and I won't see you again until Danny and Jen's wedding next week. I want you to know I do love you and I always have. We can work things out. Please think it over." She gave him a quick kiss and headed out the door.

Jon was frozen with uncertainty. *Dear God, why now? I want to be with Peggy and Mickey. They're the ones I feel centered with.* He rubbed his head. *I haven't seen Peggy for hours.*

He tapped on Peggy's door and softly called her name.

She didn't answer as she sat motionless in the rocking chair, staring out. *I can't talk to Jon now.*

The others chatted at breakfast while Peggy silently sipped her coffee, wondering if and when Jon was going to tell her about the kiss.

In Jon's mind nothing had happened, so he said nothing. He was still trying to sort things out.

Molly studied him as she poured his coffee. "It was great to see Kelly last night."

Jon glanced at Peggy, who turned away. He decided to change the subject.

"Danny, your whole family is proud of you. You did it, man!" Jon raised his coffee cup and the others cheered.

Peggy stood up. "Good job, Danny. Well, I've got to excuse myself and get Mickey ready for his bath."

"Do you want any help?" Jon asked.

"No, thank you. I'm in a hurry this morning and you play with him too much."

Catherine picked up on Peggy's coolness and decided to follow her upstairs.

"Peggy, is everything all right?"

"I thought it was, but last night... after seeing Jon and Kelly together again...." Tears came to her eyes. "I don't think it's wise for me to tell Jon about Mickey. Jon needs to decide where his heart is. Unfortunately, we can't choose who we love."

"I understand how you feel, but Jon loves you and Mickey. I just know it."

Peggy wasn't convinced. "I've made so many mistakes. For Mickey's sake I have to be sure about this."

Catherine hugged her and left the room.

The wedding was only a few days away, and everyone had left Dublin for Tuscany. Peggy was staying behind because Mickey had a cold. Jon insisted on waiting for them.

"You'd better go on without us," Peggy said as she cuddled the little one. "Mickey can't seem to get over this congestion, and flying will be hard on his ears."

"Well, I'll stay here with you."

"Nonsense! It's your sister's big day and you're in the wedding party."

"Peggy Girl, I don't feel right leaving you two alone."

"If you don't go, I will feel responsible for ruining Jen and Danny's wedding. Now go! Mickey and I will be fine."

Jon moved in closer to give her a kiss, but Peggy subtly avoided it by turning slightly. He simply said, "I'll miss you."

"We'll miss you, too."

The long hours alone on the flight gave Jon plenty of time to think things over, but not arrive at any solution to his dilemma. After a long cab ride from the airport, he finally arrived at the villa to find a bustle of activity, with people setting up tables and chairs, and decorating anything that stood still. He overheard his mother mention that Kelly was soon to arrive, and that was all Jon needed to quickly make himself useful.

"Is there anything I can help with, Father?"

"Yes, son, you and Liam can take the van and go pick up the champagne. The delivery man is apparently way behind schedule, and I want to get it on ice right away."

Jon grabbed the keys and slipped out the back door, narrowing avoiding Kelly, who was just arriving by taxi.

Liam immediately sensed Jon's stress. "All right, what's on your mind?" Jon shrugged his shoulders. "You're not nervous about Jen's wedding; it's something else. I'm here now if you want to talk."

"I guess you know me better than I know myself. I wish I could figure this out."

Liam looked at him quizzically. "You mean, with Peggy?"

"No, she's wonderful and I love her and Mickey. It's Kelly."

Liam nodded. "Hmmm. Let's see, she wants you back now?"

Jon looked surprised. "You know about that?"

"Well, Molly told us that Kelly's boyfriend dumped her. I figured she might realize what a good thing she'd had with you."

"I should have known I was being used."

"Don't get me wrong, Jon. I'm sure she cares about you very much. Who's to say… it could work out."

"What about my feelings for Peggy and Mickey? I really do love them."

Liam put a hand on Jon's shoulder. "Do you truly love Kelly?"

"I truly don't know. When she kissed me I could feel all the old emotions stirring. But I don't trust her and… I don't feel safe with her."

"Jon, you know I wouldn't try to tell you what to do. But I will say you need to step back and look at the whole picture. Forget the passion of the moment. This decision could affect the rest of your life."

Jon said no more about it until the return trip from the winery.

"I know in my heart Peggy has always been important to me. Ever since we spent the night stranded in the snowstorm, we've had a special bond. It's been a deep friendship, but now it's become... a warmth; comfortable and secure. I trust her and believe she'll always be there for me. I want to be there for her. We share so many things, and now there's Mickey to love."

When they arrived back at the villa Liam gave Jon a hug. "I can see you've had a lot of clear thinking about Peggy. You've always said you wanted what Laura and I have. Well, the love between Laura and I started with friendship, comfort, trust and believing we would always be there for each other."

"Liam, my guru. I love you, man!"

The cathedral in the Tuscan village provided a magnificent setting for the wedding. Danny stood nervously at the altar with his best man, Liam, and groomsman, Jon, at his side. The maid of honor, Laura, and bridesmaid, Kelly, were in their places. The organ began to play, and Robert Bianchi lovingly kissed his daughter.

"Jennifer, your mother and I are so proud of you. You have grown up to be a beautiful woman. We love you and Danny very much."

When Danny first caught sight of Jen, his heart fluttered with a newfound intensity, fueled by the memories they had created together. The joy he felt at that moment seemed to eradicate any and all of the old doubts: the feeling that her family was above his, the angst when she still lived with them across the Atlantic, and the fear that she would never come back to him.

Jen was radiant in her elegant lace gown and veil that gently covered her face. Danny had to suppress the urge to run to her, to scoop her up and smother her with kisses. He knew the ceremony was to be traditional Catholic with a full mass, and it would be a very long time before they were together in the way he wanted.

As expected, everything was fairly regimented, spoken mostly in Latin, which Danny couldn't tell from Italian. Bride and groom dutifully participated, squeezing each other's hands when they could and stealing a smile with their eyes at each other often.

Finally the conclusion was drawing near, and the priest lightened things up with his pronouncement in English.

"You may kiss your bride!"

There was a raucous applause as Danny lifted Jen's veil and gave her a passionate kiss. Then he picked her up in his arms, presenting her to the congregation like a trophy. "I accept with honor the blessing of being Jen's faithful and loving husband for as long as I live." He kissed her again and gently placed her alongside him. The two blissfully strolled down the aisle together as husband and wife.

Elizabeth Bailey was beside herself with emotion. Catherine patted her arm.

"We have two of the most wonderful children, and they are now united. Robert and I couldn't be happier. Danny is like a son to us."

Elizabeth dried her eyes. "You've been so kind to our Danny. Sean and I feel blessed to have Jen in our family." Elizabeth watched as Jon escorted Kelly out through the front doors of the church. "I wonder if we will be blessed again by Jon and Kelly."

Catherine bit her lip. "Oh, you never know what's in store for the future."

Jon had decided to be polite to Kelly for Danny and Jen's sake. He would be the perfect groomsman, participating in all the traditions of wedding and reception.

The afternoon had slipped into evening, with everyone dancing on the terrace of the villa in the balmy Tuscan sea breeze. Jon was indulging in more than his share of the champagne, trying to ease his mind, but it only added to his uncertainty.

With moonlight gently illuminating her rose-colored gown, Kelly was stunning. They danced together under the stars, and she seemed to melt into Jon's arms. Although he was tempted by her closeness, a little voice was warning him not to go too far.

Every move Kelly made seemed to stir Jon's emotions. She danced closer and spoke softly into his ear, recalling a line from one of Liam's songs. "*Falling stars whisper secrets to the wind.* Jon, this is such a magical night for me. Can we go somewhere to be alone?"

Kelly didn't wait for an answer. She took Jon by the hand and led him to her room, locking the door. She gazed into his eyes as she slowly removed his tie.

"Jon, I hurt you and I'll never forgive myself. But do you think you can still love me?" She kissed him passionately. He did not resist at first, but then pulled back.

"Kelly, I care about you. But we can never be like we were."

"Jon, let's make this a night to remember. Make love to me. It's what we've both wanted for so long now." She pulled him in closer.

Jon stood motionless. *After all the nights I've dreamed of this–of her–and now she wants me. What's wrong with me?*

Kelly reached to unbutton his shirt, but Jon grabbed her hands. Something deep in his soul chilled him to the bone. "It's too late–it's over, and it has been for a long time. I can't explain it, but all that's left are old feelings. There's nothing to build on. I'm sorry if I gave you false hope, but I'd be fooling myself if I thought we could make it work."

"Jon, you can't mean it!"

"Oh, I mean every word I say, and I think you should be honest with yourself, too. Maybe you're just coming back to me on the rebound."

Jon grabbed his jacket and tie and exited the room. Back on the terrace, he walked up to Liam and patted him on the shoulder.

"You'd be proud of me, my guru friend." Jon smiled confidently and walked over to the bar, not waiting for Liam's response.

Laura looked at Liam curiously. "What is he talking about?"

Liam smiled, having seen Jon leave the terrace with Kelly. "I think Jon has finally found what he's been looking for. My guess is she's back in Dublin."

"If you're talking about Peggy, I'm all for it. They both deserve love and happiness. I was really beginning to worry that Kelly was back in the picture."

"Oh, she was in the picture, but now she's fading into the shadows."

Their focus soon shifted to Jen and Danny, who were saying their goodbyes, leaving for a honeymoon in Capri.

Most of the guests were flying back to Ireland the next morning, but Jon decided to stay an extra day to talk with his parents.

"Father, Mother, I've made a decision. I'm not asking your permission, but I would like your blessing." Robert raised his eyebrows, while Catherine bit her lip. Jon cleared his throat and continued. "You've probably noticed how close Peggy and I have become. And Little Mickey... he lights up my heart. Anyway, I'm going to Dublin tomorrow to ask Peggy to marry me."

"Congratulations!" Robert broke into a smile and hugged his son. "She's a wonderful girl, and you know we're crazy about the baby."

Catherine was in tears, and Jon put his arms around her. "Please don't be upset."

"I'm happy for you, Jon. I'm just overwhelmed that both my children are all grown up! Jennifer just got married– and now you, too."

"Well, that is if she agrees to marry me."

"Oh, I'm sure she'll agree," Catherine smiled. "And Little Mickey will have his father–a father."

"I can't tell you how much it means to me to have your blessing." Jon embraced his parents. "I'm headed to town right now to that special jewelry store, Antonetti's."

"Ahhhh," Catherine replied. "Only the best for Peggy."

Jon left the villa with a smile on his face and a spring in his step.

Robert faced his wife. "Peggy hasn't told him yet, has she?"

"No, and I almost slipped up. This will all be so much easier when it's out in the open and we can claim our grandson to the world."

Peggy was preparing herself for the worst. Jon had not called and the wedding was over. *He must be back with Kelly now.*

From the nursery Peggy thought she heard the front door open. She wondered if it was Molly and Brent, but she heard no voices. Peggy tucked the baby in for the night and decided to go downstairs. There was a light on in the kitchen and she heard running water. Peggy opened the door, and much to her surprise, there was Jon, arranging a beautiful bouquet of exotic flowers.

"Peggy Girl! I've come bearing gifts. The flowers are for you, and the package is for Mickey."

"Thank you." Peggy's heart was pounding. She tilted her head to the side. "How was the wedding?"

"Jen made a beautiful bride, and Danny was floating on cloud nine. But I wished you and Mickey could have been there."

She looked at him cautiously. "How did the rest of the wedding go?"

He took her into his arms. "Do you mean, how did things go with Kelly?"

Peggy blushed. "Well... yes."

"Honey, I'm over her. She's part of my past now. You and Mickey are my future." He pulled her in for a tender kiss.

Peggy wanted to give in, but she was still guarded. "Jon, please don't say the words unless you mean it."

He pulled a small box out of his pocket and knelt down before her. Slowly he opened the lid, revealing a stunning emerald-cut diamond ring. Peggy gasped, putting her hand over her mouth.

"Peggy Girl, I would honored to be your husband, and Mickey's father, if you'll have me."

Peggy was sobbing. "Oh, Jon, we would love to marry you." He rose up to place the ring on her finger, then reached up to gently wipe her tears away. She took his hand and placed it over her heart. "I love you, Jon–I've always loved you." He kissed her, tenderly at first, then passionately. They held each other in silence.

"Honey, I want to marry you right away. Mickey will be talking soon, and I don't want to be Uncle Jon. I want to be his father."

Peggy looked into Jon's eyes. "You never were Uncle Jon. Mickey is your son."

Jon hesitated. "What, exactly... do you mean?"

"Don't you remember our pity party, after I found out Garrett had cheated on me and you were rejected by Kelly?"

Jon rubbed his head. "I think I can still feel that hangover."

"Yes, you were very drunk, and I wasn't far behind you. I'm not proud of what happened, but I'm very grateful for the results." Jon raised an eyebrow. "Jon, we had unprotected sex that night. Mickey is your son."

Jon sank down on the kitchen chair, putting his head into his hands. "Oh, my God. I thought I was having a fantasy about us making love that night. And when you never said anything, I was sure it was my overactive imagination."

"Oh, my God!" Peggy repeated. "I was waiting for *you* to say something. I assumed you were too drunk to remember anything."

Jon put his arm around her waist and pulled her into him. "This is more than I could have ever prayed for. I've felt like Mickey was my own son from the moment he was born."

"I'm sorry I didn't tell you sooner. I didn't want you to feel obligated to us when you were... in love with someone else."

"Peggy Girl, it's been you for years and you know it. We've always been there for each other. I just never thought you would go for me."

She laughed. "I've always wanted you, along with thousands of other girls. But I was happy to be your best friend." She stroked his hair. "I can't believe this is happening. Will you pinch me so I know this not a dream?"

"How about another kiss instead," he replied, standing up.

"My parents are going to be so thrilled about Mickey!" Jon said after the kiss. "They already love him."

A satisfied smile came to Peggy's face. "They already know. Your mother figured it out months ago. I made her promise not to tell."

Jon's jaw dropped. "No wonder they were so happy when I announced I was going to ask you to marry me." He shook his head in disbelief. "This has been some day…."

Peggy took his hand. "Would you like to go visit your son?"

Jon lifted his head up high with pride. "Absolutely."

They went upstairs and gazed lovingly at their sleeping child.

"He looks just like you," Peggy whispered as she stroked Mickey's head. "He looks like an angel."

"We better get married tomorrow," Jon said suddenly, "before I wake up from this dream and find you've changed your mind."

"That won't happen, and I'm anxious too. Of course we have to tell Mother and Aidan first."

"Of course. Tomorrow we'll go to Montrose and tell the world."

Peggy laughed softly. "I hope Mother doesn't have a heart attack. I always seem to be shocking her."

"Come on, now. She can't still believe Mick is the father?"

"I'm not sure what she thinks. Even if she thought Garrett was the father, she would never admit it. She loves Mickey, and it would upset her to think his father was a commoner."

"Wait till she finds out his father is a wild American rock star, and her grandson may grow up to be just like him." Peggy shook her head, smiling as she rolled her eyes.

"We should get some sleep, tomorrow will be a big day," she sighed.

With his most charming smile, Jon looked deeply into her eyes. "I don't want to spend one more night without you. Can I stay?"

As if to shut out the world, Peggy closed the door. She turned to face Jon, and a gleam came to her eye.

"If you wake him, you get up with him."

# ᴄ⁓Chapter Twenty-Seven⁓ᴐ

I ris answered the phone when Peggy called, then put the receiver down to go find Laura. She'd been asked to simply tell Laura there was a call for her and not announce who was on the line. Laura got up from the breakfast table, shrugged and left the room to take the call.

"Hi Laura! It's Peggy."

"Hello, big sister, how are things in Dublin?'

"Funny you should ask," Peggy replied coyly. "Everything's brilliant! Jon and I have some news, and we're driving to Montrose today to tell Mother and Aidan, but I wanted you and Liam to know first."

"Hmmm," Laura mused, "let's see... you and Jon finally got together?"

"Well, yes! I wasn't sure how much you suspected, but yes! But don't tell the others just yet, only Liam."

"Mum's the word."

"Thanks. And there's a bit more to the story as well, also for your ears only."

"More?" Laura asked. "What could be more exciting than that?"

"Well…" Peggy proceeded to tell her about the pity party with Jon that turned to a night of passion; and the stark contrast between that and the unconsummated marriage she'd had with Mick.

"You mean…."

"Yes, Laura, Mickey is Jon's son." Laura was instantly laughing through tears of joy. Peggy suggested Laura dry her tears, reminding her to conceal her emotions from the others, and then put Hannah on the phone.

Peggy only told her mother that she would be at Montrose in a few hours and that she had some important news. She would say nothing more. Hannah asked for something more specific, but Peggy would reveal nothing, saying it was best told in person.

For hours Hannah sat in the living room trying to read the paper, but found herself staring at the same paragraph. She soon gave in to worry, nervously wringing her hands as she sat and waited for Peggy's arrival. She quickly stood up when her husband entered the room.

"Aidan, I just know this is going to be bad news."

He reached for a section of the newspaper. "Now Hannah, Peggy said she was coming today to give you some news. Why do you assume it's bad?"

She frowned. "You know Peggy has always done things her way… and look where she has ended up."

Aidan rubbed his chin. "Let me see… she has graduated from law school with top honors while caring for her baby. She's bright, beautiful and always a pleasure to be around." Aidan faced Hannah deliberately. "In my book she's done brilliantly."

Hannah shook her head in dismay. "You always take her side."

"My dear, when it comes to your children, there should never be any sides. You can only hope to be a part of their lives. Peggy has always included you, and that's more than I can say for your other daughter. Whatever news Peggy has for us, we should feel honored she wants to share it."

Rather than admit Aidan could be right, Hannah chose to look out the window and nervously pace. When she saw the car coming up the driveway she sat next to him, taking his hand.

❧

Laura had told Liam the story, and he was pleasantly surprised. He chose to wait with her on the front porch for the arrival of what he would now think of as the "new family" at Montrose Manor.

The moment they drove up Liam was on his feet to meet them at the car. He gave Jon a bear hug and Peggy a kiss on the cheek. Laura gave Jon a hug then gently took Mickey from Peggy.

"Come to Aunt Laura. If it's okay with your mother, I've got some kittens to show you." The boy cooed at her and gleefully accepted.

"That's a good idea," Peggy said, giving her sister a quick hug. "Jon and I need to have that talk with Mother and Aidan anyway."

Laura stopped to study Jon's face for a moment, and then Mickey's. She then gave Jon a wink and a smile, while Liam patted him on the back.

Jon leaned into Laura and whispered softly. "This is a summer for weddings."

Laura almost cried out but caught herself. "We'll be at the Callahans' with Mickey and the new kittens. ' Bye, you two!"

Peggy and Jon walked together into the living room.

"Mother, Aidan, I've got a couple of things to tell you, and I hope you'll be happy for me–for us." She smiled at Jon and took his hand. "We're getting married."

Hannah stifled her shock and smiled. "That is lovely news, dear. Jon, you will make a wonderful father for Little Mickey."

"Mother, he is Mickey's father. Haven't you noticed how much they look alike?"

Hannah gasped. "Are you telling me you and Jon have been... lovers?"

Peggy and Jon smiled at each other before she answered. "It's a long story, but we had... a special night together. There was a lot of compassion, and some drinking. The truth is, Jon and I have always been close, but he didn't know Mickey was his."

Aidan stood up to shake Jon's hand and then he hugged his stepdaughter. "I'm happy for you both. Of course you're welcome to get married here on the estate, and we'll do all we can to help out."

Hannah was still in shock. "Mickey is not... Mick's child?"

"Mother, Mick is gay. We never slept together."

"Oh, good Lord! Why did you marry him?"

"I knew you would be upset that I was an unwed mother, so I decided on what I thought at the time was a sensible solution. Besides, it looked like Jon was getting back together with Kelly, so I didn't want to tell him it was his child. I couldn't ruin his life, too."

By now Hannah had tears running down her cheeks, and Aidan put his arm around her. "Peggy, why don't you go share your news with the others and give your mother a chance to compose herself."

"Thanks, Aidan," Jon said. "We'll be at the Callahans'." He took Peggy's hand and they left the room.

Aidan passed his handkerchief to his wife. "Peggy and Jon have had a wonderful relationship for years. It's obvious to me it has grown into a strong love. I couldn't be happier that Jon is Mickey's father. I suggest you count your blessings. Your daughter loves you and wants your approval."

Hannah sobbed. "She does have my approval. I feel terrible that my daughter would marry someone she did not love because she was afraid to tell me the truth. What kind of mother have I been?"

"You must have done something right. She keeps looking for your approval."

Hannah dabbed her tears with the hankie. "I am happy for her and Jon. I have come to care a great deal for him. I must admit it took awhile for me to get used to his wild behavior, but he has grown up to be a responsible young man."

"Good—that's just what you need to tell them. Shall we go to the Callahans'?"

Jon laughed as they walked along the river to the Callahan cottage, which was the nearest to the manor. "Honey, I think that actually went well, but I have to admit the expression on Hannah's face was priceless. Wait until she comes to the realization that Mickey may grow up to be just like me."

"It was a shock to her," Peggy laughed. "But Aidan seems to be happy for us."

Jon nodded. "Aidan has always been great. He's one of the most fair-minded people I've ever known."

"Amen to that!"

Mrs. Callahan's exuberance at the arrival of Peggy and Jon was a dead giveaway that Laura had already told her the news about their engagement. The head gardener's wife hugged them both and invited them in. They turned to see Mickey gently holding a kitten, with Laura's help.

Peggy sneezed. "Dear Lord! I hope Mickey doesn't have my allergies."

Jon chuckled. "C'mon, our son needs at least a couple of kittens and a dog."

Peggy poked him in the ribs. "Where am I supposed to live?"

Liam laughed and then jumped up from where he'd been sitting. He wrapped his arms around Peggy and Jon at the same time. "I guess it's official now, you two are getting married."

Jon nodded excitedly. "I can't wait for us to be a family. And now you'll be my... stepbrother-in-law?" Jon scratched his head.

"You've always been like a brother to me, and now you really will be."

"I like that! My brother, will you be my best man?"

"And I want my sister, Laura, to be my maid of honor," Peggy added.

Laura proudly answered for both of them. "We'd be honored."

Peggy smiled and embraced Laura, but then stepped back. "I hope you don't mind, but we want to get married now–well, as soon as Jen and Danny are home."

Laura smiled. "Of course! The sooner the better. God knows you've been patient enough."

Mr. Callahan got up from his easy chair. "Miss Peggy, the flowers are all abloom! I can have plenty for your weddin'."

"Thank you very much." Peggy picked up her son and twirled around. "We're getting married next week! I feel like life couldn't get much better."

There was a knock on the door and Aidan poked his head in. "May we come in and join the celebration?"

"Yes, do!" Mrs. Callahan replied.

Hannah reached for her daughter, then Jon. "You took me by surprise, but I want you to know I am happy. Peggy, can we please have a nice wedding here at the manor?"

"Only if you can put it together in a week."

"One week!" Hannah gasped. "Good Lord! I will need more time than that."

"One week," Jon said firmly. "I think we've already waited too long." He kissed Mickey. "We need to be a family as soon as possible."

Mickey hugged his father and then pointed at the frolicking kittens. "Kitty!"

Jon smiled. "You can have whatever you want, my son."

Peggy rolled her eyes and laughed. "It is easy to see who's going to be the soft touch in this family. Jon, he's too young for a kitten."

Jon gave her his most charming smile. "Oh Ma', pleeease?"

"Kitty!" Little Mickey said, giving her the same smile.

Everyone laughed, including Hannah. "Peggy, I think you will have your hands full with the two of them."

Peggy threw her arms up. "I don't stand a chance with my guys ganging up on me. I guess I need a little girl to even things out." She winked at Jon.

"Peggy, please tell me you are not...."

"No, Mother, but Jon and I would like another child as soon as possible, to be close in age to Mickey."

Hannah blushed. "Peggy, can we please get through this wedding first?"

Jon winked at Hannah. "Come on, wouldn't you love a little granddaughter to fuss over?"

"Of course, but one thing at a time, please. Aidan, I think I need to go back to the manor and rest. This day has been overwhelming."

Jon had agreed to Peggy's wishes that their marriage be non-secular. He wanted things to move right along anyway, as did his parents, so convincing them to deviate from a traditional Catholic ceremony was not difficult.

Peggy had made the arrangements for a judge to marry them on the patio overlooking the river. Everything else was up to Hannah, and it was amazing what she was able to put together in such a short time.

The afternoon of their nuptials couldn't have been lovelier. A gentle breeze caressed Peggy's long auburn hair, crowned with a wreath of yellow flowers that matched the ribbons cascading down her back. In her off-the-shoulders cream chiffon dress, Peggy looked like the princess out of a fairy tale. Jon, every bit the Prince Charming, wore his new black Armani suit with a cream-colored ruffled shirt.

The ceremony was short but sweet, with bride and groom speaking vows they had written themselves.

At the conclusion the judge had hardly begun to pronounce them husband and wife when Jon gave Peggy a passionate kiss, to the delight of everyone. Just then Mickey jumped off Hannah's lap and ran to join the embrace.

The judge smiled. "As I was saying, I would like to present Mr. and Mrs. Jon Bianchi–and son!"

Applause filled the air and Jon scooped Mickey into his arms.

For the first dance, Liam played his acoustic guitar while singing a love song he'd written just for Jon and Peggy. The newlyweds danced to the waltz as if they'd rehearsed it together a hundred times. The lyrics told the story of a beautiful maiden lost in the forest who was rescued from the darkness by a handsome prince. Of course, they married and lived happily ever after.

Laura and Mickey, along with Little Philip and Beth, blew bubbles while the bride and groom gracefully spun around.

Liam made the first toast of the intimate reception.

*Always remember to forget*

*The things that made you sad.*

*But never forget to remember*

*The things that made you glad.*

*Always remember to forget*

*The friends that proved untrue.*

*But never forget to remember*

*Those that have stuck by you.*

"You've always stuck by each other through sad times and glad times. May there be only glad times. For the truest of friends. Sláinte to my brother and sister."

---

Robert followed with a heart-warming welcome. "And now the Bianchi and Meegan families are officially joined together." Everyone cheered.

---

There was no delay in getting to the next phase of things: the honeymoon. Having Robert and Catherine accompany them to Italy was the natural solution, and a blessing. The grandparents helped with Little Mickey during the traveling and at the villa. The newlyweds were able to spend time alone together, taking day trips to the village, the foothills of Tuscany, and on one balmy evening, the yacht harbor.

Jon never actually took out the Bianchi sailboat, instead opting for a candlelit dinner aboard her with his new wife. After the meal they gazed out over the bay, enjoying the solitude. Jon finally spoke.

"Out there is where it all happened."

Although she hadn't been with them, Peggy knew he was talking about the day an appendicitis attack had stricken Laura when they were out for an afternoon cruise for Danny's birthday nearly four years ago. She gently stroked Jon's arm.

"The way I heard it, your skills as a sailor, and a communicator with the local Coast Guard, saved the day."

"Thanks, honey. But the truth is, it was a team effort. Even Danny got a crash course in seamanship that day. I'm so glad Laura came through it okay. We all learned a lot then, and we bonded closer than most families ever do."

She leaned into him. "I've got a feeling this new family is going to be pretty close." Jon gave her a tender kiss, and they both turned to watch an incredible sunset.

In just the few short days that Mickey spent time with his new grandparents, they had become inseparable. In fact, the child had become so attached that he cried as much as his grandmother when it was time to return to Ireland.

Just days after the newlyweds got back to Dublin, Second Wind began a six-week United Kingdom concert tour to promote the new album, *Storm*. European dates were scheduled for late fall. Unwilling to be separated from his new family, Jon had convinced Peggy to go on the road with the band and study for the bar during the tour. Catherine would join them later and help out with Mickey.

359

Although Patrick had grown accustomed to not having Liam and Danny around to help with things at Montrose barn, he really found himself in a jam one morning as he pulled out the antique wedding carriage. He'd guessed there would be some repainting, along with leather conditioning, but did not expect to find such a level of disrepair in the chassis of the carriage that had not been used in quite some time. Some of the steel parts had rusted, and several bolts were loosening.

With Laura and Liam's wedding only weeks away, Patrick did not want to take a chance on sending the carriage out for restoration in Dublin. He had an idea, but he had to run it by Aidan first. He telephoned his boss, asking him to come down to the barn at his earliest convenience. Aidan said he was ready for a break from looking at business projections and would be right down.

After crouching down to look at the rust, Aidan stood up and spoke. "It never ceases to amaze me how our moist air on the Emerald Isle can eat away at metal."

Patrick scratched his head nervously. "I feel a bit of a fool for not havin' pulled the carriage out sooner for a once-over."

Aidan shrugged. "Don't be too hard on yourself, Patrick. You've had plenty on your plate with the boys gone at Trinity and on the road with their band."

"Well, thank you for sayin' so, sir. And even though we don't have time to send her out, it shouldn't put us in a bind. There's a guy from Galway–he came to another farm I worked at–and he's got a repair shop on wheels, you might say. I think he could do all the work right here. And word is he's nearby re-workin' carriages at another farm."

Aidan raised his eyebrows. "Is he a… traveler?"

"Well, yes, sir, he is–a traditional tinker, with a wagon and all–and he's got all the parts with him, and a forge. But best of all, he's got experience."

A small tinge of doubt crept into Aidan's mind, but he didn't give in to it. "I think that's a fine idea, Patrick. Go ahead and put out the feelers, and let's get this guy here as soon as possible."

"Will do," Patrick replied, somewhat relieved.

◦◦◦

The concerts were quickly sold out, thanks to the ever-growing fan base. Together Jon and Robert exercised their creative talents as the sets and special effects became more elaborate. It came to be known as *The Storm Tour*.

The last song of each show ended with the set turning dark and the impression of lightning crashing across the backdrop. A specially illuminated sheer curtain gave the effect of rain coming down. Laura had programmed her new DX-7 synthesizer with the sounds of lightning cracking and rain pounding. The others all fell into step, Danny with a thundering arpeggio on the bass, Jen with a sustained roll on the big floor tom using mallets, and Jon with a haunting broken chord. Liam then came in with the highest note his vocal chords could produce. The finish was dramatic beyond anything the fans had ever seen.

◦◦◦

The morning following the Webley Stadium performance, the *London Times* called the show "uniquely theatrical and way ahead of its time." The major music and publicity magazines featured articles with vivid photos of the band. While there were obvious rewards in promoting record sales, it came with a price: the invasion of privacy.

The record producer had arranged for an exclusive story with *Rock n Roll* magazine to cover Laura and Liam's wedding. As bandleader, Jon had authorized it.

Liam was furious. "Jon, how could you take the most important day of our lives and turn it into a media circus?"

"Calm down, it won't be a circus. They've promised just one photographer and one reporter. And guess who the reporter is?"

"I'm not in the mood for games."

Laura spoke up. "Jon, you know this wedding has already gotten out of control. Hannah has invited over five hundred guests. We don't even know half of them."

Jon put his arm around her. "It has become a big event, and it'll be covered by reporters, no matter what. I say let someone cover it who we know and trust."

Liam sighed. "Jon's right, there's no stopping the press. Now who is this mysterious reporter?"

"The one and only, our favorite *Dublin Times* reporter, Eoin McKee! He was offered a job working for *Rock n Roll* a few months ago. Since he personally knows us and he's a hometown boy, he got the job covering the wedding."

"He's always been good to us," Laura remarked. "And the magazine is professional. We probably won't even notice them."

Liam sighed. "All right, whatever you want."

# Chapter Twenty-Eight

L ooking like a multi-colored barrel on wheels, the unusual wagon, pulled by two Gypsy Vanner horses, pulled off the road and up the drive to Montrose. The driver, a lean man in his late forties, skillfully steered the rig to an open area alongside the tractor barn. Patrick had heard the jingling of the harness and walked out of the main barn to greet him.

"Welcome to Montrose," he said cheerily. "Don't know if you remember me, I'm Patrick O'Brogan."

The man set his reins and nimbly jumped down to extend his hand. "Aye, but it's been some years back. Bartley Doyle of Galway, and this be me son, Lunny."

Patrick felt calluses on the man's muscular hand. "Pleased to have you. And thanks for makin' the journey with all your gear and such."

"Don't go anywhere without it,' he chuckled.

Patrick eyed the intricately crafted harness, and noticed the perspiration on the Vanners. "If you need to unhitch and rest your horses, you're welcome to put them in the corral just over there. We'll have water and feed for them as well."

"Thank ye for that," Doyle replied, and nodded towards the wedding carriage. "Looks like ya got a pretty lass over there that needs some lookin' after. We'll know in a few minutes just how much."

"Looks like we've got the right men on it." Patrick winked at the teenager and the boy smiled. "Well, I'll leave ya to it. Oh, and the missus says she's got some scones and jam for you whenever you want."

"Thanks to ye. Maybe a bit later."

The younger Doyle went straight to the back of the wagon–called a *vardo* in some regions–and removed a wooden table with a sheet metal top, an anvil and several tool boxes. Doyle senior grabbed a small wooden mallet and walked over to the carriage to begin his inspection. Every few seconds he would tap two or three times on part of the frame or wheel while listening intently. After a few minutes he gestured to his son to unhitch the horses. He knew they'd be awhile.

Hannah gasped. "What on Earth?" She was just returning in the limousine from a meeting she'd had with the wedding caterer and couldn't help but notice the wagon parked over by the barn. Instead of seeing a couple of skilled men working their craft, her mind's eye saw a full gypsy caravan with thieves and hooligans.

The moment the driver stopped the car in front of the manor, Hannah marched up the steps and straight into Aidan's office.

"Since when did we start inviting gypsies onto the property?"

Aidan looked up from his spreadsheet. "Since we found the best tinsmiths out of Galway!" He had guessed Hannah would react this way and was more than a little amused with her protest. "Not to worry, dear, I haven't invited them to the wedding."

Hannah shook her head, uncharmed by his humor. "Well, I hope they're not spending the night!"

"Only if they have to order parts." A gleam came to his eye with the tease.

"Oh! You're impossible!" She turned and stormed out. Aidan simply chuckled.

The sun was low in the sky when the repairs were finally complete. Lunny was touching up paint on the wheels, much to Patrick's delight. "You fellows are very thorough," he commented. "You can't know how much I appreciate this. Young Laura Meegan's weddin' is the end of August, and now I can be sure I'll be drivin' a carriage that's not only sound, but also fittin' of a beautiful bride."

Bartley Doyle rubbed his chin. "Ah, yes, daughter of Fey, if memory serves."

Patrick raised his eyebrows. "I didn't know you knew any of the Meegan family."

"Well, not the Meegans," he replied. "But Maura we knew: Fey's mum. Just a minute." Bartley turned and walked to the front of his wagon, reaching up to pull out a small case from under the driver's seat. He returned with two brasses in his hand.

"These are the Claddagh symbols–Love, Loyalty, and Friendship–and young Lady Laura has a heritage that goes back quite a ways. If it pleases you, it would be my honor to affix these to the carriage."

Patrick held one of the brasses up to admire it. The setting sun danced off the heart, hands and crown, causing them to shine brightly as if they were gold. His first instinct was that he would have to run it by Lord Meegan, but an impulse took hold of him instead.

"I think Laura would be most honored to have these adorn her weddin' carriage."

He handed them back to Bartley, and within minutes the man had them securely fastened to the carriage, one each on either side.

"Very fine, indeed!" Patrick remarked. He reached into his pocket and pulled out a large roll of bills. "This is what you estimated, and then some. Courtesy of Lord Meegan."

Bartley's eyes widened. "Thank ye! And thank Lord Meegan for us as well." Then he furrowed his eyebrows. "Too bad Laura's grandmother can't be here for all this." But then a curious smile came to his face. "Well, we'd best be hitchin' up and on our way."

Patrick watched the wagon roll off into the darkness, the clip-clop of hooves signaling the end of a long but fruitful day. He thought about Doyle's mentioning of Maura and just shrugged his shoulders. His dinner was waiting up at the cottage.

Days had passed since the visit from the gypsies, and Hannah had more important things on her mind. She was busy planning what she was sure would be the event of the year: Laura and Liam's nuptials. Laura, knowing Second Wind would be home from touring only days before their wedding, called Hannah from the road.

"I know you're doing a brilliant job coordinating everything, but there are a few special things I want."

"Of course, dear. Lavender roses and white gardenias... and what else?"

"I want Little Philip and Little Mickey to be ring bearers and Beth to be the flower girl."

"Laura, it would be proper to have Olivia as flower girl. She is family."

"I suppose... but I hardly know her. Emily never brings her to visit. I feel closer to Beth. How about this: Beth and Olivia can do it together."

"That will be fine, dear."

<hr />

Laura and the others were amazed by the changes to Montrose when they returned from the Great Britain leg of the tour. The splendor of the upcoming event was laid out before their very eyes the moment they drove through the gates. What had once been pleasing landscaping was transformed into luscious and vivid opulence. Now embellishing the huge estate were enchanting garden paths, now leading to a newly built gazebo overlooking the river, which would serve as a dance pavilion with a stage for the orchestra.

Inside the manor, Hannah had work crews cleaning and polishing everything down to each crystal of the ornate chandeliers. Laura and Liam had known Hannah would make their wedding special, but this far exceeded their highest expectations. The majestic castle had come alive in all its grandeur.

Hannah greeted Laura and Liam at the entryway, proudly sweeping her arm across the room in a personal unveiling. "Well, what do you think?"

"It's unbelievable!" Laura said in awe. "This could be for a royal coronation."

"My dear, to the peoples of this county you *are* royalty. You and Liam deserve the best. Your father and I are proud. We want this to be the quintessence of all weddings."

Laura gave Hannah a warm hug, and then stepped back to smile at her.

"Thank you for everything. You are a master of your craft."

Hannah beamed. "Why thank you, dear."

The day before the wedding, the grand entry was brimming with wedding presents on display. Liam came down the stairs to find Laura looking over the gifts.

"I can't believe this," she sighed. "We've been opening these for days and they keep coming–not that I'm complaining or anything." She picked up one of the envelopes. "But I don't even know half these people."

Liam gently took the card from Laura's hand, placing it back on the gift box. "I never knew you were supposed to open them before the wedding, anyway. Let's get out of here for a while. We need some time alone–in our special place."

❧

At the barn they were greeted by Chloe and the children, who were decorating the wedding carriage, and Patrick, who was bathing Copper Crown, the warmblood horse she had helped to save from lameness, retirement–or worse–years earlier.

"He'll look like a royal coach horse tomorrow," Patrick said with pride.

Laura patted the gelding on the neck and spoke to him. "I'm so happy you'll be pulling our carriage. It's been my dream for a long time." Copper nuzzled Laura.

Patrick, do you need any help?" Liam asked.

Patrick winked. "You two go on your ride. Enjoy a little peace and quiet."

Laura walked over to admire the carriage, and the handiwork by the children. "Well, Beth and Little Philip, you're doing a fine job!"

"Thank you!" they sung out in unison. Laura stooped to give them each a hug, and when she stood up her eye was suddenly level with one of the new brasses installed by the Galway tinsmith.

"Oh! When did we get this? It's the Claddagh symbol!"

"It's a matchin' set, there's one on the other side," Patrick replied. "We had a tinsmith–a tinker, I guess some'd call him–here to repair the carriage while you were still on tour. It was his idea to put them on: said there was some meanin' in it for you."

"How did he–? Wait, was he from Galway?"

"As a matter of fact, he was. Seemed to have known who your mother was–I mean Fey."

Liam and Laura looked at each other at the same moment, but Liam wondered if any further conversation would only get Laura's hopes up.

Laura turned back to Patrick. "Did he... mention Maura?"

"Well, yes, but I didn't get the impression he knew anythin' else, like it was all in the past or something."

"Thanks, Patrick," Liam said. "The brasses look good. Laura, let's get Rose and Sky ready for that ride."

Laura was predictably quiet while they got their horses ready. Liam knew that if she had more to say on the subject, he would just try to be a good listener. With the wedding the next day she probably had enough on her mind already.

Although the path was the same one they'd always used, the journey seemed somehow different to them, even as they entered the cave.

"This will be the last time we come here as innocent children," Laura sighed.

Liam tipped his head back and laughed. "We haven't been innocent or children for quite some time." Laura pouted and Liam took her hand to give it a kiss. A wistful look came over him. "I know what you mean, though. Where did those young children go? Do you realize we've been coming here for ten years?"

Laura threw her arms around him. "I'll never forget our cherished moments in this haven. Most of all I'll remember your songs that mean so much to me."

Liam kissed her tenderly. "Sweetheart, without you, my life would be shades of gray, instead of the vibrant colors that surround me every day. I would be empty of all inspiration. You taught me friendship, trust, loyalty and passion. You gave me faith and confidence in myself. I owe it all to you."

She took his hand and they touched the inscription on the cave wall. *My Friend, My Life, My Love.* Laura smiled. "I remember when a handsome young poet wrote this for me. It will always be a treasure in my heart. From that day I knew I had been touched by my one and only love."

Liam pulled her close. "I knew we'd need this private time today to say what's in our hearts. With so many guests, tomorrow won't be as intimate as we wanted, but I want you to know all my prayers have been answered, and every dream has come true. The day has finally come when I'll be yours and you'll be mine."

She kissed him, then softly repeated the words. "My friend, my life, my love."

They rode their horses slowly through the woods on the return trip to the barn. A new chapter in their lives was about to begin, and even Sky and Rose seemed to know.

$$\sim$$

Everyone in the manor was aware of Emily's arrival from the moment she stepped through the door with her husband and daughter. Even Hannah was perturbed by the commotion her eldest daughter brought with her. In contrast, the other weekend guests were settling in peacefully.

Aidan's brother and sister-in-law, Aengus and Rachel, were delighted to be there, and none of the tension between the two brothers from years past was apparent. They counted themselves among family of the bride, and in keeping with Irish tradition, they had brought a special offering for Fiona to prepare for the rehearsal dinner.

$$\sim$$

The evening had begun in fine style with a relaxed atmosphere. Fiona and her assistant cook, Aine, had just carried in a large platter of roasted goose with apple-potato stuffing.

Aengus stood up, tapping his glass to get everyone's attention.

"Rachel and I are proud to have brought this addition to the menu," he cheerfully announced. The aroma filled the room as the man continued.

"This is what they call *aitin' the gander*, and Liam should know that this is where the expression *his goose is cooked* comes from." Everyone laughed.

"Now, all kidding aside," Aengus went on, "I have made some wrong judgments in my day, but I always try to admit it when I do. Liam, I'm afraid I judged you unfairly in the past. You have proven to be the best son my brother could ever have. I'm proud to call you my nephew." Aidan was surprised, but truly pleased.

Aengus smiled broadly at Laura and Liam. "Rachel and I have decided that after the New Year we'll retire and move to our manor at Lakes of Killarney. What does this mean to you? Well, you and Laura have been the only ones in the family to show interest in Feyland Stud. Therefore, our wedding present to you is our interest in the farm."

There were cheers from everyone as Laura and Liam, somewhat dazed, thanked Aengus and Rachel repeatedly. Aengus tapped on his glass again.

"I'd like to make a toast to the bride and groom:

*May your pockets be heavy and your heart be light,*

*May good luck pursue you each morning and night.*

*Sláinte!*

Aidan jumped up and hugged his brother while glasses continued to clink. "This is wonderful–more than generous. I can't believe you did this. What about your sons?"

Aengus shook his head. "They've never been interested in the horses, or living in Ireland, for that matter. Don't worry, they'll inherit plenty when we're dead and gone someday. I hope you and Hannah will visit us at the lakes. Maybe we can go fishing together, like the old days."

Aidan smiled. "I'd like that very much."

The chatter in the room soon died down and then Aidan placed two small packages on the table, asking Laura and Liam to open them. The first contained two gold coins.

Aidan spoke. "For any one of our American friends who might not know... the Irish tradition of Lucky Money calls for the bride and groom to exchange the special coins right after the wedding rings. If the coins clink as they are passed, the couple will be blessed with children."

The second package contained two handkerchiefs, one with the Meegan crest embroidered on it, the other a Magic Hankie.

Hannah smiled at Laura. "It was your mother's. Aidan tells me that Fey carried it on their wedding day, then it was stitched into your christening bonnet. I have made it back into a hankie for you to carry on your wedding day."

Laura gave Hannah a tearful hug. "Thank you so much. I love you for this." Hannah blinked back her own tears as Aidan looked on.

"Son, the hankie with the crest is for you. I carried it on that special day."

"I will carry it with pride," Liam proclaimed.

⧽

It was a heartfelt evening with everyone in good humor, except Emily. She wasn't the center of attention, and her spoiled child whined most of the night–which was no surprise to Laura and the others. On the other hand, Little Mickey never stopped laughing until he fell asleep. Hannah volunteered to help put him to bed.

⧽

She spoke candidly to her younger daughter once they were upstairs. "Peggy, dear, I am so delighted with Mickey. He's always so happy. Olivia, I am afraid to say, always seems to be miserable. I want you to know how very proud I am of the woman you have become, and I thank you for not giving up on me."

Peggy hugged her mother. "That means so much to me. We always want to be included in your life, and I believe the reverse is also true. I hope you have room for one more, though. We just found out we're expecting another baby in April."

Hannah was pleased. "I hope you have another just like this one."

With Peggy upstairs, Kelly took the opportunity to talk to Jon. "I'm happy for you and Peggy. Mickey looks just like you, and I can see he's the center of your world."

"That's true, and Peggy *is* my world. We're expecting another baby in the spring. Who would have ever figured–Jon the family man."

"I wish you the best, and I hope we can always be friends. I'm dating Chase, Brent's brother. We have a lot in common, and things seem to be going well."

Jon gave her a warm smile. "I'm happy for you."

A few minutes later Iris brought a package into the dining room. "It's for Laura and Liam. The delivery man said it was to be opened right away."

"Is it perishable?" Hannah asked. "Who is it from?"

Laura examined the package. "I don't see a return address."

"Let's open it and see," Liam suggested.

Laura unwrapped the ornate gift box. She carefully held up a pair of engraved Galway crystal champagne glasses. "Oh my! They're exquisite!"

Liam picked up the small card that was enclosed and read it aloud.

*The uniquely Irish Claddagh symbol means:*

*The crown, for loyalty–the hand, for friendship–the heart, for love.*

Added to the embossed script was a handwritten message, which Liam also read.

*And... a Gypsy's Blessing.*

Laura almost dropped the glasses, and Liam was sorry he'd read the last line aloud. He carefully took the crystal from her trembling hands.

"Sweetheart, they're lovely. We'll use them for toasting tomorrow."

Laura knew he was trying to cover for her shock. "Yes... they are lovely."

"What about the Waterford crystal glasses I bought for you?" Hannah asked.

"We'll use yours for the champagne toast and these for the Bunratty mead toast," Liam quickly replied.

Hannah was satisfied with his answer, but wondered about the gift. *Who could have sent them? The card was unsigned. And what was that part at the end?*

Aidan picked up the box. "Hmm... the Irish Claddagh symbol?" He looked at Laura curiously, but she did not meet his eye.

The dinner party went on for several hours before Liam finally had a chance to get Laura alone on the terrace. He'd noticed the melancholy look on her face.

"Sweetheart, I know what you're thinking, and maybe you're right. But if the glasses are from your grandmother, she must have her reasons for being... mysterious. We should respect her wishes and just accept her blessings."

"You're right. I won't let anything darken our special day tomorrow."

"Laura Lye, I want the world to shine for you on our wedding day. After tomorrow's events, saying goodnight will never again mean we are parted."

# Chapter Twenty-Nine

The early morning sun was generous with its warmth, and the air was sweet with fragrant flowers. Mr. Callahan was busy arranging fresh blossoms around the gazebo. His wife Anna approached, her assistants behind her, carrying linens to the tables.

"Evan Callahan," she remarked with a sparkle in her eye, "you've done a brilliant job! Many a day you've been plannin' this glorious weddin'. Laura will love the lavender roses, the gardenias... and especially the Bells of Ireland."

Evan beamed with pride. "I've even trained the swans to stay close to the gazebo. I've been feedin' them here by the river."

Anna laughed. "Glory be, when did we get swans?"

"Oh, they aren't just any swans, they're royal swans. Lady Meegan ordered them special for the weddin'. She also has a piper and some Irish dancers. They're goin' to perform in full regalia."

"That'll be a wonderful touch of pageantry and color," Anna smiled. "Well, I'd better be on my way. The Lady of the Manor wants all the tables covered with the white damask linens, the best china and crystal–and all before the floral arrangements arrive." Anna tilted her head up, imitating Hannah. "The atmosphere must be sophisticated and elegant." Evan chuckled and Anna did a little curtsy.

Liam stood anxiously in front of the mirror. *I sure wish Laura and I could have a more private wedding.* His thoughts were interrupted by a knock on the door. It was Jon. "I'm here to make sure you get to the church on time."

"I've been ready for an hour. Let's go." Jon started singing *Goin' to the chapel and I'm gonna get maaarried.* Liam shook his head. "It's more like going to the cathedral and having a royal ceremony, with the BBC and all the reporters there."

Jon waved his hand. "That shouldn't bother a big rock star like you!" He looked at his watch. "C'mon, we have to be out of here before the bride gets into the carriage. I don't want to get fired as best man." Liam laughed nervously.

It was unusual for a small village to have such a grand place of worship. It was the same church they had all attended mass in so many times before, but today it had earned the title of cathedral, which it truly was. From the double doors at the entryway all the way to the altar, it was fully adorned with lavender roses, gardenias and white candles. The ornate stained glass windows illuminated the altar in a mystical array of colors which seemed to come alive with the prelude music that was playing as the congregation of friends and family began to take their seats.

In the small vestry, Chloe was putting the finishing touches on the children who were to be in the wedding party. She beamed as she straightened her young son's tie. "Philip Liam O'Brogan, you are going to be quite the handsome man in the weddin' if you'll just mind your fidgitin'."

377

"Yes, Mum!" he replied dutifully. Satisfied, she went on to Beth, who seemed to be keen on her impending role as flower girl and needed no reminders.

Since Peggy was in another room with the bridesmaids, Chloe was also in charge of little Mickey, who was to carry the silk pouch with the coins. He was not fussing at all, but would certainly need guidance when the time came.

Chloe glanced at her watch, wondering why Peggy's niece, the other flower girl, had not shown up yet.

Suddenly the door burst open and Emily came in, thrusting her daughter Olivia into Chloe's arms. The young girl had been crying, and as usual, Emily couldn't be bothered to do anything about it.

"I'm not going to apologize for coming at the last minute," Emily quipped. "I'm here under protest anyway."

As the former upstairs maid, Chloe had endured Emily's terse nature without revealing her displeasure. But today was Laura and Liam's day, and her maternal instinct kicked in.

"Well, perhaps your less-than-cheery disposition is what's causin' this poor girl's unhappiness." She turned away and did her best to comfort Olivia.

Just then Hannah walked in and Emily spun around to face her. "Mother, I want this woman fired! She just insulted me!"

Hannah could clearly see that Chloe had her hands full and was doing nothing offensive. "Now, Emily, perhaps you have overreacted. We do not need any conflicts on Laura and Liam's special day."

Emily scoffed. "Oh, Laura and Liam, Laura and Liam! I'm so sick of hearing about them–like they're your own flesh and blood, or something. Well, they're not!"

Fully aware that things were past the boiling point, Chloe shuffled the children into the adjacent anteroom and closed the door behind her.

Hannah slowly shook her head as she looked at her eldest daughter with disgust. Emily had been unsupportive throughout the whole planning process, and was once again demonstrating her arrogance. Hannah was finally fed up.

"Emily, you have crossed the line of decent behavior one too many times. Chloe Bailey-O'Brogan was more of a mother to young Laura and Liam than I was. But I learned to love them after Aidan taught me that compassion and decency are what every person on this Earth should expect from one another. I am afraid you never learned that lesson, and as such you are less of a daughter to me than Laura or Peggy. I am ashamed to be your mother!"

Emily's husband, Elliot, had just entered the church after parking the rented Mercedes, and had heard the sound of voices raised just before he entered the vestry. Coincidentally, Olivia had just returned from the anteroom, opening the door herself.

"Elliot, we're leaving now!" Emily barked. "I never wanted to be part of this tawdry affair anyway!"

"No!" Olivia answered firmly. "I want to be a flower girl!"

The girl's father quickly intervened. "Olivia, dear, of course you can be a flower girl." He reached down and picked up his daughter. "Your mummy is not feeling well, and I'll take her back to the manor. You can stay with your Grammie Hannah and help Auntie Laura get married."

Olivia grinned with delight, and the reaction infuriated Emily even more.

"Well! Isn't this just perfect!" With that Emily turned on her heels and left the room.

Elliot just shrugged and patted his mother-in-law on the back. "I'm sure it's best this way."

Hannah nodded, but was still in mild shock, surprised by her own forthrightness. As Elliot brought his daughter back to the other children, Hannah stood in place drying her own tears. Chloe had emerged from the anteroom and did something she never would have thought was appropriate–until now. She gave Hannah a hug.

∞

Everyone was in place when the pipe organ began to play the processional music.

All the attendants did brilliantly, including Olivia, who initially refused to walk down the aisle with Beth, but finally cooperated after gentle guidance from Chloe. Emily was nowhere in sight, and nobody cared. Mickey, only fifteen months old, marched down the aisle with Little Philip as if he'd rehearsed it for a movie. He carried the Lucky Money in the silk pouch, holding it up like a badge of honor.

Aidan stood with his daughter in the foyer, tears in his eyes.

"Laura darling, you are absolutely the essence of perfection. I am so proud of you. I'm sure your mother is watching and sending her blessing from heaven." Laura gently kissed him on the cheek.

"Thank you, Father, thank you for everything–but especially for Liam. You gave him a chance, and I will always love you for it."

∞

Liam's heart filled with pride as he lovingly watched Laura glide down the aisle on her father's arm, radiant in her white satin gown with its flowing train. The diamond tiara and veil gently held back her golden hair, her soft curls cascading over her shoulders. This was the moment Liam had been waiting for. The ceremony was deeply spiritual, and Father O'Malley embellished the traditional Catholic ritual with a personal tribute to Laura, Liam and the Meegan family.

"If ever there was a testament to faith in family and faith in God, it is here amongst these families from our local counties who have come together from every walk of life and every background to honor the sacrament of holy matrimony. ' Tis not often that we can look out and see a blurring of the lines that separate peoples into different classes, different factions, different circles. It takes the will of those who have seen that

God has created us all equally. Blessed are those who carry that lesson, that faith, into their daily lives."

Although she knew Father O'Malley was addressing everyone, Hannah felt at that moment that he was speaking directly to her. She allowed a gentle smile to come to her face. The priest continued, "And finally, blessed are those who cannot be with us today in body but who are with us in spirit. We hold them in our hearts now with the knowledge that we would not have come all this way, on this fine day, without them enriching us along the way."

Liam found it difficult now to hold back his tears as images of his father and mother flooded his memory. He knew they would be proud of him.

Without disturbing the ongoing ceremony, Little Mickey had quietly sat down on the steps in front of the altar, but he was still clutching the silk pouch. Father O'Malley then turned to the boy, motioning for him to hand over the treasure. Little Mickey pulled the pouch to his chest before relinquishing it, which elicited a delighted snicker from the congregation.

The boy watched the proceedings intently as the priest blessed the coins and handed one each to Laura and Liam. They finished the ritual by clinking the lucky coins loudly, which resulted in a cheery applause from everyone, most of whom were aware of Laura's desire to be blessed with children. Suddenly Little Mickey scrambled out to front and center and took a bow. Father O'Malley laughed out loud, along with the rest of the congregation.

Catherine leaned over and whispered to her husband. "Looks like Little Mickey's got his father's flair for being a star." Robert chuckled with delight.

The priest pronounced them husband and wife, and Liam didn't wait for permission to kiss his bride. He took Laura into his arms, dipping her dramatically for the grand finale. The emotional reaction soared through the cathedral with thundering applause, animated laughter, and heartfelt tears.

Father O'Malley turned the newlyweds to face the ecstatic crowd, and a moment passed before the priest was able to speak again.

"I'm quite certain there are many here today who've watched these young hearts grow through the years. You've all waited for this blessed event as much as I have. So, it gives me great pleasure to present to you Mr. and Mrs. Liam Delaney!"

The couple nearly floated down the aisle while the elated onlookers cheered. After doing a quick Irish jig, Patrick attended to the newlyweds as they boarded the wedding carriage.

It was only after they were seated that Laura and Liam became aware of the adulation they were receiving from the townspeople.

Liam turned to his bride. "It's a shame there wasn't room inside the church for all of them. They belong here as much as anyone."

Patrick overheard the remark. "You know, there's nothin' that says we have to go straight back to the manor. Perhaps we could give these fine people the show they deserve."

Laura nodded and Liam spoke. "Take the long way home."

Taking the reins with pride, Patrick clucked briefly to Copper Crown, and off they went at a gentle pace through the old town that, as a small child, Laura had known as the only world beyond Montrose Estate. It was more than just a step back into her own history, with the thatched cottages and shops lining the main boulevard serving as reminders of a village that could trace its roots back to 1200 A.D. The old Gaelic traditions that afforded Aidan the title of Lord Meegan were still alive, as his ancestors had existed in harmony with the forefathers of these modern-day onlookers.

Today's picturesque journey was indeed a personal trip down memory lane for Laura and Liam. Mr. and Mrs. O'Grady were waving from out in front of the body shop where Danny had lived and worked years earlier. Then there was the ice cream parlor-one of Liam's favorite spots–and several of the boutiques Laura had shopped in as a child. One of the old shopkeepers had always called her mother Lady Fey.

The gentle motion of the carriage put the newlyweds into a comfortable euphoria, with the warm afternoon breezes caressing them.

"Sweetheart, I can't wait until we're alone tonight."

"Alone?" Laura pouted. "On a flight to New York?"

Liam replied with a twinkle in his eye. "Who says we're flying to New York?"

Laura tilted her head, looking at him suspiciously. "I thought we were going to America for our honeymoon."

"We are," Liam replied matter-of-factly. "But not until we go to Paris first."

Laura's eyes lit up. "Mr. Delaney, whatever do you have in mind?"

"Well, Mrs. Delaney," he replied with a wink, "it's certainly not spending our entire wedding night on a plane. We'll be in the honeymoon suite of the Hotel Napoleon before midnight." Laura gave him *that smile*, and for the first time in his life Liam knew that soon he would be able to fully surrender to it in all its seductive glory.

They returned to the manor to cheerful greetings and flashing cameras, the bride and groom then being escorted through the rose gardens to the waiting guests. After the formal presentations of wedding party members, Jon made the first toast.

"It is a great honor for me to be the best man today. Liam has always been my best man. Years ago he turned my life around–or, I should say, saved my life. He inspired me to be like him: good, honest and motivated. There has never been a more loyal friend, and he truly is my brother. His lovely bride, Laura, has always been like a sister to me. She is the sweetest and most generous person I've ever known. These two have been in love forever, and now they have joined hearts as husband and wife. Raise your glasses, please:

*You don't marry someone you can live with.*

*You marry someone you can't live without.*

*Laura and Liam, that's just what you did!*

*May your life be filled with happiness and joy.*

*Today and always.*

*Sláinte!*

The newlyweds stood to hug Jon, and no tears were spared. Liam took a few moments to regain his composure before taking the microphone.

"First, I'd like to thank all of you fine people for coming to share the day that I have held in my dreams for what seemed like an eternity.

"Next, thank you, Hannah, for all of the splendor, for all of your expert planning and coordination. And, for years ago, accepting this stable boy into your home, and ultimately into your heart." Hannah had now surrendered to tears and Aidan had his arm around her. Liam continued.

"And, what can I say about the man who saved my life, Lord Aidan Meegan? You literally pulled me from the inferno that would have left me without a home and without a family. Your love and guidance went far beyond the duties of legal guardian. There are no words to describe my boundless gratitude. But, they say actions speak louder than words. I am therefore committed, with every fiber of my being, to showing my love and honor for your angelic daughter each and every day of my life." He faced the guests again. "Please raise your glasses to the Lord and Lady of Montrose Manor. May they reign in peace for all eternity."

Liam embraced Hannah and Aidan as everyone cheered, and then he asked Laura to stand. He took her hand and placed it on his heart.

"Laura Lye, my mother and father are looking down from heaven, and their love shines on you. You've always been the love of my life, even before I knew it. I'm sure I first felt you in my heart when all else around me was dark. The night I lost my father you came to me with open arms. You held me close, showing me warmth and compassion, giving me the power of your love when I felt there was no reason to go on.

"Without you there would be no me. You give me reason to dream and inspiration to create, the wisdom to give and the power to love... my friend, my life, my love, my Laura Lye."

Liam gently wiped Laura's tears as music began to softly play nearby. To Laura's surprise, Danny and Jon were playing their guitars. Liam began to sing *That Smile*, with all the depth and emotion the day had unveiled. It brought tears to the eyes of many, and Laura wept with joy.

After his song was finished, Liam led his new bride to the center of the dance pavilion. The orchestra began playing *That Smile*, in a musical arrangement that Liam had prepared. It was truly an enchanted scene, the bride and groom waltzing gracefully across the floor of the ornately decorated gazebo.

At the finish of the first dance, Laura then surprised Liam when she led him to the orchestra's piano. She released his hand, seating herself on the bench and taking the microphone.

"My special gift to Liam today is a song that he wrote about two young children and their growing love. Most of you know this as Liam's first hit, *Remember When.*" Liam was filled with pride as Laura began to play and sing. Liam could barely speak when the music was finished. Above the din of everyone's applause he simply said to her, "You are amazing."

After a minute Danny decided it was a good time for him to take the mic.

"Hello everyone! I'd like to say a few words if it's all right with these fine people. And ask you to find your glass again if it got away from you." There were a few laughs and then people began to quiet down. While he paused for a moment Danny tapped on Liam's shoulder and pointed to the gift box containing the specially engraved glasses that had been mysteriously delivered the day before. Liam waved the wine steward over and pointed to the bottles of Bunratty Mead, which the waiters began to open and pour for everyone.

"For those of you who don't know me, my name is Danny Bailey. My sisters have worked for Lord and Lady Meegan for several years, and my eldest sister Chloe married Patrick O'Brogan, bless him. I count myself as one of those who was saved by Laura and Liam, and Jen, of course, the love of my life. Back in the day I was, shall we say, uncomfortable around people who I thought were in a class above me, until they all showed me they were just *people*. If it hadn't been for the guidance–and the employment–from Aidan Meegan, and the acceptance from their extended family the Bianchis… well, I certainly wouldn't be a college graduate with a beautiful American wife on my arm."

Jen gave him a hug and a kiss, and there were a few hoots and hollers.

"So, to make a long story short–"

"Too late!" Jon hollered out, to the delight of many.

"As I was saying," Danny continued, "I would like to thank them all for showing me the way, but I will never forget my roots, which includes the traditional toasting of the bride and groom with the Bunratty Mead. So if the rest of the bridal party will gather 'round… And if everyone will now raise their glasses.…

*Friends and relatives so fond and dear*

*'Tis our greatest pleasure to have you here.*

*When many years this day have passed*

*Fondest memories will always last.*

*Sláinte!*

There were cheers and hollers, along with many a pat on the back for Danny, who years before had been known as the shy young man of few words.

After giving Laura another kiss, Liam suddenly felt the urge to walk towards the edge of the large gazebo and gaze out towards the River Maigue. He was still holding the Galway crystal glass engraved with the Irish Claddagh symbol. His eyes focused on a lone figure standing on the bridge, with long gray hair gently flowing in the breeze. Liam realized it was a woman and that she was holding a glass, which she slowly raised towards him. His natural response was to do the same, and they both took a sip. But suddenly his spine tingled and the thought flashed in his mind: *Could it be her? Could it be Maura?*

Liam quickly turned to see where Laura was, but when he turned back… the mysterious figure was nowhere in sight.

The caterers spoke briefly to Hannah, and she nodded her approval for the meal service to begin.

The lavish buffet provided the guests with everything from lobster and salmon to rack of lamb and beef Wellington, the exceptional staff catering impeccably to everyone's needs. The elaborate wedding cake towered ten layers high, topped with a crystal castle and flowers cascading down the sides.

Hannah took great pride in the extravagant event, gracefully accepting compliments from the elite of Dublin society among her guests.

Aidan had been a man of few words that evening, often overcome with emotion. Gazing out at Laura and Liam as they glided to the Vienna Waltz, Aidan smiled, knowing how much his Fey would have shone at her daughter's wedding.

Sensing his emotion, Hannah reached for her husband's hand and led him to the dance floor. At that moment, Aidan was not troubled by the loss of Fey, but rather imbued with fulfillment. The woman who now held his heart had worked the magic that allowed this glorious scene before him to come together. Aidan whispered to Hannah.

"My dear, I would say this is certainly an affair to remember."

Many hours of celebration had passed, and it was at last time for the bride and groom to leave for the airport. As they said their goodbyes, the reporter, Eoin McKee, made his way to the couple, notepad in hand.

"I understand you'll be honeymooning in America."

Liam winked at his bride. "That's right."

The newlyweds stepped into the limo, the world of activity finally silenced with the shutting of the driver's door. Liam heaved a sigh of relief.

Just then light suddenly flooded in as Jon jumped inside. "Driver, let's go!"

Liam signaled for the driver to stay put and looked at Jon in disbelief.

"What do you think you're doing?"

"I need to run an idea by you before you leave, then I'll hop out at the gate."

"This had better be good," Liam cautioned. He shook his head and motioned for the driver to get underway.

Jon had that gleam in his eye. "Well, we've come a long way with the band, and our new material is really good, and I think we're going to be stars. So I was thinking the new album should say something about shining stars, and maybe something about, you know, where we're going."

Liam was listening and he quickly nodded, but his yearning to hit the road for Shannon airport would not allow him any further distraction.

"Okay, sounds good. We'll think about it later. Now goodbye!"

Jon opened the door and begrudgingly stepped out, disappointed in Liam's lack of enthusiasm. But a moment later Liam rolled down the window. Jon could plainly see a curious smile on his friend's face; a smile that seemed to project more than the contentment of finally being married or more than the satisfaction of a job well done. It was the look of serenity that comes from a life well lived; knowing that you've carried every burden without question, that you've earned every milestone, every reward, and every prize.

The car began to slowly roll away, and Liam poked his head out.

*"Hey Cowboy, Who's To Say Where The Stars Will Shine?"*

# ᘒAbout the Authorᘓ

Carol Carpentier's interest in horses was passed
down from her maternal grandfather, who was
a coachman for Lady Buxton in England
during the late 1800s. Young Carol was fascinated with his
stories of rail travel throughout the U.K., which required him
to load the team of horses onto a railcar along with the ornate
carriage, and to care for them along the way.

Carol's sense of the equine spirit led to a successful career as an Arabian horse breeder for over forty years in Santa Cruz County in California. During that time she also worked as an equine veterinary assistant, and the combined careers allowed her to interact with a diverse complement of trainers, riders and breeders from all over the world.

Carol was born on Mare Island, California, to a U.S. Naval officer and his wife. The relocation of their small family every few years instilled in her a fondness for travel which she has shared with her husband, Bob, for 40 years. Carol and Bob now reside in Kissimmee, Florida, which serves as a sunny home base for their continued travels.

CPSIA information can be obtained
at www.ICGtesting.com
Printed in the USA
LVHW042201251119
638495LV00001B/47/P